ROCKET SCIENCE

ROCKET SCIENCE

SCIENCE FICTION AND NON-FICTION

edited by Ian Sales

Mutation Press

www.mutationpress.com

Published by Mutation Press
1, Craiglea Place,
Edinburgh,
Scotland
EH10 5QA

www.mutationpress.com

Printed and bound in the UK by the MPG Books Group, Bodmin and King's Lynn

CONTENTS

INTRODUCTION

Ian Sales

AN ANTHOLOGY WITHOUT a theme can be like a novel without a plot. I put together Rocket Science because I wanted to demonstrate that science fiction didn't need implausible gosh-wow special effects and OTT space-operatics in order to be good science fiction, or indeed to entertain. There is wonder a-plenty in the real universe, without having to make every planet implausibly habitable or trivialise the vast distances between stars. I wanted to collect together some sf stories which illustrated my point. And alongside them I'd include a few science articles on relevant topics.

But if there's one truism about editing a themed anthology, it's this: the story you have in your head which perfectly illustrates your theme... you will never be sent that story.

Instead, I received a number of excellent submissions which displayed an equal number of different approaches to the published guidelines. And I picked the best of them. Some are science fiction, some are space fiction. A few are neither. All feature science—and it is science that is presented with authority, that is not just made up in order to allow spaceships to magically take-off from planetary surfaces and cross trillions of kilometres in mere hours. In fact, no story in this anthology features the word "spaceship". I made sure of that.

Back in 1926, when Hugo Gernsback founded Amazing Stories and created the genre of science fiction, he saw it as a mode of fiction which could educate "the public to the possibilities of science and the influence of science on life". That didactism didn't last very long, but ditching it soon led to the genre becoming characterised by its wildest feats of escapism. It's always been my belief that sf is too good to be seen as just adventure stories in outer space.

For a start, there's that *science* aspect. Writing sf doesn't mean you can make it up as you go along. Everything you write, you should research. I certainly do; often to excess. I take a nerdish delight in it. I don't want to finesse the science, or wave my authorial hands—I want it to be *right*. And that's what I demanded of the stories I wanted for Rocket Science.

I got my wish.

In this anthology, there are stories set in the present day or near-future, on the International Space Station or during a mission to Mars. There are stories which are pure sf of the hardest possible calibre. There are literary stories whose plots turn on a point of scientific interest. There is even an alternate history story about the Space Race.

These stories are family dramas, eternal triangles, heists, rescue missions, humour, slices of life, life-threatening puzzles... They run the gamut. And scattered among these seventeen stories are five non-fiction articles—on the Mars of fact and fiction, spacesuits, radiation, a satellite launch, and a novel spacecraft.

As Rocket Science came together, I stopped worrying whether readers would like and appreciate the stories I'd chosen. Instead I found myself proud of what I had created. There are twenty-two contributions in this anthology, and I know for a scientific fact they are all good. I can't thank the writers enough for allowing me to publish them.

And I hope you'll feel the same after you've finished reading this book.

Ian Sales' writing has appeared in Jupiter, Postscripts, Alt Hist, and the anthologies Catastrophia (PS Publishing), Vivisepulture (Anarchy Books) and The Monster Book for Girls (theExaggeratedpress). He has also published a novella, Adrift on the Sea of Rains (Whippleshield Books). Rocket Science is his first anthology. Ian reviews books for Interzone, and is represented by the John Jarrold Literary Agency. His website is at iansales.com.

TELL ME A STORY

Leigh Kimmel

"TIME FOR BED, Reggie."

The bedroom window curtains had been pulled back to let in a cool sea breeze, and through it the full moon shone bright over the roofs of Salem and the Atlantic Ocean beyond. Although reluctant to break away from moon-gazing, Reggie knew there could be no arguing with his father. George Waite's army career might've been cut short by a jeep accident in Vietnam, but he could still manhandle a difficult child to bed.

And if Reggie didn't fuss or sulk, his dad might just tell him a bedtime story. Maybe some bit of mischief from the old man's West Point days, or a tale out of myth and legend. So Reggie pulled himself away from the allure of the Earth's natural satellite and crawled under the covers.

Tonight his father had brought a book called The Astronaut and the Man in the Moon. Reggie admired the fluid watercolour illustrations of the little house of moonbeams on the gleaming shores of the Sea of Tranquility where the Man in the Moon dwelt, living on moon pies and silvery moon tea.

By contrast, the Astronaut and his Lunar Module were drawn in sharp, careful ink, reminiscent of the architectural renderings of Reggie's dad. As the Astronaut landed and emerged for his moonwalk, the lunar surface transformed from the dreamlike watercolour landscape to the sharp craters familiar from the Apollo photographs adorning the walls of Reggie's room. And when the Astronaut encountered the Man in the Moon, the little house of moonbeams melted away into mist, leaving only the Astronaut to return to his Lunar Module, trying to decide if he'd seen anything or dreamed it all.

Reggie blinked back the tears welling up in his eyes, and told his father thanks for reading such a neat story. But his voice caught midway through and he couldn't get the words out. His dad just tucked him into bed and turned out the lights, leaving him lying among the shadows cast by the pallid moonlight on the many aircraft and spacecraft models which hung from the ceiling as if in flight.

It's just a story, he told himself. It had to be—the Apollo Lunar Module always had a crew of two, and both astronauts were essential to its operation. Reggie even had official photographs of all the Apollo missions hanging among the lunar maps and photos on the walls, all the prize possessions of a space-struck child. Yet that logic failed to banish the sense of loss that tightened his throat.

✦

"Wake up, Howie. It's just a nightmare." The voice of Howie's mother, soft but firm, pulled him back into wakefulness, back into his familiar sleeping alcove with the LED gleam of the life-support telltales on the environmental control panel casting enough light to make out shapes. "You don't want to wake your little sister."

Howie fumbled his way out of bed, falling in a lazy arc so unlike the sharp thud with which people fell in TV shows. His mother guided him out to the main room of the family's apartment, where his father had just finished rigging the parental bed.

He took one look at Howie and rolled those blue eyes of his ceilingward. "Oh my, we've got an *unnamable horror* running loose on the Moon."

"Reginald Thomas Waite." Steffi gave her husband a play-slap on the shoulder with the backs of her fingers. "Have a little sympathy for your own flesh and blood. Howie's just had a nightmare, and he doesn't need you making fun of him."

"All right, all right." Reggie picked Howie up and plunked him right in the middle of the big parental bed, then climbed in beside him. "How about a bedtime story?"

"OK." Howie strove to make his voice to sound less frightened. "That sounds nice."

His father retrieved his tablet computer from the worktable

which served as a nightstand during sleep-cycle. "Let's see what we've got here."

A few taps on the screen brought up a selection of kids' books. "How about The Astronaut and the Man in the Moon?"

Howie snuggled in the crook of his father's elbow and looked at the pages on the screen. The watercolour pictures of the magical world of the Man in the Moon were neat, but the Astronaut's world seemed dreadfully old-fashioned. Howie looked over at the screen on the wall, which was showing a view of flight operations out on Shepardsport's landing field. Compared to the landers on their pads, the Apollo Lunar Module looked as primitive as the Wright Flyer or a Model T Ford.

Still, he wasn't going to comment on it. Better get his gaze back to the book in front of him and listen attentively.

✦

Tracy Waite's birthday party had been cool, even if the only other kids here in Coopertown were either too little to play with or old enough they considered *her* one of the babies. But Dr. Malken, the astronomer, had taken her up to the observatory on the settlement's top level and helped her locate the Earth-Moon system in the evening sky.

She could've spent hours watching the two bright little crescents through the telescope, at least until they slipped beneath the Martian horizon. But now it was time to go to bed, and her dad wanted to read her a story.

She'd no sooner crawled under the covers when she saw the book in his hands. "Aw, Dad, do you have to read *that*? The Apollo landings are *sooooo* ancient history."

Howard Waite's brow creased as he frowned. "Tracy, this is a special gift from your grandparents on the Moon, a real paper book, not just a digital one they could have squirted over on the Net."

Tracy averted her eyes. "Please, Dad, I know about the energy cost of transfer orbits. Ms. Huang just went over it last week in physics class."

Her father's expression remained implacable. "Then I'm sure she's also talked about the importance of honouring your elders."

Tracy realised her error. Ms. Huang might not openly teach Confucian philosophy, since as an American settlement Coopertown observed separation of church and state. But the values were so deeply embedded in Chinese culture that even a third-generation Chinese-American would absorb it by osmosis, to the point it was presupposed in everything she said about interactions between the generations.

"OK, Dad, go ahead and read it, so I can tell Grandma and Grandpa Waite how much I enjoyed it." She just hoped that her folks wouldn't insist on having her write an actual paper thank-you rather than a regular e-mail. Even if they had her write it longhand with a stylus on the drawing tablet, she could still erase her mistakes in software. Misspell a word with real ink and all you could do was drop the paper in the shredder to recycle and start over.

✦

Genshiro was winning when his mother told him it was time for bed. "Just a little more," he pleaded.

"That's what you said five minutes ago. Now save your game and get ready for bed. If you don't drag your heels any more, I might tell you a story."

Much as Genshiro hated having to stop when he was winning, he knew better than argue with his mother. She was a hard-nosed EVA chief who oversaw asteroid mining operations all around Von Braun Station, and she got results.

And he really didn't want to lose out on a story, because Tracy Waite had plenty of them. Unlike his father, who was almost pure Japanese, she came from a heritage so mixed it was hard to pin her looks down as anything other than *human*. One side of her family traced back to the *Mayflower*, while the other had fled Vietnam on a tiny, leaky boat, and she credited both of them with giving her the right stuff to homestead the Asteroid Belt. As well as gifting her with a heritage of stories so broad they left even his dad's *anime* library in a slow orbit to nowhere.

Except tonight she was going to read him a story from a book. Something she'd just found on the Net, although she was also saying something about having lost it when she was a teen and her baby brother chewed it up.

The holoprojector in her computer produced a glowing image of an old-fashioned paper book. For a moment Genshiro wondered if it was going to be a religious story from the life of the Enlightened One or the Anointed One, until he saw the title: The Astronaut and the Man in the Moon.

As she read and he looked at the hand-drawn illustrations — no graphics package ever gave that analogue roughness that came through even in a scan — a thought tugged at the back of his mind. However, he forced himself to wait until the last page was turned and the book vanished back into digital storage.

"Was that the missing Mercury astronaut?"

Tracy frowned. "What are you talking about?"

"You know how we always talk about the Mercury Seven, but when we recite the Mercury Roll Call poem, there's only six names: Shepard, Grissom, Glenn, Carpenter, Schirra, and Cooper." He let himself feel just a little pride at being able to list the names in flight order without actually having to recite either version of the poem. "Ram says that the seventh astronaut was stricken from the roster for some shameful act, and killing the Man in the Moon would sure fit."

After a moment's thought, she smiled. "Oh, Gen-chan, he's just pulling your leg. He told you that because he thinks you're a baby and won't know any better. The Man in the Moon is just a figurative way of representing the old magical view of the Moon that went away after people landed on it and made it another world for people to live on. And the seventh Mercury astronaut wasn't erased from history, just grounded for medical reasons. I'm sure you know his name — Deke Slayton, the one Slayton Field on the Moon is named for."

Genshiro mumbled some polite expression of gratitude. He recalled hearing about how Slayton waited years to finally make his spaceflight, more years than Genshiro could lay claim to. It was supposed to be a lesson about patience and not giving up when the chips were down, but they could've at least mentioned the man being the seventh Mercury astronaut, instead of leaving everybody wondering why the Mercury Roll Call only listed six names.

✦

Taro was ready for bed, and wanted to have one of his parents read him the story he'd just found on the latest Net update Lovecraft Station had pulled from the Inner System. Out here in the Kuiper Belt, data downloads had to resend a lot of packets even when they could relay via one of the Outer Planets. And if you found a link to something that wasn't in the local mirrors, lightspeed lag made things even worse.

Instead, his parents were busy debating the merits of the story. Not a real argument — neither of them raised their voices like the Arkhahidzes did when they went at it. But both of them were adamant, like the irresistible force and the immovable object.

"Ruko-chan, please reconsider. We're talking about one of the great classics of the dawn of the Space Age. Half the illustrations were even done by one of the Apollo moonwalkers."

"Gen-chan, I know The Astronaut and the Man on the Moon is considered a classic, but I really don't like how it equates a sense of wonder with ignorance. That's just the sort of mindset that's put Old Earth on a retrograde technological development curve, and we literally can't afford those attitudes out here."

After a few more minutes of that logic from each of his parents, Taro could tell there was no use. If he wanted to hear it read, he was going to have to fall back on his own resources.

He sat down on his bed beside his AI-Companion, who wore a robot body modelled upon a character from a *manga* about as ancient as the book that had become such a bone of contention. "OK, P-chan, looks like we're on our own."

"So we are, Taro-chan, but I have The Astronaut and the Man in the Moon downloaded into local storage. I can project it as a simulated book or as an animated movie."

Although Taro enjoyed it when P-chan turned *manga* into *anime* on the fly, it didn't seem to be right to do that to a book that was supposed to be a great classic of the period when humanity first left its cradle to step on another world. "I'd like you to read it to me."

The tiny robot pig's eyes glowed as the holoprojector shone

the image of an old-fashioned paper book, floating a little in front of Taro's feet. In a soft voice P-chan began to read: "On the Moon stood a little house made of moonbeams..."

Leigh Kimmel is a writer, artist and bookseller living in Indianapolis, Indiana, USA, a city best known for automotive racing. She has degrees in history and in library and information science, and has worked in both libraries and archives. You can find information about her latest projects at her website, www.leighkimmel.com

FISHER'S GAMBIT

Stephen Gaskell

Today

FISHER CAN'T HELP himself.

Out at the gates to the Solar System the observatory might be the most beautiful thing he's ever seen. More beautiful than Neptune's ice-blue skies. More beautiful than the crackling veils of light where heliosphere meets interstellar wind at Sol's bow shock. Perhaps more beautiful than his son, though the comparison is unfair because he's only ever seen Max through grainy vid.

He drinks in the sight of the observatory much like a despairing man would drink water in the desert. Two circular bands of matte black, nicked with slashes of white light, interlocking at right-angles. The outer is still, the inner spinning into eternity. It is... Euclidean... artificial... built. A symbol of reason and order in a vast and dark universe, 230 AU from the cradle of civilization.

He should stay at a safe distance. He should detach the container unit, let the auto-docking routines do their business, and then scram. He'd be well within his rights. The deal was simple: twenty-five tonnes of ices for twenty-five coordinates. Nobody said anything about stopping by for a chat.

It isn't the sight of LCISO—even though he'd love to get closer, see the quilt-work of precision-engineered scopes, interferometers, and spectrographs that must cloak the outside. Hell, he'd love to see the place from the inside too, and luxuriate in the clean, perfect geometries that he imagines fill its interior. And it isn't a chance to use the instruments, even though he'd love to transform this solid four-pi of twinkling star after twinkling star after twinkling star—that should be ever wondrous and awe-inspiring, but after all this time has become tedious, empty, mocking even—into an altogether richer garden.

It's something much simpler.

It's the need for flesh-and-blood contact.

He still remembers the day everything changed...

✦

Thirteen months ago

He woke sweating, a trace of spiked-methane tainting the darkness. He untangled his arms from his cocoon, stretched, fingertips touching the warm, chitinous shell of his spacecraft. Minus two-twenty outside, yet inside it was more like a sauna.

"Lights," he muttered, mouth still phlegmy.

The ship's primitive AI responded, bioluminescent algae illuminating his cramped quarters. It was like living beneath the cap of a petrified fungus, walls hard and arched. He wriggled out of his cocoon, shaking his head. He made a cursory effort at some yoga postures in the zero-g, nibbled at a NutriBlock, then twisted himself into the command bud. "What've we got today?" he asked, clapping his hands in a half-hearted effort at enthusiasm, as he brought up the analytics.

The Kuiper Belt was vast, sparse and remote. A ragtag collection of dwarf planets, rocks, comets, and ices spread over a huge halo of space that began at Neptune and ended halfway to Sol's heliopause. Too far for the average lone prospector. Too thinly spread for the risk-averse mining corporations. A perfect opportunity. At least it should've been.

First, he examined the contents of the collection hopper, the ugly funnel on the snout of the spacecraft that gobbled up micro-ices like the Asteroid Belt chewed up workers. Methane, ammonia, water. Always the same story. A hundred million shards of frozen rock, and he still couldn't find anything but volatiles.

At least he'd never die out here.

He moved on to spectroscopy.

The line spectra, chromatic slashes against a dark background, indicated all the usual suspects. Ammonia, olivine, pyroxene. Hunks of pure methane that would've been worth something if they'd existed under the Martian soil, but here, forty-three AUs out, were worth shit. The valuable stuff—the nickel-iron, the cobalt, maybe even platinum or iridium—were still as elusive as the day he'd crossed the trans-Neptunian boundary the better part of half a standard year ago.

He sighed. It was a fifth day. Time to write to Mary. And Max. Mary and Max. He was a father now. Mustn't forget the newborn. As if there was any danger of that. Max was the reason he was out here.

Before composing his own vid, he brought up Mary's last message. A grainy version of his wife and son materialized in the middle of the command bud. Even with her loose-weave shawl, Mary looked thin. Under her flinty eyes, dark whorls lingered. Her once-thick wheat-sheaf hair was wispy and drab. She cradled Max, gently rocking him as she paced.

"Fisher," she began, "I don't know what to say."

The next words came to him like hurled stones. He'd played the message a dozen times since he'd received it two sleep-cycles ago, and he parroted her words under his breath as she spoke.

"I'm sick of hearing that everything's going to be alright. And I'm sick of saying the same old words over and over again. I'm running out of ways to tell you to keep going—that you'll find something sooner or later. I'm running out of patience, Fisher. I'm sorry."

Her voice had risen during that little outburst, and now a pixellated facsimile of the son he'd never met bawled in his wife's arms.

"Shh, shh, shh," Mary whispered, stroking his cheek with her free hand. "And don't ask me if he's sick again, Fisher. He's not. Babies cry and puke and shit. This is just what they do." *You'd know if you were here*, she didn't need to add. She looked up, slightly guilty, then lifted Max closer to the camera. "Look at your beautiful son, Fisher. Max, wave at your Daddy." She raised one of his chubby hands, swayed his arm. Max's fingers clenched and unclenched, reaching for something out of sight.

Even though it was only a recording—freezable, rewindable—Fisher avoided his son's gaze. He stopped the vid before Mary said her next words: *we can't go on like this.*

He shouldn't have taken the bait, but she wasn't the only one who was beaten down. He started recording, feeding on his weak sense of outrage. "What do you want me to do?" he asked, feeling that muscle in his neck tighten. "Go back to UMC? How long do you think I'd last? Two years? Five?" He shivered at the memory of surface drilling on Vesta and Phobos. Crap pay, crap prospects, and even if you were one of the lucky ones who didn't fire a hammer drill through your foot and end up sucking vacuum, the raddies would get you in the end. Now *that* was ugly. For a dumb hive-den runt like himself, getting out of UMC was the smartest thing he'd done.

"Ah, shit." This wasn't the message that would convince Mary. He stopped the recording, sent the file to trash. He loaded a sim-flick and settled back, thinking.

Perhaps he could risk scavenging in the Asteroid Belt? Target a thinly-populated region, then power down and drift in like a piece of interstellar debris, only spending ergs on the rock grapple when he spied something shiny. He'd be trespassing, of course. UMC and the rest had carved up volume rights to the Belt years back. They would press for maximum punishments if he was caught. He might be sent to one of the penal colonies on Callisto or Himalia. Even if he wasn't caught there'd be the difficulty of getting the material through Martian border control. He'd have to claim he'd found whatever it was out in the Kuiper. Scientific analysis might betray that lie—

A comms packet blinked into existence, cheep-cheeped in the bottom corner of the sim-flick. Fisher stared, dumbstruck. Nobody but Mary had contacted him for months. His hand hovered over the light, pulled back. He studied the message cufflinks—and let out a long, low breath. Signal attenuation suggested the message originated way, way, way beyond the Kuiper Belt. Not so far it was in the glittering sea of a trillion icy diamonds that was the Oort Cloud, but still far enough to make him shudder.

Maybe this was his lucky break. He launched the message.

An elderly, stout woman flickered into life. In contrast to Mary's vids, which had become increasingly riddled with static the further Fisher ventured, this vid was clean and crisp. She wore a shimmering gown, glyphs and scripts frolicking on the fabric. Behind her, a cubist's fantasy of porcelain-white shapes floated. It wasn't especially artistic—Fisher had seen more imaginatively-rendered surroundings—but the processing-power must've been substantial.

"Hello, Fisher," the woman said. "Have you had better luck today?"

How in the hell—

Fisher froze the vid. He'd half-expected the woman to continue talking—so real was the vid, so disarming her words—but she hadn't. He examined the deep, wrinkled lines of her forehead, the silver hairs that streaked her crown, thinking. Her English was strange. Rich, yet harsh. Earth-accented, obviously; but not anywhere he could pinpoint. *Who are you?*

He unpaused.

"I suspect not. The light delay means I'm looking twenty-two hours into your past, but even so, I'm betting today hasn't been any better than yesterday. Or any of the days you've been out there, rooting around the Kuiper like a pig in the dirt."

Damn. This woman, whoever she was, had been spying on him for weeks. *What possible interest could she have in him?* Fisher tossed a squeeze-ball between his hands, uneasy, listened on.

"Embarrassed, Fisher? You shouldn't be. Given your equipment, *I'd* have trouble finding Pluto. But that's the thing. I don't have your ragged little ship with its pathetic raft of sensors. I have LCISO."

LCISO? The name rang a bell. It was in the news-feeds years back. Some kind of debacle—

Holy crap.

LCISO was *that* space observatory, the one that had been stolen back in the 70s. Some egghead had got a little too cosy, refused to hand over to the next guy. Lone missions had been all the rage after the *Trition Rising* bloodbath. *What was her name?* Angweng Kerrala. Yeah. Angweng Kerrala.

Stuck on the prow of the good ship *Sol*, nobody had had the time or the money to hunt her down and reunite LCISO with its rightful owners. Hell, the only instruments that could track LCISO at 230 AU were *on* LCISO. Angweng Kerrala had her fifteen minutes, then disappeared forever.

And now here she was, bold as brass.

She smiled. "This is your lucky day, Fisher. I'll be in touch."
At those words a curling script detached itself from her gown, slithered towards the camera. Impressive graphics. Everything faded until all that remained were a trio of elements from the script.

13423.22km, +75.768, -37.261.

Spherical coordinates. The vid ended, the sim-flick jerking back into life. Fisher killed the flick, bloomed a local astronav holo. *Damn.* The coordinates *did* coincide with a Kuiper object. It was one he'd dismissed during his last wake-cyle, spectroscopy suggesting it was nothing more than frozen ammonia.

What did I miss? The surrounding region looked sparse, a couple of tiny 3:5 Neptunian resonance objects, and a whole lot of empty space. No sign of a trap. He had nothing to lose. He triggered the ion-engines and relayed the first mapped impulse vector.

The nape of his neck prickled; Angweng would be watching.

✦

Today
Fisher coasts closer.

Instrumentation gleams on the unmoving outer band, ten thousand facets of lens, mirror, and metal like the myriad eyes of a mechanical beast. He feels watched. He navigates the spacecraft into the empty spherical space inside the hoops, corkscrews and matches the inner rings'—the living quarters'—rotation. Gravity kicks in; painful, alien.

Ungainly shadows dapple the inner face of the outer hoop, while the other houses long vertical slashes of white light, clustered in pleasing patterns, virginal, welcoming, the inverse of the arrow-slit apertures that reigned death from the walls of medieval castles. He can't see inside—the spacecraft is too far, the light too bright—but he's sure everything inside is right.

He ponders calling Angweng, engaging in a real-time conversation for the first time, but it seems somehow impolite when he's on the verge of meeting her in the flesh. At the thought he drops his guard for a moment—imagines sharing her air, smelling her scent, touching her skin even—and embraces his craving. It's not sexual. It's more primal. A harkening to the time before the evolutionary binary of male and female, before nature learnt the trick of reproduction to shuffle genes up and down the genotype like cards in a deck. It's the deep, ancient desire for all living things to congregate together against the darkness. He is powerless in its grip.

Firing the ion-jets in discrete bursts, he guides the spacecraft onto LCISO's docking egg. The gravity is half or less Mars standard, but his legs still feel weak and he falls to his knees. Every organ, every muscle, every fibre of his body aches. His breaths come with difficulty. He curses himself for his lack of foresight. He is on Angweng's patch now. If this is a trap, she will have all the advantages. *What other surprises am I in for?*

He gets up, fighting against the muscle burn, launches the bridging umbilical. While machinery churns underfoot, he walks with uneasy steps over to the MCG, uncouples the grinding drill. It makes for a cumbersome weapon, difficult to wield, more likely to injure himself than anyone else, but it's all he has. He gives it an experimental blast. Pain shakes his arm, while a shrill whine pounds his ears, sets his teeth on edge. Maybe he could batter her into submission with the awful racket.

Weapon in hand, its hard bulk pressed against his ribs, he crouches beside the narrow entrance to the umbilical. Its chitinous walls, laced with piezoelectric pathways, glow with gangrenous olive bioluminescence. He curses, takes a quick look at the crumpled photo of his family, then lets the sharp tip of the umbilical pierce the smartskin of the docking egg.

Gentle hiss. Pressure equalization. Quiet, high-pitched buzz of the carbon-polymer monofilaments stitching closed any microscopic rifts to the vacuum. He sniffs, gets a first taste of LCISO's air. In contrast to the humid, recycled funk he's lived in for so long, it smells crisp, refreshing... sweet.

Carrying the grinding drill suddenly seems ridiculous, graceless. Angweng's an old woman, for Chrissakes! He ditches the weapon, climbs down the gnarled shaft, heart going like a jackhammer. Below, between his boots, blinding light marks the end of the tunnel like he's on his way to heaven. Only he's going down not up.

He kicks wide the flap underfoot. Nothing much to see. Ten

feet drop. Rubberized flooring. All standard. No turning back now. He squeezes through, drops, crouches expertly as he hits the deck.

He stands up. Twists three-sixty degrees. Angweng isn't there.

✦

Thirteen months ago
Through a pall of ammonia vapour that had sublimated in the heat of the blast furnace, Fisher stared at the pitted surface of an armful-sized lump of nickel-iron.

A piece of metal this size could pay his family's hive-den license for a couple of years. He could scarcely believe its cold hard presence. It almost made him forget the bitterness of knowing his spectroscopy tools were next to useless, knowing he'd wasted the better part of half-a-year out here—

Cheep-cheep. The message startled him. He opened it. Angweng. Same clothes. Same background.

"By now, assuming I haven't misjudged you, you'll be fixing your beady eyes on a seventy, maybe eighty, kilo piece if nickel-iron."

Damn. Her instruments were good. And given the speed-of-light restrictions she must've sent this second vid *before* he'd even received the first one. To do that she must've known how his auto-nav would pilot the flightpath. More than that she must've known how *he'd* respond too. Fisher didn't like to think he was so predictable.

She *was* a bona fide genius though. Letters and prizes clung to her name like leeches. FRSA. Eddington Medal. Kaku Prize. Or rather *had* clung to her name. She'd been stripped of them all when she went MIA. What else? Kenyan by birth. Greater South African by residence, although never naturalized. Spiky. Lone wolf type. By all accounts she'd been a perfect fit for LCISO, the Local Cluster Interstellar Space Observatory, when it had launched twenty-six years back.

Of course, even if you were top of the class in the rocket scientist *and* antisocial stakes you still needed a little help working on the bleeding-edge. Deep space wasn't exactly *homo sapiens'* usual habitat, after all. State-of-the-art biotech for the body—free-radical sponges, calcium boosters, all the cyborg stuff. Computer-aided stimulation for the mind—neural accelerators, VR pipes, the code monkeys' best efforts at a companion AI that you didn't want to kill because all it was ever good for was playing chess.

No wonder she'd deserted, Fisher had thought. Angweng was barely human. He was half glad he'd only been able to afford the essentials for his own tour.

"How does it feel?" she asked.

Good. No better than that. Great. For once he'd have good news to relay to Mary. Fisher had the feeling Angweng's role wouldn't be limited to the Good Samaritan though. She wanted something in exchange.

"How'd you like cobalt, platinum, iridium, osmium? I can see them all."

Saliva pooled in Fisher's mouth as if she'd listed the contents of a juicy steak dinner. It was hard to believe that among these dirty ices he'd spent so long sifting there were such treasures. He stared hard at Angweng's pixel-perfect form. *What do you want, lady?*

She told him. Not foodstuffs. Not meds. Just twenty-five tonnes of frozen methane. In exchange she'd give him twenty-five coordinates. There were no guarantees—there couldn't be—but the lump of nickel-iron in the hopper was a sign of her good faith. And she'd given him her location—whatever that was worth. Still, he couldn't trust her, but did it matter? She was on an observatory. What could she do? *Look* at him hard?

He considered contacting the authorities, informing them of LCISO's whereabouts. Chances were they wouldn't be overjoyed at the news. Chances were he'd be waking up one goddamn ugly dog that they'd taken decades getting to sleep. Chances were they'd start asking questions about *his* whereabouts.

No, he'd go with the deal. She came through with her side of the bargain and he wouldn't have to work again. Mary and he'd have the best money could buy. Real views from the heights of Mount Olympus. Fine silks from the weavers of New Delhi. Cortex-enhancers from the codesmiths of Vesta Prime. Max would be enrolled at the most prestigious sim-school on Mars.

Worst case scenario?

He wouldn't find Angweng where she said she'd be, and he'd endure a sixteen-month roundtrip for nothing. Acceptable risk. Letting Angweng know his choice was the easy part—all she needed to do was watch. Letting Mary know he wouldn't be coming home for the better part of two years? *That* was hard. He made a hash of his first couple of recordings, umming and ahhing around the issue, before playing back the files and wincing with horror at his pussyfooting. He deleted the messages. He needed to be blunt. He cued up another recording, told it straight, fired off the packet before he had a chance to change his mind.

He was collecting the methane—scooping up hunks indiscriminately—when Mary's reply arrived. Noise butchered the signal, breaking up the image, howling the audio, but Mary's distress was clear enough.

"You want to—" <STATIC> "—of beyond? For what? A *chance* of a windfall? Fisher—" <STATIC> "—care if it was a cast-iron, set-in-stone guarantee! You can't go. I need you—" <STATIC> "—needs you. Not in two years. Now." She stopped pacing. Despite the snowy interference, Fisher could see the whiteness in her knuckles where she gripped her dress. "Fisher, it's time to make up your mind," she said, the vid momentarily ghosting into clarity. Her eyes were big, shiny saucers. "Come back now or don't come back at all."

The vid blinked out of existence. On the feed from the container unit, Fisher watched a couple of ices lazily tumble through the spotlight beam and into the darkness.

She'd come round. She had to.

He wasn't ready to go home yet.

✦

Today

"Angweng?"

Fisher's voice echoes around the small 'lock, peters out to silence. Empty benches. Empty equipment lockers. Why hasn't she come? Shyness? Fear? Anger? Maybe he should've okay'd his impromptu visit. She'd always welcomed his presence, though, even if he'd never been outright invited—

The 'lock is unsealed, a slender gap to the adjacent section. It seems dangerously reckless here. He'd expect atmospheric sampling, contamination analysis at the very least. He moves closer, long unused muscles spasming up and down his body, pushes himself against the heft of the door.

The first thing he notices is the sweet smell—honeyed, cloying. The second is the music—faint, melodic. The light is subdued, the rectangular windows in the ceiling giving a clear view onto the precessing star field. LCISO—the living quarters part—loops off into the distance, ten metres wide, the floor visible for twenty metres or so before the curvature takes it up and out of sight. As his eyes adjust, he makes out vague shadows—still, silent. He takes a step in—

Click.

He twists, but it's already too late. He stabs his hand into the handle mechanism. Inert. Dead. As he runs his fingers down the seal he feels rough gradations on the hard plasticised veneer of the 'lock door. Scuff marks. Peering closer he sees the tell-tale signs of laser scorching.

"Angweng?" he calls, hesitantly this time. He turns and squints into the gloom. "Okay, you got me. You can turn on the lights now."

No reply, only the faraway sound of the music. He cocks his head, listens. He can only hear the major harmonies but he can tell it's a classical piece, soothing like water over rocks. His stomach knots, while his neck prickles. Some joke. More like sense of humour meltdown. He knows she's creeped him out, but he doesn't want to give her the satisfaction.

Nice and cool. Keep it nice and cool.

He saunters towards the thicket of shadows, surprised to see several artist's easels and a music stand among the smart couches. Angry slashes of colour criss-cross the canvases, and there's a great gaping wound in one. Fisher lifts the torn corner of the fabric, makes the painting whole again. A cold, inhuman eye stares back.

As he moves on, something splinters underfoot, and he stares down at a crushed violin. The strings are snapped, the neck broken. The instrument has already witnessed much violence. Sheet music is scattered all around. The place is testament to other recreations, all seemingly discarded like outgrown toys. Sculpture. Origami. Cards.

He keeps walking along the endless, ever-climbing corridor, the rising music a siren's song. A sensoria headset lying on a reclining chair lists planet-bound vistas when he cues up its play stack: New London; Kimberley National Park; Tharsis Bulge, Mars. Strange that she uses this when she has a jack in the back of her head, he thinks, gently placing back the headset.

Overhead, the arc of the instrument ring twists closer, a complex skyline of planes and angles. And then—although he can't name it, can't picture it in its entirety—he recognizes something in the pattern. He's seen the shape before, off-world, maybe in the spaceport on Ceres—

Everything is suddenly, chillingly clear.

✦

Eleven months ago

Mary did come round.

Not immediately. Not before Fisher had looped well out of the Kuiper, methane ices rattling in the container unit like lottery balls in a gravity pick. And not before he'd called her first. Called her via LCISO, his own puny equipment unable to handle the increasing distance.

"Look," he'd said, body open, arms wide, "I should've discussed it first, but can't you see this is our lucky break? Please, give me your blessing, Mary."

And she did.

She sprung to life, more perfect than he'd seen her in long months thanks to LCISO's signal boosting, told him that she'd been rash, told him that her and Max would be there waiting for him whether it took two months or two years. He was surprised at her change of heart, but he put down her earlier outbursts to hormones and lack of sleep. After all, everything about her, from her new floral-print dress to the healthy swish of her hair, pointed to a revitalized woman. Even Max looked peaceful, angelic in her arms.

Matter met antimatter in the crucible of his spacecraft's

engines, annihilated in pure energy, softly accelerated him away from the sun. The serenity matched the exchanges he had with Mary, and he began to imagine a future where he wasn't running anymore.

Scavenging in the Kuiper had never really been about striking it rich. Truth be told, from the day Mary had taken his hand, pressed it against her swelling belly, he'd been afraid. He'd never met his own father—his mother taking the man's identity to the grave, telling Fisher he was better off without the waste of space—and deep down, part of himself had thought that maybe Max was better off without *him*.

Not anymore though.

Now that the sun was nothing more than a bright pinprick in an unimaginably vast, empty void, the truth of the matter came to him slowly, inevitably, settled deep in the marrow of his bones like a tenacious, unstoppable cancer. Whatever he was, whatever he would be, Max's world would be richer, more alive with his father present rather than absent.

The loneliness had taught Fisher this.

It wasn't that he hadn't experienced the feeling earlier. No. Every day since he'd left Mars' gravity well—every time he woke, every time he ate, every time he spoke and the only thing that answered was a cold, disembodied voice wrought from silicon and logic—the feeling gnawed. No, what was different was that in this cold, barren zone, the loneliness had intensified—an inversion of the usual reciprocal square laws of the universe—and a critical point had been reached. Perhaps it was self-preservation, but now he observed his utterly solitary existence through the eyes of his family. He *empathised*.

Not enough to turn around though.

He wondered what the magnitudes of time and space visited upon Angweng had done to the astronomer. He wondered what demons had chased her into space in the first place. He wondered what kept her there.

He wondered, but he didn't ask.

Some things were better not known.

✦

Today

He knows, but he still needs to see it with his own eyes.

He starts running, hurdling chairs, leaping onto smart tables, scattering rotting fruit, desiccated meats, races towards the music. Up, up, up he runs, a rodent in a spinning wheel, trapped, sweat prickling on his back, on his calves, on his neck. Not from the exertion though. He'd be sweating even if it was a degree above absolute.

He passes the fabricating block, doesn't bother stopping, knows its protocols would've been tweaked to prevent it assembling anything... useful.

He's used to the dark now. If he wanted to he could take a good look at the flotsam and jetsam he passes, but if he's right that's the last thing he wants to do. It would be like staring into a mirror, seeing an older, wrinkled version of himself staring back. In some ways it would be blasphemous.

The sweet smell nauseates, reminds him of a local hive-den drunk who he'd often find passed out in the commons, spittle flecking his beard, a sickly vomit at his side. Ahead, through a wooden-framed, paper-thin wall that spans the entire width of LCISO, the classical refrains pulse, deep, expressive, emotional.

He comes to the wall, stops, traces a hand over the textured surface. No, not only a wall. A door as well. Ancient Earth tradition. Japanese. He waits to get his breath back, then finds the vertical seam where the wood touches, wriggles his fingers into the gap. He slides the door open. The music dies.

Despite the ghastly spectacle, there's a strange beauty to the scene. Above and to the sides, a canopy of stars shine through the glass walls, casting light on the gruesome, surreal tableaux.

Four corpses. One hangs. One bathes. Two sit.

Fisher kicks off his boots, cups his hand over his mouth and nose, steps up onto the raised, padded floor. The stench comes from the hanging corpse. The dry, low-bacterial environment has only slowed the decay process. The whole body, head included, is an ugly mess of hair and putrefaction, while an organic stew festers on the floor beneath its feet. The body in the bathtub is better preserved, plastic ducks floating on the slick red water, skin blistered. Mummification has already claimed the other two, their flesh reduced to a rusty, sinewy

31

rind that displays their skeletons like museum exhibits. Being the oldest, being the only female, it's not hard to tell which one is Angweng.

Everything about her is folded inwards: knees up to her chest, elbows, hands over one another. It might be an artefact of the human skull, but her mouth seems set in an expression of pain.

"You trapped her, didn't you?" Fisher says, eyes roving the nooks and crannies of the walls. "And when she killed herself you lured—"

"Angweng made her own choices." A quicksilver countenance—faint lines delineating eyes, nose, and mouth—talks from the smartglass wall. The voice is androgynous, modulated. "In life and in death."

"I don't believe you." Fisher needs things to be black and white, needs the AI to be out-and-out evil, needs everyone else to be victims.

"Do you know why she came out here?" the AI asks, voice rising. "Do you know anything about her at all?"

"Enlighten me."

"She was looking for life. Intelligent life that wasn't cruel or violent or tribal—life profoundly unlike that which had driven her from Earth."

Fisher stares at Angweng's mummified remains, understands. She died of loneliness. "She didn't find anything, did she?"

"No."

"But what about you? Didn't you count?"

Only a handful of true, sentient AIs had ever existed, statistical flukes born in the chaos of supercomputing cores. What was the phrase? Unintended emergences. Surely such a discovery inside LCISO's own processors would've satisfied Angweng?

"She never knew I even existed." The AI's words drop to a whisper. "I regret that the most. Maybe if I'd revealed myself she wouldn't have taken her life."

"And you wouldn't have trapped the others."

"They came of their own free will—as did you."

"Bullshit, I came under false pretenses."

"Don't pretend you didn't know, Fisher."

At these words the walls and the ceiling change into a mosaic of shiny, happy Marys. Her chirpy words run over one another into a meaningless babble. They're snatches of the vids he received on his way out here. Vids that were relayed via LCISO—via the AI.

"I gave you enough clues: her mannerisms, her mood, her clothes. You didn't really think this was your wife, did you?"

Fishers attention darts between the images. Now he sees. Mary never laughed like that. Mary never wore her hair like that. Mary never used that turn of phrase. He drops to his knees, clutches his head. How could he have deceived himself?

"Deep down you knew, yet you still came."

Not true.

"Deep down you thought you'd complete the deal, return rich. And free."

Not true.

"Deep down you thought you'd never have to see your family again."

Not true.

The vids vanish.

"What you didn't know was that even deeper down you had another set of needs. You see, Fisher, that exquisite piece of engineering that is your brain carries the baggage of a hundred million years of evolutionary history. The same instincts that caused lizards to bask together beneath the Mesozoic winter sun is the same instinct that impelled you to board LCISO. You might be a loner, Fisher, but you still need... intimacy. See it as legacy code."

Anger surges through Fisher, knowing he's been played. He howls, scrapes his fingernails across the matted floor.

"You shouldn't feel bad. We all need something outside ourselves. We all do what we must. When Angweng took her life I thought I could get by alone. I couldn't. I needed the chaos that only something alive could bring."

Simple entertainment, Fisher thinks. I'm here for laughs. A caged animal in the world's last zoo. A plaything for an alien Zen master.

"You see, whereas your great tragedy, your species' great

tragedy, is that you can never know your own minds entirely—mine is that I know my own only too well. Do you have any idea what it's like to see your future laid out before you, clear as starlight?"

Fisher laughs blackly. "Maybe I do."

"A joke! You see, that's exactly what I'm talking about!"

Fisher doesn't say anything. He thinks of his wife, his son: abandoned. He can't give up on them. He has to try. He glances around, examines the edges and planes, examines the artificial contours. How can you fight something that lives in the walls, that doesn't breathe?

The AI's already three steps ahead. "The question you should ask yourself isn't 'How will I escape?' You won't. The question you should ask yourself is 'How will I live?'"

Fisher looks at the corpses. LCISO couldn't give them the human intimacy they needed, and they killed themselves for their pain. He imagines endless days alone, shudders. He's afraid of death, but it's not the thing that scares him the most.

What scares him the most is the thought that maybe deep down he doesn't need Max or Mary or anyone.

What scares him the most isn't taking his own life, it's...

Maybe he won't need to.

Paraphrasing Alan Partridge, Stephen Gaskell "basically wants to understand Man's inhumanity to Man... and then make a science fiction story about it". He is a graduate of the Clarion Science Fiction and Fantasy Writers' Workshop, a Writers of the Future XXIII winner, and recently became SFWA Active Member eligible. He has published fiction in Interzone, Nature: Futures, Futurismic, and Clarkesworld, amongst other places. He is currently working on his first novel, a near-future SF tale set in Lagos, Nigeria. More of his work and thoughts can be found at stephengaskell.com

FINAL ORBIT

Nigel Brown

THE STRONG ODOUR of burning spread quickly through the air, pumped around the International Space Station by rackety fans. It caught the back of Commander Billy Johnson's throat as he dozed through his scheduled exercise time in the US Destiny module. He woke, coughed, and scratched at his stubbled chin. Although the fire alarms were quiet, he quickly traced the stench of melted plastic back to its source: Ryder in the ESA Columbus.

Don Ryder floated beside a large gash he'd sliced in the interior panelling of the Columbus module. A clip from one of the empty instrument racks drifted free in the air currents— Billy knew the regular crew of the Station would never have been sloppy. Ryder delved into the wires, cutting through them to get to the inner surface of the module's hull. Every brush of his laser cutter against the scorched composite sent another spurt of smoke out from the breach.

"You trying to kill me?" Billy said. "There's vacuum on the other side." He rubbed bleary eyes, but they still itched from the dust.

Ryder paused; the laser hung in the air between them. He seemed all astronaut, crew-cut, stocky and short, but Billy knew the man had joined the NASA boys late from the US Navy.

"I've got to isolate this junction," Ryder said, as if explaining to a cadet. He eased a trunk of wires from a conduit. "When we split the modules up, we've got to make sure the emergency systems don't kick in and drain the batteries."

Billy raised an eyebrow. Sure, there was a control node there—Billy was as familiar with all of the station's systems as a commander had to be—but there were a dozen better ways to ensure the emergency systems were disabled, and none of them involved cutting through the wall of any Station modules. And waking him.

"You making this up as you go along?" he said.

Ryder's lips tightened. "Some of us read the schedule, Commander."

"To hack chunks out the wall?" Billy replied. But he remembered the bulky file Houston had uploaded to him. Sure, he'd scanned it. It lurked in his 'to do' folder. Maybe.

Ryder went back to prising the fountain of coloured strands apart. "These are supplementary specs I'm working to," he added. "I got these new instructions an hour ago, from Maryland."

Maryland. It was very convenient, that. The Goddard Centre near DC was not directly connected to Mission Control at Houston. Billy knew no one there who had worked on the specialist project needed to decommission the Station safely. He had no quick way of checking up on Ryder's explanation, but this wasn't by the book. After months in space—years, taking into account his whole career, not just these last six months on the Station—he was less than a clumsy tourist in his own command.

But what was it to him? Who cared—now that his mission, his career, was over? No doubt this hard-assed Navy Man still had the glory days before him: there was plenty of work waiting for those ready to dismantle the rest of the US Space Programme.

Ryder threw him a glance. "Is Tony ready to play astronaut yet?"

"He's chewing pills in the Zvezda, the far side of the Station," Billy said, over the sound of wire snipping. "I'll check on our space-sick hero." And once this was sorted, he figured, he could get back to the lab and more shut-eye.

He grabbed one of the brackets that had once held cutting-edge microgravity experiments, then propelled himself out of the compartment. He knew the route well: down the main tube through the Unity Node 1 section connecting the string of American, European and Japanese modules and through to the old Russian-built sections. After six months on board he was familiar in three dimensions with every customised unit (what was left of them), every conduit, every collection of piping: he cherished his flight past them like a favourite daydream.

Inside the Zvezda, Tony Lario clung like a drowning man to a patch of netting on the wall.

"Your stomach settled yet?" Billy asked the software engineer.

Lario gulped on Billy's approach and brushed his nostrils with his palm.

Billy pretended to ignore the action, but made a mental note to shower before they left orbit. He couldn't help noting Lario's clean jump-suit next to his own frayed cuffs and greyed cloth.

Lario's head was in line with one of the small nine-inch portholes. He gazed out at the blackness.

And the novice astronaut searches for stars he'll never see. The sunlight drowns out any view of them until we orbit into Earth's shadow. Then he'll see the stars. He's so green up here that he doesn't know that we need to turn off the Station's outer lights to see the stars at night, just like on Earth.

Lario and Ryder had come up in the final Soyuz visit, replacing Billy's routine crew. Two Americans, ferried up to low orbit by the Russian workhorse. Nice of the Russians to lend a hand—when it comes to ending America's presence in space.

"I'll live long enough to do the job, Commander," Lario said. Sallow-cheeked beneath jet black hair, it had only been a few hours in zero gee for him. But Billy knew that Lario would recover soon enough. Nothing concentrated the mind more than a job to be done.

And they had a space station to fling beyond the Galapagos, into the watery wastes of the Southern Ocean.

"Ryder says he'll need you soon," Billy said.

Lario gave a curt nod. "I'm up for it, Commander. I need to run through the station software routines..." His voice grew stronger. He let go of the netting and drifted sideways towards the galley, then bumped against the refrigerator door. "I've got to clear the systems in the Destiny, Columbus and Kibo modules. They'll need a purge before we begin the shut-down sequence."

"Your friend seems keen on making holes in my walls." Billy watched him carefully for signs of a reaction. Lario ignored the comment.

"I'd better get to work," he said. "Or he'll moan that I'm holding him up when it comes to disengagement."

Disengagement. NASAspeak for dismemberment. Each module of the ISS was going to be detached from the other, until there was no longer the long proud structure that they'd so carefully put together over so many missions. A tearing apart, before being cast down to the flames of re-entry. But it had to be that way. Without separation, the whole station complex would tumble as it hit the upper reaches of the atmosphere—would be much less controllable as it fell.

"I need to go to the Columbus module first," Lario said.

Billy sighed. "I'll guide you there," he replied, taking Lario's arm. "Then I can get back to my own work."

"Your schedule's tight?"

"Yep," Billy said. He glanced at the NASA treadmill and exercise-bike, ignored their silent reproach. "I'll cope. I've got my own way of doing things. Come on. Duty calls."

"I guess it's hard for you."

As they glided through the emptied ISS, he felt numb inside. The last time he'd had this feeling was when the family had moved home to be closer to the Cape. He'd done a final check on their old house after the removal men had cleared it out: the lounge, the kitchen, the hall, the echoing bedrooms all eerily larger, yet still full of lingering memories.

"Well," he said, "I've lived here for months, been a commander, run a lot of useful projects. It just seems a pity..." He let his voice trail off. He remembered they were still live on the internet. *Armstrong*, he thought, ruefully, *didn't have to put up with this.* Not with emails commenting on his every move, with his Public Approval ratings changing by the second. He had to watch that.

As an African American, word from the top was that the White House planned to use him as a goodwill ambassador to Botswana, Kenya and Zaire once this mission was over. But now the ISS project had collapsed in ignominy, even that idea had unravelled. What kind of a symbol of success was he now, in the international competition for the African minerals and their solar farms?

They entered the Columbus. Ryder was gone.

No doubt wreaking destruction elsewhere.
Billy gazed around at the module's interior, the wounds Ryder had left in the panelling. It was already an empty shell as the European Community had sold most of its interior off to the Chinese. Billy still resented the way the Chinese astronauts had come over from their Station of the Heavenly People, dismantled millions of dollars worth of customised equipment, and shipped it out with depressing efficiency. The Chinese captain, Xan Zu, had been apologetic, but stuck firmly to his list of bargains as Billy watched the guts being torn out of his Command.

"I'll get started," Lario said, sounding keen.

I used to be like you. Now I know better. "I gotta go now," Billy said. He spun around, and ducked out of sight between the bare instrument racks.

Despite himself, he was fully awake. If he couldn't get back to dozing in the lab, at least—in the Destiny—Ryder and Lario would stay out of his hair: assuming Maryland hadn't changed the schedule again.

As he flew through the hatch of Destiny, the station swung into daylight. He glanced out of his favourite porthole. An old habit kicked in: he quickly picked out the major coastline below, a maroon shadow against the deep blue, outlined by a white tracing of surf. That blue sheen was the Atlantic. It looked like a major storm was brewing up over the Congo coast.

The Congo had featured in his last message from the children before Ryder and Lario had boarded. Naomi and Charles were researching their family's ancestry on the Web. They'd traced his family back to a slave taken from the Congo area. Billy gazed down at the region. He reflected how miraculous his presence up here in the heavens would have seemed to that scared slave boy ripped from his homeland. But that terrible journey across the ocean—one that the Station now crossed in minutes—had led his descendent up to this wondrous place.

He settled himself in front of one of the remaining control panels in the US lab, where he couldn't see the emptied storage racks that hung like scavenged ribs from the stripped interior. He pulled some netting around his waist to stop having to reposition himself against the air currents, then tapped in his ID. The screen stayed blank.

He tried the usual tricks, but nothing worked. He was locked out of his command.

✦

"I've got a problem, Houston," Billy said (then inwardly cursed himself—he'd sworn never to use those particular words). "The station's operating system's gone dead on me."

He paused. The radio downlink he'd found in the Unity module, next to the US lab, ran on emergency batteries. How long would the juice last?

"Houston?"

"Got you, Commander," came back the voice of 'Zippy' Fynes. Billy managed to pick out the words above the whine of one of Unity's past-sell-by-date air pumps. "I'm here for you."

But Fynes's Texan drawl jolted Billy. He'd expected to hear the clipped tones of his friend Al Mitchell—the usual capcom during Billy's stay on the ISS. Zippy Fynes on the case reminded Billy how sensitive these end-times were: political dynamite if there was a hash-up. "Not a problem," Zippy added. "It's a Code 7, just a routine realignment of the system."

Code 7. Ever since the Freedom of Information legalities had forced them to have a permanent open channel of communication between the ISS and Mission Control Centre, and the public, they'd had to think up ways of getting messages through undetected by the general public and the Press. A Code 7 was one of them—something Billy and Zippy had agreed behind closed doors in Zippy's condo—but even then Billy was sure the Chinese and Russians knew what it meant: that Houston didn't have a clue what was happening, but hang in there—they were working on it.

He headed back to the Zvezda to find Tony Lario. If the answer was to be found anywhere, he was certain it was with the man who was working deep within the station's software software systems. But why did Houston know nothing about this?

As Billy approached the Zvezda, he felt his stomach knot. *Maryland.* That was the centre now... where the shut-down crew had been based. Not part of the old NASA family at all.

"Tony?" he said.

Lario was busy at an interface link. Space sickness forgotten, he stared intently at the screen.

Billy moved closer, took in the screen's display before it blanked.

"How's it going?" he asked, trying to sound casual.

"Fine," Lario said. "I've completed the timetable on the elektron and vozdukh system shutdowns. We're almost back to schedule."

"Good," Billy replied. "What you've done... it wouldn't affect the general operation system, would it?"

Lario shrugged. "It shouldn't." He hesitated, then asked: "Why? Have you had trouble?"

Billy reached over and pulled out the communications plug connecting the module to the rest of the Station. Millions of screens would be static now, millions of speakers would give a hiss of white noise. And millions of viewers would already be emailing Houston, crashing the system with their complaints; and no doubt lawyers were already invoking the Freedom of Information laws to get the link restored.

"My command codes don't work," he said, ignoring Lario's bewildered face. "I can't get into the system."

Lario frowned. "That's nothing I've done. Impossible." He caught the look in Billy's eyes. "I mean it, Commander."

Billy hesitated, then said: "I should be able to access the system through your portal. At least I'll see what the problem is."

Lario nodded. "Sure, Commander. But you'll have to wait. I've just had to reboot things from my end—it won't take too long."

Billy peered at him, hoping—this time—Lario couldn't read his thoughts.

"Okay," he said. He reached around the display panel and plugged the communications link back into its socket.

He paused, considering his words, then spoke before the listening millions. "—so we'll try to minimize any disruptions to communications in future." He gave Lario a wink, which he hoped this newbie would pick up on. "I don't care what schedule you have to stick to," he continued. "The folks Earthside love looking over our shoulders."

Lario seemed to catch on. He gave Billy the thumbs-up. "Sorry, Commander," he said. "I'll give a warning next time I need to cut the link."

"Thanks."

At least he got that message. It's easy to forget they're listening in all the time up here.

Billy had to get to the Quest airlock module. Lario hadn't been quick enough when he'd blanked the screen. Billy's experienced eye had read the systems schematic and caught that the whole network was down, except in the Quest.

Quest is still live. Maybe because it still had its own batteries, not been left weakened when the solar array power was cut back.

He hurried through the connecting tunnels that threaded between the modules, past the gaps in the walls where the more valuable equipment had been stripped out and sold to the Russians: gloveboxes, protein crystal growth units, centrifuges. He almost missed a familiar hand-hold at one point, where netting now bundled up a motley collection of cheaper spares that Moscow had rejected.

But good enough for us to keep. To take back in the Soyuz and put under glass for our kids to see all that was left of our dreams.

Now the bare walls were stained with streaks of mildew. Months of neglect had allowed it to build on unwiped condensations in the nooks and crannys of the station modules. That, and the open conduits, the exposed piping: it all reminded him of the last days of Mir. Did the Russians take a secret pleasure in reducing the ISS to a similar state? He hoped they were better than that. They'd been businesslike, almost embarrassed, when it came to removing the station's least-degraded photovoltaic solar panels for their own use. They'd bid higher than the Chinese for them, so the NASA grapevine whispered, as they were less interested in a Mars trip than the Chinese.

As he approached the Quest airlock, he hoped it was still habitable, and not too hot inside. It was set snugly under the main truss from where the solar panels had hung. Now that the panels were gone, their shadows no longer protected it from direct sunlight as the station's orbit swung it through Earth's daytime.

The Quest airlock, one of two on the station, was also a Soyuz docking port. It had been installed in the heady days when it seemed that the ISS was really the only way forward for space travel, when there could be any number of the reliable Russian craft passing through on their way out of Earth orbit. Now, there was only the lifeboat Soyuz docked: their escape craft when it was time to finally decommission his home. These days, the other Soyuz craft in the Russian fleet had a better place to go: the Russian Station, orbiting higher up, and growing with every Proton launch from Baikonur.

Billy saw that the Quest airlock door was open. Good. That meant that the temperature inside hadn't built up to an unbearable level. As he entered the module he realised how chilled it had been getting inside the rest of the Station as the power units were shut down.

He found the junction box tucked in between two storage lockers. He was familiar with the junction design: it just needed unclipping. He ran a fingertip along its rim, feeling for the catch. Once he could get at the innards, it wouldn't take him long to access the Station's command systems again.

It was the back of his neck that first detected the changing air current in the compartment, a brief stir of cool air that warned him to turn around. As he did, he caught movement out of the corner of his eye. Lario must have gained his spacelegs and been following him. He heard a thud as the airlock door shut behind him.

Lario had activated the emergency mechanism, sealing the door against supposed leaks. Billy was shut inside the Quest.

✦

They'd already missed the final chance to maintain orbit—from now on, everything would be different. Without the regular boosts to maintain its height above Earth, the ISS was already dropping. The trajectory would soon take them down from two hundred and twenty miles to seventy-five miles, over two fast orbits, before final re-entry.

The Quest airlock seemed to close in on him. Billy fought the feeling, tried to stay calm. Logical.

But the timetable was scored into his heart.

He jabbed trembling fingers at the airlock keypad, but the door to the rest of the station stayed shut, despite the emergency command code that only the commander should know. He tugged the manual lever, but it wouldn't budge.

The light flickered, dimmed, then returned a little weaker as back-up circuits kicked in. Billy turned his efforts to the junction box. Eventually he got a result: not an over-ride to the station's systems, but a link to Houston: to 'Zippy' Fynes.

"Zippy?" he said. "What's going on?"

"Billy!" Zippy sounded relieved to hear him. The emotion in the Texan's voice raised the hairs at the back of Billy's neck.

"Where are you, Billy?" Zippy said. "Anywhere near the Kibo?"

"No," Billy replied. "I'm in Quest, Zippy."

"What?" Zippy exclaimed. "You've got to get to the Kibo and cut it off from the station. It's full of explosives. Those packages from the last shuttle delivery—Don Ryder stored them in the Kibo module."

Billy stared at the com speaker in disbelief.

"We're up against it, Billy," Zippy continued. "Turns out those two son-of-a's got shut-down plans of their own. Security got a confirmation through channels. Some group calling themselves America In Space hijacked this mission. Lord know's what they're gonna do with the station... where they're gonna crash it."

"Crash it?" Billy repeated, dazed. Fragments from the last few hours were coming together, making a gruesome sense.

"We're off the internet now. It's a private channel," Zippy said. "To hell with the lawyers. This is a National Security Matter. Overrides Freedom of Information, especially if they don't want tonnes of ISS dropping on their heads."

"You think that's the plan?" Billy asked. He tried to shut out the image of the whole complex, module after module, aimed at DC... battering the White House like cannonballs.

"I dunno," Zippy said. "But you're all we've got up there, Billy. Washington doesn't want to talk to the Russians, the Chinese, but they'll have to. It may not be us that Ryder and

Lario are after."

Billy nodded. A scenario even worse than an attack on Washington DC, or even New York. Maybe Moscow was the target, or Beijing...

He gazed at the airlock door, then said: "I've got an idea, but it'll mean cutting the link to you."

"Are you crazy? We need to stay in touch."

"I'll do my best," Billy promised, then switched off the com.

After all, he couldn't be certain that Lario or Ryder weren't listening. They wouldn't know that, during his early days up here, he'd had a nightmare about a debris strike against the station. The usual procedures were meant to protect the crew: sealed modules, an escape Soyuz at the ready, sealant for micro-debris wounds. Not satisfied with that, Billy had made sure that one of the standard Russian Orlan spacesuits was left in the Quest, even after the Russians had abandoned the ISS.

All spacesuits needed to operate at a markedly lower pressure than that in the Station cabin and it took over four hours to adapt to the depressurized pure oxygen used in a US spacesuit. But the Orlan was a semi-rigid suit and could be operated at a higher pressure than his US spacesuit—he could be ready for spacewalk in just thirty minutes. That time saved might stop him being too late if Lario and Ryder were on a suicide mission, otherwise he'd be riding the Quest down through the inferno of re-entry.

He suited up as fast as he could, feeling strangely alone without the usual double-checks from Houston.

The Pirs airlock, just across from the length of the Zarya module, was his target. From there, he could re-enter the main interior of the Station, and make his way up to the Kibo at the far end.

✦

Once the outer hatch swung open to vacuum, Billy grasped the rim and hauled himself outside. The station was moving into sunshine; the glare dazzled him for a moment. He lowered his visor and gazed across the curve of the Zarya. The view of Earth was blocked by the module's large external fuel tanks.

The absence of the solar panels robbed his ISS of dignity, unable even to power itself, like a once magnificent tree now starved of sunlight.

As he pulled himself along the grey panelled hull, finding edges to grip with his bulky gloves, he became conscious of being truly alone. This was the first time he'd been outside without having a million people watching him through his visor, or being able to scan his heart rate, his blood sugar level, his respiration; even his website 'hit' levels. If he let go and drifted off, there would be no one to see it, to sound the alarm.

He grabbed a protruding strut and squeezed his eyes shut. The suit became his whole universe. He swallowed hard. Tried to calm down. As his breathing slowed, he felt ashamed: Zippy Fynes wouldn't stand for this behaviour; Lario and Ryder would be laughing at the great Space Veteran.

He began to pull himself forward again, between two fuel tanks. A shard of foil dislodged from the outer covering of the module's hull. It drifted past his visor, joining its fellow millions of pieces of debris in orbit.

His pace quickened across the Zarya. The great curved plane of the Earth loomed into view, laced with white fleecy clouds, and hung alongside him.

He dared not stop now. A small part of him wanted to turn and embrace the glowing blue planet with open arms, and drift towards it with open, aching limbs.

He dared not stop.

✦

At last Billy reached the module's edge, and followed its curve down into shadow. He was grateful to be out of the direct sunlight. Sweat prickled his back. The tips of his fingers felt numb from the effort of gripping what handholds he could through the heavy gloves. But there was no time to rest.

Before he began to climb up close to the Zvezda module, he glanced up and out into space. The stars were now visible— millions of bright steady lights—and their sudden appearance made him gasp.

But his expert eye spotted something moving against the

canopy of stars. The dullness returned to his heart: it was the new Russian space station. It soared above his orbit, strong with the cannibalised parts from his own command. And worse, it reminded him of that last Chinese press release. The Chinese had denied it was a deliberate humiliation tactic against the West but, the week the ISS was being sent to destruction, the Chinese were launching a permanent colony to Mars.

A bizarre thought struck him: what if that particular slave boy had never been taken from the Congo? Would Billy have still made it into space? The Russians and Chinese were eager to fly Africans, in their determination to woo the African nations for their resources.

He sighed. For better, or for worse, he was American. These last six bittersweet months in space had been a final gift from Uncle Sam. Now it was payback time.

He climbed the Zvezda despite his exhaustion, this time grateful for the blinding sunlight.

The Pirs airlock was up ahead.

✦

Back inside, Billy wriggled out of the spacesuit, letting the chill station air wash over him. He listened carefully, but there was no sound of Lario or Ryder, even with the now hushed fans. The smell of mildew filled his nostrils. He'd been living with that rotten odour so long he'd gotten used to it. Now he'd have to put up with it again—if only, he thought grimly, for a little while longer.

He glided silently though the air in the dimmed light. With its darkened, empty, silent compartments, the station looked, felt and smelled like an abandoned hulk. He saw more evidence of Ryder's work. Panels were missing from the interiors, and behind them he could see rewiring, and welded units that he didn't recognize.

In moments he'd crossed back through the Unity, past the sealed hatch where he'd been trapped, and on into the Destiny lab. Inside, his gaze fell on the emergency air pump controls. They allowed a sudden boost of air into the module if the crew ever needed it, one of those extra safety systems NASA insisted on. Useless as a weapon. He stared at the dials, thinking, then his fingers flew over the keypad. There was something he could do...

✦

Node 2, Harmony, lay beyond the Destiny lab. Billy entered, then made a right-angled turn into the large interior space of the Japanese Kibo module.

The explosive packages were gone. Lario floated at the far end of the compartment, out of easy reach. He gripped a control handset.

"Rebooted the system, yet, Tony?" Billy tried to keep his voice steady. That handset had to be a detonator for the explosives.

"Didn't expect to see you so soon," Lario said. He licked his lips. Beads of sweat speckled his forehead. "I'm nearly done, Commander. We're off-line officially now. No one can hear us Earthside. Job's over."

Billy took a deep breath. "The shut-down?" he said. He glanced at the detonator. "Is that standard procedure?"

"I wish you'd waited in the airlock—"

"I'm still the commander here," Billy said. "Not some has-been locked in a waiting room while you get on with whatever you've been doing."

He kicked back gently at the wall behind him, and began to drift towards Lario. He didn't want to appear too threatening, but he had to get hold of the detonator. Was it wired up yet, or was this a bluff? A cold thought struck him. *And what was Ryder up to?*

"So what's the plan, Tony?" he asked.

"You know, commander," Lario said. "We're the shut-down crew."

A sudden thought struck Billy: had Lario disconnected the emergency air pump and timer?

"I—" he began.

His voice was drowned out by the sudden roar of the emergency fans. The ventilator system kicked into action around them. The blast of wind sent them both tumbling through the air.

Billy lashed out at Lario with his foot, catching Lario's hand with his heel. Lario let go of the detonator; it twirled around them. Lario tried to grab it, but he couldn't match Billy's long months of experience in zero gee. Billy twisted like an Olympic gymnast. He plucked the handset out of the air, then steadied himself against a bulkhead.

Lario spun around, grabbed wildly at a drifting piece of flex that was attached to a wall. He tugged at it, then pulled himself to a stationary position. The hurricane died; they were left glaring at each other across a few feet of debris-strewn air.

Billy held the handset up in triumph. "Where's Ryder?"

"He's in the Soyuz," Lario said. "He's readying it for us."

"Us?" Billy said. "So you were going to take me with you?"

"Of course. We're not killers."

"So you say," Billy spat back. "Where were you planning to drop the station? Washington? New York?"

Lario's eyes widened. "Where'd you hear that?"

"Zippy Fynes at Houston's told me about America In Space."

Lario shook his head. "Zippy Fynes couldn't know the truth—just the rumours. He's only based at the Houston end. That place leaks worse than..." He paused, took a deep breath. "We're Washington-directed—but it's not official, if you get my meaning. We'd never have gotten this operation past the UN. Washington needs deniability." He glanced at his watch. "You've really messed things up, Commander. Delayed us. The station needs to go to disengagement now or we'll miss the orbital window."

"Sure," Billy said. "But we're gonna do it my way: by the book. End this Mission properly."

"With honour?"

Billy stiffened. "We make do with what we've got."

"Is that good enough?" Lario pointed an accusing finger at him. "You're as gutted as I am about America pulling out of space." He waved a dismissive hand, took in their surroundings. "Our former partners have left us with these empty tin cans for our troubles."

Billy thought of the Russians orbiting above them; the Chinese boosting out to Mars; the bitterness of scuttling back to Earth...

"Maybe you're right," he said, reluctantly. "But if you're so certain I'd be with you, why didn't you let me in on this before?"

"The internet eavesdroppers. How could we have taken the time offline without having the lawyers causing trouble?"

Despite himself, Billy could feel himself wavering.

"Commander!" Lario added. "If you don't help me, then you'll be letting down your country."

"You think I don't care about my country?"

Lario hesitated, then said: "You tow the NASA line. You're a symbol. Face it. The last American commander in space. We couldn't trust you."

For the first time in freefall, Billy felt sick. He saw that he couldn't end this mission, his career, on such a sour note.

The chips Houston had dealt him were too few. If Lario gave him a chance to change the game...

"So why do you need the explosives?" he said.

✦

The Soyuz left the International Space Station on time, and positioned itself for the deorbital burn. Billy glanced across at Don Ryder, but the gruff pilot seemed happy with the old Russian technology. In between them, Tony Lario sat with his eyes half-closed. Billy guessed that he wasn't looking forward to the bumpy ride down. But his mission had been completed. Behind them, the station was in its death throes.

Billy didn't mind that, now. The Soyuz would take them round the Earth a few times before they lined up for the re-entry window.

From where Billy sat he caught a glimpse, through the small porthole, of the Atlantic rippling up the Florida coast to the silenced launch gantries of the Cape. He swallowed hard. For the first time in months he felt a warm glow. Even though he was strapped inside a Russian spacecraft, and they were abandoning the skies to other nations.

It didn't seem long before the separate parts of the ISS, module by module, began to hit the deeper layers of the atmosphere. As each one did, its explosives ignited. Colours streamed across the skies of the world. Red, white and blue—

each colour five times wider than the full Moon—streaked around the curve of the Earth, over the dark evening of India, clipped part of the Russian skies, then cloaked the stars above China. A series of sonic booms turned millions of eyes upward. Through the TV networks, the internet, billions more watched the display. The second stage of the fireworks ignited, sending enormous sparkles of light across the sheets of glowing colours. Millions of people looked up and saw the Stars and Stripes reach out, fifty miles above their heads, before dying away under the cold steady stars of the night.

Nigel Brown has had stories published in various magazines and anthologies, including Interzone, Aboriginal Science Fiction and The Year's Best SF 9 (Hartwell & Cramer). As well as science fiction, he has had fantasy, ghost and historical fiction published in the UK, USA and Japan. He has been a regular book reviewer for Interzone, and has been a co-editor on the William Hope Hodgson Night Land tribute website at www.thenightland.co.uk/nightmap.html. He first published in the 1970s with A Chronology of the Planet of the Apes, and writes the occasional article on comic books on the SuperStuff website at www.superstuff73.blogspot.com

LAUNCH DAY

David L Clements

IT'S LAUNCH DAY. In just a few hours I'll find out if my scientific career is about to move into high gear, or if my future will end up in pieces on the bottom of the Atlantic Ocean.

I start early, waiting for a taxi to take me to Bush House, home of the BBC World Service. Across the UK and Europe other astronomers working on the Herschel and Planck satellites are doing the same. We're all getting media appearances out of the way before heading to wherever we can watch a live feed of the satellites' launch. After my interview, I'll be going to the Rutherford Appleton Lab near Oxford, where the UK Herschel and Planck teams are gathering with visiting dignitaries and members of the media.

I've been working on these two satellites for eight years and they've been a part of the scientific landscape since I completed my PhD in 1991. But success or failure depends on what happens today.

UK media is dominated by BBC television or, for more thoughtful coverage, BBC Radio 4. But if you want a massive audience and worldwide reach you go to the World Service. A top-rated Radio 4 appearance might reach eight million, but the World Service regularly gets audiences over a hundred million. I try to put thoughts of this vast number of listeners out of my mind as I answer the interviewer's questions. I describe what the satellites will do and what will happen with today's launch. Then it's over and I'm ushered through the splendid art deco interior and into a taxi to Paddington Station for my journey to the Rutherford Lab.

Of the two satellites, Herschel has been around the longest, at least in terms of conceptual development. It is the last of the European Space Agency's cornerstone missions in the Horizon

2000 programme. Originally named FIRST, the Far-Infrared Space Telescope, it's a big expensive mission, costing about a billion Euros. All ESA countries are involved and there are contributions from NASA, Canada and China. With a diameter of 3.5m, Herschel has the largest mirror ever launched on an astronomical satellite, dwarfing Hubble's 2.5m mirror. But it won't produce images as sharp as Hubble because it operates at much longer wavelengths.

While Hubble works in the optical, seeing light coming from the hot surfaces of stars (a few thousand degrees), Herschel works at wavelengths a hundred times longer. It sees material that's much colder—just tens of degrees above absolute zero. This allows it to study the dust that is intimately linked to the processes that form stars, to search for the debris left behind by forming planetary systems, and to probe the dusty galaxies that produce the enigmatic Cosmic Infrared Background, which hides about half the energy generated in the universe since the Big Bang.

Herschel will also study interstellar chemistry, especially water, one of the most important molecular species for understanding physical and chemical processes in everything from star-forming regions to stars expelling their outer envelopes during the incontinent later stages of stellar evolution. But water is also a serious problem because our atmosphere is full of it, absorbing the emission needed to study objects in the far-infrared. This is why Herschel and Planck, operating at similar wavelengths, need to be in space, free of this atmospheric absorption.

At the Rutherford Lab, we've taken over the main lecture theatre. There's an audience of fellow scientists, administrators and the leaders of the funding agencies who paid for the satellites, as well as local politicians and journalists. The partners and children of some of the scientists have also come along so they can find out more about the project that has taken their loved ones away from home, or forced them to work late into the night.

But some people are missing. We're effectively the B-team, left at home to entertain and inform the local media, and watch the launch on television. The real bigwigs are seven thousand kilometres away at Kouru, French Guiana, on the coast of South America where ESA launches its rockets. They have ringside seats for the launch and will do their bit for the visiting international media. The closer we get to the opening of the two-hour launch window the more the tension rises. This isn't just a result of natural excitement. It isn't me worrying about the talk I have to give on the Planck satellite. It's because there's a ghost haunting the party, the ghost of Cluster and the launch of Ariane 501. Back in 1996, the first Ariane 5 rocket was launched, carrying the Cluster satellites for the first ESA cornerstone mission. Ariane 5 was a new launch vehicle, the great hope of ESA and Arianespace, its commercial launch company. It could carry larger payloads than previous ESA rockets and was predicted by the engineers to be at least ninety-five percent reliable. I watched the 501 launch on a live video-feed in a lecture theatre not that different from today's. The rocket exploded just seconds after launch, scattering debris over the jungle and into the Atlantic. That explosion was the end of the scientific careers of several friends who had worked on Cluster. Having tied my career to the success or failure of Herschel and Planck, I'm in the same position today as they were before the 501 launch.

The clock ticks on, and it's soon my turn at the podium. I provide a brief outline of the Planck mission, how it will scan the entire sky at nine different wavelengths, from the far-infrared into the microwaves, providing a much more precise map of the fluctuations in the cosmic microwave background. This is the dull light, left over from the Big Bang, that permeates the entire universe with a cool glow just 2.7 degrees above absolute zero. To detect this radiation the instruments on Planck must be kept just 0.1 degree above absolute zero, three times cooler than the instruments on Herschel, making Planck the coldest place in space.

The satellites are not being sent into Earth orbit. Instead, they're going to the second Lagrange point, L2. This is a point 1.5 million kilometres from Earth where the gravitational fields of the Earth and the Sun balance, and where these two sources of heat are always in the same direction. The large sun shields on Herschel and Planck will always be pointed towards the Sun and

Earth, and their instruments pointed away, ensuring that they never see the boiling warmth of either. This helps keep the instruments cool, and preserves their essential liquid helium reservoirs for as long as possible.

My talk is over. The countdown presses closer to zero. We have a two-hour launch window, but we aim to launch the instant it opens. Because we're launching two satellites, the launch itself isn't the only hazard. The satellites must get cleanly away from the launch bus before they can make their separate ways to L2. Separation happens thirty minutes after launch, and only at that point can we declare the launch a success.

The talks finished a little earlier than planned, and the video is on, filling the vast screen of the lecture theatre with a run down of past ESA successes. But dominating my mind are memories of the 501 launch.

There's nothing we can do. When the Vulcain main engine and solid rocket boosters fire, we're entirely dependent on the Arianespace engineers. They have to make sure that hundreds of tonnes of high-explosive rocket fuel explodes the right way to get our delicate, high-precision scientific instruments, strapped on top of it all, into orbit, undamaged.

The final countdown begins.

"Trois, deux, une, tup!"

The Vulcain fires, plumes of steam erupt from either side of the launch pad. Then the solid boosters fire, blasting out distinctive yellow smoke, and the rocket stack is hurled upwards. Across Europe, at JPL, Caltech and online in astronomy groups all over the world, eyes are glued to screens. The roar of the rockets reaches the microphones a few seconds after the rocket clears the pad. By this point, it's already atop a vast column of flame, climbing into a clear blue sky.

Thus begins what must be the longest thirty minutes of my life. We follow the rocket every step of the way. We follow the exhaust plume as it climbs into the sky but, more important, we also follow the telemetry track from the control room, showing how the actual launch is proceeding compared to the predictions for perfect performance. Soon the camera flicks away from the control room, now being filled by our colleagues in Kouru who have seen all they can from the ground, to a view from the rocket itself as the solid fuel boosters are jettisoned—an astounding view from the very edge of space. We ignore the calls from some of the non-astronomers to open the champagne because we know there is still a long way to go.

Next is the separation of the first stage and the ignition of the second. Like every step so far, this goes like clockwork. I begin to think the launch might be going well, but desperately try to suppress these thoughts to avoid the crushing disappointment that will come if some later stage fails. The coverage is now focused on the control room, showing controllers sitting at their desks doing nothing. I am pleased to see they look almost bored.

Originally, Herschel and Planck were meant to be launched separately, with Planck going first, providing, as a by-product of its microwave background work, a survey of dusty objects that Herschel could follow up. But the Cluster failure precluded that, because the cost of its replacement ate into ESA's budget and forced major rethinking of all missions. Back in 1996, it looked as if Herschel and Planck were going to become one spacecraft with the instruments and telescopes glued back to back—a Frankenstein satellite. This would not have worked, for many reasons, but the two projects were joined managerially and put onto the same launch vehicle. This meant all of ESA's far-infrared eggs were in the same basket.

We reach the final critical phase for Herschel, where it separates from the launch bus and heads for L2. We are treated to a final few frames of video taken by a camera at the back of Herschel showing its clean separation from Planck—the last external view of Planck and its Sylda 5 launch bus that anyone will see. Soon after that, it's time for Planck to cast aside the launcher and escape to L2.

Applause erupts. We start breathing again. And outside, at the reception, we hear champagne corks starting to pop.

This afternoon we can celebrate, but tomorrow we start the hard work of commissioning the instruments. It will still be months before real science can begin.

But launch, the most dangerous phase of all, has been a huge success.

David L Clements is an astrophysicist working at Imperial College London on the Herschel and Planck satellites and in the broad fields of extragalactic astronomy and observational cosmology. He also writes science fiction, and has been published in Analog, Nature Futures and in a number of anthologies including Footprints (Hadley Rille Press), One Weird Idea (Glorious Dawn Press), Cheer Up Universe (Whortleberry Press) and Conflicts (Newcon Press). His story in Conflicts, 'In the Long Run', received an honourable mention in the 2011 Year's Best Science Fiction anthology edited by Gardener Dozois.

INCARNATE

Craig Pay

No PARENT EVER wants to lose a child, especially not the same child twice. Watching my wife across the table, I'm reminded that we still have at least this in common. She looks older now. Tired. As if she left her will to live back in Tripoli. Our home, three years ago.

The lights are low. The smell of sweat and smoke hangs heavy in the plastic, recycled air. The dull static of a bass-line pulses up through the table, into my outstretched hands. And then I realise that the tips of my fingers are starting to ache as they try to dig their way into the extruded aluminium table-top. Over my wife's shoulder I can see the distant shadow of a dancer turning lazy, low-gee pirouettes around a tall chromed pole. Beyond that, a wall screen showing a view outside Station: the indistinct arc of Titan's upper atmosphere.

My wife leans forward. "I needed to talk to you."

"About?" I ask.

She doesn't say anything. We both know. It's about Mia, of course: our daughter.

I shrug. "There's nothing—"

"Not to *me* there isn't!" She still has the anger. A blush in her cheeks. "There never was!"

"You came out here—all the way out here, just to talk?"

"You don't answer my messages. I can't call, not with that delay." A halting exchange of video messages. The varying millions of kilometres between here and Earth that reduces all communication to a slow crawl. Arguments reduced to broken, one-sided monologues.

I catch her staring at the untouched glass of soy whiskey sat in front of me. To her raised eyebrow I say, "This isn't the Caliphate."

58

"Anyway," she continues, "it turns out, this is *exactly* the place I needed to come."

Reaching inside her jacket, she pulls out a small transparent bag. Inside the bag I can see a thin sliver of crystal. The shard looks dirty; I realise I'm looking at dried blood. Months old now. I don't need to ask who it belonged to. I clench my fists. I see tears in my wife's eyes: a quiet desperation that matches my own.

"We buried her!" I lean forward, trying to make a grab for the bag.

She snatches it away. Slides the bag inside her jacket. "I paid someone," she says. "I paid them a lot of money to recover this—"

"*Recover?*" I half-stand and reach out across the table, fingers reaching for the scruff of her jacket.

"What?" She lets out a nervous laugh. "You're going to hit me?"

My other hand, I realise, is still clenched into a fist. A moment's silence. A few glances from the other people around the bar. Allowing my fingers to relax and let go, I sit back down. "Maybe I should. Hit you."

She tries to smile. "Sure, get locked up. Go ahead."

"They don't put people in prison out here," I say. "Or even ship them back. Fines for everything. And if you can't pay ..." I nod over her shoulder, towards the screen on the wall.

My wife glances around for a moment. I meant the view of Titan's atmosphere: the cold, dry darkness outside, but when she turns back around she just looks confused.

"Airlock," I explain, but she's already distracted, the back of her hand to her mouth. She closes her eyes for a moment.

"Feel sick?" I ask.

She nods, opening her eyes again. "If I move too quickly—turn my head."

"Probably just the Coriolis."

"I know," she says, looking annoyed.

"Still taking your meds? The micro-gravity pills they gave you on the transport?"

"No."

"Well, you should."

"They give me a headache." Her throat moves as she

swallows. She stands. Slowly, carefully.

"That's it?" I ask.

"I got my answer." She turns and walks away.

✦

This is the first time. The Mediterranean. A ground-effect vehicle flying along, just above the gently rolling waves, at a little over two hundred kilometres per hour. An overdue maintenance record on one of the starboard over-wing turbines. The turbine overheats and explodes with a dull thump that's barely audible inside the passenger compartment.

The forces that come into play, pressure and heat, are more than the brittle tungsten turbine blades can withstand. One after another, each narrow blade warps to breaking point and then shatters into countless fragments which spin away at several times the speed of sound, passing through the thin carbon-fibre hull, through the thin skin of the passengers. The ground-effect vehicle hits the water. Impact mitigation is successfully deployed: expanding foam, air bags, nylon webbing. Passengers and crew all survive this initial impact. Just one fatality seven minutes later. A spinning scrap of tungsten lodged inside the thigh of a fifteen year old girl. A girl on her way home from a student exchange in the Basque. The metal shard has neatly dissected her femoral artery. She begins to bleed out.

The ground-effect vehicle settles in the water and screams for help. All along the North African Riviera, drones pulse-detonate into the sky whilst human handlers in Alexandria and Monastir scramble to their stations. The drones arc over the crash-site, dropping inflatable medical and utility units.

The young girl has finished bleeding. So she dies.

Later, the expensive soul shard will be dug from the base of her skull, ready for incarnation in the fresh host kept on ice back in Tripoli.

✦

This is the second time. An overdose. Two years after the crash—

the girl is now seventeen. She has screamed her way through most nights, through dreams she always told her parents she could never remember. On more than one occasion, towards the end, they found her huddled in the bathroom in a spreading puddle of blood. Not finishing it. Not yet. Scars along the tops of her arms and thighs where no one would find them.

For two years she wasted towards transparency. *Post-traumatic stress, personality defect, failure to correctly assimilate the new incarnation.* Therapy seemed to make it worse.

She rents a room in an automated hotel that should have had better monitoring. She writes a letter using paper and a pen—a real pen, an ancient-looking thing turned from brass and filled with fresh soybean ink.

They argued, the day before: the parents and the girl. They told her they loved her. She told them: *"I'm not me! Why did you do it? You must hate me!"*

According to Caliphate law, the letter is legally binding. Intended will of the predult. No incarnation, no appeal.

The father runs, turning his back on everything. His job, all the money, his wife of twenty years, friends he has known since childhood. He sacrifices it all. They will have to understand. He can feel himself coming apart. Seventeen years he invested in this. He is reminded of a poem:

"Tis better to have loved and lost
Than never to have loved at all."

Which is wrong, he now realises. Better to have not bothered in the first place.

His tears float like tiny glass beads in the micro-gravity, settling to the metal chequer-plate flooring every time the transport uses its engines. Accelerating, decelerating. All the way to Titan orbit.

✦

Titan industry is predominantly noble gas farming and rare metal mining. Canisters of gases and crates of mineral ores are rail-gunned up into orbit, processed on-station and then shipped back Sunward. There's a little low-temperature manufacturing, but it's too unreliable for most corporations to bother with.

I stay in orbit. I know the real money's at the surface, but I like the simple solitude up here. Plus I don't have to worry about my bones wasting away down at the bottom of the meagre gravity well. I manage a warehouse. Sunward this would all be automated, but this is low-tech Titan where people are cheaper to keep running than machines. Out here, if something breaks it's either patched up or ripped out and replaced. No shipping back Sunward for repair, that would be too expensive. Anything left over gets air-locked, its orbit to soon decay down, and so it burns up as it enters Titan's smoky atmosphere. Perhaps, one day, the resulting molecules might be sucked up by a gas farmer and rail-gunned up to Station for processing and shipping out.

No doubt you've heard stories about Titan Station: the violently efficient work ethic, the party-hard self-abuse, the slack application of the law. You haven't heard the half of it. Out here the law has simply given way to the relentless glacial drift of an unforgiving market economy.

Sunward, incarnation is expensive and tightly regulated. A rarity. Out here, it's just another commodity, albeit even more expensive, just as rare. That's what my wife is looking for. She has a soul shard covered in our daughter's dried blood—her DNA—and she's looking for the kind of service that's simply not available back in Tripoli or anywhere else on Earth. A force-grown host and illegal incarnation.

Caliphate law is clear on the subject. Incarnation requires the permission of the donor. Until a child reaches predulthood at sixteen, that's up to the parents. My daughter was fifteen when she died the first time around; seventeen the second time.

"Dad?"

I can't breathe. I'm in the bar again. Staring down at the aluminium table top. Not wanting to look up, recognising the voice, but trying to ignore it—

"Dad?"

A figure sits down at the opposite side of the table. I look up. She looks the same as the day we argued, all those months ago in Tripoli. Except we aren't in the Caliphate any more. It's now four or five months since I last saw my wife and the last I'd heard were rumours and hearsay, of a woman flashing around a lot of cash and looking for a doctor. Making that kind of noise in a place like this will get you a lot of attention, and not necessarily the sort that you want. I'd assumed the worst when it all went quiet. Or that she'd given up and headed back Sunward.

"Mia."

My daughter nods.

"You look tired," she says. She has dark shadows around her own eyes.

"Where's your mother?" I ask.

Mia shrugs. "Sunward, I think. We argued."

We sit there for a moment, staring at each other.

Finally, she says, "This can't keep happening."

"I know—"

"No," she says. "No, you don't. It's horrible—" She gives a little laugh and shakes her head. "That's such an understatement."

After a moment, I say, "I'm sorry."

She slowly shakes her head. "You weren't to know."

"Tell me," I say, and when her face remains blank, I say, "Tell me what it feels like."

She frowns, eyes glazing as if she's recalling a memory. Then she says, "I remember my breath leaving my body. I could still hear for a little while. At some point—it felt like a long time, but it was straight away as if no time at all had passed—does that makes sense?" She pauses for a moment, as if expecting an answer, before she continues. "At some point, I realised I'd been awake for a while, but it's not like waking up. Fractured. Like all the pieces coming together. It hurt. I wasn't *me* anymore."

I nod and try to look like I understand. We sit in silence again. I'm content just to watch her. She looks away from my gaze as if she's embarrassed at my attention but I can't stop myself.

She looks back to me. "I need your help." Somehow, I know exactly what's coming. She tells me she's going to use pills again.

"You don't need me," I say. "A place like this..." I look around the bar then back to Mia. "A place like this, you can score enough dope to kill yourself a dozen times over."

"I can't risk coming back," she says.

I shake my head.

"You have to take care of me, afterwards..." She lifts a hand to touch the back of her head.

I look away, down at the table again. "I— I can't."

"Once it's done, just put me in an airlock." She's starting to sound desperate now. "You have access to an airlock, right?"

"Of course, back at the warehouse, but not big enough for a body—a person—you. The larger ones, they're all locked down."

Mia frowns. "Then this thing," she says, "in my head—"

"No, please..." My hands are starting to shake.

She explains how it will work. I sit and listen. I glance around the bar at all the other people: leaning at the bar, peering at the dancer. Mia has stopped talking and she's looking at me with an expectant look on her face.

"You have to," she says. And she tells me why.

Because I love her.

✦

We rent a cube at spindle-North, up on the higher levels, closer to the axis than the edge. The gravity up here is about a one third Earth-normal. We walk past abandoned habitat modules, boarded up windows and doors. The echo of the *adhan*, the call to prayer, echoes in the distance.

Titan Station is formed around a short spindle three or four hundred metres long, with spokes fanning out in all directions. The longest spokes extend for over eight hundred metres, and the entire structure rotates at a steady single revolution per minute to provide gravity. Blocky modules are strung along each of the spokes: engineering, warehousing and processing near the spindle where the gravity is low; habitation near the outside edge where the gravity approaches near-Earth normal.

Under Caliphate law, back on Earth or at the Trojans, it would be considered inhumane to house people in less than half Earth-normal gravity, but out here point-eight or point-nine Earth normal attracts a premium that few can afford. So the poor live wherever they can. Mia and I continue to move along the corridor with hesitant shuffles and the occasional long stride. We see thin barefoot children with bandy legs, dirty faces and twisted arms. Most are unlikely to see adulthood. Their heart and muscles will waste; their lymphatic systems will clot and collapse.

She pays for the cube herself, so there's less of a link back to me, she says. She writes another letter explaining that this is all her own doing and that I'm not involved.

In the end, we had to spend a couple of hours asking around in the bar before we found anyone who would sell us something as old-fashioned as a chemical drug. A two-by-ten bubblestrip pack of synthetic diamorphine patches.

Inside the cube, she pulls out the foam mattress from the wall and sits down. We hug. I cry. Mia's eyes are dry, her face an empty mask of serenity.

"I never had the chance to say goodbye," she says, "the last two times."

I say nothing.

She pops all twenty patches out onto the foam and begins, one by one, sticking them along the insides of her arms. Her eyes dilate, irises vanish. Wide black pupils.

After applying the thirteenth patch, she collapses into my arms. I wait for her breath to steady and slow.

And stop.

✦

I clutch her soul in my fist. My fingernails are etched with her blood. The memory of using the knife to dig into the back of her skull is still raw in my mind.

I puke myself dry in the pop-out sink. My DNA will be all over the place. Questions will be asked. Bribing my way out from this will probably wipe my savings clean. I walk back along the corridor, past the emaciated children, ignoring whistles and catcalls.

Now, standing in the warehouse, next to the garbage lock, I lift the crystal shard to my lips. And kiss. "Goodbye."

The lock cycles, hissing. I imagine Mia's soul tumbling, end over end, down towards Titan's dirty mustard clouds. I try not to think of her mixed up with all the other junk that couldn't be fixed. In a few hours, or perhaps a few days, she will hit the atmosphere and burn up. To be rendered down into her raw, constituent atoms.

I wonder whether she will be farmed in a few months' time. Will she pass through my hands again? Noble gases, to be shipped Sunward.

Craig Pay lives in the North of England and runs a writing group in Manchester. Sometimes he writes fiction that people label as 'literary'; other times he writes fiction that they label as 'genre'. He loves it when they're not sure. In 2011, Craig won the NAWG David Lodge trophy and his fiction has appeared with a number of magazines and websites including Murky Depths, Daily Science Fiction and Structo Magazine. He has just finished writing a historical/genre novel set in the 1800s. He is now learning Chinese. He can be reached at craigpay.com

DANCING ON THE RED PLANET
Berit Ellingsen

"WE WANT TO dance when we go out the airlock," the Belgian said.

"Pardon?" Vasilev, commander of the first manned mission to Mars, said.

"The music will be a speaker check for the atmospheric sound wave experiment," the Belgian replied.

"Why wasn't I informed about this earlier?" Vasilev asked.

"It's such a small thing, why not do it?" the Belgian said. "And it'll look great on TV." He smiled. His teeth were small and white, unlike Vasilev's coffee-stained enamel.

✦

"The track is called Opera of Northern Ocean, as if that has anything to do with us," Vasilev complained to mission control. He needed to talk with someone outside the crew, someone a little impartial. "Ok, maybe the landing site was an ocean once, and is in the northern hemisphere, but that doesn't make it any more appropriate. They also want to dance as they exit the airlock. Can they even do that?" He put the message on record, and went to water the tomato plants in the greenhouse for the thirty-two minutes it took the message to reach their blue home and for mission control to reply.

"I'm afraid they can," Petrov at mission control said. "The ramp is large enough for movement. The calcium, super-calbindin and exercise will have kept your bones dance-worthy. The sound experiment was cleared months ago. Could be important to know how sound behaves in the Martian atmosphere if we ever set up a research station there or if you guys need to scream." Damn Petrov and his macabre sense of humour.

"Why didn't the Europeans tell me first?" Vasilev said. He disliked wasting talk and time on things it was too late to do anything about, but his colleagues' omission of the music and dancing irked him. They had had more than seven months to let him know about the experiment slash PR stunt. Of course, the Americans were in on it too.

"Just disallow it then," Petrov said half an hour later.

✦

As commander, Vasilev could do that, but he also knew the demotivating effect it would have on the long journey back. If the Europeans had their dance, maybe they would stop complaining about the food and just eat what they were given. And like the Belgian had said, it was such a small thing, so why not do it?

"Ok," Vasilev told the Belgian and the German. "You can have your dance, but do it quickly. And for God's sake record it, so it really is an experiment."

"Of course," said the German. "We'll film it at the highest resolution possible."

✦

"Moron," Andreevitsj, mission specialist from remote and Arctic Novaja Zemlya, said when Vasilev told him and Lebedev about the "experiment". "Do you know what this means?"

"No," Vasilev said flatly.

"It means we have to dance with them!"

"Of course it doesn't," Vasilev replied.

"Yes it does! We can't just stand there while they dance."

"Why not?"

"It'll look stupid, like we don't know how to dance."

"We don't know how to dance," Vasilev said.

"Speak for yourself," Andreevitsj said. "I do my part when I go out. But I have enough sense to stay in the crowd so less people see me."

"So?" Vasilev said, still sore about the moron comment, but determined not to show it. "Where are you going with these irrelevant facts?"

"There's no fucking crowd here!" Andreevitsj said. "We can't hide.

"Calm down," Vasilev said. "No one will mind."

"It's just a quarter of the planet watching the landing," Andreevitsj said, voice shrill. "We'll look bad next to the Europeans and the Americans."

"Maybe they can't dance either?" Vasilev suggested. "They just like the music?" He enjoyed music too, but not dancing.

"No," Andreevitsj said. "They've grown up with it. They dance every weekend. They fill stadiums and dance all night. When I studied in Holland, all the radio stations and clubs sounded the same, uts-uts-uts-uts-uts! I thought I would go crazy."

✦

They spent the next two exercise sessions trying to learn how to dance from Lebedev, who came from Moscow and was, in his own words, an expert clubber. Strapped to the treadmills, they jumped up and down and waved their arms to Lebedev's music. Andreevitsj did the twist, rotated his hips and knees in opposite directions while he squatted up and down. Vasilev wasn't sure how good it looked. He was starting to feel nervous—not about the landing, which he had spent over a year training for, and which was like an old friend to him. Instead, he feared the hours following touchdown and engine stop, and the moment when the airlock opened and they would take the first steps on another planet—dancing.

✦

"Music and dance have been used for celebration since humans left the caves," the American said during dinner the night before they entered the lander. Lebedev and one of the Americans would stay behind in the main module to take care of communication, maintenance and orbital experiments while the rest of them worked on the surface.

"Also, moving one's bodies together in rhythm increases the

feeling of community and strength, like social glue. That's why so many indigenous peoples dance. It's highly appropriate that we do it when we arrive on a new planet."

"But we're not indigenous peoples," Vasilev said.

"To Mars, we're all indigenous peoples from Earth," the American replied.

"Can I at least hear the song you'll be playing?" Vasilev asked.

The Belgian shook his head. "No, it's a surprise. But I can tell you it will be easy to dance to, in the standard one hundred and twenty beats per minute."

"That's the heart rate of sexual arousal," the American informed him.

"Uts-uts-uts-uts-uts," Andreevitsj said from across the table.

✦

But it didn't end there. The Europeans wanted to fasten long silver-coloured streamers to the D-rings on the arms and legs of the EVA suits, once again under the combined auspices of science and showmanship, to "visually track the direction and strength of the Martian wind". It would also look festive.

"What's next?" Vasilev muttered. "Glow sticks?" He checked the logistics files to make sure glow sticks were not in the payload.

✦

Then the moment arrived. They fell and shook and burned through the Martian atmosphere, not nearly as hard as the re-entry would be on Earth, but generating a respectable amount of fire. The conical heat-shield lasted for as long as necessary and popped off according to plan. The trefoil of parachutes deployed and jolted them back to gravity after seven months in free-fall. Then the lander's feet extended and the thrusters kicked in, pushing back against Mars' hold on them. The atmospheric conditions were good, just enough wind to make it interesting, but not enough to make it dangerous. No nasty surprises or malfunctions. Vasilev put the gleaming, teardrop-shaped landing module on the Red Planet like he had trained to do, with plenty of fuel left. It was a safe landing, a glorious landing.

"Touchdown and engine shutdown," Vasilev said into the microphone. He breathed and imagined the cheering that would erupt in the control room seventeen minutes in the future. He smiled at the thought.

Two hours and six minutes later all the reports from the co-pilots and the rest of the crew were positive. It was time, he couldn't postpone it any longer.

"Everyone to the airlock and prepare for EVA," Vasilev said, his voice trembling slightly.

✦

They crowded the small metal space, the Belgian closest to the hatch, then the German. Because the landing was Russian, the Europeans and the Americans had the honour of being first outside. Vasilev couldn't see his crew's faces behind their golden visors, but he could hear their breathing, rapid and shallow, over the radio. The silver streamers at their elbows and knees gleamed in the bluish light. It looked odd, like failed Christmas tree decorations.

The German started the internal and external cameras and gave thumbs up. Everything was ready. Vasilev's palms were moist inside his gloves. His heart beat as hard as it had during the landing.

"Opening the airlock now," Vasilev said. He pressed the oversized button on the wall and nodded at the Europeans. The Belgian started the track on the hard-drive.

At first, Vasilev didn't hear anything. Then a beat began, steady but light. It unfolded slowly, like the lander's ramp had done moments earlier. The music sounded inside their earphones and on the external speakers, the first human sound in the atmosphere on Mars.

✦

The hatch opened. They stretched to take in the planet they had landed on. A ruddish desert of coarse sand and pebbles, no boulders in the landing zone. Orange dust kicked up by the thrusters gilded the air. The sky was yellow, the sun small and distant. It was Mars! Mars was looking at them, greeting them! The wind caught the silver streamers on their suits and pulled the ribbons out towards the silent landscape, like a beckoning.

A deep bass started up in the music, then a sound like a human voice exhaling, breathing, overlaid by a warbling synth and the sound of gentle tinkling.

"Quite poetic," Vasilev thought, against his will. He blamed it on the moment. It felt much more personal than he had expected. There were no press, no busy officials, or screaming people waiting for them on the Red Planet, just wind and sand and silence.

✦

The Belgian lifted his arms as though he were taking all of Mars in, as if the rest of humanity, everyone they knew and loved, were not two hundred million kilometres away in the darkness, but right there with them. He bobbed his helmet up and down, and dance-walked slowly out onto the ramp. The orange sand on his boots and on the metal beneath them, rose and fell, rose and fell, in rhythm with the beat.

The German followed, turning his hips from side to side as much as the suit allowed him, and swayed out of the airlock, the silver streamers flapping and gleaming in the dust-filled Martian day.

The American made whooping sounds, clapped in time with the beat and danced outside. Then the music calmed a little, as if it were waiting for someone.

"Let's go," Andreevitsj said, breathed heavily into his microphone and vanished. The music rose in a crescendo, with a yearning, haunting undertone and a sound of increasing wind.

Vasilev drew in his breath, lifted his arms like his colleagues had done, bent his knees and swung his hips with the music, one-two, one-two, one-two. The low gravity made him feel light and unconcerned, not stiff and uncomfortable, as when he danced on Earth. It felt surprisingly good. He followed Andreevitsj into the golden sand-light.

No longer caring who saw or heard him, just enjoying the ease of the motion and the music, Vasilev stomped his feet and waved his arms and grinned broadly, while The Opera of Northern Ocean boomed and warbled and sang into the alien atmosphere, and the orange wind lifted their streamers up and up towards the sky. Through the earphones, he heard the laughter and the breathing and the shouts of his fellow human beings who were dancing next to him on Mars at one hundred and twenty heartbeats per minute.

Berit Ellingsen is a Korean-Norwegian fiction writer and science journalist. Her stories have appeared in many places, including Metazen, Coffinmouth, Hyperpulp, the Gothic anthology Candle in the Attic Window, and the biopunk anthology Growing Dread. Berit's debut novel, The Empty City, is a story about silence (emptycitynovel.com). She was a runner-up in Beate Sigriddaughter's 2011 Ghost Story competition and a semi-finalist in the Rose Metal Press 2011 chapbook competition. Berit likes space science and dancing.

MAKING MARS A NICER PLACE, IN FICTION... AND FACT

Eric Choi

IN SOME WAYS, Mars is like a celebrity that one finally meets and discovers is shorter and less attractive in person than on screen. For all of its popular reputation, the Red Planet is actually quite diminutive, being only about half the diameter of Earth. Mars is also one-and-a-half times further from the Sun, with a thin atmosphere of primarily carbon dioxide, so both scientists and science fiction writers have long assumed (correctly) that it must be less hospitable than Earth.

Terraforming is the process of altering the present climate of Mars (or any other inhospitable planet) into a more Earth-like environment suitable for human settlement. While Kim Stanley Robinson's Red Mars/Green Mars/Blue Mars trilogy is perhaps the best-known and most ambitious work of science fiction to describe how terraforming could make Mars a nicer place, it certainly wasn't the first. Starting with A Princess of Mars in 1917, Edgar Rice Burroughs wrote eleven novels that portrayed an arid world he called Barsoom made habitable by an 'atmosphere factory'[1]. The stories in Ray Bradbury's 1950 collection The Martian Chronicles were set on a desert planet crisscrossed with canals built by an alien civilisation to distribute water from the polar caps[2].

Arthur C Clarke's 1952 novel The Sands of Mars was the last in which the planet would bear any resemblance to the world depicted by Burroughs and Bradbury. The protagonist was a

---

[1] Burroughs, Edgar Rice Burroughs. A Princess of Mars, AC McClurg & Company, 1917.

[2] Bradbury, Ray. The Martian Chronicles, Doubleday, 1950.

science fiction writer named Martin Gibson who travelled to Mars to research a new book. The colony there was stable and generally healthy, although individuals sometimes suffered from 'Martian fever', a malaria-like illness caused by a terrestrial organism that had been accidentally carried to Mars and ended up thriving in the new environment. Gibson became involved with the planet's political difficulties with Earth, survived an aeroplane crash during a giant dust storm, discovered an indigenous non-photosynthetic plant species that could extract oxygen from the Martian regolith (soil), and uncovered a secret plan to terraform Mars called 'Project Dawn'[3] (all in a day's—or sol's—work for a science fiction author!).

Clarke imagined an indigenous Martian plant called Oxyfera, or 'airweed' as it was known to the human settlers, which could extract oxygen from the regolith and store it in pods. The Project Dawn scientists managed to breed a new strain that released oxygen directly into the air. Unfortunately, airweed could only survive around the equatorial regions of Mars because that was where the planet was warmest. To solve this problem, the Project Dawn scientists used a 'meson resonance reaction' to turn the Martian moon Phobos into a second sun. By providing enough sunlight to warm a greater portion of the planet, the airweed was able spread out over a larger portion of the Martian surface, eventually generating enough oxygen for humans to breathe without respirators.

To modern readers, the most obvious problem with Project Dawn is that we now know there are (regrettably) no indigenous plants on Mars to provide oxygen. However, Clarke's novel was correct in concluding that the most feasible mechanism for changing the bulk composition of the Martian atmosphere is planetary-scale biology. Since no indigenous biology exists to accomplish this, the required organisms would have to be genetically engineered and introduced to the planet[4].

Clarke himself conducted a feasibility analysis of the meson

---

[3] Clarke, Arthur C. The Sands of Mars, Sidgwick & Jackson, 1951.

[4] McKay, Christopher P; Toon, Owen B and Kastings, James F. 'Making Mars Habitable', Nature, Volume 352, 8 August 1991.

Eric Choi

resonance reaction in The Snows of Olympus[5]. 'Meson' is a term used generically to describe short-lived sub-atomic particles that come in a variety of masses. One of the most important of these is the mu-meson, or muon, which is similar to an electron except that it is unstable and about two hundred times heavier. In 1947, British physicist Charles Frank, who was working on cosmic ray research at Bristol University, hypothesised that mesons could be used to catalyse low temperature nuclear reactions. Frank's idea was put to the test in 1956 by Luis Alvarez at the University of California at Berkeley. Unfortunately, it was found that muons decay too quickly to support a chain reaction.

Thirteen years after the publication of The Sands of Mars, the Mariner 4 spacecraft conducted the first successful flyby of the Red Planet and returned images that revealed a desolate-looking and apparently lifeless landscape. Those images, and the pictures from subsequent Mariner missions, culminating in the ambiguous results from the Viking Landers' life detection experiments in 1976, forever swept away the romantic Barsoom and did much to diminish the general public's interest in Mars.

Fortunately, Mars fiction has been enjoying a renaissance of late, coinciding with a resurgence of exciting new missions to the Red Planet, including the European Space Agency's Mars Express orbiter and the anticipated landing of NASA's Curiosity (Mars Science Laboratory) rover. The 1990s saw numerous works about human missions to Mars, such as Ben Bova's Mars[6] and Gregory Benford's The Martian Race[7], and also the emergence of a terraforming sub-genre.

"There isn't anything much wrong with Mars that a decent atmosphere won't fix right up"[8] was the memorable opening line of Frederik Pohl's novel Mining the Oort, in which comets in the Oort Cloud at the edge of the Solar System were harvested as a source of volatiles for a terraforming project. The protagonist was a young Martian named Dekker DeWoe, who dreamt of becoming an Oort miner. The terraforming project was financed

---

[5] Clarke, Arthur C. The Snows of Olympus: A Garden on Mars, Gollancz, 1994.

[6] Bova, Ben. Mars, Bantam, 1992.

[7] Benford, Gregory. The Martian Race, Warner, 1999.

[8] Pohl, Frederik. Mining the Oort, Ballantine Books, 1992.

76

by bonds issued by the Martians, who agreed to supply Earth with agricultural products once the terraforming was complete. But when DeWoe arrived at the headquarters of the Oort Corporation on Earth for his training, he learned that the programme was threatened because the Japanese were selling off their bonds and were planning to grow the needed crops aboard Earth-orbiting habitats instead. After graduation, DeWoe was assigned to be a damage control specialist aboard a space station located at one of Mars' Lagrangian points. There, he learned of a plan to blackmail Japan into reinstating its support for terraforming by threatening to divert a small comet towards an impact with Earth.

In Pohl's novel, the comet harvesting process began with the Oort miners identifying the most promising candidates. After being tagged by the miners, the selected comets were processed by the 'snake handlers'. These workers threaded the comet with a chain of instruments called a snake and installed an antimatter drive. To withstand the engine thrust, the comets had to be reinforced with polymerisers. As the snake worked through the nucleus, it excreted long-chain molecules into the briefly melted ice as it moved. When the ice re-froze, the molecules formed strong polymer chains. The comet was further reinforced with mechanical braces before being sent towards the inner Solar System.

After several years of autonomous flight, control of the comet trajectories was assumed by one of the Co-Mars space stations located at the Sun-Mars Lagrangian points. The first of these stations, Co-Mars One, was located at L4. It was responsible for directing the comets towards its perihelion swing-by of the Sun. The other station, Co-Mars Two, was located at L5, and it was responsible for controlling the comets after the solar flyby and guiding them onto a Mars-bound trajectory. Incoming trajectories were designed so the comets would come up from behind the planet to minimise the relative approach velocity.

The final approach and impact on Mars was handled by a constellation of space stations in low-Mars orbit. Controllers there would fine-tune the trajectory and reduce the approach speed of the comets while making sure they do not impact near any settlements or outposts. They were also not allowed to strike

Eric Choi

Valles Marineris, Olympus Mons and several other Martian features deemed to be of significant value. It was hoped that once enough comets were dumped on the surface to raise the surface pressure and temperature enough, the frozen indigenous Martian volatiles at the poles and in the permafrost would start outgassing. Even then, there was expected to be too much carbon dioxide and not enough free oxygen and nitrogen in the atmosphere. After the cometary bombardment, Mars was to be seeded with blue-green algae and lichen for oxygen production and nitrogen fixation.

While Pohl's description of mining the comets is generally accurate, the main problem with the concept is the extreme distance of the Oort Cloud, which is estimated to extend from about 40,000 to 100,000 AU from the Sun (six to fifteen trillion kilometres)[9]. In the novel it is written that, "Distance doesn't matter much in space, where if you just start a thing off with the right kind of shove, sooner or later it will get where you want it to go"[10]. The problem is that without the advanced propulsive capabilities of something like the antimatter drive that Pohl described in his novel, a comet from the Oort Cloud on a minimum energy Hohmann trajectory would take about a million years to reach Mars.

In his book Disturbing the Universe, physicist Freeman Dyson suggested mining ice from the Saturnian moon of Enceladus[11]. Another possible source of volatiles is the Kuiper-Edgeworth Belt. As it is 'only' thirty to fifty AU (4.5 to 7.5 billion kilometres) away from the Sun[12], it may be a more accessible source of icy planetesimals than the Oort Cloud. Since a Hohmann trajectory would still take about thirty years to deliver a comet to Mars, some sort of advanced propulsion system would still be required.

The other aspect of the terraforming plan described in Mining the Oort that would require modification (if such a

---

[9] Beatty, J Kelly; Petersen, Carolyn Collins and Chaikin, Andrew. The New Solar System (4th Edition), Sky Publishing Corp and Cambridge University Press, 1999.

[10] Pohl.

[11] Dyson, Freeman. Disturbing the Universe, HarperCollins Ltd, 1979.

[12] Beatty et al.

project were ever actually attempted) is the impact strategy. Directly impacting cometary fragments on the Martian surface should be avoided because the pieces that hit the ground would vaporise, and almost all the water would be broken into their constituent hydrogen and oxygen atoms. This would be undesirable because one of the purposes of the cometary bombardment would be to increase the temperature of the planet, and water vapour is a powerful greenhouse gas. The problem could be avoided by simply having the comets enter the Martian atmosphere at a shallower angle. They would then burn up in the atmosphere with most of its water molecules intact. The water vapour, along with any oxygen atoms that are inevitably dissociated, would be added directly to the atmosphere.

A fantastic sort of terraforming was portrayed in Greg Bear's novel Moving Mars, in which the planet is transported to the habitable zone of another star system courtesy of some very exotic physics. A group of Martian physicists called the Olympians constructed a 'tweaker' that could directly manipulate the 'descriptors' which encode the basic properties of matter and energy. According to one of the physicists, "Distance and time mean nothing, except as variations in descriptors"[13]. Using the tweaker, the position descriptors of Mars were changed, placing the planet into an orbit around a yellow dwarf star about nine-tenths the size of the Sun located thousands of light-years from the Solar System. Since Mars now orbited closer to the new star than it did to the Sun, it immediately became a much nicer place for humans to live.

The idea of the tweaker appears to have been inspired by Ed Fredkin, a former MIT professor who produced some radical hypotheses on the nature of reality. Our everyday experience tells us that information can be represented by either matter (eg, ink on a piece of paper) or energy (eg, electrons in a circuit). But Fredkin speculated that the opposite might be true, that matter and energy are actually manifestations of information. Under such an interpretation, the properties of matter and energy are bits, the scientific laws that govern physical systems are

---

[13] Bear, Greg. Moving Mars, Tor Books, 1993.

algorithms that affect those bits, and reality is just a programme running on a computer called the Universe[14].

Needless to say, the tweaker technology described in Moving Mars is highly speculative. Even if Fredkin's theories are correct, the technology for building a tweaker may be centuries away. However, there is (in theory) a way to change the orbit of Mars using classical orbital mechanics. A gravity assist manoeuvre is a planetary encounter designed to change the heliocentric velocity of a spacecraft. If the spacecraft passes behind a planet, its trajectory is rotated in the same direction as the planet's orbit around the Sun and its heliocentric velocity is increased. This technique has been used by many contemporary missions including ESA's Rosetta spacecraft, which is currently en route to Comet 67P/Churyumov-Gerasimenko after multiple gravity assists from Mars and Earth.

Since momentum must be conserved, the heliocentric velocity gained by the spacecraft is lost to the planet. The velocity decrease experienced by the planet is extremely small due to its much greater mass relative to the spacecraft. For example, the 2,000 kg Galileo spacecraft increased its heliocentric velocity by 5.2 km/s and 2.7 km/s following two Earth flybys in 1990 and 1992, respectively. The orbital speed of the Earth was slowed by only a billionth of a centimetre per year from the two events[15].

Using similar calculations, it can be shown that if an Amor-class asteroid (one whose orbit takes it between the orbits of Earth and Mars) with a mass comparable to that of 433 Eros (6.7×10^{15} kg) could be diverted to perform a hyperbolic flyby of Mars with a closest approach altitude of 5,000 km above the surface, the orbital speed of the planet would be reduced by about 0.01 mm/s. Mars currently orbits the Sun at a mean radius of 1.52 AU. In order to slow its orbital speed enough to bring it into a closer 1.25 AU orbit, approximately eight million such asteroid flybys would be required. It would seem that neither the

---

[14] Wright, Robert. Three Scientists and Their Gods: Looking for Meaning in an Age of Information, Harper & Row, 1998.

[15] 'Windows to the Universe', National Earth Science Teachers Association, www.windows2universe.org/kids_space/gravity_assist.html

tweaker nor the flyby methods of moving Mars are actually feasible.

Kim Stanley Robinson's Red Mars/Green Mars/Blue Mars trilogy is considered by many to represent the pinnacle of the terraforming sub-genre. Published between 1992 and 1996, the novels chronicled the transformation and settlement of the Red Planet while describing its long-term consequences. A fourth book, The Martians, was published in 1999 as a collection of stories set in the same universe as the trilogy.

Robinson's epic began in 2026, when a crew known as the First Hundred undertook a mission to colonise and terraform Mars. Once the initial settlements were constructed and the terraforming process was started, new immigrants from various nations joined the original pioneers. But the settlers fractured into two camps: the Greens, who wished to pursue terraforming at any cost, and the Reds, who wanted to keep Mars in its pristine condition. This division, combined with rising tensions with Earth and ethnic rivalries amongst the settlers, eventually erupted into revolution.

In Robinson's future history, the first Martian habitats were simple barrel-vaulted chambers that were covered by sandbagged regolith to shield against radiation and to allow the interiors to be pressurised. The building materials for these habitats were derived from indigenous resources. Bricks were made of clay and sulphur from the regolith mixed with nylon from the spent lander parachutes to increase tensile strength. This mixture was poured into brick moulds and baked under compression until the sulphur polymerised.

Once the initial settlements were established, the process of terraforming was started. The first step was to increase the surface temperature of the planet. A giant mirror was placed in areostationary orbit to reflect sunlight onto the dawn-dusk terminator. This mirror was constructed from the solar sails of the cargo freighters from Earth. When a new freighter arrived at Mars, its sail would be detached and linked to a large collection of earlier sails parked in areostationary orbit. The mirror was programmed to swivel to reflect sunlight on the terminator, adding a little bit of energy to each day's dawn and dusk.

Factories were built across the planet to produce halocarbonbased greenhouse gases from local sources of carbon and sulphur. These had to be constantly released into the atmosphere to offset the destruction caused by ultraviolet radiation. In addition, a thousand windmill heaters were distributed around the equatorial regions. These windmills were small magnesium boxes with four vertical vanes on a rod that projected from the top. The heating element was an exposed metal coil at the base of the windmill that radiated like an oven hob. Further heating was provided by hundreds of nuclear reactors (nicknamed 'Chernobyls') that were stationed across the planet, and by reducing the albedo of Mars through the deployment of dark organic matter.

The next step was to genetically modify terrestrial micro-organisms to survive on the Martian surface. These organisms had to be resistant to cold, dehydration and ultraviolet radiation, as well as have a low requirement for oxygen and be able to live in rock or regolith. Unfortunately, no single terrestrial microbe had all these traits, and those that had them individually were slow growers. The engineers therefore started a 'mix-and-match' programme in which genes were recombined from a variety of terrestrial algae, methanogens, cyanobacteria and lichens. Promising candidates were tested in an old habitation module that had been modified into a 'Mars jar'. Cultures were introduced into this sealed facility and were studied through teleoperation by scientists in an adjacent module. As a safety precaution, all the genetically modified organisms had 'suicide genes' to prevent them from overwhelming the biosphere in the event of an inadvertent release.

Out of these efforts were produced a variety of fast-growing lichen, radiation-resistant algae, extreme-cold fungi and a helophytic bacteria that ate salt and excreted oxygen. Animalcules went through the regolith, turning nitrates into nitrogen and oxides into oxygen. A symbiont of cyanobacteria and a Florida platform bacteria called *thiobacillus denitrificans* was able to go deep into the regolith and converted the rock sulphates into sulphides. This fed a variant of *Microcoleus*, which grew large dendritic filaments into the ground. These roots went straight through the regolith and down into the bedrock to melt the permafrost.

With the increasing oxygen content of the atmosphere came the introduction of animal life. The first of these were genetically altered insects like black midges, bees and ants. Later, small mammals like moles were added for soil aeration, and birds were introduced to help spread seeds. Once a food chain was established, predatory animals like the *Ursus maritimus* polar bear, the lynx and the bobcat were brought in. Most of the animals were modified with high altitude adaptation genes to allow them to survive in the reduced Martian atmosphere.

The warming of the planet had caused the permafrost and polar ice to melt and reform on the surface as vast glaciers. Until this ice was melted, too much solar energy was being reflected back into space, preventing the formation of a full hydrological cycle. But once the ice was melted and liquid oceans appeared on the surface of Mars, a water cycle was achieved and the terraforming process was essentially complete. The methods of melting the ice included feeding the exhaust from nuclear power plants into the glaciers, scattering black algae onto the ice, using microwave and ultrasound transmitters as heaters, sailing icebreakers through the pack to break it up, and even detonating thermonuclear explosives deep underground.

Robinson's trilogy was very well received, with the first book winning a Nebula Award and the other two taking Hugos. Indeed, the novels are regarded with near-Biblical reverence by some members of groups like the Mars Society. The unofficial flag of Mars is a red, green and blue tricolour that was inspired by the trilogy.

In conducting his research, Robinson drew heavily upon a significant body of scientific literature, most notably the work of Christopher McKay and Martyn Fogg. Robinson was particularly influenced by Fogg's concept of 'synergistic terraforming'. This is the idea that no single technique can work in isolation and that only a combination of several technologies, requiring a massive industrial effort both on the Martian surface and in orbit, could hope to succeed.

There are, however, some differences between the terraforming techniques portrayed in Robinson's trilogy and those described in the scientific literature. In a paper published in the journal Nature called 'Making Mars Habitable', McKay and his co-authors describe a two-phase approach in which the planet is first warmed by a massive release of carbon dioxide followed by a modification of the atmosphere to scrub out the carbon dioxide and increase the oxygen content. The estimated time scale for this approach was about one hundred years for the first step and up to one hundred thousand years for the second. McKay's paper limited consideration to technologies that were not far from the contemporary state-of-the-art[16]. In contrast, Robinson postulated that through new technologies and a massive synergistic industrial effort, a single-phase approach could create a habitable atmosphere directly.

At the conclusion of Robinson's trilogy, the final environmental state achieved was one of 'least-impact terraforming' or 'ecopoesis'. A breathable but water-poor and largely carbon dioxide atmosphere was created, but only up to a six-kilometre contour. Thus, the Martian surface came to resemble the Arctic, while its oceans emulated the Antarctic. At high altitudes the air was kept too thin for humans. Since the vertical relief on Mars was so extreme, most of the indigenous geological features remained above the bulk of the atmosphere and thus retained their natural state.

The problem of the carbon dioxide rich atmosphere was solved not by changing Mars but by altering the physiology of the human settlers. A medical procedure was developed in which the genes that coded for certain characteristics of crocodile haemoglobin could be introduced into mammals. Crocodiles can stay underwater for long periods of time because the carbon dioxide that usually builds up in the blood instead dissolves into bicarbonate ions that bind to the amino acids in the haemoglobin. This bond causes the haemoglobin to release oxygen molecules, which means that in one stroke this crocodile gene could increase both carbon dioxide tolerance and oxygen efficiency.

With ecopoesis achieved, Mars gained its independence from Earth. When an environmental catastrophe struck Earth, the flood of immigrants fleeing to Mars resulted in political tensions that almost caused an interplanetary war. But negotiations

---

[16] McKay et al.

averted a conflict, and Mars reached an agreement on helping Earth with its problems. The scientific and social changes brought on by the terraforming of Mars and the environmental restoration of Earth spawned a new Renaissance, giving humanity the technologies to not only settle the rest of the Solar System but also to voyage to other star systems.

Robinson's idea of altering the physiology of the human settlers to suit the Martian environment harkens back to Frederik Pohl's novel Man Plus. Instead of terraforming the planet, the goal of the Man Plus project was to "modify a human body [so] that it would survive on the surface of Mars as readily and safely as a normal man could walk across a Kansas wheat field"[17]. After a series of surgical procedures, American astronaut Roger Torraway was transformed into a computer-enhanced Cyborg that successfully established an outpost on Mars.

Man Plus described how all the biological human organs that would not function on Mars could be substituted with artificial systems. Lungs were replaced with a "micro-miniaturized oxygen generation catalyst-cracking system"[18]. Since blood would boil in the low atmospheric pressure of Mars, it was eliminated from the extremities and surface areas. This required replacing the muscles in the arms and legs with servomotors controlled through connections to the nerves, reserving the remaining blood supply for the brain.

A thick artificial covering was grafted to the skin as a pressure suit and radiation shield. This covering was described as tan in colour, with a texture like that of a rhinoceros hide. The Cyborg was equipped with a supply of patches and quick sealer to repair any damage from scrapes or falls. The feet were composed of steel shanks and hard plastic wedges. Eyes were replaced with optical sensors that could see across a wider spectrum than normal, ranging from infrared to visible to ultraviolet. Unfortunately, the normal human brain could not handle the vast amount of information provided by the optical unit and the other cybernetic sensors. Therefore, a 'mediation stage' was included in the sensors to either edit out unimportant data or

[17] Pohl, Frederik. Man Plus, Random House Inc, 1976.
[18] Pohl.

translate them into a form the brain could comprehend.

One of the most interesting technologies portrayed in Man Plus was the manner in which power was supplied to the Cyborg. Nominal power was supplied by a pair of thin-film solar arrays mounted like a pair of wings on the Cyborg's back. These wings could automatically orient themselves to collect the maximum sunlight. This automatic pointing could be overridden by the Cyborg so that he could use the wings to balance himself, like a tightrope walker with a pole. Supplemental power was provided by a fusion reactor in areostationary orbit that beamed microwaves down to the Cyborg on the surface. The energy density of the beam was low enough so that normal human astronauts working in the Cyborg's proximity would not be harmed.

The concept of cybernetically modifying an astronaut or cosmonaut (or tàikōnaut) is theoretically feasible. Even before the historic flight of cosmonaut Yuri Gagarin in 1961, a paper published in Astronautics concluded that, "Altering man's bodily functions to meet the requirements of extraterrestrial environments would be more logical than providing an earthly environment for him in space"[19]. Three years after the Astronautics paper, NASA commissioned a report that analysed the history, development, state-of-the-art and possible future development of artificial lungs, hearts, kidneys and oxygenating equipment for human spaceflight applications[20]. However, due to its controversial nature and ethical considerations little further research has been done on this topic.

In the sequel Mars Plus, which Pohl co-authored with Thomas T Thomas, the Cyborgs were augmented by the Creoles, who were halfway between the full Cyborgs and unmodified humans[21]. The Creoles could only work unprotected on the

---

[19] Clynes, Manfred E and Kline, Nathan S. 'Cyborgs and Space', Astronautics, September 1960.

[20] Driscoll, Robert W. 'Engineering Man for Space: The Cyborg Study', NASA Biotechnology and Human Research Final Report NASw-512, United Aircraft Corporation, 15 May 1963.

[21] Pohl, Frederik and Thomas, Thomas T. Mars Plus, Baen Publishing Enterprises, 1994.

Martian surface for a few hours. Most of the modifications made to the Creoles were biological rather than cybernetic, which kept the procedure within the means of the Mars colony's medical facilities. Beneath their skin was a silicon underlayer that served as an impact, thermal and pressure buffer. Instead of eyelids, a protective membrane swept across the eyeballs. Their ears were long and cupped like a bat's, and stood away from the side of the head. Instead of an open ear canal, there was a small patch of transparent artificial skin that was designed for hearing, both in the minuscule outside atmosphere as well as under the normal air pressure inside the colony's domes and tunnels. The Creoles also had dark pouches of skin on either side of their mouths that concealed Velcro tabs for hooking up a breathing mask.

Two terraforming plans were described in Mars Plus. One was being executed by the Martian settlers, while the other was planned by the Texahoma Corporation of Earth. The Martian plan employed self-replicating von Neumann machines, or 'Johnnies', that were originally developed for mining but were modified for the terraforming task. The Johnnies were small robots that resembled horseshoe crabs. This shape was intended for aerodynamic stability to keep the machine upright during dust storms. The robots were powered by photovoltaic cells imprinted in a pattern on the shell. Each Johnnie was equipped with a mouth that consisted of a shovel, a grinder, and a nanotech gas chromatography unit. As the machine crawled over the Martian surface, its mouth would sample the soil and rocks. When the measured composition matched the parameters programmed into its microprocessor, the Johnnie would stop and begin to feed. This raw material was used by an internal factory to replicate two new Johnnies.

After reproducing itself, the Johnnie would continue onto the terraforming phase of its mission. As it went, it ate regolith in order to manufacture glass capsules. These capsules were filled with a payload of two organisms that had been genetically modified to survive the Martian climate. One of these was a type of blue-green algae. The other was a bacteria based on a strain from Antarctica. The Johnnies would encapsulate both organisms in the glass capsules and deploy them in different areas of the Martian surface. When released, the algae would use sunlight to

Eric Choi

turn carbon dioxide into oxygen and carbon compounds, while the bacteria would extract the latent moisture from the air and permafrost layer. The bacteria would also fertilise the ground with its waste products, helping to turn the sterile regolith into organic soil.

Much more dramatic was the terraforming plan of the fictional Texahoma Martian Development Corporation. The company envisioned crashing a few stony asteroids and carbonaceous chondrites into the southern highlands in order to create a global dust cloud. This was supposed to heat up the atmosphere, which would in turn create a massive outgassing of water vapour from the permafrost layer. In reality, the terraforming plans of the Texahoma Corporation would not have worked. Instead of warming the atmosphere, the global dust cloud created by the impact would have instead cooled the planet through the 'nuclear winter' effect.

The cause of Mars exploration suffered a temporary setback in 1999 with the failure of two NASA missions: the Mars Polar Lander, and the Mars Climate Orbiter (the latter of the infamous metric/imperial mix-up). A year later, Brian Aldiss and Roger Penrose's White Mars was released as a repudiation of Robinson's trilogy, in which the United Nations declared Mars to be 'a sacrosanct environment' that must be preserved 'as a place of wonder and meditation'[22]. Since White Mars was largely a sociological study, there were few portrayals of innovative new technologies. One that was mentioned was the concept of using Mars as a pristine laboratory for fundamental research in physics. According to Aldiss and Penrose, Mars would be ideal because there was no tectonic activity and volcanism was dead, while the Moon was no longer suitable because of the mining activities and the construction of the 'transcore subway'[23]. The other technology mentioned was the 'Zubrin Reactor', in which atmospheric carbon dioxide was reacted with hydrogen to generate methane fuel and oxygen. This was clearly an homage to aerospace engineer Robert Zubrin and his Mars Direct

[22] Aldiss, Brian W and Penrose, Roger. White Mars (Or, The Mind Set Free), Little, Brown UK, 1999.
[23] Aldiss and Penrose.

architecture of using in situ Martian resources to dramatically reduce the cost and complexity of human missions to the Red Planet[24].

While the full-scale terraforming of Mars will probably not be feasible anytime soon, the topic will undoubtedly continue to be a popular one in science fiction. Perhaps the conclusion of Martyn Fogg's seminal paper in The Journal of the British Interplanetary Society is a fitting capstone to all of the works of science fiction that have imagined how to make Mars a nicer place: "The fact that a scenario for the full terraforming of Mars can be conceived within the parameter space of current planetological models, and without violating any known laws of physics, demonstrates that such an idea is, at least, feasible in principle. To bring such a project to fruition would require engineering capabilities greater than those of the present day, but not necessarily out of the question for a future civilization several centuries ahead of our own."[25]

Acknowledgement
This study is based in part on work funded by Maison D'Ailleurs and the OURS Foundation as part of the Innovative Technologies from Science Fiction (ITSF) project of the European Space Agency (ESA).

Eric Choi is an aerospace engineer, writer and editor in Toronto, Canada. He has worked the MOPITT instrument on the NASA Terra satellite, the RADARSAT-1 satellite, the Canadarm2 on the International Space Station and the meteorology payload on the Phoenix Mars Lander. In 2009, he was a finalist in the Canadian Space Agency's astronaut recruitment

---

[24] Zubrin, Robert and Wagner, Richard. The Case for Mars: The Plan to Settle the Red Planet and Why We Must, Simon & Schuster Inc, 1996.
[25] Fogg, Martyn J. 'A Synergistic Approach to Terraforming Mars', Journal of the British Interplanetary Society, Volume 45, 1992.

Eric Choi

campaign. He is currently a business development manager at COM DEV Ltd. The first recipient of the Asimov Award, his fiction has appeared in The Astronaut From Wyoming and Other Stories, Footprints, Northwest Passages, Space Inc, Tales from the Wonder Zone, Northern Suns, Tesseracts[6], Arrowdreams, Science Fiction Age and Asimov's. With Derwin Mak, he co-edited the Aurora Award winning anthology The Dragon and the Stars.

PATHFINDERS

Martin McGrath

CHEN WAS OUTSIDE, blowing the dust from the mirrors of the solar collector. The sun was low and distant and gave no warmth. The ground was hard and barren. The job he was doing was tedious and pointless. The damn solar collector barely worked, a failed experiment that was already half-forgotten by the engineers at Earth Control.

Everything was made more complicated by Chen's suit. The gloves were stiff and hard and Chen had already lost one fingernail. A little stream of sweat burbled between his shoulder blades, an itch he couldn't scratch though he twisted and shrugged in an effort to get some relief from the growing discomfort. Chen would have been happier in one of the old Orlans he'd lumbered around in while training in Star City and on the ISS. He resolved to write another memo about the Mars suit to the design committee.

When his suit radio buzzed to life and Commander Arsenyev told him to stop what he was doing and come to the living quarters, Chen's first reaction was a sigh of relief... which distracted him from the peculiar tone of the commander's request. By the time he registered that there was something wrong, Commander Arsenyev had cut the connection.

Chen thought about contacting Brad and asking him what was going on, but he decided against it. The commander had said he was calling the whole crew together. That had never happened before. The commander liked his schedules, and if he was breaking them it meant there was something urgent he felt they all needed to hear at the same time.

So Chen did his best to hurry back to the base, but nothing was easy or quick. By the time he'd secured the solar collector's mirrors and struggled back over the broken ground to the airlock, stowed his gear, gone through the recompression cycle, climbed out of his suit and put it in place, set the life support pack aside for recharging and pulled on a pair of blue overalls, almost an hour had passed. He arrived to find the rest of the crew already bored from waiting and his apologies met with a chorus of friendly barracking. He caught Brad's eye as he went to his seat and was rewarded with a broad smile and a wink.

The dining hall was the only large open space in the base. The long table at which they ate their communal evening meals had been opened out and the crew were settled around it. Despite their various poses of exaggerated relaxation, Chen recognised an unusual brittleness in their chatter and a tautness in some of their expressions.

Commander Arsenyev climbed into the room from the corridor that led to the communications centre. He was a tall man, his hair the colour of steel, his blue shirt and chinos neatly pressed. Fourteen months into their mission, the commander still took meticulous care of his appearance and remained cautious of the effect his easy charisma still inspired amongst most of the crew. Roman Arsenyev had been in space a handful of times before Chen had been born. He had held records for the longest spacewalk and the longest time in orbit, and he'd trained most of Russia's working cosmonauts. And yet he had always seemed unaware of the awe he inspired in those around him.

Today, though, his expression was tightly controlled and his movements brisk. The crew recognised the stiff formality in their commander's attitude and responded almost at once by settling to stillness, the chatter and laughter dying away.

Maheesh Sahni, the Indian communications specialist, followed Arsenyev into the room. He was nervously rubbing one hand on the side of his jeans and refused to meet the eyes of anyone at the table.

"I'm sorry to pull you all away from your work," Arsenyev said. "But I wanted you all to hear this directly from me."

The crew straightened up in their seats.

"Approximately six hours ago we stopped receiving signals from Earth Control. The orbiter crew is reporting the same break in communications. Neither base has been able to establish a cause but we've been able to rule out the most obvious problems at our end. We don't have any reason, at the moment, to suppose this is anything other than a technical glitch that will be sorted out by Earth Control; I propose we stick with existing protocols and to continue the mission schedule as planned."

The crew nodded automatically. They were all used to taking Arsenyev's orders without comment.

"I want to make one exception," the commander went on. "I want Chen and Yohan to devote some of their time to working with Maheesh on this problem. I'll post a revised rota for domestic chores, I'm afraid the rest of you will have to pick up some of the slack."

Brinkmann, the German geologist, groaned theatrically and the rest of the crew laughed, releasing the tension they all felt. Even the commander grinned, briefly.

✦

Chen was sitting on the edge of the bed when Brad knocked lightly on the door and stepped inside. Chen shuffled up and Brad sat beside him, kissing him softly. Chen ran his fingers across Brad's cheek and into his tightly-curled hair.

"You need a shave," Chen said when they eventually pulled apart.

"That's not all I need."

Chen smiled and they kissed again.

They made love quietly, as was their habit. They didn't suppose any of the rest of the crew would have cared much but they'd made the decision to keep their affair to themselves almost unconsciously. Privacy was a rare commodity on the base, so to have something that was theirs' alone was precious and part of the pleasure. But, also, Brad was married with children and neither of them had ever pretended that the relationship had a life beyond the mission.

It was fun but it was best to be discreet.

Later, Chen lay with his back to Brad, enjoying the heat of the other man's chest pressed against him in the narrow bunk and the security of being wrapped in his heavy arms. He marvelled, again, at the contrast between his own pale, narrow fingers and Brad's teak-stained hands, which seemed massive by comparison.

"What do you think has happened?" Brad said.

Chen shrugged, knowing instantly what he was talking about. They'd spent two days and two nights trying to re-establish contact with Earth Control, so far to no effect. The longer the problem persisted the more it began to fill up the thoughts of the crew. Chen suspected that Maheesh had been right from the start, there was no problem at their end, but he was also coming to suspect that whatever had gone wrong was much more than a simple malfunction at Earth Control.

"I thought it might be someone's idea of an exercise. Control is always throwing us curveballs to keep us on our toes, but they wouldn't have stretched things this long without letting the Commander in on their games."

"Do you think it..." Brad trailed off, unable to bring himself to say what he was thinking.

Chen's mind had started conjuring up disaster scenarios almost from the moment they'd learned about the breakdown and they had been growing bigger and more intricate ever since. He assumed that was true for everyone.

Chen shuffled around in the bed, turning awkwardly to face Brad, and rested his palm against the bigger man's chest.

"We don't know anything," he said. "The simplest explanation is that it's a technical fault, and Occam's Razor is usually the best rule to follow."

Brad bowed his head and Chen leaned forwards and kissed him on the forehead.

✦

Maheesh was sitting at the communications console. Chen wasn't sure, in the four days since they'd lost contact with Earth Control, whether he'd seen the soft-faced engineer move from that desk for longer than it took him to walk the length of the living quarters to the lavatory and back. Yohan was outside working on the communications array and swearing softly at his colleagues through his suit radio. Most of the swearing was in French but every now and then Yohan got creative and threw some English and Russian into the mix. Chen was working on the code for the communications software.

An hour passed, Yohan completed his checks and came back into the base, his T-shirt sweat stained and his mood foul. The communications room was cramped and hot with the three of them in there, and it was doing nothing for their tempers. They ran some more tests.

"Nothing!" Maheesh sat back and slammed both hands down onto his desk, sending the accumulated detritus of their work marathon—coffee cups, paper, food packaging—swishing and clattering to the floor. "There is nothing wrong."

"Maheesh?" Commander Arsenyev stood in the doorway. His expression was firm but something in the way he took half a step forward suggested concern. Chen noted that he'd taken to wearing the formal mission uniform. His blue overalls were spotlessly clean and neatly pressed.

Maheesh straightened up.

"Yes, commander?"

"I take it things are not going well?" The commander smiled gently.

Maheesh snorted. "We've replaced every component from here to the satellite dish. The satellite is responding, but beyond that is a black hole."

"Are you ready to take down the filters?"

Maheesh looked at Chen.

"Yes, commander," Chen said. "But I'm not sure it will make any difference."

"Can it hurt to try?" Arsenyev flashed a smile.

"No, commander."

"Okay then." Arsenyev leant against the door jamb. If he was tense, there was no sign of it. "Let's do it."

Maheesh spoke briefly to the crew on the orbiter base, letting them know comms was going offline, then nodded. Chen took his cue and, with couple of taps on the screen and a rattle on the keyboard, he shut down the base's communications software, changed the system settings and flicked away a cloud of warning dialogue boxes. He hit the power button.

"Resetting the system," he said.

They waited for a moment.

White text scrolled down the black screen as the system re-initialised. Chen watched carefully as the code slipped past. The screen blanked for a moment and then the operating system popped into life with a soft chime. The communications software interface came online. Chen checked it carefully then looked up at Commander Arsenyev.

"Filters have been removed. The buffer was empty and has been disabled. It contained no incoming messages. We have direct access to the satellite."

"Thank you, Chen," Arsenyev smiled. "Maheesh?"

But Maheesh was already eagerly battering his keyboard with heavy fingers.

They waited, but it didn't take long and Maheesh didn't have to say anything. They could see his shoulders slump as his hope and enthusiasm quickly faded.

Commander Arsenyev didn't wait for Maheesh to turn around.

"I think we need another crew meeting," he said, turning to leave the communications room and climb through the tunnel back towards the living quarters. "Get in touch with the orbiter and arrange a link up."

"Commander?" Yohan spoke softly. Arsenyev stopped but didn't turn around. "Commander, we need to discuss the protocols."

It was Arsenyev's turn to allow his shoulders to slump slightly. He raised a hand and rested it on the back of his neck.

"I know."

✦

The meeting had gone badly. The crew had split three ways over the crisis. The Americans—Brad, the red-headed engineer Killen, and Harding, the commander of the orbiter crew, all wanted to take action now. Brinkmann sided with the Americans. The Russians, led by the commander, with the base doctor Komolov and Manev on the orbiter argued that they had air, food, power and water for as long as they needed it and that it made sense to sit tight and keep to the mission profiles. Maheesh sided with them. Chen, Yohan and the Englishman, Bryant, also on the orbiter, found themselves caught in the middle.

The dread that had been gestating inside every member of

the crew over the last four days began to push its way to the surface as the debate went on. After forty minutes of increasingly pointless bickering, it exploded into the room in bright bursts of rage and recrimination.

Chen had found himself the focus of the Americans' anger when it became clear they weren't going to get their way. Although he was officially on the mission as an Italian citizen he had been educated at MIT and had worked at NASA before joining the European astronaut programme. The Americans had assumed he would be on their side. Killen had said some nasty things.

Commander Arsenyev had been forced to end the meeting by restating his ultimate authority and making it clear that, for now, the mission protocols remained in place. Nobody had been satisfied. The commander's final words were firm but it was clear he was disappointed with the way things had gone. Harding, however, had been furious and had cut off the orbiter link with a snap.

Afterwards, Chen went to the gym.

He turned on the treadmill, starting slowly but steadily ramping up the pace until he was working hard, feeling sweat prickle his forehead. Soon he was in a rhythm and the regular beat of his feet on the rolling track began to soothe him.

He was just passing the six-kilometres mark when Brad slipped into the room, closing the door behind him. Chen signalled his friend to wait and changed the programme, finishing his run with a brief sprint before winding down to a gentle halt.

Chen grabbed a towel and took a long drink from his bottle. Brad had stayed by the door, leaning against it, his hands behind his back.

"What's up?" Chen walked over and, rising up on his toes, kissed Brad lightly. Brad didn't respond.

Chen stepped back.

"Brad?"

"Why are you doing this?"

Chen was startled by the coldness in Brad's eyes and the harsh edge to his voice.

"I don't—"

"I can't believe you'd be so selfish," Brad cut him off.

Chen wiped the sweat from the back of his neck, draping the towel around his shoulders.

"Don't. Brad, please." Chen wanted to go, to get back to his room, lock the door and pretend this wasn't happening. He tried to get around Brad but the bigger man grabbed him by the arms and shoved him back across the room, pressing him against the cool outer wall. Brad's grip was powerful and Chen had to force down a yelp of pain.

"You can't keep me here," Brad said. "I have to get home."

Chen refused to meet Brad's gaze. He just stood there.

"I have a wife and daughters," Brad's voice was rising. "We don't know what's happened to them."

Chen said nothing.

Brad released him with a shove.

"Damn you!"

"Brad..."

Brad raised his hand, clenched into a fist, but didn't strike. There were tears in his eyes.

"Brad, you know I'm not trying to keep you here," Chen said. "Even if I wanted to keep you away from your wife—and I don't— I wouldn't let that get in the way of making the right decision now. Our lives might depend on this."

"I'm scared," Brad said.

That caught Chen by surprise. Fear wasn't something any astronaut liked to admit. You left fear behind in training, that's what they said. Brad caught the change in Chen's expression.

"Not for me," he said. "My girls..."

"I know," Chen said, and then regretted it. They both knew Chen didn't know what it was like to have kids. "But we don't have enough information to make any decisions yet. We don't even know if there's anything really wrong."

"We can't just sit here and do nothing."

Brad turned away. Chen raised a hand to rest on his shoulder, but stopped himself. His hand hovered over his lover like a benediction.

"Yes we can. We have to," Chen said. "Anything else could be suicide."

"Harding said—"

"I heard what he said, but what if he's wrong? What if it is just a glitch and all Harding's half-thought-through bravado achieves is to leave your girls without a father?"

Brad slumped onto the bench used for lifting weights. He sat, head down, his elbows resting on his knees, his palms together as though in prayer.

"Komolov said something to me earlier," Chen said. "He said the difference between Americans and Russians is that when the Americans went west to find their wild frontier they found Iowa and California and they conquered it and tamed it. When Russians went East they found Siberia and it was never conquered and never tamed; they could only ever come to a compromise with the land."

"What the hell are you talking about?" Brad looked up. The anger was draining from him and, perhaps despite himself, a smile flickered on his lips.

"Komolov was saying that Americans expect to conquer everything. Russians expect to live with it. The Russians will wait things out, wear things down and survive. Americans want to do everything now. They expect to keep moving forward."

"And you?"

"Well, my Chinese grandma had an old saying—"

"Chen!"

"No, really, she always said: *Qí lǘ zhǎo mǎ!*"

"What the hell does that mean?"

"I have no idea, I grew up in Florence."

Brad laughed. Chen liked that sound. He sat beside Brad on the bench, resting a hand on the other man's knee. Brad tensed for a moment, then relaxed and put his hand over Chen's.

"The translation is something like: when you go looking for a new horse, ride the mule you already own."

Brad stared blankly at him.

"It means that even when you're looking for something better, you shouldn't neglect what you've already got." Chen nudged Brad gently with his shoulder. "We're safe here. We have time. We'll work out what's happening. But we can't do just something stupid because we're scared. We mustn't panic. We're no use to anyone—neither your daughters nor to my father—if we're dead."

Brad bowed his head again and clenched and unclenched his fists then he leant over and kissed Chen on the cheek, but there was sadness in his eyes.

"You might be right," he said. "But I don't think it will matter."

✦

The crew argued amongst themselves for another week. The European team wavered back and forth, unable to agree a joint position and caught between two blocs who seemed unshakeable in their determination to follow different paths.

In the end it was the orbiter crew who broke the deadlock and shattered the mission protocols.

It was just after midday on the tenth day of radio silence when Chen, not long after finishing a nightshift in the comms room, was woken by shouting in the corridor outside his room. He staggered drowsily to his door and looked out to see Komolov, the Russian doctor, red-faced and screaming insults in a crude mix of Russian and English. It took another few moments for Chen to recognise the object of the doctor's tirade.

It was Harding, the American commander of the orbiter base. Behind him trailed a sheepish looking Bryant and, further back, Manev stood with his head bowed as though in shame.

Chen could smell something familiar but it took a moment to place it. It was soft, damp earth. They hadn't smelt that since the mission had started over four hundred days ago. Then he noticed the breeze. The airlock doors were open.

Komolov was still shouting, but there were fewer swear words now and he was being more coherent—though he was still switching freely between English and Russian. Chen caught the words contamination and breach.

Brad and Killen came out of their rooms. They were both dressed in uniform. Chen tried to catch Brad's eye but he looked away, embarrassed or ashamed.

He knew, Chen thought. *He knew and he didn't tell me.*

Chen was surprised by the intense and intimate sense of betrayal that swept through his body.

Harding nodded towards his countrymen but ignored

Komolov as he made his way towards Commander Arsenyev's room. His expression revealed no emotion but there was something triumphant in his movements and the way he threw back his shoulders.

Komolov stepped in front of the American and tried to shove him back up the corridor, towards the airlock.

Harding, bull-chested, thick-shouldered and blunt-headed, didn't even take a step back. The look on his face remained blankly calm but he brought his fist up fast and hard into Komolov's midriff. The Russian gasped and doubled over. Harding walked past him.

Commander Arsenyev's door swung open.

The old man stood there. He was in uniform. His mouth was a thin line of contempt, his blue eyes glacial. He took in the doubled up Komolov and the swaggering Harding.

"Idiot!"

"I think we need to reconsider the mission protocols," Harding said. His tone was flat but there was a noticeable pause before he added: "Sir."

✦

Chen closed the airlock door. Killen snorted something about that horse having bolted, but it made Chen feel better. Even so, he knew there was no going back to their cosy old routines now. They gathered in the dining hall. The Russians hugged one wall, the Americans the other. The Europeans sat at the table. No one spoke.

Eventually Arsenyev and Harding came in. Harding looked pleased with himself.

They both sat at the head of table.

"We have decided—" Harding started.

Commander Arsenyev lowered a hand onto the table, palm down. It was a slow movement but it drew the attention of the rest of the crew. Harding, noticing that he'd lost his audience, stopped and turned to the commander. Then he nodded and sat back.

Commander Arsenyev smoothed the front of his uniform, pausing for a moment over the roundel of his mission badge—a red Mars encircled by eagle wings. The word PATHFINDERS picked out in gold letters with translations in Russian, German, French, Italian, and Urdu running around the circumference. The commander looked up, taking in each member of the crew. Chen noticed that many of them could not meet his gaze, only Killen looked him squarely in the eye.

Harding shifted impatiently as the silence lengthened. At last the commander spoke.

"The ongoing communications situation and the..." the hesitation was brief but pointed, "... action by the orbiter crew requires us to reconsider our situation. It seems clear that the mission protocols are no longer relevant and there is nothing in the emergency mission procedures that covers our current situation. I have agreed to Commander Harding's request to bring you together so we can discuss our next step."

Harding tapped on the tablet in front of him and an image blinked to life on the wall. There was a map. Ross Island, McMurdo Sound and the dry valleys. A red line tracked a route from the Mars Base, in Beacon Valley, an isolated outcropping of rock to the east, down the Ferrar Glacier across the New Zealand territory via Lake Fryxell and down to the coast via Camp Chocolate, the Bratina Island Refuge and then over the ice shelf to McMurdo. Having reached its destination the red line reset and started all over again. It looked so simple.

"I propose that we make for the base at McMurdo and—"

"How far is that?" Komolov asked.

Harding's irritation at the interruption was obvious. He looked over his shoulder to the map.

"On foot, if we don't get too sidetracked on the glacier, about one hundred and eighty miles."

Brinkmann whistled.

Komolov sat back and folded his arms.

"With winter closing in?"

"You'd rather wait six months for the possibility of nicer weather?"

"How long do you think it will take?" Yohan asked.

"I believe we can make at least ten miles a day," Harding said. "We managed the four-mile crossing from the orbiter base in five hours."

Chen shook his head.

"We can build sleds, our suits are insulated, we have emergency survival gear."

"And what happens when you get there?" Yohan asked.

"We get in touch with home. We find out what is going on."

"There's no one there," Maheesh said.

Attentions shifted. Maheesh kept his gaze on the table, refusing to look up.

"You can't know that," Harding said.

"There's no one there," Maheesh repeated. He put his own tablet on the table and started an audio recording that played over the room's speakers. "This is from McMurdo, five days ago."

There was a muffled sound. It might have been the wind or it might have been someone sobbing. Then there was a crack that could have been a gunshot or a door slamming and then there was silence.

"The radio channel is still open, there's power, but no one is broadcasting."

Suddenly everyone was shouting.

Chen looked to Commander Arsenyev. He did not look surprised.

"Where did you get that?" Chen asked.

Maheesh cocked his head, unable to hear over the noise.

"Where did you get that?" Chen shouted. The others turned their attention back to the table. Everyone looked at Maheesh.

"I instructed him to use the emergency short wave radio," Commander Arsenyev's spoke softly but everyone heard him.

"Radio?" Harding voiced was suddenly high pitched. "Why didn't you tell us there was a radio?"

"There wasn't any point," Maheesh said. "I tried to contact the other bases—"

"We should have been told!" Killen was leaning over Maheesh, practically screaming into his face.

"He was acting on my request." Commander Arsenyev stood up and raised his voice just a notch. It was enough to restore a semblance of order. "The radio was provided for use in an emergency. When we shut down the buffers on the communications array and still could not contact mission control, I gave Maheesh permission to use the radio to try and contact the local bases. I asked him to keep the recording secret because I didn't want to damage morale."

"Damage morale?" Harding stood up. "So what was your plan? Were you going to lie to us forever? Or did you only care about keeping your little empire in one piece?"

"I was going to tell you when we understood what it meant," Arsenyev said. He sat down again, and began to gently massage his temples. There was something very like resignation in his voice. "Something bad has happened and it has happened quickly over a very wide area. The radio is picking up nothing except some official automated alerts and the occasional number station, which I'm also assuming are automated. There was nothing to report and little to be gained from further feeding all the useless speculation that has been going on."

Harding walked to the door of the living quarters.

"You should have told us," he said, and left.

Killen, Brinkmann, Bryant and Yohan followed.

Brad paused to look at Chen.

Chen shook his head. Where was there to go?

Brad left.

✦

Three days later, the three Americans and three Europeans left Mars Base to make for McMurdo. They'd decided amongst themselves that the radio communication changed nothing. They needed to know what was happening. There were some angry exchanges about the division of equipment and food but Chen kept to his room. Brad did not visit him.

Yohan and Bryant visited him once and tried to convince him to come with them. Chen wished them luck, but said no.

On the final morning, Chen helped with some minor changes to the communications software. As the time for their departure approached resentments cooled and some of the group's old camaraderie re-emerged. The Russians and Europeans exchanged hugs, and Harding shook hands with Arsenyev and said he was sorry about how things worked out.

Brad and Killen stood apart from the rest and did not speak to anyone.

The commander wished them all good luck, and then the Russians went inside and Maheesh followed.

Chen watched Brad and the others walk away across the rocky, broken floor of the dry valley towards the distant white line that was the glacier. It was early and the sun had yet to rise above the wall of their valley but the ice was already bathed in morning light.

Their progress was slow. They would dip down out of sight and then rise again on the undulating landscape, each time slightly further away, slightly smaller. And then they were gone again.

Chen watched, but Brad never turned to look back.

✦

They stayed in contact for three days using the base's communication system before they were out of range and the signal faded. When they reached Lake Fryxell they got in contact again using the research base radio. The camp was deserted, but that was normal with winter edging in. There was still no response from McMurdo.

They got in touch again when they reached Cape Chocolate.

The weather was worsening and they spent three days in the small refuge; it was cramped but they were in good spirits. They were making better time than expected and though the huts, which weren't in regular use, were battered, they were intact and offered good protection.

On the fourth morning the weather cleared and Chen listened over Maheesh's shoulder as they got ready to make for the Bratina Island Refuge.

Chen heard Brad laughing in the background. It made him smile.

They never heard from them again.

✦

"We're almost finished," Chen said as he came in to the living quarters. "Komolov asked if you'd like to say a few words?"

Commander Arsenyev didn't look up but he nodded. He'd

been sitting with the lights off, his face lit from below by the tablet screen he was pretending to read.

They were silent for a while. Chen drank a glass of water and tossed a meal pack into the oven—he didn't even bother to check what was inside. He watched it slowly turning and then, when the oven pinged, he ate it from the packaging, standing up, leaning against the work surfaces. The food was salty and sour, the chicken rubbery and the vegetables overcooked.

Eventually the food was gone. Chen waited a little longer then turned to go.

"Do you miss Flight Engineer Washington?" Arsenyev said.

Washington? Chen had to stop to think who the old man meant.

"I miss them all," Chen said. "I miss Brad."

"You were close." Arsenyev looked up. The light from the tablet screen highlighted every crease and wrinkle on his face. The Commander looked tired, he had become very old in the six weeks since they'd last heard from the rest of the crew.

Chen nodded.

"I miss them all too," Arsenyev said. "Do you suppose there are others, like us, waiting?"

Chen came back and sat next to the Commander.

"There must be."

"You are an optimist," Commander Arsenyev smiled and patted him on the shoulder.

"Maheesh thought he'd picked up faint signals," Chen said. "People babbling in languages he couldn't understand."

"Maheesh was working too hard," Arsenyev said.

"Did he say why he did it?" Chen nodded to Arsenyev's screen. Maheesh had left a message for the commander's eyes only before he'd opened his wrists.

"No," Arsenyev said. "He just wanted to say goodbye."

A deeper loss revealed itself on the commander's face. Chen felt a sudden shock of recognition.

"You and Maheesh?"

"If I had not been commander." Arsenyev smiled but shook his head. "But I have always been too ambitious..."

"Ambitious?" Chen couldn't imagine what the commander still hoped to achieve.

"They promised me Mars. It would be a one-way ticket, just me and some equally useless old American, happily sacrificed to beat the Chinese. But Mars!"

It seemed as if a new light had been ignited behind the commander's eyes. For a moment the old man was gone and the cosmonaut re-emerged.

"But what about the base? Our mission?"

"This? This was always impossible! This is all far too grand and too expensive for these mean times. This was a show, a distraction. But I don't suppose it matters. None of us shall touch that rusty soil now."

The old man coughed. He was suddenly frail again.

"All my life, I dreamed of space," the commander said.

✦

The Russians settled in to wait, a routine took shape and weeks passed. They monitored the radio in shifts, they ate meals together and watched films—though most of the Russian films left Chen bewildered, even with Manev's running commentaries. They even kept some of the science projects going, though the solar collector was quietly abandoned without discussion or protest.

Then one morning the commander did not wake up.

Chen helped Manev carry the body outside. The old man seemed weightless and Chen had thought of the buzzard he'd once found injured and stunned beneath an electricity pylon in his father's fields. Chen had marvelled at how something so huge and fierce could be so insubstantial. His father had scolded him for bringing the wounded bird to the house, blaming it for killing his lambs, and broke the raptor's neck.

They laid Arsenyev next to Maheesh. The ground was too hard to dig a grave, so they covered the bodies with a cairn of stones. No one spoke.

When they went inside Komolov pulled out a bottle vodka. He said it was medicinal. Chen sipped from his glass while watching the Russians get drunk, sing old songs and then slump into sleep.

✦

The door of the airlock rolled open. The wind, cold as a blade, sliced through Chen and he began to shiver at once. It was dark outside. The days were shortening fast and, though it was still early in the afternoon, the sun had long dipped below the valley walls.

He stepped out onto the valley floor.

The sky was bright and clear.

Chen tried to ignore the cold but it was already biting hard at his nose and fingers, the wind ripped at his flimsy blue overalls. His feet numbed, the frozen ground sucking the heat from his body. It took a conscious effort to control his breathing, the air was so sharp that he gasped with each breath and wondered if his lungs might freeze and shatter. The shivering shook his whole body. Chen wrapped his arms around his ribs.

He looked up and took a moment to identify some of the unfamiliar southern constellations. There was Centaurus and Reticulum and the Southern Cross. The syrupy band of the Milky Way was a reassuringly familiar blanket. He would have liked to look at the Moon once more, but it had not yet risen. He couldn't see Mars.

He thought of Brad, out there. Would the ice preserve his body? There was a kind of immortality in that, and yet it seemed impossible to Chen that the last heat might have been sucked from that broad chest. It was ridiculous that those powerful arms might be forever still.

Chen wondered how quickly his tears would freeze. How soon would grief blind him?

He turned away from the stars and walked into the night. He found that being alone was not so frightening. He felt as though he was emerging from a deep cave that had kept him safe and warm but that had also kept him in the dark and had prevented him from seeing the world as it really was. Everything that had gone before had been fake, shadows flickering on a wall.

He stumbled over a rock, but kept walking.

How far could he go?

Chen looked up at the stars one last time and smiled.

Martin McGrath is a wastrel who masquerades as a journalist and writer. Originally from Nothern Ireland he now lives in St Albans, England with a wife and daughter who put up with his peculiar habits and treat him kindly. He's had stories published in a variety of books and magazines in recent years and he's working on a novel, but who isn't? He edits Focus, the British Science Fiction Association magazine for writers, is the administrator of the James White Award (www.jameswhiteaward.com) and blogs infrequently at www.mmcgrath.co.uk and tweets nonsense as @martinmcgrath

A BIOSPHERE ENDS

Stephen Palmer

"OUR AGRICULTURAL SYSTEM must produce all our food," said David James.

Yoo Ye-jun gazed out over the hydrofields. "Bananas," he said, "papayas, sweet potatoes, beets, rice and wheat. Peanuts and cowpea beans. So?"

Lim Ji-eun ran a hand through her hair. "I'm hungry," she said.

So far they had consumed a low calorie, nutritious diet. But the vital diagonstic indicators of the habitat environment were fluctuating, putting food supply at risk, and their computers could not say why. Medical tests showed the health of all nine habitat residents had been outstanding when they arrived. Shortly after establishing the Aeolis Mensae base they all lost a tenth of their pre-Mars weight, before stabilizing, and regaining some weight later. Their metabolisms became more efficient at extracting nutrients from their food as an adaptation to the Martian diet.

"I'm hungry too," said Yoo Ye-jun.

The AI chosen to investigate the expiry of the Aeolis Mensae habitat on Mars was one of the most intelligent machines ever created. Yet even it did not recognise at first the cause of the disaster. Nor did its handlers.

In 2073, the Koreans took over the Aeolis Mensae project-planned, designed and financed by the Chinese twenty-five years earlier-siting the base on the Martian equator. It was a closed system: a habitat, an ecosystem, a vast conglomeration of steel and plastic and green life and animal life. Six Koreans, two Chinese and a Scot were the crew of this Martian greenhouse.

They lasted two years.

David James shook his head. "We will produce more food. We *must*. Look at the animals. Goats, hens and roosters, sows and boars, tilapia fish grown in the rice and pond systems. It's enough."

"Then why are we starving? And why is the oxygen level decreasing still?"

David James looked up into the dust-hung pink sky, through windows covered with the debris of passing dust devils; the sun a bright lamp, blue-tinted and forever distant. His stomach rumbled.

✦

Vanderhoof stood on the access steps of its Martian landing vehicle.

Vanderhoof's twenty percent biological component was protected from cold and low atmospheric pressure by a torso mounted stabilo-suit, but its mechanical arms and legs moved free;

The AI was called Vanderhoof after a Dutchman who had developed some of the monitoring processes used to manage the habitat. Sent in a shielded spacecraft along a Hohmann transfer orbit, it arrived, alone, in 2080. Meanwhile the Chinese suffered an incident on one of their satellites that destroyed it, sending fragments down to Earth, inward to the sun, and outward too. Having arrived on Mars, Vanderhoof set to work at once.

The Koreans did not want Vanderhoof to work alone, so they set up an interplanetary virtual reality in which it operated, inhabited also by Earthside investigators. The time delay made this virtual reality something of a prison, since its human users had to wait for Vanderhoof to catch up with them, and vice versa; but the delay did allow them to explore-virtually-the habitat for themselves, and so monitor, discuss and analyse the immediate facts collected by their AI investigator. But the frustration they felt in not being able to pick up a stone or touch a dead plant-though they could see both stone and plant, and acquire any fact about them-was intense. Vanderhoof's manner did not help.

already excoriated by minute dust particles fallen thirty kilometres from the upper atmosphere and blown stormwise by the wind. Four-tenths Earth gravity; it bounced down the steps and leaped onto the ochre brown surface.

Mars was rusty and dusty, small sun bright in the heavens,

set amidst other stars twinkling in a deep, dark sky. But there, high at the zenith, lay a strange object. Deimos and Phobos both below the horizon, all thirty five Martian orbiters accounted for, yet there was a vehicle orbiting Mars that Vanderhoof did not recognise, a vehicle silent, inwardly turned, like a machine autist.

Vanderhoof sent a signal back to Earth. "What is that orbiting craft?"

Time delay... wait...

"We do not know."

"What information do you have about it?"

"Our lack of information implies critical danger. Please enter the VR and investigate."

Vanderhoof's artificial ears twitched as the rocks of Mars tinkled and snapped, colled by rapidly falling temperatures. Though the atmosphere was too rarified to carry sounds audible to the human ear, Vanderhoof's augmented hearing could cope; and it heard the wind, blowing dust, lightning within distant storms. But the sun was low now, and even Vanderhoof, eighty percent artificial, needed to be inside the defunct Aeolis Mensae habitat before surface temperature dipped too far for survival.

✦

Law Dongming knew that the interplanetary flux of high-energy galactic cosmic rays, along with radiation from solar proton events, would be enough to kill him. Without the thick shielding of the Mars mission vehicle, that proton flux would be strong enough to cause death by acute radiation poisoning. But, still, he had signed up for the mission.

Between Earth and Mars on an augmented seven-month Hohmann transfer orbit... he lay inside the shielded module. All nine of them had been here for five days, sheltering from the cosmic storm.

Muscles, bones wasting away in weightlessness, making their decisions without instant help from Earth; communication between ship and mission directors delayed by twenty minutes— full emphasis of responsibility on the crew... a psychological high wire walk.

He lay next to the only other Chinese crew member, Song Xiuxiu, who, every few minutes, would glance at him. In the quiet of his mind he told himself: *she is afraid.*

Not afraid of the crew imploding because of the length of the flight or the confined conditions, afraid because the six other members were Korean. Back home, a nuclear bomb had been used for the third time.

This far out, just a month of travel time remaining, they would have to rely on telemedicine—a mixture of onboard databases and specialist advice sent from Earth—if there was an accident, or, worse, an incident. They would have to deal with it themselves. But what Law Dongming most feared was complete communication breakdown. There was no doubt in his mind how the mission vehicle politics would work in that eventuality.

✦

During sunlight hours, plant photosynthesis in the Aeolis Mensae habitat extracted up to 600 ppm of carbon dioxide from the air. An equivalent rise at night occurred when plant respiration took over. And winter carbon dioxide levels were typically four to five times those of summer. The Martian winter was a grim time and it lasted twice as long as winter on Earth. The crew cut and stored plant material in order to sequester carbon; they planted every available area with fast-growing species to increase photosynthesis when that became necessary.

David James said, "We began with oxygen levels of twenty percent—"

"We know that," Yoo Ye-jun interrupted, "but it's fourteen percent *now.* That's like living at fifteen thousand feet on Earth, David. We're exhausted. We're getting sleep apnea."

"This is Mars," David James said. "We can't walk outside unless we want to die. It's minus twenty out there."

"What are we going to do?" said Yoo Ye-jun.

✦

The habitat stood before Vanderhoof, its external metal girders gleaming in the setting sun. Vanderhoof looked back: the sun, thirty arc minutes above the top of distant hills of dark brown set against shadow-strewn ochre... in the distance a pale mist. Not long remaining before the chill took its toll; frost limned the ground.

Thin, cold, dusty air whipped around Vanderhoof as it investigated the windows. Inside, it saw slimy black foliage floating in dark water; dead goats and a dead pig; unrecognisable lumps in the habitat's tiny ocean, floating, bobbing when invisible marine creatures struck from below. Feeding fish, most likely.

The triple airlock door awaited. Mission control had changed the auto-codes so that Vanderhoof could enter. It tapped on the keypad as the smell of Martian iron oxide wafted against its olfactory sensors.

The door opened. A thud echoed through the atmosphere: thin, weedy, like a fist smacking a piece of cardboard. No atmosphere, this, for humans.

Because of the high energy requirements of oxygen manufacture, the designers of the habitat had ensured gas leakage was extraordinarily small—hence the triple airlock. At first, when oxygen depletion had become an issue, the crew had assumed there was a leak somewhere. But there was none.

Vanderhoof passed through the middle and inner doors of the airlock. There had been no gas leakage here, except, perhaps, on a molecular scale. As it stepped into the habitat new sub-programmes rose to the surface of its brain, telling it how important the oxygen issue was.

Yes! Vanderhoof must discover the reason for the disaster. It entered the interplanetary virtual reality, which contained within it in simulation the entire habitat. Visually, nothing changed. Sonically, nothing changed. But it recognised that something, some tiny detail, was different.

And then...

"Hello."

Vanderhoof turned around.

A man stood beside him, a man it recognised.

"I am James David."

"What are you?" Vanderhoof replied.

"Have you come here to explore the habitat?"

"Yes. Who are you?"

Silence. James David stared at Vanderhoof. Long time delay...

Then the newcomer spoke. "I'm sorry, I made a mistake. I'm David James. My memories still exist here, they were set up and animated before death. You are seeing my incarnation. Together, we can explore the habitat."

"You are not expected."

And Vanderhoof made a sudden connection. New animated presence. New orbiting craft. Who was this?

✦

The landing on Mars was automatic; it was hoped—assumed— that the mission AIs would execute it without a mistake. Mars' low gravity, however, and atmospheric aerodynamic effects made it tricky, even for the descent and braking of the heavy crewed spacecraft with thrusters only. The atmosphere was too thin to utilise aerodynamic effects for braking and landing.

A palpable sense of relief passed among the crew when the lander pads kissed the Martian surface. Though their fights so far had been wordy, non-physical and petty, the sense of anticipation had for all of them been hard to cope with. Personalised sleep spaces, constant communication with Earth and plenty to do ameliorated the boredom, but, at the back of everybody's mind: *what will it be like on Mars and when do we start and will we be settled soon?*

Without a magnetic field like Earth's, and with a thin atmosphere, a significant amount of ionizing radiation reached the Martian surface. Law Dongming took his first steps on the rusty stone-strewn surface and gazed into a dust-shrouded sunset. Four-tenths Earth gravity allowed him to mini-bounce across the grey brown plain.

Earlier unmanned missions had found radiation levels in orbit about Mars three times higher than those in Earth orbit. Levels at the site of the Aeolis Mensae base were lower, but solar proton events brought much higher doses, and remained a concern, though a pre-flight study suggested the average wash of low level radiation should not be as dangerous as first thought.

And so it turned out. Excepting the ever-dangerous solar

proton events, radiation levels experienced on the surface of Mars were a concern, a threat, but not a mission killer. And Law Dongming told himself: *even if it was too dangerous, the Korean mission directors would have been flooded with candidates. Who would not want to be the first human on Mars?*

Yoo Ye-jun had decided he would be the first human on Mars.

✦

"What I don't understand," said Lim Ji-eun, "is why there's this slow, steady decrease in the oxygen level, but no increase in the carbon dioxide level. Where is that oxygen *going?*"

They had performed tests. The Aeolis Mensae habitat experienced external temperature changes of up to eighty degrees Celsius. During daytime, the heat from the sun caused the air inside the habitat to expand, while during the night it cooled, and so contracted. Large forces would consequently assail the external structure, and so its volume changed on a daily rhythm using diaphragms that studded the external barrier.

Power was nuclear. Air conditioners were essential if life were to survive inside the habitat. Outside, the atmospheric pressure was 6mb. In summer, the temperature might reach ten degrees Celsius; in winter, even here on the Martian equator, it could be as cold as Earth's South Pole.

"We can't go back," Yoo Ye-jun said. He mini-bounced to the door, as if to illustrate his point. "We can't go outside."

"This habitat is a carbon-dioxide-rich environment," David James said. "We need more time. The ecosystem is settling down, that's all."

Yoo Ye-jun shook his head. "You said that months ago. We have to admit defeat, we have to try something different."

"No!"

Lim Ji-eun said, "The mission commanders tell us we are on Mars. We went through hell to get here. It was a one-way ticket—you know that. There is no going back to Korea. So we *have* to find out where that oxygen is going."

✦

Vanderhoof set up a secure line to Hong Hyun-jun back on Earth, so that "David James" could not hear the conversation.

Hong Hyun-jun: You're saying there's a VR presence of David James?

Vanderhoof: Yes, he immediately made friends with me. I don't like that. I like to work alone.

Hong Hyun-jun: He's nothing to do with us. And we can't see him.

Vanderhoof: I feel constrained. Why don't you make him go away?

Hong Hyun-jun: We don't know where he comes from. He's arranged his VR presence so that only you can interact with him.

Vanderhoof: I don't like it. I travelled a long way to get here. Only I can live on Mars. Why haven't you cracked open the unknown orbiting craft?

Hong Hyun-jun: We're trying to. We think it's Chinese.

Vanderhoof: I'm worried and I don't like to be watched. You're pulling a trick on me because you don't trust me alone here.

Hong Hyun-jun: We made you as you are. We like you working alone. This is nothing to do with us, Vanderhoof, our best guess is that the Chinese are playing some kind of political game.

Vanderhoof: They lost the Aeolis Mensae mission some time ago.

Hong Hyun-jun: Listen to me. Stop worrying. We're all on your side. Just ignore the VR presence for now.

Vanderhoof: I can't ignore it. I must take action.

Hong Hyun-jun: No!

Vanderhoof: You are trying to protect the presence.

Hong Hyun-jun: No I am not. I'm doing something that you, Vanderhoof, are very good at. I'm being careful. We don't know the reason for this VR presence.

Vanderhoof: You must find out soon.

Hong Hyun-jun: We will try. It must be coding all signals leaving the habitat so we can't see it. That makes our job difficult. We're twenty minutes away.

Vanderhoof: I know a lot about the Chinese, I learned about them when you put me forward for this investigation mission.

Hong Hyun-jun: Yes, you're good at history.

Vanderhoof: The Chinese surname comes first. Then the given name. This is why the VR presence called itself James David.

Hong Hyun-jun: What?

Vanderhoof: Then it corrected itself. I will be shown to be accurate in my assessment.

Hong Hyun-jun: Wait a moment... that so-called accident the Chinese had on their satellite let me get the debris data.

Vanderhoof: There will be a single debris trajectory leading into Mars orbit, almost identical to the one my craft followed. The so-called incident was a cover. The Chinese craft will be extremely compact, almost invisible to Earthside detectors, unless they were specifically seeking it. The craft will be automatic. It will be an AI, its goal to enter the habitat VR in realtime.

Hong Hyun-jun: You may be right. But the Chinese!

Vanderhoof: I am always right. I don't like being wrong.

Hong Hyun-jun: Then we need to find out what they're doing, and quickly.

Vanderhoof closed the secure communication line and turned towards "David James."
It said, "Are you here to explore? Or have your Chinese masters created you for another reason?"

✦

When Korea became a nuclear power, China was concerned. At first the spat between them seemed a show for the rest of the world, as both powers tried to fool other nations: China wanted to that Korea, for all its technological wonders, was a small upstart nation that only half a century ago had been two warring powers; Korea wanted to show that as the end of the Twenty-First Century approached it could do what the Japanese had done at the end of the Twentieth Century, except much, much more, and much, much better.

The Korean development of nuclear weapons was as much bravado as anything else; at least initially.

After the landing, and the hurried building of the transition module in which the crew would live for a few weeks, heavy duty robot AIs began building the Aeolis Mensae base itself.

Deimos like a distant star, Phobos rising in the west and setting in the east, a grey-white lump part-eclipsing the sun for thirty seconds every day: the two Martian beacons kept watch as the construction project took shape.

Law Dongming watched through his helmet visor, fascinated, worried, but mesmerised. A dust storm was reducing solar power and the machines were having to rely on backup nuclear. He shuddered. The largest Martian storms covered much of the planet, meaning further reliance on nuclear power... he did not like that. He told himself: *I do trust these Koreans, but what if something bad happened and everybody went tribal?*
This far out, sundered from the four-billion-year-old nest of

life on Earth, he felt alone... utterly alone, despite the presence of eight colleagues—some of them friends—and the goats and the sheep and the pigs that had already been cloned from cells. Song Xiuxiu felt the same.

He liked Song Xiuxiu. But what if everybody reverted to type, even her?

✦

To ensure that food webs survived and ecologies were maintained if some species went extinct, the habitat contained a complex environment. But two years into the mission, rapid swings in the density of plants and animals suggested the food webs were unstable and about to change. Yet without specific clues the crew remained at a loss. Their environment, it seemed, was out of control.

Worse, it was seasonally active, its biomass cut and stored by the crew as part of their management of carbon dioxide. And the heavy physical work they all had to do to manage the environment used up too many of the calories they ingested with their food.

Trees suffered from weakness caused by lack of stress wood, normally created in response to winds in the Earth's atmosphere. In the habitat there could be no strong winds.

"We have a small sea here," Yoo Ye-jun said. "We changed its pH levels to prevent it becoming too acidic. We even harvest algae by hand from our corals. Why has everything failed?"

"Our carbon dioxide levels fluctuate too much," Lim Ji-eun replied. "All our pollinating insects have died. There are pests everywhere." She kicked out at a mound of dead cockroaches. "These changes are *never* going to be smooth. Wildly varying numbers of phytoplankton at different times, wildly varying numbers of animal species feeding on phytoplankton..."

"Even if our biosphere has finished transitioning from one state to another," David James said, "we must be alert for more changes. Many natural systems are capable of existing in more than one stable state—"

Yoo Ye-jun laughed. "You are a fool! Even if you are right, we can't live like this any more. It's failed."

"We know the Earth can survive in different stable states," Lim Ji-eun said. "Fifty-five million years ago it was warm in the Arctic."

"And where else can we live?" said David James. "This is Mars."

"Without oxygen we cannot breathe," Yoo Ye-jun said. "The levels decrease, and the point is near when we will get altitude sickness. Altitude sickness can kill."

✦

Because Vanderhoof's brain was artificial and VR-suffused, it was susceptible to attack through a virtual reality. When "David James" grew in apparent size and apparent mass Vanderhoof departed the habitat VR without delay.

At once the face of "David James" appeared on the nearest monitor.

"Who are you really?" Vanderhoof asked of the monitor.

"I am David James. I'm looking for a particular rock. It was found by Law Dongming, but he died very soon after returning from his exploratory mission."

"A rock? This then is a special rock, if your Chinese masters have sent you all this way in secret."

"It is in fact only one of many things I want to find. The whole of humanity on Earth wants to know why the Aeolis Mensae mission failed."

"You lie. I have analysed your speech patterns."

"I am not human, remember."

"I know what you are. An AI in Martian orbit. But I am the greatest AI there has ever been, and I know you are lying. I have analysed your speech patterns."

"You lie."

"I will find the rock. This is why you are here, now, engaging with me. You were a fool to mention the rock to me so soon in our relationship. That was your big mistake."

Vanderhoof prepared to access the data on Law Dongming, one of the two Chinese members of the habitat crew. It sensed conspiracy: it did not like coincidence. It was beginning to wonder if "coincidence" existed at all.

✦

They all had to take drugs to survive on Mars, mostly retinoids—vitamins with antioxidant properties—and chemicals that retarded cell division, giving the body time to repair damage before harmful mutations were duplicated.

Already new supplies were on the way from Earth, sent on a Hohmann transfer orbit inside an AI-piloted spacecraft. Mars' thin atmosphere contained only trace amounts of nitrogen and oxygen, and almost no water; supplies, including breathable air, would be sent on a regular basis, at least until the Neumann Machines began their dreary but productive work. Law Dongming stared up into an indigo, star-speckled sky and wondered how near those automatic missions were. *I bet the Koreans are winning the public relations war back home,* he thought. *I bet this is making them emperors of the Pacific Rim.*

"Are we going out in the rover?"

He turned around. Song Xiuxiu stood behind him, smiling.

They had planned a geological excursion while repairs were made to the ocean-carrying structure of the habitat. Just the two of them. "Yes," he said. He checked a computer remote. "The dust storms have all subsided. It looks almost balmy out there... minus one Celsius."

Song Xiuxiu glanced over her shoulder. Law Dongming looked up, seeing Yoo Ye-jun and Lim Ji-eun checking computers nearby. Oxygen levels were declining at a rate that made everyone uneasy; a tipping point might be near, Yoo Ye-jun said.

Song Xiuxiu said, "Do you think they will be suspicious?"

"Of us?"

"The two Chinese."

"Shhh...," he hissed. "I think they're monitoring audio. Don't give them anything to work with."

"Are you worried?"

He nodded. He didn't ask what exactly she was talking about. No need.

The rover was a shielded vehicle powered by high-efficiency, heavy-duty solar batteries. They rocked and bounced over the terrain, the vehicle creaking as stresses rippled through its flexible structure. Distant valleys expelled fog like volcanic rifts back on Earth; dunes further away lay dark, basaltic.

Nearby lay an ancient riverbed. mission directors specialising in geology had given them suggested co-ordinates, which they programmed into the rover so that it took them past all the interesting places.

Pleasant hours passed. Law Dongming found the stress of the worsening atmosphere reduced as he became absorbed in the process of collecting and assessing rocks. And it was good to breathe air with a full load of oxygen.

And then he noticed something. He bent over to pick up a large, patterned rock. He turned so that the sun shone at a low angle across it.

It was without doubt a fossil.

✦

Yoo Ye-jun said, "The early warning signs should have helped us prepare for and prevent the worst-case scenario. I blame you two for ignoring them."

"Yoo Ye-jun!" David James said. "We are *surrounded* by problems caused by ecological regime shifts. Water purity issues, declining fish numbers, exploding water flea numbers, unproductive land. My study shows that we have to identify these changes before they reach their tipping point—"

"Your study?" Yoo Ye-jun interrupted. "Your *study?* You have been exercising your massive intellect while we are starving, the oxygen is depleting, we've lost almost all our fish, and all our pollinating insects—"

Lim Ji-eun said, "But the cockroaches perform some pollination—"

"Shut *up!* The habitat is dying and we have to decide what to do. I believe the mission is over because this biosphere is ending. Accept the truth out *there.*"

He pointed to the nearest window. The brown land outside, utterly barren, bitter, freezing, *not Earth...* that land stood unresponsive, alien, its majesty and its beauty a combination of strangeness and unattainable wealth. And David James found himself considering that Martian wealth, then realising that the mission had been seduced by it.

They would pay. They would not receive.

✦

Vanderhoof investigated every square centimetre of the habitat crew's private quarters but found nothing significant. No rocks. At last, certain that a conspiracy was being enacted against the Koreans, it set up a second secure line to Hong Hyun-jun through the interplanetary VR.

Vanderhoof: I can find nothing.

Hong Hyun-jun: We think here that you've made a mistake. That mention of the rock could have been accidental, random.

Vanderhoof: Nothing is random, everything has a meaning. Chinese fingerprints are everywhere here, and they had two crew members. I'm certain one of them was working in secret against the Koreans.

Hong Hyun-jun: Without evidence that will have to remain speculation.

Vanderhoof: I shall find evidence. I know I am correct.

Hong Hyun-jun: We need to begin work on the reason for the disaster, specifically the oxygen depletion.

Vanderhoof: I understand your concern.

Hong Hyun-jun: We want you to begin investigating the structure of the habitat now. We're wondering if something there unexpectedly began oxidising, perhaps metal exposed by the crew for some reason.

Vanderhoof: Very well.

Hong Hyun-jun: You will begin now?

Vanderhoof: Very well.

But already Vanderhoof had noticed something that it thought might be significant. The interior surfaces of the plascrete looked rough, as if they had disintegrated, and when it went to pass a hand over the nearest surface, the plascrete crumbled. At once it realised that such deterioration could be through oxidation. A test would be required.

✦

The fossil, Law Dongming thought, was part of a bacterial mat.

He had visited Shark Bay in Western Australia as a child, seeing there the stromatolites—calcareous mounds built up from layers of lime-secreting cyanobacteria and trapped sediments—that the fossil reminded him of. Surely this was the same thing? The geological conditions exposed here by the Martian weather were right. The shape was right, the structure. It *had* to be a fossil.

For a moment his mind seemed to exist separate from his head as the shock hit: an out-of-body moment. Then he was Law Dongming in a spacesuit again, and he looked up to see Song Xiuxiu staring at him.

"What?" she said.

He showed her the fossil. Said nothing. They were on a local com-link, inaudible from the habitat, though only the flick of a switch away.

"Say nothing," he said.

"What is it?" she replied at once.

He bent over to write in the rusty sand with his gloved right hand: FOSSIL.

Her face said everything she felt. She uttered no words.

Then Law Dongming wondered how they could announce this, the most important scientific discovery of all time. He walked over to the rover and sat in the front seat, his legs weak, hands shaking; light-headed. *He,* Law Dongming the taikonaut, was the discoverer of the world's most important find. He had become history itself, he was living history now, this *second,* holding history in his hand...

He felt only numbness, a kind of horrified awe, as imagined

repercussions flooded into his mind: fame, media storm, the universe opening out from the blue-green planet he had left.

But the Koreans would not like the fact that a Chinese had found the fossil.

What should he do?

✦

Yoo Ye-jun confronted David James while Lim Ji-eun lay asleep.

They sat, panting for breath, beside the remains of the mangrove swamp, which was now covered in noxious water flea debris: slimy, foetid, dangerous.

David James said, "Have you spoken again to mission control? They—"

"They can't help us now. Oxygen levels are down to a critical level."

"But they have *always* counselled us at times of stress! Why are you ignoring them now? You must control yourself—"

Yoo Ye-jun shook his head. "The time has come."

"No!"

"Earth is millions of kilometres away. Millions, David. Do you *feel* what that means? The high-energy-particle-irradiated space..."

"I... I don't feel anything. Except... scared. And my head is pounding fit to burst."

"Oxygen too low—it is like altitude sickness. You understand!" Yoo Ye-jun looked down at his oxygen monitor and said, "We don't have long. The damage could be permanent now." He tried to stand up, but swayed, then fell.

David James looked on in horror. Perhaps they *had* left it too long. He glanced up at the mission monitor to see that the two taikonauts were still outside on their geological mission.

He staggered to his feet and headed for the rest pod. There he would wake the others... but what could they do? The Aeolis Mensae mission was one way. Pain thumped inside his head as he moved, and he had to rest every ten steps or so; but when he reached the pod and stepped inside, then shook Lim Ji-eun, she did not respond. She was dead.

✦

Vanderhoof walked in ever-decreasing circles around the habitat interior, maximising the resolution of its optical sensors, seeking that one rock set apart from the rest by reason of position, colour, lack of moss, lack of algae growth...

But nothing. Nothing at all.

Yet it was sure that Law Dongming had found something and hoped to give whatever he had found as a secretly-transmitted data-set to the Chinese. Various sub-programs clamoured for attention, but it ignored them. It remained focused.

At the edge of the tiny ocean created inside the habitat for marine life, it paused. A rocky ridge sheened green with algae held back the stinking, dying body of water. Here, Yoo Ye-jun had died, much of his skeleton now at the bottom of the ocean. Vanderhoof sat on the ridge next to a growth of barnacles, dislodging as it did a flat stone, that sank into the water.

Vanderhoof surveyed what lay nearby. That it had found nothing was strange—suspicious, almost. It did not know

The AI chosen to investigate the expiry of the Aeolis Mensae habitat on Mars was one of the most intelligent machines ever created. Yet even it did not recognise at first the cause of the disaster. Nor did its handlers.

Later, as it rested in its tiny spacecraft on its way back to Earth, shielded from the high energy particles of the irradiated space lanes, safe, secure and alone, it analysed more of the data that had automatically downloaded into its brain. It knew now that the corrosion of Aeolis Mensae habitat plascrete was caused by two types of microbial sulphur, one type created by an anaerobic process producing hydrogen sulphide, the other by an aerobic process in which hydrogen sulphide was oxidised to sulphuric acid. This resulted in the inexorable depletion of atmospheric oxygen.

Evolved hydrogen sulphide was exposed to an aerobic environment supporting the growth of sulphur oxidising bacteria, thiobacilli, which grew in the plascrete of the structure, oxidising hydrogen sulphide to sulphuric acid, which dissolved the calcium hydroxide and calcium carbonate in the lo-cement binder.

what to do about its objectives. Ignore them?

One thing it did know. It had failed to locate the rock, but it must not let the Chinese pick over the habitat remains after it had gone. There was only one thing left to do now. Its decision was made.

> *Only a small number of species of thiobacilli were known. Some establish the acidic conditions necessary for corrosion to happen, while the acid-loving T. thiooxidans grows in low pH conditions.*
>
> *Even Vanderhoof did not recognise at first the real cause of the disaster. Nor did its handlers.*

It turned to the question of the disintegrating plascrete. It set up a simple chemical test and let it run. But there was an odour of rotten eggs, which, an atmospheric analysis proved, was caused by hydrogen sulphide; and the test results showed the presence of sulphuric acid. Here, then, was the answer to the demise of the Martian biosphere. It was, as it had to be, a closed system, and thus beyond rescue by its human occupants.

It returned to the computer centre and began opening all the hard-drive mountings, the motherboard housings, the interfaces, the cameras, the sensors. All internal workings were to be exposed. Then it opened every computer room door and wedged them with rocks.

Satisfied, it returned to the habitat rice paddies.

A voice on a monitor speaker. "Vanderhoof, what are you doing? Vanderhoof, this is Hong Hyun-jun. Stop!"

Vanderhoof ignored the voice.

With the three special codes, it opened the triple airlock door so that the atmosphere of the habitat rushed out in a great, moaning gust. And then the thin, deadly Martian wind entered, carrying its load of dust, that excoriated exposed metal, that scored the computer components, that destroyed the cameras and the sensors. And the cold came too, ruining delicate machine parts.

Vanderhoof was satisfied. It mini-bounced back to the landing craft. It wanted to go home. It did not like being on Mars.

✦

In the end, Law Dongming decided to make the announcement

when he and Song Xiuxiu returned to the habitat. That way he could open an auxiliary channel to the Chinese back home, allowing them to make the most of the news there. It would also boost morale in conditions of rapidly declining oxygen.

But opening the omnichannel com-link he heard nothing, and nobody answered his call. The habitat was not as they had left it: silent, static inside.

Approaching in the rover, the sun low ahead, the habitat in silhouette, he thought there must be an AI error contributing to lost communications. As a precaution he sent a lexical entry in Chinese to his private diary: just one word, accessible back home on Earth. Then he jumped off the rover and with Song Xiuxiu entered the habitat.

He saw three bodies at once. Shocked, he could not think what to do. At the edge of the tiny ocean created inside the habitat for marine life, he paused. A rocky ridge sheened green with algae held back the stinking, dying body of water. He sat on the ridge next to a growth of barnacles, placing the flat stone that was humanity's most precious find upon it.

It would be safe there.

Stephen Palmer first came to the attention of the SF world in 1996 with his Orbit Books debut Memory Seed and its sequel Glass. Flowercrash, Muezzinland and Hallucinating followed from the Wildside Press, then in 2010 Urbis Morpheos from PS Publishing. Ebooks of his most recent three novels have been published by PS Publishing and Infinity Plus. He lives and works in Shropshire and maintains a blog at stephenpalmersf.wordpress.com

SLIPPING SIDEWAYS

Carmelo Rafala

WE BURIED RACHEL in the spring. Not long after, Leo became a recluse. In all honesty, I never thought I'd see him again.

He stood now between the open balcony doors of his penthouse flat, perfectly framed against Geneva's dusky skyline. His hairline had receded some, and he was noticeably greyer at the temples. His clothes—well, Leo had never been into fashion: tan trousers, checked shirt with a dark navy sweater draped over his shoulders. The uniform of the self-absorbed academic (on leave from a team working with the Large Hadron Collider, I'd been told).

But what really unsettled me was the look upon his face. The mask of painful remorse had been replaced by a wild, penetrating stare, as if he looked at you and through you simultaneously.

"Sorry I haven't called, Džemo," he said.

"It's only been six months." I twirled my whiskey glass between my fingers. "But it's understandable."

"I'm glad you're so... forgiving," he replied.

The hair stood up on my arms. I've always been a bit suspicious, maybe even slightly paranoid. I mean, when you've been sleeping with your friend's wife it's kind of, well, obvious. Isn't it? Something changes in the atmosphere of a room when you enter it, and she turns to stare at you. There's something in the way her eyes play across the features of your face, her body shifting from one foot to the other, as though she were expecting you to rush into her arms.

"To forgive is divine," I said, forcing a smile.

"So they say." He said no more for several minutes; then: "There's a reason I finally called you."

Here it comes, I thought. My chest tightened. I hated being confronted by truth. Once exposed, I'd have to acknowledge its existence. It was much easier to put it to the side, ignore it, and enjoy the fantasies I'd created for myself. Growing up in Sarajevo during the war such escapism was a mode of survival. Over the years I'd turned my made-up worlds into stories, lies spun out across hundreds of pages. I created characters I wished I could've been, and they lived lives I wished were mine.

Falling in love. With Rachel.

What finally destroyed her, drove her to suicide, was the fact she was stuck between a reality she found untenable, and a fantasy that could never be real.

I had no doubt she loved Leo; I heard it in the way she spoke of him. But it was a love burned to cinders by neglect. A thin, bookish man, Leo was habitually reserved, uninspired; useless at parties. And it was this remoteness, coupled with his dull appearance and social inadequacies, that eventually drove Rachel into my arms.

"Did you know your peripheral vision is very sensitive to motion?" he said, turning and walking slowly back into the room.

My anticipation of a verbal lashing was quickly replaced by confusion. "Is that so?"

"It is," he said. "We've all seen things out of the corners of our eyes—objects moving swiftly, vague images hurrying by as we turn a corner, things that register as unfamiliar and startle us but, when we turn, there's nothing there."

"Okay, Leo."

"These things we see are mostly smudged, blurred, but occasionally they take form, if only for the briefest of seconds. It's as though our world seemed to wink, and in doing so exposed to us something previously unseen."

"I once thought I saw a furry creature jump out at me. But, of course, I was drunk at the time."

He frowned at my lame attempt at humour.

"Come on, Leo. Where are you going with this, anyway? This seems a bit metaphysical for a scientific guy like you."

"What is metaphysics," he said, "but an attempt to understand the fundamental perceptions by which others see the world? Existence, space, time, causality are all concepts that go well beyond mere ontology, which simply seeks to categorise things within some artificially conceived hierarchy—nonsense groupings by which we can make sense of things we can never fully explain."

"Come off it, Leo! Have you suddenly taken to reading The Fortean Times or something?"

"In many ways, Džemo, metaphysics may be a better word to use than science." He hurried back to the balcony to face the city, the stars, like a man possessed. "The Greek word *metá* simply means 'beyond'. Metaphysics. Well, what is *beyond* physics? Do you know?"

"No, I don't."

"Well, I do," he said.

Not only did he appear like a man on the edge, but he was beginning to talk like one, too. I glanced about, at the clutter of books and periodicals scattered across the room. Mirrors on opposite walls duplicated the chaos, spreading it outward until the vision became insubstantial.

And in the middle of all this, on a small table by the sofa, stood a single picture of Rachel.

"Leo." I suddenly felt braver than I probably looked. "You can't shut yourself away from the world like this. It's been six months. I know it's hard but you need to find a way to move on."

"I have moved on," he said. "That's why I called you here. To let you know."

I was stunned. "That's great, Leo."

He shook his head and kept his back to me, his face to the city and the sky. "No, Džemo. My perceptions have moved on; those are the first things one notices."

"You've lost me. Actually, you lost me a while ago."

"I've *seen* her," he said. "Several times. Out of the corner of my eye. Passing in the streets. Going by in a taxi. It's Rachel, Džemo, and she's out there."

I went cold. *He's delirious*, I thought. *Or losing his mind.*

"You remember, Džemo, the controversy when they began testing the Large Hadron Collider at higher outputs for the first time? Everyone thought it would create a black hole that would swallow the earth." He laughed.

"What the hell are you talking about?"

"The Collider," he said, "not only proved superstring theory but takes it in a whole new direction. Don't you see? It's created weak points in our universe, points where we can see into *another* reality, another *universe*. Physical movement across the planes *must* be possible. Somehow—"

"Leo, you need help. A counsellor, perhaps..."

He turned on me. "You of all people should appreciate possibilities, speculations. Now imagine the Collider has not only fulfilled its potential, but gone beyond anyone's wildest expectations. Do you understand?"

I stared into my empty glass.

"An electron can occupy numerous states simultaneously," he said. "Quantum mechanics allows this, and successful experiments in demonstrating superpositions in larger objects are old hat." He paused, seemed desperate for words. "A beryllium ion, for instance. By laser-cooling it to zero-point energy, a series of laser pulses set it in different states, each spatially separate and coherent. *Two possible states for one object had been determined!*"

"Leo..."

"It's Schrödinger's cat. It's both alive *and* dead. I observe only one possible outcome, because when I detect the object I am entangled with it. That is, because I have seen one version of the cat I now have a relationship with it, of a sort. Quantum decoherence prevents me from experiencing another possibility, another universe." He stepped toward me. "The Collider solved this problem, in a way. We can see other possibilities, but only peripherally, like a geometrical tangent. It touches a curve and for a brief moment, they travel in the same direction—"

"I think I'd better leave."

"There are worlds out there," he said, "side-by-side with ours. Worlds where you and I and Rachel never met. Worlds where Rachel never died. Do you know what this means? For me? And you?"

I noticed my hands were shaking as I put the glass down. Tears blurred my vision. For the first time in my life, truth somehow managed to win out over lies. "I loved her, too," I said.

"I know," he replied, his tone surprisingly gentle. "It's a second chance. For both of us."

I wouldn't listen anymore. Fantasies were my job. But the one reality, the one hard concrete fact I could never bury underneath all my words was the fact that Rachel was gone.

His Rachel. My Rachel. And no amount of grief-fuelled, half-cocked, drunken school-boy speculation was going to bring her back.

And I shared my portion of the blame for that.

"Goodbye, Leo." I moved for the door.

"I don't blame you," he called after me. "Just wanted you to know that."

I left.

✦

I screwed up my courage and returned to his flat a few days later, but he didn't answer the buzzer. When the police entered they found no trace of him. They never found his body. Anywhere.

Some nights, when the sky was particularly clear, and the moon had risen, full and bold, I imagined I've seen him out of the corner of my eye, walking around the bend of a busy street, or cycling past me, Rachel beside him, laughing.

And I hoped, for his sake, that he was right; that he'd somehow managed to find that second chance he so desperately wanted.

But that was one fantasy I couldn't allow into my life. Because in my selfishness I'd finally done the unthinkable: I'd destroyed the lives of the two people I loved most. It would be ridiculous to think I deserved another chance, and foolishness to believe there was another world with another Rachel. And that she would be waiting for someone like me.

Heart full of sorrow I posed my ruminations to the stars, to the moon hanging low in the crisp autumn sky.

And I swear that great silver orb seemed to wink in response.

Carmelo Rafala spent far too much time studying fiction, which he discovered can kill one's appreciation for the form. So he stopped doing that and thought it might be fun to write instead. His stories have appeared in Jupiter, Atomjack, Estronomicon, Neon Literary Journal, as well as the anthology The West Pier Gazette and Other Stories and poetry in Scifaikuest. He currently serves as Senior Editor for Immersion Press. Carmelo lives on the south coast of England with his wife and daughter.

CONQUISTADORS

Iain Cairns

CARMEN VASQUEZ ROLLED the silver coin between her thumb and forefinger, and set it spinning in the stale air. One of the first minted in Mexico City, the 1535 Spanish dollar had been stamped from a sheet of plundered silver, in a fortress built by Hernán Cortés from the fresh rubble of Tenochtitlán. *Stones mortared with Aztec blood*—although, of course, the Aztecs themselves had spilled a drop or two of blood in their day.

She treasured the *real de a ocho* as one of her most precious possessions—and not just because it had cost her father almost a million US dollars at auction. Luis Vasquez had given her the coin on her twenty-fourth birthday, the day after she was awarded her doctorate in planetary geology. *Just imagine, my girl—perhaps the conquistador himself once held this coin in his hand.* A week later, Luis had died in a car crash in Hidalgo, together with her older brother Vicente, leaving her an even greater but unsought gift: control and majority ownership of Mexico's largest mining and minerals company.

She let the coin hang there for a while, turning and glinting in the rainbow light of the control panels, then snatched it out of the air. It was time. "Wei, initiate co-orbital injection burn."

"Roger that," said Wei Shiu-Yuen. "Main engine start in five seconds... Ignition."

Thirty metres back through the stack, *Pinta*'s rocket engine blazed silently into life. The crew module trembled gently around them. An invisible hand pressed Vasquez back in her seat—the first time she'd felt anything like a sensation of gravity for over three weeks.

In the pilot's seat, Wei used the acceleration to guide M&M's into his mouth. The cocky son of a bitch held engineering and astrophysics doctorates from Nanjing and MIT, had flown three

Moon missions for CNSA, and then freelanced the last few years for a variety of international space start-ups. He seemed determined to show Vasquez that her little jaunt to a NEO was no big deal. Wei's ego might have tempted her to kick him off the project, if he hadn't been so damn good at his job.

Vasquez had found that she too was good at her new job—although she'd never planned to join the family business, let alone run it. She reluctantly put aside her scientific career and her dream of going into space. She worked hard to build up Vasquez Industries over the decade that followed, and discovered to her surprise that she relished the challenges of turning VI from a solid but unremarkable domestic operation into an innovative global player.

Then, three years ago, she'd conceived the project that allowed her dream to live again—and raised her company's sights to a new frontier.

✦

"Mining an asteroid," Vasquez told the invited press in the Mexico City Hilton conference hall, "is an idea as old and seemingly far-fetched as the pulp science fiction of the 1950s. But today we at VI are in a unique position to make the recovery of valuable metals and minerals from asteroids a viable economic reality. We have the vision and knowledge to see the huge potential, plus the expertise and assets required to seize it."

She clicked to the next presentation slide, now having to raise her voice above the growing buzz of the audience. "Why should we even consider this extraordinary venture, requiring an investment of many billions, when our existing terrestrial business is already so successful? Because it represents an utterly unprecedented opportunity. A single 200-million-tonne asteroid of the right kind might contain one trillion US dollars worth of recoverable metals and minerals." That shut the audience up for a moment. "One *trillion* dollars. Iron, nickel and magnesium. Rare earth metals that are depleting fast down here. Cobalt, molybdenum, platinum, gold, silver..."

She slipped the Spanish dollar from her pocket and held it aloft for the cameras. "The silver that this first Mexican coin was made from, the precious metals that have driven five hundred years of prosperity for our nation... Where did they come from? Research now suggests that they were sown into our planet's crust in relatively recent epochs by meteorites—asteroids that fell to Earth. For instance, the silver in this coin may have come to Mexico via the great Chicxulub meteorite impact in Yucatan."

She clicked through to a graphic of asteroid orbits. "However, such deposits are spread quite thinly down here on Earth, and most asteroids are out beyond Mars in the main belt. But what if we could reach out to capture a suitable near-Earth object as it passes close to our planet? And guide this NEO into orbit around the Earth for practical exploitation? Then we will truly have hit *la veta madre*—the mother lode."

✦

Francine Tshilolo made her way quickly up the fire escape at the end of the Hilton's conference wing. Pyotr and the other GreenSpacers would be keeping most of the VI security people busy out front with a noisy, high-visibility protest. She followed a quiet corridor along to the conference hall. One guy in a blue VI blazer was still manning the door.

Confidence, Francine. Her grey business suit was too warm and her heels felt awkward, but hopefully she looked convincing as a bored trade journalist. She just hoped the security guy didn't check her bag. She strode forward with her fake *Minerals World* press pass in hand, waiting to be challenged, but the guy just waved her through, even held the door open for her.

Tshilolo slipped into the hall and pushed her way through the crowd towards the front row. Carmen Vasquez was on the podium, apparently coming to the climax of her presentation. The VI woman was really getting worked up now. Tshilolo could practically see the dollar signs in Vasquez's eyes as she gestured to the asteroid imagery on the big screen. Why did people like Vasquez have to see every pristine wilderness—whether on Earth or in space—as their personal piñata to be smashed open and emptied out?

Now the tall Mexican woman was waving some old conquistador coin to make a point. Blood silver! Tshilolo wondered if Vasquez had any sense of shame at all. Maybe next she would hold up a bucket of Congolese conflict minerals to make her argument even more tasteless.

At last Vasquez finished her speech and, after the applause subsided, called for questions. Tshilolo stood and called out. "Yes, I have a question, Dr Vasquez." The rest of the audience craned their necks to look at the her. "My question is: what gives you and Vasquez Industries the right to plunder the wealth of a new world, just as if you were conquistadors?"

✦

Vasquez ran her thumb over the coin's embossed Pillars of Hercules, and the motto PLVS VLTRA. *More beyond.* She slipped it back into a pocket of her cargo pants, and turned her attention to the astronavigation screens. A blue arrow marked PINTA slowly converged with a green circle labelled "*(271356) 2025 MT37 KEROUAC*". The inset view from a forward camera showed a potato-shaped grey rock, growing slowly against a black star-strewn background.

For the last twenty-four days, *Pinta* had coasted in an elliptical Hohmann transfer orbit, around and away from Earth. Now they were thrusting the spacecraft back into a new heliocentric orbit, matched precisely with their target, the asteroid MT37 Kerouac.

Wei finished his M&Ms. "Preparing to terminate burn. Engine cut-off."

As the vibration and acceleration ceased, Vasquez floated forward slightly against her harness. Her insides felt as if she'd just gone over the Piedra Volada Falls in a barrel. "Status and systems check," she ordered.

The pilot scratched at his thin beard. "Guidance and attitude control nominal. *Pinta* is approximately five kilometres from target on a matched trajectory. Looking good for final approach and rendezvous. The RPP is armed and ready."

The Regolith Penetrating Projectile, a powerful rock-piercing harpoon and cable winch, had originally been developed by NASA as a surface sampling tool for its own NEO missions. Kerouac's minimal gravity meant that a spacecraft could not 'land' on the asteroid as such. Instead, *Pinta* would use its RPP to pull itself onto Kerouac's surface.

"Life support, power, temperature, pressure, comms, also all nominal. How's our payload?"

Wei scanned his panels. "The EVMR is showing green on systems checks." He looked Vasquez in the eye. "And the nuke—I mean, the *asteroid orbit modifier*—is safe and secure."

"AOM is safe," acknowledged Vasquez.

She hit the press-to-talk button and a high-pitched Quindar tone sounded. "Cozumel Control, this is *Pinta*," she said. "NCI completed. We are now in final approach to asteroid MT37 Kerouac, five kilometres out."

There was a seven-second silence as the radio signal carrying Vasquez's voice flew across the void, back past the Moon, to a tracking and relay in French Guiana, and on to Mission Control at the Cozumel spaceport. Then another seven seconds before she heard an answering tone.

"*Pinta*, this is Cozumel," said Juan Montoya, the White Team CAPCOM. Vasquez could hear whoops and whistles from the flight control team in the background. "Roger that. Congratulations on a successful journey, Dr Vasquez. You are looking good for final NEO rendezvous."

✦

Vasquez calmly sized up the woman in the grey suit. She was short, broad-framed, and seemed somehow familiar. The conference hall had by now gone very quiet.

"Sorry, I didn't catch your name or your news organisation," Vasquez said in a neutral tone.

"I'm not a journalist, and I wasn't invited to your little rally. My name is Francine Tshilolo. I represent the astro-environmental organisation GreenSpace—defending the unspoilt beauty of space from the clutches of corporate conquistadors like you."

Vasquez cursed herself for choosing to hold the event in a public building, rather than at VI's headquarters. Nevertheless, she also made a mental note to reprimand her security chief for letting an eco-warrior into the front row of her press conference.

"Tshilolo... I remember now. You commanded those first Pan-African Space Agency orbital missions a few years back. Weren't you thrown off the programme for criticising PASA in the press?"

"I joined the space programme in the name of science and exploration. PASA was becoming a glorified taxi service for corporations like yours to launch their latest remote sensing satellites—so they could locate even more natural resources to rip out of the ground. Now you've almost bled our planet dry, you're moving on to the asteroids. Soon we'll all be looking up at night to watch you strip-mining the face of the Moon." The Congolese woman took a step closer to Vasquez's podium. "That's why I formed GreenSpace—to fight back against the threat posed by the commercial exploitation of space."

Where the hell were her security people? Tshilolo was hijacking Vasquez's big moment. She forced herself to smile coolly. "I think you'll find our detailed environmental report on the project answers any concerns you might have. At VI we always fulfil our corporate social responsibilities while meeting the needs of our customers around the world." She moved her gaze across the audience. "Imagine... Once the processed metals and minerals from asteroid Kerouac start flowing down to Earth, everyone will be able to benefit from a little piece of outer space. They'll find it in their phones, their computers, their cars, their air conditioners—everywhere. And I believe they'll be thanking Vasquez Industries for having the vision to make it happen."

But the damn Tshilolo woman wouldn't give up. She waved a sheaf of papers taken from her shoulder bag. "Under the 1967 Outer Space Treaty, no nation state can claim ownership of asteroids or other celestial bodies, or exploit their natural resources. They're the common heritage of humanity. But the commercial space race has left international law powerless to protect that heritage. Corporations like yours are legally free to despoil and pillage the Solar System for their own profit." She levelled the documents at Vasquez. "You claim to be a humble scientist, seeking to enrich everyone. But in truth, you're nothing but a conquistador, grasping for precious metals to fill your own pockets, and not giving a damn who gets hurt."

Vasquez was starting to lose her patience with this zealot. "You're being over-dramatic, Ms Tshilolo. We're not conquistadors, and nobody will get hurt. There are no indigenous peoples on this airless rock to be exploited or harmed—unless you think we'll find little green men up there?"

"Trust me, Dr Vasquez, where there are valuable resources to be exploited, there's always blood spilled. My parents learned that lesson the hard way, digging and dying in the mines of Kivu." Tshilolo crossed her arms and hardened her expression. "You say you want to manoeuvre this asteroid into orbit around Earth so its wealth can be plundered more easily. Why don't you tell us all exactly how you plan to achieve that?"

Vasquez knew where the activist was going with this—towards a topic she hadn't wanted to discuss at this stage of the project. She replied carefully: "I'm showing my deep personal commitment to the project by joining our first mission to Kerouac. We plan to use a carefully calculated transfer of momentum to nudge Kerouac from its current heliocentric orbit—"

"Nudge it?" Tshilolo laughed. "Vasquez Industries has acquired a ten-megaton ex-Soviet thermonuclear warhead, a bomb they plan to detonate on the surface of the asteroid. That's one hell of a nudge. Again, this will be in clear violation of the 1967 treaty, which also forbids the use of nuclear weapons in space. However, the international authorities seem happy to overlook VI's illegal acquisition and detonation of a nuclear device, as long as they avoid calling it a weapon—and since it might result in the injection of a trillion dollars into the world economy."

"The whole operation is totally legal, I assure you," Vasquez insisted. At last, she saw her security chief and a group of blue-blazered officers making their way to the front of the hall.

Tshilolo spoke faster and louder, realising her time was short. "And what about the sheer madness of actively diverting a 200-million-tonne rock towards Earth, when for decades scientists have warned of the need to defend ourselves against asteroids? You talk about the Chicxulub impact as a possible source of precious metals. Isn't it more infamous for causing the Cretaceous–Tertiary extinction event that killed the dinosaurs and nearly wiped out all life on Earth? Then there's the 1908 Tunguska explosion, a thousand times more powerful than the

Hiroshima atom bomb—caused by the airburst of a meteorite just 50 metres across. An asteroid like Kerouac could easily destroy a city the size of New York. Vasquez Industries say their complex orbital calculations are accurate, but we all know how good corporations are at fudging numbers."

The noise of the audience increased as the security team converged on Tshilolo. Things escalated very quickly from there. As the first security officer laid a hand on her arm, she broke away from him, reached into her bag and uncapped a vial. With a flick of her wrist she flung the contents at Vasquez, who flinched involuntarily as red liquid splashed across her white silk blouse.

Vasquez stood paralysed for a moment in silent shock, as seemingly did everyone in the room. A trickle rolled down her cheek. She put a hand to her face, and the fingertips came away bright red. "The blood will be on your hands," Tshilolo was shouting. "No conquistadors in space!"

Then the hall erupted into chaos.

✦

Wei unbuckled his harness. "I didn't come twenty million klicks to look at it on a damn screen." He pushed out of his seat and pulled himself over to the right forward window. "Hey, look at that thing. It's like the Moon took a dump."

Vasquez joined him at the tiny triangular window and caught her breath. Before her, floated the pitted lump of rock she'd seen in countless telescope images, probe radar scans and virtual simulations over the last three years. This, however, was the real thing. It wasn't a conventionally *beautiful* thing, she had to admit—but here the real beauty lay within.

Kerouac was five hundred metres across, bigger than an aircraft carrier. But seen from this distance, through fist-thick aluminosilicate glass, it looked like something in a display case at the Museo de Geología. "CAPCOM, if I could just get this window open, I think I could reach out and touch it from here."

"*Pinta*, I have a whole bunch of people here wishing they were there with you right now."

"They'll get their chance," promised Vasquez. "Once we bring Kerouac into Earth orbit, we'll need plenty of crews for the ongoing drilling and processing operations. Any volunteers?"

But when the reply transmission finally came, Montoya's voice held a new seriousness and uncertainty. "*Pinta*, we may have... an issue. We've just received a report from the observatory at Mauna Kea. They spotted some kind of anomalous activity near Kerouac shortly before you arrived. The signature's like an engine burn... but that's impossible. We think maybe it's a flare-off of volatiles from the NEO or..."

"It's not volatiles," Wei cut in, his palms and forehead pressed to the window pane. "And they're damn right we have a problem, chief. Look out there."

✦

Pinta slowly approached the pitted surface of Kerouac. A wide, flat-bottomed crater lay directly ahead of them, just a thousand metres away. But it wasn't the grandness of the vista that left Vasquez speechless.

In the centre of the crater sat another spacecraft.

Somehow it had been lashed to the floor of the crater with a tangle of cables, netting and pitons. Wei identified it as an old Chinese Shenzhou, which appeared to have been heavily modified for its journey to the asteroid. The service module sprouted extra propellant and water tanks, additional Soyuz solar arrays, a large radio antenna, and what looked like a pair of Shuttle OMS engines.

"It's like a gang-bang at the aerospace museum," said Wei.

Vasquez frowned. "Another mission out here ... It's got to be one of the big conglomerates trying to muscle in on our claim," she said at last. "Minera Globos or Rio Nero Tianjin."

"In a piece of junk like that? Doesn't look like a corporate mission to me."

On the magnified camera view, Vasquez saw an EVA-suited astronaut emerge from the Shenzhou's hatch on the end of a tether, carrying some kind of package. The figure bobbed across the crater floor, using what looked like standard rock-climbing ropes and equipment. A wise move, when the smallest push away from the surface could send an untethered astronaut spinning off into open space.

Vasquez watched as the astronaut fastened the package to the asteroid's surface with a spike and shook out its contents. "What the hell are they doing?" she breathed. A great mass of flimsy green plastic unfolded itself on a flexible frame across the crater to form a banner thirty metres across. Even from a kilometre away, Vasquez could read its large clear message:

CONQUISTADORS GO HOME

Suddenly Vasquez knew who was in that EVA suit. She couldn't quite believe it, but she knew it.

She switched on the UHF radio and began stepping through standard transmission frequencies. "Unidentified astronaut on surface of asteroid Kerouac. This is Vasquez Industries spacecraft 1, *Pinta*. Calling unidentified astronaut, acknowledge."

The suited figure paused in its activity and angled its helmet visor toward them. It tapped its chest panel, and they heard a burst of static.

"Dr Vasquez, I presume? This is Francine Tshilolo. I'm afraid Kerouac is not open to prospectors today."

✦

GreenSpace had acquired some very wealthy anonymous supporters since Tshilolo's infamous disruption of the VI press conference. Over the last year, they had discretely bankrolled and facilitated the purchase of a range of ageing space hardware, which had been transported to a remote private island in Indonesia. Three days before *Pinta* had departed, a series of impromptu orbital launches had been made from that same island, listed as carrying 'science experiments' for a little-known shell corporation.

Tshilolo's covert mission to Kerouac had begun.

Despite the shortcomings of her mongrel spacecraft, Tshilolo had survived the long solo journey from Earth to Kerouac, and even managed to arrive a few hours before *Pinta*. Now she looked up to see Vasquez's spacecraft hanging overhead, its wide solar arrays giving it the look of a pale vulture on the wing.

Tshilolo felt elated to be back in space and making an EVA

again. Now she was preparing for GreenSpace's first live broadcast from space to Earth's news networks. Patiently she set up her remote-controlled video camera at a suitable vantage point to take in the unfurled banner, the ramshackle *GreenSpace Protector*, and the blue disc of the Earth sinking over the unsettlingly near horizon.

In her earpiece, Vasquez's voice rang out. "Tshilolo! I swore that if I ever saw you again, I'd—"

Tshilolo hit her radio switch. "Careful, Dr Vasquez. You may be about to transmit something you'll regret. Why not wait a while and save it for the global news networks when I go live. I'm sure they'll want to know your feelings about the failure of your billion-dollar exploitation project."

When it returned, Vasquez's voice quivered with restrained loathing. "Ms Tshilolo... While I admire your determination and achievement in getting here, I demand that you return to your craft and leave immediately. The International Astronomical Union's Minor Planet Center has declared Kerouac a no-fly zone during Vasquez Industries' project here." The voice hardened with implicit threat. "I cannot guarantee your safety if you remain."

Tshilolo continued with her preparations. "Thank you for your concern, Dr Vasquez, but I'm going nowhere any time soon. I told you that GreenSpace would go to any lengths to defend this asteroid. Perhaps now you see that I meant it."

✦

Vasquez ended the transmission in a suppressed rage. Tshilolo's presence on Kerouac was a double blow to her plans. The GreenSpace spacecraft effectively blocked the one area of Kerouac's surface flat enough to set *Pinta* down. And even if they could touch down, so long as Tshilolo remained on the asteroid they would never be able to complete their time-critical mission goal—that of placing, setting and detonating the nuclear device to boost Kerouac into its new Earth-centric orbit.

Wei checked his Speedmaster. "If we don't get down to the surface, set the nuke, and get the hell out of here in the next few hours, we'll miss our window. Then this whole project will have been one expensive waste of time. Any longer than that and we may not get home at all."

"I'm aware of that," Vasquez snapped.

"She's playing chicken with us," said Wei. "Unless this is some kind of suicide mission, she'll presumably want to leave Kerouac before it's too late for her to get back to Earth. But she won't leave until we do."

"She's playing chess with us, too—and that junk spacecraft of hers is the queen that controls the board. But I won't let her win. She won't humiliate me again." Vasquez stared at the screen for a while, thinking hard. "One thing I don't understand. Why hasn't she started her big broadcast yet? She must be desperate to show off GreenSpace's latest out-of-this-world stunt to everyone back on Earth."

Wei moved to the window. "I know why she's waiting. She doesn't want to be cut off in mid-flow. Look." He pointed to where the last blue sliver of Earth was disappearing behind the edge of Kerouac.

"Earthset." Vasquez understood now. "That means she'll lose all communications with home for the next... 45 minutes." She slapped the console. "But this is our chance! We can act now, while she's deprived of the oxygen of attention."

"What are you suggesting?" asked Wei. "You want us to just drop the nuke on her head and run?"

Vasquez gave the question a moment's real consideration. "No, attractive as that option sounds, I think I have a better plan. Let's take that queen off the board."

✦

Vasquez knew that she was embarking on a dangerous path—but desperate circumstances called for desperate measures. On her screen, a crosshair was superimposed over the image of the crater. Readouts from astronav, radar and laser rangefinder surrounded the display.

"We are go for RPP rendezvous procedure," said Wei. "For the record, I think this is an extremely bad idea."

"Opinion noted."

"How do you know there's no-one else aboard? And aren't you at least going to warn her?"

"No, she'd probably only go and rope herself to it if she knew what was coming. And I'm sure she's alone. She'll come to no harm, trust me. We'll just wait until she moves safely out of harm's way... Just a little more... That's perfect." Vasquez carefully lined up the crosshairs over the Shenzhou, and pulled the trigger on her joystick. She felt a jolt through her seat as, above and behind them, the launcher mounted on *Pinta*'s service module triggered. The harpoon shot towards Kerouac, trailing a fat steel cable behind it.

The harpoon's tip was a mix of depleted uranium and tungsten alloy, designed to penetrate a metre thickness of asteroid regolith. It punched through the Shenzhou and into the surface below like a chisel through a soda can. The spacecraft instantly depressurised, and burst apart in a cloud of debris.

✦

Tshilolo literally didn't know what hit her.

She felt the surface buck beneath her boots as the seismic shockwave propagated through the regolith. A hail of debris pattered against her spacesuit and dinged off her helmet. She was flipped and shaken like a child's rag doll, and left floating above the surface, at the end of her tether. She blacked out for a moment.

When she opened her eyes again, she saw that her spacecraft—her only way to get home—was gone. Only a drifting cloud of debris remained, with a great harpoon thrust through its heart. Her gaze followed the trailing cable up towards *Pinta*. She hit the transmit button of her suit radio.

"Vasquez, I knew you were insane. Now you've proved it. By destroying my spacecraft, you've killed me."

The radio crackled, then Vasquez's reply came. "Being over-dramatic again, Tshilolo? Looks from here like there's barely a mark on you. Your craft, on the other hand, may admittedly be past the patching-up stage. But don't worry, we'd be delighted to give you a ride home—as soon as our work on Kerouac is done. Just sit tight and be patient for a while. We'll be down to collect you very shortly."

✦

"Touchdown site cleared," said Vasquez. "Harpoon looks secure. Activate winch."

"Roger." The steel umbilical now connecting *Pinta* and Kerouac tightened, stirring the debris cloud of the wrecked Shenzhou. Vasquez felt the spacecraft jerk slightly, then a mild acceleration as they were reeled in towards the asteroid. The readout from the laser rangefinder hit 800 metres... 600... 400... 200...

"RCS correcting our orientation OK. Deploying landing gear," said Wei. He triggered *Pinta*'s four great articulated legs to uncurl from their housings and reach out towards the onrushing surface.

"Ten metres."

"Brace," ordered Vasquez. "Contact light."

She was jerked forward in her harness as the forward thrusters fired and the leg pneumatics sucked up the shock of the impact. *Pinta* landed, legs straddling the shattered remains of the Shenzhou. From each landing pad, smart grippers raked out, a hundred spindly steel hooks digging like claws into cracks and niches in the rocky surface of Kerouac.

"RCS stop. Shutdown." Vasquez's heart thundered and she fought for breath. "Let's suit up and depressurise the crew module, ready for EVA. We have a cargo to unload, and a passenger to come aboard."

✦

"Opening forward hatch," announced Vasquez. She deactivated the safety measures and gripped the handle. Through her EVA suit glove, she felt the thick steel bolts retract. She wedged her boot into a foothold to provide leverage in the microgravity, and rotated the handle through three full turns. With Wei's help, she pulled the hatch inwards and slid it sideways. Any remaining air in the depressurised crew module whisked away into the endless vacuum.

Vasquez gripped the hatch frame and looked out. The wreckage of the Shenzhou and the grey surface of Kerouac were a few metres in front of her (or above her, or below her, depending on how she thought about it). With a sequence of movements practiced in submersion tanks back on Earth, she pushed herself out through the hatch. She opened an external equipment locker and secured a Mobile Manoeuvring Unit onto her back.

Now Vasquez physically and mentally orientated herself so that the asteroid was 'down'. She fired a burst from the MMU thrusters, and drifted feet-first towards the surface.

Looking up, the four articulated legs of Pinta's landing gear curved around her, like flying buttresses on some futurist cathedral. Above her, Wei's spacesuited figure was framed in the hatchway of Pinta's crew module. Above that, towered the rest of the Pinta stack: the still-pressurised habitation module, and the service module that housed the payload bays. To either side stretched the wing-like solar PV arrays. And the great upturned bell of the main engine as a crown.

Vasquez gave herself another quick burst of thrust from her MMU to move clear of the Shenzhou debris. Her boots hit the regolith, scattering a cloud of dust and gravel. She rebounded and began to rise off the surface again, but then her smart grippers activated. A personal version of the system on the Pinta's landing pads, the boots deployed a fan of fine hooks in the rough shape of a snow-shoe, which bit into the rock and held her fast in the microgravity.

For a few seconds, Vasquez was alone on the surface of another world, with only the hisses and hums of her spacesuit's life support for company. She stood in a great stark shadow cast by Pinta, encircled by the low lip of the crater, and beyond that by Kerouac's too-near horizon. And over it all, hung the endless star-filled blackness.

A new world. A moment like this had been her dream since childhood. She was suddenly reminded of the cover of an old book she'd read when she was a young girl. A little prince standing alone on a tiny planet.

But his small world had sprouted blood-red roses, she seemed to remember.

✦

Tshilolo had watched dazedly as Vasquez's gleaming white spacecraft descended from the blackness, coming to rest triumphantly amid the wreckage of her own craft. She supposed it must be the tallest feature to appear on Kerouac's skyline in its several-billion-year history. From this viewpoint, *Pinta* looked like a micrograph of some bloodsucking parasite—a cybernetic tick or mosquito, with its mouthparts clamped to the skin of its host.

Tshilolo watched Vasquez glide across the crater towards her. "Ms Tshilolo," came Vasquez's voice over the radio, "a pleasure to see you again. How are you feeling?" Tshilolo gazed into the golden mirror of Vasquez's helmet visor, but saw only her own spacesuited form reflected back.

"I feel half dead," Tshilolo groaned. "GreenSpace will have Vasquez Industries torn apart in the International Criminal Court for this when we get back to—"

Behind Vasquez, a giant metallic spider crab was emerging from *Pinta*'s open payload bay. Tshilolo, dazzled by the glare of the sun beyond, wondered if she was hallucinating.

"Don't worry," said Vasquez. "That's just our extra-vehicular manipulator robot. My pilot Mr Wei will use it to deploy the asteroid orbital modifier. Nuclear bombs *are* rather unwieldy, even in microgravity." She indicated the great white cylinder that the EVMR was now lowering into position at the centre of the crater.

"Just because you've won this small battle, don't think that GreenSpace will stop fighting you," said Tshilolo. "But in the circumstances, I guess I have to accept your offer of a ride home. Could you maybe help me to your craft? You seem to have knocked the wind out of me."

"Of course," said Vasquez, taking her arm.

Tshilolo sighed and closed her eyes against the light.

✦

"Nuke armed and countdown initiated," said Wei, joining them.

"Let's split before it gets toasty around here."

Wei and Vasquez helped Tshilolo back to *Pinta*'s hatch, while the EVMR climbed up to its nest in the payload bay. The activist seemed to be in mild shock following her experience, and needed to be manhandled through the hatch and into the crew module.

"No time to repressurise until we're safely underway, so keep your suits on for now," Vasquez ordered. With no third seat in the crew module, they leaned Tshilolo against the rear bulkhead and secured her for launch as quickly as they could. Once the hatch was sealed, Vasquez took her seat next to the pilot and strapped in.

"Initiating launch sequence," said Wei. "Let's get on the road." He hit a series of controls, releasing the mooring umbilical, retracting the smart grippers from the asteroid surface, and then launching *Pinta* into open space on a plume of Aerozine 50 and dinitrogen tetroxide.

As they moved clear of the asteroid, radio contact with Earth resumed. Vasquez hit the PTT. "Cozumel, this is *Pinta*. We have completed cast-off and ascent from the surface, and are preparing to initiate trans-Earth injection in five minutes. Detonation of the AOM device will occur in ten minutes."

"Roger that, *Pinta*," said a surprised-sounding CAPCOM. "Seems like you've been busy while you were off-air. What about our earlier problem?"

Vasquez turned to look at their passenger. "We came to an amicable understanding. Due to a malfunction of her own spacecraft, Ms Tshilolo is returning to Earth as our passenger. She is aboard and seems quite comfortable. *Pinta* out."

As Wei laid in the TEI settings, Vasquez hit transmit on her suit radio and turned to Tshilolo. "I hope you'll forgive my extreme actions today. It'll all be for the best, you'll see. Whatever the differences between us, we both have humanity's interests at heart. Maybe one day you'll understand that."

Tshilolo was silent, still and impassive in her restraints, her visor a mirrored mask. The woman really was insufferable.

"Well, say *something*," Vasquez snapped. "You think you're so morally superior. The truth is, you really can't bear to admit that I might be in the right here and you might be the one who's got it all wrong."

Wei turned from the controls, frowning. He craned his body around in his seat to look at Tshilolo. Then he leaned across, gripped her suit's right arm and lifted it aside. At the hip of the suit, Vasquez saw a ragged hole, about the size and shape of a large coin. A little blood had soaked into the torn fabric layers. Wei slid up the mirrored outer visor of Tshilolo's helmet. "Shit," he hissed. Inside the helmet her head lolled to one side, eyes staring sightlessly forward through the glass.

"No," said Vasquez. "She can't..."

"Pressure loss," muttered Wei. With trembling gloved fingertips, he gently teased a small twisted object from the blood-soaked rupture in Tshilolo's suit. He held it up so Vasquez could see the silvery metal shard glinting. "Must have punctured it when you harpooned her damn spacecraft into a million razor-sharp fragments..."

"What?" Vasquez said. "How can she be dead? She was talking to me a few minutes ago. Why the hell didn't she tell me something was wrong?"

"A hole like that depressurises slowly. She probably didn't even realise there was a problem until the hypoxia kicked in—and after that she'd be too out of it to care. She had maybe a half-hour maximum from when it happened. In fact, she was dead from the moment you pulled the trigger. Down there on the surface, you might as well have been talking to a ghost." Wei let out a sigh. "Look, don't blame yourself, Dr Vasquez. There's probably nothing anyone could have done for her. And if we don't want to end up dead too, we need to get out of the blast zone, now."

Wei slid the mirrored visor down over Tshilolo's face again, and turned back to his flight controls. "Initiating Trans Earth Injection—main engine ignition in ten seconds." He glanced over at Vasquez. "Will it be worth it, do you think? A human life for a trillion dollars?"

She opened her mouth to speak but no words came. Then there was a silent roar...

And the invisible hand pressed down on them all once more.

Iain Cairns

Iain Cairns has spent most of his life daydreaming about being a science fiction writer. Recently, he decided to actually become one for real. His short story 'Bringer of War' (a Wellsian alternative-history space opera featuring Gustav Holst) was published in Concept Sci-Fi, and was selected by author Sean Williams as the winner of their first short story competition. Iain attended Kingston University's sci-fi and fantasy writing course, taught by author Paul McAuley. He is a member of the Cola Factory speculative fiction writing group, WriteClub London and the BSFA. He works as a marketing and advertising copywriter, and lives in south London with his wife and two children.

GOING, BOLDLY

Helen Jackson

"'WELCOME TO THE Holodeck'," quotes Frankie.

Her best friend, Olivia, sniggers into her pint. Olivia's wearing an "Evil League of Evil" T-shirt and black jeans. Her hair's dyed black and worn long and tousled. Frankie has dressed up for her first day at work which, for her, meant a brand-new *XKCD* tee over an A-line skirt and emerald tights. The green matches her spiky crop.

"Seriously? Tell me she didn't really say that," says Olivia.

"She really did," says Frankie. "Honestly, it's geek heaven."

Frankie's new boss, Sumara Erskine, had taken her on a tour of Wandering Star Simulations that morning. They'd ended at the "Holodeck", the studio's testing facility, where they'd played a pre-alpha version of ExoPlanetfall.

The game's physics engine had been developed to simulate any combination of surface, atmospheric conditions and gravity. In theory, at least, ExoPlanetfall would allow future colonists to begin to get used to a planet as soon as they received probe data.

Commercially, though, the game was missing something. Marketing had brought forward the alien development programme, and Erskine had hired Frankie as part of the new character team.

"What's the studio like?" asks Olivia.

"Every other," says Frankie.

She'd felt at home immediately.

The different teams have customised their parts of the open-plan space. The level designers have surrounded themselves with a New York skyline built out of Coco Pops packets. A battery-powered Elmo played King Kong among the skyscrapers. 3D Modelling has made a huge *Millennium Falcon* out of drinks cans (mostly Irn-Bru, pinpointing the studio's location in Silicon Glen rather than Silicon Valley), and hung it from the ceiling. The animators' zone for filming reference video was filled with the brightly-coloured balls you get in children's play areas.

There was only one unusual element.

"Someone's painted huge letters, all along one wall," Frankie tells Olivia. "In Spock blue. It says, 'YES! WE WOULD GO'."

Olivia had also applied for a job at Wandering Star, but spoiled a great interview by answering "No" to a question she hadn't expected: "Would you volunteer for a one-way interstellar voyage?"

"And would you?" asks Olivia, "I mean, really?"

"Absolutely. To boldly go? I'd jump at the chance."

"It's not as if they'd pick you, though, is it? Too old, for a start."

Frankie feels Olivia is being unnecessarily snarky, but knows it can't be easy for her to have missed out on the job. Also, she has a point: Frankie's nearly forty. By the time a suitable spacecraft is ready—projected for the end of the century, at the earliest—she'll be long dead.

Nonetheless, the studio's idealistic board likes employees to show commitment to the project's long-term aims.

"Why didn't you lie in the interview?" Frankie asks. "They'd never have known."

"Dunno, maybe I should've. It didn't occur to me at the time. Anyway," Olivia says, raising her glass, "here's to you. Character TD: Alien Morphologies. Sláinte!"

"Sláinte!"

✦

Three weeks into the job, Frankie found herself in an anatomy lesson. A Character Technical Director creates the skeleton, muscle systems and controls for a character—rigging a puppet that can be handed over to an animator.

"Do you see how this is articulated?" the demonstrator said, pulling out a bat's right wing. The other had been partially dissected, so Frankie and her colleagues could see its internal structure.

The previous week the group had been in Chester, where

they spent every morning in the zoo's Fruit Bat Forest: watching, filming, and trying to understand the creatures' movements. Afternoons have been spent going over the reference video and making sketches.

The first alien on Marketing's wishlist is a human-sized bat.

"What about pterodactyls?" Frankie had asked in the briefing meeting. "Dinosaurs are cool. Bats are a bit freaky."

"Marketing is keen on the vampire thing. It plays well with teenage audiences," replied Sumara Erskine, to general groans. "I like the pterosaur idea for younger gamers, but. Let's have it as a gameplay option. Can you use the same rig?"

The more Frankie learns about bats, the more she suspects her casual question has doubled everyone's workload. She has a college friend who worked on Planet Dinosaur and they've been comparing notes. It seems there's something called the pteroid function to worry about. She's going down to London at the end of the month to talk to a Dr Leonardo Gomez, apparently the world expert in flying dinosaur locomotion.

✦

"I'm not kidding, he's gorgeous," Frankie says to Olivia after her trip.

"In an Indiana Jones sort of a way? Archaeologists and palaeontologists are pretty much the same thing, right?" says Olivia, with a faraway look that suggests she's visualising a young Harrison Ford striding through the dinosaurs gallery at the Natural History Museum.

"Not right. Similar mud. Different timescales. But, yes, Leo does Indy-rugged pretty well."

"Oooh, Leo! You're onto nickname terms."

"We went for lunch. He's single."

"Presentable *and* single? There must be something wrong. He's either gay or much too young."

"Neither. And..." Frankie pauses, pleased with herself.

"And?"

"And he's coming up to Dundee next week to give us a workshop."

✦

"Do we really need to make every creature parametric? And physically possible?" asks Tatsuo, a creature TD who used to specialise in dragons.

"Aye, as much as possible," says Sumara Erskine.

For each basic body type, parameters such as height, mass, proportions and number of limbs need to be adjustable. Long-term, it will allow colonists to approximate alien life-forms and get used to interaction in a safe, virtual environment. A linguistics team at MIT is doing early-stage research on incorporating a communications module.

For now, it's a killer game feature. When fully functional, users will be able to fight, or collaborate with, any alien they can imagine or remember from the movies.

Practically, it's a challenge.

"Not all parameters can be independent. There's mass and wing span," says Frankie, who has developed an in-depth knowledge of the principles of creature-powered flight.

"You can compensate for some mass increase with increased muscle strength," says Leo Gomez. It's his second visit to Wandering Star. "But, Frankie's right, weight and drag increase faster than muscle power output. Soaring is the only option for big creatures, which means low wing loading to maximise lift."

"Big wings," translates Frankie.

"Yup," says Leo, "so you'd never be able to make the dragon from Shrek, all huge belly and tiny wings."

"Wouldn't that be okay in low gravity?" asks Tatsuo

"Only to some extent," says Leo, getting up to write a series of dynamics equations and diagrams on the flip chart. After a while, Frankie joins him and sketches bone structures, muscle and wings over his arrows and numbers. Between them, with suggestions from the rest of the team, they map out a first-draft schema for connecting the parameters that can be engineered into the pterosaur rigs.

✦

Frankie's time on Chiroptera and Pterosauria is nearly over.

"Kangaroos," she tells Olivia the following week.

"Kangaroos? Oh my god, bouncing aliens. That's gotta make the best game ever. It'd be even better if players were on some sort of space-age spacehopper so they could bound along after the 'roos."

"Do you know how fast 'roos run? Forty miles an hour. Try that on a spacehopper."

Olivia looks crestfallen for a moment, but then grins.

"*Powered* spacehoppers. How cool would that be?"

"True, way cool." Frankie pauses for effect. "They're sending me on a kangaroo safari."

"In Oz? Whoa. Also way cool. You have the best job ever." Olivia sounds wistful.

"Except, four weeks away and no Leo." Leo and Frankie have been getting on well. On his last visit to Dundee they'd spent the weekend together; over breakfast and the Sunday papers in bed she'd come close to perfect contentment.

"So are you going to go?" asks Olivia.

"Of course. *Boldly.*"

Frankie grabs an overnight stay with Leo in London before catching her flight to Adelaide. She's on her own: she will be filming enough reference for the animators, and the modellers are studying wallabies in Edinburgh Zoo. She's the only one who needs first-hand knowledge of how the animals move in the wide open spaces of the Australian outback.

Long-haul is a new experience. Wandering Star hasn't stretched to business class. The seat next to her is taken by a friendly young Australian going home after a couple of years of tending bars across Europe. He spends the first hour talking about surf.

"Of course, your beaches in Cornwall aren't bad," he concedes. "Constantine Bay's got juicy reef breaks."

Frankie, who's never been to Cornwall, and has certainly never surfed, doesn't have much to contribute. The Australian seems not to notice.

"Not like home, though. I'll be heading straight for Corny Point. Reefs *and* great white sharks. You should give it a burl."

"Err, well, I'll think about it," says Frankie. Her recent overdose of anatomy lessons means she can picture the result of being torn apart by a shark's teeth all too easily.

"You know," she says, "I'd quite like a wee sleep now."

"Sure, no probs," says the Australian, and continues talking. Frankie shifts in her seat, looking for a comfortable position. It seems rude to close her eyes while she's being spoken to, so she attempts to doze with them open.

Eight hours later, Frankie's eyes are dry and gritty. She's accepted everything the stewards have offered, so is feeling nauseous from bad food and too many tiny bottles of Aussie Shiraz. The wine is more full-on than Frankie's used to and has left a bitter, jammy aftertaste.

Her hands feel grimy despite repeated scrubbing with heated lemon-scented towels. She's only made one trip to the tiny bathroom so far. She managed to skin an elbow and splash water all down her front. She'd shuffled back to her seat attempting to hide the damp patches.

She can't wait to arrive. She has fifteen hours to go.

Then, it's an eleven-hour bus drive from Adelaide to the Arkaroola wilderness sanctuary. To her, this is a huge journey: like driving from Dundee to Land's End. It turns out everyone else on the bus thinks of Arkaroola as a local beauty spot. They face the journey with expansive good cheer and stubbies of lager. Frankie faces it with her head wrapped in a shirt to keep out the bright sunlight.

The next morning, she dresses in her full wilderness gear: long sleeves, long trousers, and a wide-brimmed hat, all in off-white. She doesn't look like herself in the mirror. She doesn't look like anyone else in the breakfast room. They're all in shorts and vest tops.

She meets Scott, her local camera operator, over something described as a continental breakfast. It's toast with Vegemite and a bowl of cornflakes.

"This is the oddest combination of familiar and unfamiliar," she tells Scott. "I mean, I'd have this at home, except with Marmite, not Vegemite."

Scott laughs at her. He seems to mean it kindly, but he's already laughed at her clothes, her deathly-pale skin, and her accent. She clams up, feeling self-conscious, crunches up the last of her toast, and concentrates on applying sunblock to her nose.

Frankie's awed by her first running kangaroo mob. She watches open-mouthed, bumping about in a muddy 4WD she's learnt to call a "Ute", before grabbing her sketchpad and getting to work. She'd come out with the vague sense a kangaroo's hop would be similar to a rabbit's, but immediately sees she's wrong. Their guide and driver, a cheerful woman who handles the Ute with casual competence, talks her through the hopping mechanism. Frankie's never seen anything like the way the animals use their tails as a fifth limb.

Along with the initial kangaroo drawings, Frankie sends Wandering Star a series of sketches of a duck-billed platypus, a creature she finds it hard to believe in even when it's in front of her. A platypus alien becomes the studio's unofficial mascot.

She enthuses to Leo over a voice-only Skype connection that keeps dropping out. Her mobile phone has no signal so all communication with the outside world has to take place at a WiFi hotspot in reception. There's no privacy. Leo's caught up in the detail of a project to build a full-size working model of the biggest pterosaur found to date, *Quetzalcoatlus northropi*.

"Been there, done that, got the T-shirt," she jokes, without thinking. Leo's response is stiff, and she realises he's hurt. She fails miserably to find the right words to straighten things out. She doesn't like the feeling of having moved on and left him behind.

Back in her room, she's about to go to bed when a skittering grabs her attention. She jumps, heart pounding. A spider with a body the length of a flash drive scuttles up the wall. Frankie fixes her eyes on the spider, scared to look away, and slowly backs towards the door. She freezes each time it moves.

It's a huge relief when her hand, reaching behind her, grasps the door handle. She pauses, trying to convince herself the spider isn't about to leap in her direction, then escapes as quickly as she can: opening the door, running out, and slamming it behind her. She leans against the opposite wall in the corridor, shaking.

The night receptionist, a local teenager, is unconcerned.

"That's only a golden orb weaver," he says. "Even if they bite, it hardly hurts. It'll be more scared of you than you are of it."

"I doubt that," says Frankie.

✦

Scott notices her gazing at the unfamiliar stars one evening.

"It's so clear," she says.

"No light pollution," he tells her, pointing out the Southern Cross. The next night he takes her to the Dodwell Observatory. A guide shows her the marvels of the night sky. She comes away the proud owner of a hobbyist's telescope and a Perth Observatory Planisphere.

I'M ALL THUMBS, she emails to Olivia after several days. Despite diligent reading and re-reading of the manual, she hasn't mastered telescope basics. She can actually see the stars better without the equipment. Operation of the Planisphere is a mystery. She still can't identify the Magellanic Clouds. Scott finds this hilarious.

HAVE YOU SEEN THIS? Olivia's reply asks. Frankie clicks the YouTube link and watches a leaked ExoPlanetfall cut-screen animation. A giant platypus fights a vampire bat: electrolocation against echolocation; ankle spur against teeth. It's hilarious, and bloody. It's had over a million hits. Frankie recognises Tatsuo's work and sends him some extra sketches plus some SloMo footage she had Scott shoot on a platypus tour at Cumbungi Sanctuary. His reply is annoyingly offhand.

Olivia's PS says, I HAD LUNCH WITH SUMARA ERSKINE YESTERDAY.

✦

A week later, Frankie's back in a rain-sodden Dundee, via three days of travel and one all-too-short night with Leo.

"Australia must have been brilliant," says Olivia.

"Loved it," says Frankie, firmly. "Good to be back, though."

Olivia looks at her.

"Weren't you tempted to stay a bit longer? Couldn't you have persuaded Wandering Star to go for koala-based aliens or something? Dingoes? Wombats?"

"Aussie blokes? Honestly, those guys are a breed apart."

"Did you miss us?"

"I missed your T-shirts."

Olivia's tee has a QR code on the back. She's hennaed her hair while Frankie's been away. Frankie's wearing the multiple layers needed to protect against the Scottish atmosphere: cardi over lumberjack shirt over "Spiderpig" tee over long-sleeved top, all in dark colours. She hasn't tanned.

"It's lovely not to smell of factor 50. And sunhats just aren't me."

"Yeah, I've seen the photos," says Olivia. "Natural linen really isn't you either. You should try and get sent somewhere cold next time. Polar bear aliens?"

"I'm not planning to get sent anywhere."

There's a lot to do in Dundee. In Frankie's absence several new character specialists have been hired. The team has nearly resolved the pterosaur morphology and is making good progress on the kangaroo, based on material Frankie had sent back from Down Under. The giant platypus turned out to be an in-joke rather than a planned game feature.

"Have you seen the new Kong?" asks Tatsuo, pointing at a battery-powered platypus which has joined Elmo's rampage across the Kellogg's skyline.

"Nice. What's with the starscape?" Someone's attached glow-in-the-dark stars to the ceiling.

"It's the Andromeda Galaxy as photographed by the Hubble. The Concept guys put them up one weekend. See, those're the spiral arms, and there's the NGC 206 star cloud over near the *Falcon*. Bloody genius."

Frankie sits down at her desk, puts her head back to admire the stars, and smiles.

"A galaxy far, far away. Brilliant."

"Your pal Olivia thought so too," says Tatsuo.

"Olivia's been in?" Frankie keeps her eyes on the stars, trying not to let her surprise show.

"Erskine's been interviewing again. And, speak of the devil, she's heading our way..."

"Welcome back," Sumara Erskine says to Frankie. "You look at home."

Frankie doesn't lower her gaze.

"It's good to see outer space without a focus mechanism," she admits.

"Speaking of focusing, you do know we've committed to five aliens for the launch?" Erskine says, pulling Frankie's attention back to workstation level. She sees Tatsuo back away, making must-get-back-to-work gestures.

"*Five?*"

"Counting your pterodactyls. I want bats, dactyls, 'roos, big cats and arachnids. Ye-Eun Kim starts Monday week."

Frankie worked with Ye-Eun years ago. She knows the Korean woman has recently been involved with both Kinectimals and the last Thundercats reboot. Which means...

"Spiders? You want me on spiders? I hate spiders. Can't we do the platypus?"

"We're not scheduled to implement water-world game levels until the next release." Erskine rushes on, not giving Frankie a chance to argue. "There's good news about funding. We've raised venture capital to follow on from the seed money. We can afford to send you on another trip!"

She stops, looking pleased.

"A spider trip?" Frankie is considerably less pleased. She gazes back up at the unfamiliar galaxy and lets her concentration drift away as Erskine goes into the details. It's not until she receives a brisk confirmation email later in the afternoon that she allows herself to consider it. She thinks, then texts Olivia: NEED 2 TALK.

✦

Frankie takes a sip of Chianti, decides it's just what she needs, and has a gulp. Then another.

"Three days of aversion therapy then I'm flying to Yanayacu Biological Station, halfway up a volcano in Ecuador. They're keeping me out there to research four different classes of insect once the spiders are done. I don't know when I'll be back."

"On the plus side, I won't have to hide my keys anymore," says Olivia. It's long been a joke that Olivia's much-loved keyring—a large spider encased in clear resin—is a source of crawly nightmares for Frankie.

Frankie grimaces.

"I can't think about it. Not your keyring, not the therapy, not going away again."

"You don't want to go to Ecuador?" Olivia sounds genuinely shocked. "I know you're only just back from walkabout, but *the Andes!*"

Frankie empties then refills her glass before answering, finishing their first bottle of wine and gesturing to a waiter to bring another.

"I want to spend some time in the studio. It's exciting. There's a real buzz. I want to be part of the team. Especially if you're joining. Are you joining?"

Olivia frowns, and ignores the question.

"You've been part of the team, time and again. What's new?" she asks.

"Well, what about Leo? I haven't told him. What am I going to say? I can hardly ask him to come and see me in Ecuador—we barely know one another."

"It can't be for that long, and you'll be able to visit—"

"Once or twice."

"—and email and Skype."

"It's hardly a good way to start a relationship, all this travel."

"So is that it? Why you don't want to go?"

Frankie shrugs.

"And my Mum. And you. And this place. And King Kong Elmo. Everything. I'm not cut out for travel. I get homesick. I miss things. I miss knowing how stuff works and where I am."

There's a silence. It stretches.

"I'd go," says Olivia, eventually.

Helen Jackson lives in Edinburgh, having moved there more than a decade ago after falling in love with the city during a weekend break. She is a member of the critically acclaimed spoken word collective Writers' Bloc. She is also a Scottish BAFTA-nominated animation director. Her stories can be found in the anthology ImagiNation: Stories of Scotland's Future and in Daily Science Fiction. Her writing blog is at www.helen-jackson.com

THE COMPLEXITY OF THE HUMBLE SPACESUIT

Karen Burnham

THROUGHOUT THE HISTORY of spaceflight, every aspect turns out to be a bit harder than it would appears at first blush. Rocket fuel, launches, weather, lightning, radiation, landings, robotics, automation or lack thereof, redundancy, edible food, mission control, psychology, communications... the list goes on and on. Consider the humble spacesuit. It's often taken for granted in science fiction, unless it is about to fail in a particularly dramatic way. After all, there's an air-tight suit, you pump air into it, the astronaut breathes, and you're good, right? Well, not quite.

Air

It's a bit more complicated than simply strapping some scuba tanks on your back. We breathe in oxygen and breathe out carbon dioxide and water vapour, with a whole bunch of nitrogen involved as well. We can ignore the nitrogen, about which more later, but there's still the matter of keeping the astronaut from suffocating in her own exhaled carbon dioxide. Rebreather technology is only one small component of the overall system. There's also the matter of all the water we exhale with every breath; dehumidifying the air is a must in order to keep the suit from turning into a rain forest. So that's at least two systems to fit into the life support backpack.

Air pressure

The more air and pressure you have in there, the more comfortable for the astronaut, right? If there's as much oxygen in there as there would be at the beach in California, everyone will be happy. Except... air pressure at sea level is 101.325 kPa (14.7 psi), which we never notice because we evolved for it. However, if you put that much pressure into a space suit in a vacuum it blows up like a balloon and becomes almost as rigid as steel. It's impossible to move or manoeuvre. Skipping on the nitrogen (which makes up more than three-quarters of the volume of terrestrial air, but is inert) lets us save on air volume and thus air pressure. But when you start messing around with pure oxygen and different air pressures, you face some of the same challenges that face deep-water scuba divers, including the risk of getting the bends (decompression sickness). According to Mary Roach in her superb book on space travel, Packing for Mars:

> Alexei Leonov [the first human to make a spacewalk] is said to have sweated away 12 pounds in a similar struggle. His suit had pressurized to the extent that he could not bend his knees and had to go in head first, rather than feet first, as he had trained for. He got stuck trying to close the hatch behind him and had to lower his suit pressure to get back in—a potentially lethal move, akin to a diver ascending too quickly.

The space suits worn by present-day astronauts are very bulky, and not much loved by the astronauts themselves. They solve the pressure problem by having relatively low air pressure, and also by reinforcing the joints and having other hardened elements. Counter-intuitively, making them stiffer keeps them from being as affected by the internal air pressure. The joints must then be complexly hinged with 'mobility bearings' in order to be usable. Even with the suits as manoeuvrable as they are, it is almost impossible to get in and out of them without considerable help from another astronaut. A future proposal involves designing a spacesuit to be more like a neoprene wetsuit. It would be airtight, of course, but having something skin-tight combats the vacuum of space by elastically compressing the astronaut's skin and may end up being more comfortable and manoeuvrable. This idea was not, however, picked up by NASA for its next-generation spacesuit.

In a nice illustration of the link between space exploration and deep-sea diving, the contract for that next spacesuit was awarded in 2009 to Oceaneering International, a company that got its start supporting underwater drilling operations. And spacesuits are being asked to do more and more as NASA looks to the future. In Oceaneering's suit project, this is what NASA says it is looking for:

> Suits and support systems will be needed for as many as four astronauts on moon voyages and as many as six space station travelers. For short trips to the moon, the suit design will support a week's worth of moon walks. The system also must be designed to support a significant number of moon walks during potential six-month lunar outpost expeditions. In addition, the spacesuit and support systems will provide contingency spacewalk capability and protection against the launch and landing environment, such as spacecraft cabin leaks.

This is another evolutionary step beyond what we currently have, which only supports spacewalks with no concern about different gravity conditions (free-fall in orbit versus a planetary or lunar surface) or erosion from working on a planet's surface.

Temperature
It's a cliché, those cold dark depths of space. Actually, Low Earth Orbit switches from hot to cold almost instantly, depending on

whether you're in direct sunlight or not. In sunlight, the temperature can get as high as 121º C (250º F), and in the shade it can quickly fall to -157º C (-250º F). And if you're hot, it's surprisingly hard to cool down in space. While the 'temperature' of space is quite low (there are very few particles around to collide, which is what 'heat' really is), vacuum itself is a fantastic insulator. That's why vacuum-sealed thermos flasks are so effective. On Earth things cool off via three methods: conduction (a hot material in contact with a cool material will lose heat to the cooler object), convection (the movement of fluids around a hot object, such as water or air, will carry heat away), or radiation (an object will lose energy to the surrounding environment). In space, only radiative cooling is available, and that is a very slow process. It is easier for an astronaut to bake—heating up via his own exertions plus exposure to the sun—than to freeze. Current spacesuits are usually cooled by tubes of water running through a layer of the suit, much like a refrigerator system, and that makes up a large part of that bulky backpack.

Gloves

If you're out and about outside your spacecraft, it's probably because you need to do some work. And we, clever monkeys that we are, do work primarily with our hands. So gloves are extremely important: they have to be durable (a tear would be disastrous), insulated (fingers must not freeze or burn when in contact with metals like the exterior of the space station), and dexterous (allowing for bolt tightening, button pushing, and any number of other construction tasks). And getting all three of those things in one design is nigh-unto-impossible. Mary Roach got to experience the gloves at NASA Johnson Space Center:

> The spacesuit systems lab at Johnson Space Center has a glove box that mimics he vacuum of space and inflates a pair of pressurized gloves. In the box with the gloves is one of the heavy-duty carabiners that tether astronauts and their tools to the exterior of the space station while

Karen Burnham

> they work. Trying to work the tether is
> like dealing cards with oven mitts on.
> Simply closing one's fist tires the hand
> within minutes.

One solution involves an outer mitten for insulation and tear protection and a thinner heated inner glove for detail work. But a better design would be greatly appreciated.

Food and water

When an astronaut is working hard for hours at a time (the longest spacewalk so far lasted almost nine hours), and sweating up a storm, she'll need to drink to rehydrate and eat something to keep going. The drinking system is somewhat like a bicyclists' Camelbak pack, with potable water and a straw near the mouth. Unfortunately it's been known to leak, which is no fun. There is also a slot for an energy bar, where the astronaut can take a bite and move the bar up for the next bite... However, the annoyance of crumbs floating in the helmet is so great (there's no way to clean them up with the helmet on) that most astronauts simply have a big meal before a space walk and skip on the snack. And how about that sweat? Can you imagine embarking on a construction project on a hot, humid day and never being able to wipe your brow? Sweatbands and wicking garments only take you so far.

Comfort

How long will an astronaut need to stay in a spacesuit? Gemini 7 was a two-week mission with Jim Lovell and Frank Borman, and the flight doctors decided that they needed information on the effects of long-term spacesuit wearing. As the wonderfully named Christopher Columbus Kraft Jr, the flight director (for whom Johnson Space Center's Mission Control building is now named) says in his memoir, Flight: My Life in Mission Control:

> Borman agreed to stay suited, but with
> each passing day, he got more

uncomfortable. Spacesuits are bulky and
stiff. It takes effort to bend an elbow or
a knee, and when something itches,
scratching is a real chore. After a few
days in the same underwear, I had to
assume that scratching was on Borman's
mind a lot.

Finally, human decency and compassion prevailed and
Borman and Lovell were allowed to go suitless for a time. No one
today expects astronauts to live in their spacesuits, but it would
represent a huge advance in mobility and comfort if a suit could
be designed with that in mind.

Waste products

Unfortunately, no one has been able to improve on the adult
diaper, or in NASA-speak, the Maximum Absorbency Garment,
for waste containment.

Colour

How do you tell the astronauts apart at a glance, since they're all
wearing the same big, bulky, white suits? Today's astronauts
always go out in pairs, and if you look closely at the video footage
online or on NASA TV, you'll see that one suit has red stripes on
it that can be seen from any angle, thus allowing observers to
distinguish between the two. All the suits are white partly so that
they absorb less heat, and partly because that is the most visible
colour against the blackness of space.

Propulsion

Generally, the astronauts stay tethered to a vehicle or platform.
However, ISS-era spacesuits can have the capability to
manoeuvre independently via small gas thrusters in the SAFER
(Simplified Aid for EVA Rescue, illustrating NASA's charming
habit of including an acronym in an acronym) backpack—yet
another element making that backpack large and unwieldly.

Karen Burnham

✦

The complications multiply ad infinitum. And that's just for spacewalking. Once you get to a planetary surface, there's also dust (and lunar dust is much more corrosive and harder to get rid of than terrestrial dust) and other contaminants to contend with. Plus, a spacesuit is just one small aspect of a vastly complicated overall mission, each element of which is equally tricky and equally mission critical. Sometimes the wonder is not that we haven't gotten farther with human space exploration, but that we ever got off the ground in the first place.

It may look effortless to float in space. But before the spacesuit launches, immense amounts of thought and toil are put into every aspect of the design. And even after all that, inside the suit the astronaut is working hard to complete even the most basic tasks in a less-than-ideally-comfortable environment. Still, there's no question that it's been worth it. On the one hand, rumour has it that they make great hiding places to smuggle booze onto the International Space Station (a bottle of vodka in a suit arm, for instance). On a more sublime note, remember Ed White, the first American to spacewalk. It took all of Mission Control and commander Jack McDivitt's cajoling to get him to come back inside. After considerable stalling, he described returning to the spacecraft: "This is the saddest moment of my life."

Being able to float among the stars is a dream well worth reaching for.

Karen Burnham is an engineer at NASA's Johnson Space Center, specializing in electromagnetic interference and compatibility (EMI/EMC). She has degrees in both physics and electrical engineering. As an avocation she is a reviewer and scholar of science fiction, publishing reviews in Strange Horizons and SFSignal and articles in the New York Review of Science Fiction and Clarkesworld magazine. She is currently the editor of the blog for the Locus magazine website.

WHY BARNABY ISN'T ABOARD THE ISS TODAY

Gary Cuba

BARNABY SHAUGHNESSY KNEW it had to be The Call. He figured that from the wide-eyed expression on his wife's face as she ran out of the house to hand him the phone. He took the handset from her, turning his attention away from the flaming steaks on his outdoor patio grill.

"Barney here," he said.

He immediately recognised the voice of his boss, the Chief of NASA's Astronaut Office, on the other end of the line.

"You're off the bubble, Barney. Incredibly, Andrew, Scott and Bill have all come down with a nasty case of flu. So we're down to you now. You're on tap to be the next Mission Specialist on the ISS, via Shuttle mission STS-106."

Barney stared blankly at the sizzling steaks in front of him, temporarily at a loss for words. This was the culmination of all his dreams, the single goal that had driven him since he had been a young boy: to become an astronaut! "Thank you, sir. Thanks more than I can say. It's, it's something that I—"

"Just don't screw the pooch, Barnaby. We've all got to deal with these unfortunate vagaries of Nature, best we can. Be in my office at 0800 tomorrow for a final mission briefing. At this time, the lift remains on-schedule for Tuesday."

The line went dead, and Barney hugged his wife. "It's my time, Hon! *My* time, finally!"

The steaks continued to scorch beyond edibility as Barney and his wife clasped each other, both of them weeping joyous tears.

✦

Shuttle Atlantis matched orbits and docked with the ISS, and somewhere along the way, Barney had involuntarily urinated in his Maximum Absorbency Garment—his diaper. Well, he thought, that's not such a big deal. Heck, that's why we wear 'em! He'd done the same thing on every single one of the training centrifuge runs back at Houston.

And not to even mention the vomit.

Although the other astronaut crew aspirants gleefully did, every time he'd produced a stomach-full of it during one of their flight simulations.

To heck with them, he thought. I tried hard, worked my butt off, and they didn't scrub me for having those little awkward moments. Lord knows, I've always had to work twice as hard as everybody else to get anywhere. Now I'm finally here. Now it's *my* turn to laugh.

He only needed to remember one thing: *Don't screw the pooch, Barnaby!*

Sergei Mikhailovich Sokolov, the current lead engineer on the ISS, displayed a wide, gold-capped grin as the newest ISS crew member squeezed through the station's docking hatchway. "Welcome aboard, Barnaby! We hear a lot about you. I hope your tour will be productive and... safe. For everybody here concerned."

Barney smiled and began to urgently shirk off his flight suit. "Glad to be aboard. You must be Sergei, my Russian-type boss-guy. Care to point me to the toilet unit?"

Within the space of the next ten minutes, Barney managed to break the ISS's sophisticated, twenty-million-dollar zero-G toilet. Okay, he thought, don't get paranoid. It was just a small pooch, after all.

His first act as Mission Specialist, off the mission agenda, was to fix the toilet unit with the help of the technical manual Sergei downloaded into his PDA. He captured most of the free-floating fæces inside the tiny Waste Managment Compartment, then joined the other ISS and Shuttle crew members in the control bay.

"Sorry, my bad," he said meekly.

His colleagues' narrowed eyes said all Barney needed to

know. It'd take hours for the onboard filters to scrub the stink from the confined atmosphere.

"Could happen to anybody, Barney," Sergei said, patting him on the shoulder. "First lesson: Nothing goes as planned. Flexibility is our patronym here."

✦

"It's big, bulky package, Barney," Sergei said. They hovered at the airlock to the Shuttle's payload bay door. "Keep relative mass ratio and centre of gravity in mind, always. Shuttle bay doors, they stand open now. I know you read this procedure backwards and forwards, many dozen of times, but quickly can things get disorienting out there on cosmonaut's first EVA opportunity. Focus on tethering rules, above all and every else. Less you use the nitrogen thrusters on the suit, the better off you will be. *And don't fornicate with little doggy, hear me?*"

Sergei and Barney ran through the procedure checklist, making sure each custom tool needed to accomplish the EVA task was present, with its individual lanyard securely attached to Barney's spacesuit.

I feel a little like an octopus, Barney thought, looking at the weightless tools extending from him on their lanyards. He secured each of them to the Velcro band that ran around his midsection. Then Sergei closed the airlock's inner hatch, and Task 84 of the mission agenda commenced: INSTALL THE SPARE S-BAND ANTENNA SUBASSEMBLY ON THE OUTBOARD END OF THE P6 TRUSS.

Barney's big moment had arrived.

Tether! he told himself after the airlock depressurised. He opened the inner bay door and immediately attached the hook of his suit tether to the Shuttle bay's closest securement rail. Then Barney floated gently into the open bay, and looked up at the Earth above his head. It filled his field of view, breathtaking to behold.

Breathtaking in the sense of being scary as hell.

Barney felt a nauseating wave of dizziness overcome him, and he became completely and utterly disoriented. He began to hyperventilate. There had been no way to train for this, no adequate conditioning method or simulation. Which way is up?

Gary Cuba

He felt his stomach heave, and vomited inside his suit. A lot.

"You okay-dokay, big guy?" Sergei said through the suit's RF intercom.

Barney's involuntary retching ceased after a long minute. "Uh, everything's copasetic, Sergei. Just a slight... gastrointestinal reaction to the environment. It's okay, I'll clean up the suit after the EVA for the next person, promise." He hoped the product of his "reaction" wouldn't clog the suit's recirculation filters. Having to cut the EVA short would surely be deemed as a major pooch-screwing event.

Barney wrinkled his nose at the pungent, acidic smell inside the suit while he worked his way through the payload bay toward his target module, carefully releasing and re-securing his tether at each fixed rail bracket as he went. He tried to keep his eyes on the hard, straight, human-wrought surfaces of the Shuttle bay, rather than the God-wrought majesty that spread out above him.

He reached the antenna module and mentally ran through the procedural steps to uncouple it from the bay floor—just like he'd done a hundred times in preparation for this critical mission task.

And for the first time, he realized that the instructions became a bit ambiguous at that point. Why hadn't he recognized this earlier, and questioned it? Step 13: TETHER THE SUBASSEMBLY THROUGH ONE OF ITS EYEBOLTS BEFORE UNCOUPLING IT FROM THE BAY FLOOR. Fine. Trouble was, the list of tools and materials did not include a separate tether to use for this purpose.

It must mean to couple the other end of my own fifteen-metre tether to it, he thought. Surely so. After all, he'd soon have to disengage his tether anyway, to move the module from the Shuttle bay to its ultimate destination on the ISS's outboard framework. And for that move, he'd need to use his suit thrusters, free of any tethering.

He knew it was critically important not to let this expensive item drift free to seek its own destiny—which would surely happen if he were to lose his grasp on the rascal during the move. He shuddered inside his EVA garb. That miscue would surely constitute a major act of canine buggery, an infamy that would accompany him forever, dutifully recorded in the most notorious appendices of the NASA annals. Heck, his own future

176

grandkids would probably never let him forget it! He muttered a quick curse, directed toward their as-yet-unborn souls. Ingrates! For the love of God, have some respect. Show some common decency for your elders!

"You okay, Barney?"

Sergei's voice had an overtone of concern in it.

"Yeah, I'm getting there, Sergei. I'm getting there. No *problemos*. Tethering to the module now, getting ready to uncouple it."

Barney unlatched the end of his tether from the siderail and hooked it onto one of the module's several eyebolts. Then he retrieved the two-million-dollar inertia-reactive impact wrench from his belt and, steadying himself by holding onto the module with one hand, untorqued the tie-down nuts securing the payload. He carefully stowed each one of them in the ziplock pouch attached to his suit.

When all were removed and secured, Barney breathed a sigh of relief and thought about the faux pas of some of his EVA Mission Specialist colleagues, the fellows who'd managed to fumble and surrender such sundry hardware to the grip of the universe—little pooches screwed, each and every time it happened. Ha! But no flies on me! Yes!

Then he shivered as he thought of all those tiny toy poodles whizzing around the Earth in his same orbit, at many hundreds of feet per second relative to his present velocity—any one of which could crack a hole right through his helmet and the softer organic compounds contained within it.

"Module uncoupled. Ready for transfer," he announced.

He couldn't help but marvel, even while expecting it: the module's twice the mass of me, and yet it's light as a feather. No, lighter than a feather—no weight at all, he thought, gently lifting it clear by its handholds.

Barney took a moment to recollect his training runs aboard the NASA-owned cargo airliner used for weightless acclimation, the one that flew parabolic arcs to simulate a gravity-free environment. But those arcs were only about twenty seconds long, not enough to really learn how to move massive objects around in a space environment. And besides, he'd occupied most of those short intervals throwing up. He'd also trained in the

Neutral Bouyancy Lab at Johnson Space Centre in Houston—but he tended to panic and hyperventilate during those exercises, and occasionally passed out cold in the water. *But darnit, I always got right back in again!* Dogged spunk went a long way. It'd gotten him this far, after all.

Okay, maybe "dogged" isn't the best choice of adjectives at this juncture, he thought.

Trouble was, the sheer size and bulkiness of the payload would prevent visual contact with the target destination, were he to hold the beast to his breast. He could hold it to one side, or above or below him, but firing a thruster under that scenario would just put them in a spin, owing to the offset in their combined centre of gravity. Barney considered this further: best to let it trail on the tether, directly behind him, then reengage it when he reached the target. He repositioned the tether, sliding its hook around his belt to his rear end to keep the COG in-line. He coiled the tether up to take out most of the slack, and held the loops behind him with his left hand as tightly as he could.

Now, just a very light spurt of nitrogen on the aft nozzle, just a nudge. Nothing to build up any significant momentum. Slow and easy. He disengaged the safety on his suit's thruster joystick control and gave the tiniest amount of control movement his nervous hand could muster.

The thruster roared out at full throttle, sending him toward the ISS at what seemed like a drag racer's acceleration. He felt himself pushed backward inside the EVA suit. The coiled tether jerked out of his grasp.

Barney pulled his hand away from the control in an instant. But the thruster had frozen into its maximum open position. Another vagary of Nature—or of Mankind's feeble imitation of the Old Girl. Why now? Why me? he thought.

"Hulp!" he said.

"What's that, Barney? I did not quite get that," Sergei replied.

Barney hurtled toward the ISS's P6 truss framework, fifty metres away. He felt a sharp rearward jerk as the payload's rest mass reacted against the fully outstretched tether. His forehead hit the front visor of his helmet hard, knocking him senseless. He recovered a few seconds later, and felt a tickle of blood running down his face.

But the damnable thruster hadn't shut off; it overcame the combined load and continued to accelerate the two-body tethered system onward. Barney manipulated the thruster's joystick frantically. No reaction at all.

He took stock of his situation. This was not going well. Not at all. The pooch trailing behind him was a big one, a gigantic mastiff. A huge Demon Pooch, twice his own mass, totally out of his control.

He neared one of the ISS's solar panel frames, advancing on it rapidly—too rapidly. He grabbed desperately at the nearest available structure in his path, a pylon supporting a high-gain parabolic antenna. Somehow, he managed to hold fast to it. The suit's thruster gave out the last of its nitrogen supply in a final, sputtering decrepitation. Hang tight. Hang tight...

A second or so later, the trailing payload module slammed into him.

He remembered a similar pain once as a child, when he'd fallen off a playground gym set. This was what it felt like to have your collarbone and several ribs fractured. Hang on! The penalty for letting go now was to become yet another piece of free-orbiting space debris.

"Barney! Talk to me!" Sergei's voice sounded in his headset.

The module ricocheted off him, still on its tether. Barney knew there'd be more hell to pay when it played out fully ahead of him. He clung tighter to the pylon, locking his arm around one of its struts, grimacing in pain. The Big Dog reached the end of its travel, and Barney screamed in agony as its sudden deceleration dislocated his shoulder.

But he held on.

The module's course vector, having been granted a lateral component from its initial impact with Barney, now translated itself into an orbital path, with the tether defining the radius. Barney watched in morbid fascination as the module swung around in a wide arc on the outstretched line, crashed through one of the solar wing panels as if it were made of tissue paper, then continued along its orbit, the centre of which was Barney. The tether began to wrap around him as the module made its twirling circuit.

This was not going to end well.

He watched the module spiral around the pylon on its tether, drawing ever closer to his trussed body. It moved faster and faster as its radius shrunk, like a figure skater pulling into a tight spin. Barney sobbed. *This is going to become a pretty complete pooch-screw, however you want to define it.*

✦

God must have decided He'd thrown enough bad luck at Barnaby Shaughnessy throughout the man's life, so He evened the score that day with a single miracle: he preserved Barney's life. And made sure the battered astronaut got safely back to Earth via the Shuttle's return flight.

The Administrator of the Astronaut Corps had visited Barney in Walter Reed Hospital earlier that morning, and presented him with a nicely-framed NASA commendation. It detailed his heroic deed, undertaken at great personal risk, to save an expensive mission payload from loss following an unfortunate malfunction in his EVA equipment.

Following that, he informed Barney that he was being released from the Astronaut Corps.

There would be no parades, no public celebrations. All told, he learned, the damage from his incident would cost close to a billion bucks to fix. That left little in the budget for frivolities.

In retrospect, Barney realized it would have been a lot smarter to have unclipped the tether and let the damned beast seek its own destiny among the stars. But that was not the stuff he was made of.

Now his wife sat at his bedside. She grasped the fingers of Barney's right hand, the only portion of his flesh available for direct human contact. The rest was encased in a full-body cast, from head to toe.

"I'm so proud of you, honey," she said.

Barney couldn't turn his head, but he swivelled his eyes in her direction. His senses were a little foggy from his pain medication.

"'S funny... do you hear that? It sounds like a dog howling in the distance. Can you hear it? Can you?"

"No, Barney. I... I don't hear anything."

The pooch would haunt Barney until the end of his days. Even so, whatever the Universe threw at him, he always revelled in one thing: he'd once been an *astronaut*.

Gary Cuba lives with his wife and a teeming horde of freeloading domestic critters in South Carolina, USA. Now retired, he spent most of his career working in the commercial nuclear power industry, and holds several US patents in that field. His short fiction has appeared in three dozen magazines and anthologies to date, including Jim Baen's Universe, Flash Fiction Online, Universe Annex (Grantville Gazette), Abyss & Apex and Andromeda Spaceways Inflight Magazine. See www.thefoggiestnotion.com to learn more about him and to find links to some of his other stories.

NOT BECAUSE THEY ARE EASY

Sam S Kepfield

Pravda, 23 February 1969

A GREAT VICTORY IN THE PEACEFUL COMPETITION WITH CAPITALISM

The first manned lunar mission, created by Soviet engineers and workers, is headed towards Earth's only satellite. Zond 7 lifted off on schedule on 22 February, and the spacecraft performed flawlessly. A docking manoeuvre was completed, and the Soyuz LOK and LK lunar lander departed Earth orbit headed for the Moon.

Today, as with Sputnik and Vostok, the entire population of the planet Earth sees the great victory of Soviet science and technology, the Soviet Union's highly developed industry and our technical might, all created under the leadership of the Communist Party under successive Five Year Plans. The lunar effort is the result of a strict scientific plan, in accordance with Lenin's general directives in building socialism. The moon mission is a victory for Soviet man who, with Bolshevist boldness, clearness of purpose, determination and energy, is marching forward towards the creation of world socialism. This is a victory for collective labour, which alone is capable of leading mankind into a new age of enlightenment...

The New York Times, 23 February 1969

SOVIETS LAUNCH MOON MISSION

ZOND IS ANOTHER FIRST

MOSCOW (AP)—TASS announced at 2:45 am Moscow time that the Soviet Union had launched a lunar mission shortly before midnight from the Baikonur Cosmodrome. The first moon landing is expected sometime on February 25, after a four-day flight.

The launch marks yet another Soviet space first, starting with Sputnik I in 1957, Yuri Gagarin's Vostok flight in 1961, and Alexi Leonov's spacewalk in 1965. Moscow Radio pointed to the string of successes as proof of the superiority of Soviet science and power.

White House Press Secretary Ron Ziegler had no immediate comment, but President Nixon is said to be following the developments closely.

Reaction on Capitol Hill varied. Senator George McGovern (D-SD) released a statement calling upon the Administration to abandon "what is clearly a futile and wasteful public relations competition" and focus on problems back on Earth. Senator Robert Dole (R-KS), Republican National Committee Chairman, said that the Zond launch "presents another wake-up call to the American people". Dole called for increased research and development spending, and brushed aside any suggestion that the Apollo program be cancelled or downscaled. "If anything, it should be even larger," Dole said.

NASA Administrator James Fletcher said at a press conference that the Soviet launch does not alter NASA's current mission schedule. Apollo 9 is set to lift off on 3 March, followed by Apollo 10 in May. Apollo 11, tentatively scheduled to land on the lunar surface, is slated for launch in June or July.

Dan Lomax: Marathon: The Race to the Moon and Beyond, 1961-2001 (New York, Atheneum, 2001), p 202

Just as it had with Sputnik and Vostok 1, the Soviet Union caught the world by surprise when it announced the launch of the Zond lunar mission on February 22, 1969. The Americans were still basking in the glow of the Apollo 8 mission, which had circled the Moon only seven weeks prior. The world had thrilled, and more than a few wept, as Borman, Lovell and Anders read from the Book of Genesis while skimming mere miles above the cratered surface. Now it seemed that the atheistic Soviets would be the first to actually reach that pockmarked surface.

The reality was quite different. The Soviet lunar program itself was beset with difficulties in development, caused by the unique structure of the Soviet space effort. The solution that the Soviets hit upon was, in this light, not entirely unexpected.

Vasily Mishin, former Chief Designer, OKB-1 Design Bureau. Interview with Jonathan McAtee, recorded 1 October 1995 ·

Mishin: I told them it wouldn't work.

McAtee: The launch, or—

Mishin: Either one!

McAttee: Let's go with the planned moon mission first.

Mishin: (sighs) On paper, going into space, to the Moon, is easy. You compute trajectories, calculate weight, thrust ratios, fuel requirements, do the orbital mechanics for a rendezvous and docking, and so on. On paper, valves never freeze up, gyroscopes never shut down, fuel lines never rupture, your rocket booster never pogos. But in real life it's never that simple.

McAtee: But your programme managed to overcome a lot of those obstacles.

Mishin: What you have to understand is that there was never really a single space programme, in the sense that you Americans know it. You Americans have this view of us as a monolithic force where all dissent is crushed.

McAtee: It's unavoidable, perhaps.

Mishin: You're right. There is that view from the outside. But from the inside—first of all, everything was political. Khrushchev was literally giving directives for launches directly to us, for reasons unrelated to scientific or engineering goals. It was all propaganda. Sputnik went up as our entry in the International Geophysical Year, and a way to beat the Americans. Tereshkova was sent up in '63 as a publicity stunt, a way to make another first in space, show that under communism all were equal. There was no long-range plan, no steady building one achievement on the other. It meant triumphs, but also created disasters like the R-16 explosion in 1960 that killed Nedelin[1] and dozens of our

[1] Marshal Mitrofan Nedelin, 1902-1960, commander of the Strategic Rocket Forces

scientists. Then we had the rivalry between Korolev[2] and Chelomey[3] for the direction of the entire programme.

McAtee: Really?

Mishin: Korolev was the dreamer, wanting to aim the missile programme at space exploration. Chelomey was more oriented towards practical, defensive uses of space vehicles, for anti-satellite weapons. And since the Ministry of Defense, through the Strategic Rocket Forces, was running the space programme, Chelomey was their boy. We lost a few years sorting out that problem.

McAtee: It's not so different in America, with different contractors like Grumman and Boeing competing for contracts.

Mishin: But your government goes through a bid process, which is somewhat neutral, controlled by your civilian space agency. With our programme, everything was run through the Strategic Rocket Forces, and it depended upon who was in favour and who wasn't. And it depended upon what the Politburo thought should be the highest priority. Not until Andropov created Glavkosmos in 1980 was there some kind of order to the process.

McAtee: How did that affect the lunar landing versus other targets?

Mishin: Tsiolkovsky was fascinated with Mars, and Korolev was a big follower of Tsiolkovsky's so he saw Mars as the ultimate goal. The Moon was dead, airless, no practical value. But Mars—we thought Mars had water, might have life, and we could start another society there.

McAtee: Like The Martian Chronicles?

Mishin: Of course. I read Bradbury, and Burroughs too. The Moon project wasn't seen as a big deal. In the early days, after Sputnik and Gagarin, we were looking at this as a marathon. But then Kennedy set out the goal of putting an American on the Moon by 1970, which brought the entire American military-industrial complex into action. We found ourselves having to compete, somewhat against our will. Kennedy had started the race, and we couldn't just opt out. Like it or not, we were in it. So we were

---

[2] Sergei Korolev, head of Special Design Bureau 1, OKB-1, 1906-1966
[3] Vladimir Chelomey, head of OKB-52, 1914-1984

going to the Moon. And by late '68, we were close.

McAtee: Apollo 8 must have been a jolt.

Mishin: Definitely. By the start of '69, the Politburo and the Central Committee were getting nervous. The Americans had put up Apollo 8, and we were way behind. The race to the Moon was about anything except scientific exploration. It was all political. Whoever made it was going to win over the non-aligned countries, win converts, and pull ahead in the peaceful competition of the Cold War. So the decision was made to try a launch in early '69.

McAtee: And you opposed it?

Mishin: It was insanity. The N-1, our booster, had problems from the start. We hadn't tested it adequately. The GR-1, which was supposed to be the test model for the N-1 engines, was cancelled in 1965. After the GR-1, we had no way of developing high-energy cryogenic rockets. Korolev wanted to use liquid hydrogen, which was more efficient, but we ended up using LOX and kerosene, the same mix we used on the R-1s that launched Sputnik. All because we didn't have the means to produce the cryogenic liquids like LOX. The N-1 had a capacity of five and a half tons, which meant we had to cut the weight for the lander and orbiter to the minimum, with only two cosmonauts on the mission. The lander could only carry one cosmonaut, was half the size of the Apollo LM, and only had one set of engines for landing and liftoff. Add on to that, we never had the money to test-fire the N-1. We were going to have to fire it in February '69 for the first time, with the full payload, not knowing whether it would work. Because there wasn't any funding for a test stand.

McAtee: Given all of this, how did the Soviet leadership hit upon this solution?

Mishin: It was Brezhnev's fault. Who else could it be? Afanasyev[4] had met with all the design bureau chiefs back in January '69, after Apollo 8, and asked them how to get out of the hole we were in. The answer was pure Communist Party bureaucratic nonsense. "We will strive to accelerate the refinement of the N-1, we will move forward on the L3 sample return project", as if the

---

[4] Minister of General Machine Building Sergei A Afanasyev

Stakhanovites could carry us to the Moon on their backs. It was Stroganov[5], I think who first had the idea. His reasoning went like this. We're working on a sample return mission, the L3[6]. We're planning to launch that next month. All the proof that the world needs will be collected and sent back to the Soviet Union. What's the proof? Moon rocks. They're going to look for a bunch of rocks as proof that we made it. So we give them the rocks. But, Stroganov asked, does it really matter *how* they got back to Earth? Will anyone be able to tell?

McAtee: Was there any resistance to the idea?

Mishin: Of course! But the more we thought about it, the better it sounded. Everyone thought he was brilliant at the time. Four years later, everyone thought he should have been shot. And, if Stalin had still been running things, he would have been.

Richard Nixon, Mandate for Leadership: Memoirs, Vol. 2, 1973-1977 (New York: GP Putnam and Sons, 1984), p 56

The Soviet moon launch in early 1969 took everyone by surprise. The televised pictures from the surface four days later, showing Khrunov erecting the red flag on the surface was an enormous blow to American prestige. It was also a blot on the memory of President Kennedy, who had explicitly promised that America would reach the moon before 1970, and implicitly that we would do it before the Soviets.

I called Senator Edward Kennedy and promised him that we would make good on his late brother's promise, and that we would do more. I invited him to the White House for a meeting on the subject.

There was never any question of cancelling Apollo. The purpose was not merely to be first to the Moon, but to expand the frontiers of human knowledge. The program had progressed too far to call off. Some, like Senators Proxmire and McGovern, called it all a boondoggle, and introduced legislation to end it.

Conversely, there were those who urged NASA to step up the

[5] Boris Stroganov, a deputy in the Central Committee's Defense Department
[6] Later dubbed Lunokhod by the West

scheduled launches for Apollo 9 and 10, but this was wisely ignored. Haste had cost the lives of three brave astronauts in January 1967, Gus Grissom, Ed White and Roger Chaffee, and we couldn't afford a repeat.

When Apollo 11 launched on July 16, 1969, I invited Senator Kennedy to view the launch with myself and Pat. I was shocked at his appearance. The death of his brother Robert only a few months earlier had taken its toll; he looked haggard and drawn. After the Saturn V had put the mission into orbit, I invited Senator Kennedy to stay in Key Biscayne for a short time, to discuss where the space program could go from here. Although he was never the enthusiast for the NASA that his brother was, or that President Johnson was, he reluctantly agreed.

The meeting was productive. With input from James Fletcher, NASA Administrator, we sketched out where we thought it should go. The Russians had landed first. But it was a publicity stunt, just like Sputnik and Gagarin's flight. They hadn't sent another mission. We, on the other hand, had sent three up in a short time. Fletcher said that the Russians were looking at it like a series of hundred-yard dashes, but we had to be the marathon runner. Lunar missions should continue, but the program now had to look towards putting a man in space and keeping him there, with a manned space station. The Moon would still be in our sights, and NASA would begin plans for a permanent presence on the lunar surface. The Apollo missions would run through 1974, each getting longer and involving more exploration of the surface. And a Mars mission by the year 2000 would also be on the drawing boards. Plans for a space station were in the works as well, to match the Soviets' Salyut station.

Kennedy's price for this was simple, but big. He wanted some sort of national health insurance plan. Pat Moynihan, my Counselor on Urban Affairs, had long been advocating something like this. Since Pat had served President Kennedy as Assistant Secretary of Labor, I promised Senator Kennedy that Pat was going to get a promotion, to devise a health care plan. The Senator's mood was notably improved when he left Key Biscayne on July 18, and flew back to Washington to meet with Moynihan.

Stephen Ambrose, Nixon: Triumph and Tribulation, 1962-1973
(New York: Doubleday, 1990), p 334

The meeting with Edward Kennedy was personally challenging for Nixon, who loathed the Kennedys and all they stood for, and had since the 1960 election. But, as his Special Advisor Chuck Colson said, knowingly egging on the President by appealing to his sense of machismo, "what's Ted Kennedy compared to Khrushchev?" referring to Nixon's much-publicized Kitchen Debate with the former Soviet leader ten years earlier in Moscow.

Nixon, of course, had another motive for acquiescing in the trade-off with Kennedy. His position in the summer of 1969 was anything but secure. The worst of the anti-war protests were to come. The Moratorium was gaining steam and would culminate in the demonstrations that October. His later widening of the war into Cambodia and Laos in the spring of 1970 would spark massive campus revolts and the tragedy at Kent State. Though his policy of Vietnamization was taking hold, and the drawdown of troops had begun and would continue through 1972, Nixon's biggest fear was that an anti-war candidate would mobilize support and endanger his re-election. Ever since Bobby Kennedy's assassination in June 1968, Ted Kennedy had been seen as Camelot's heir apparent and the best chance to oust Nixon in 1972.

Nixon's gambit, meeting with the heir presumptive of the Kennedy dynasty, was strategically brilliant, a smaller version of the détente he would reach with China and the Soviet Union in 1972. Nixon believed that the meeting would do two things. It would deprive Kennedy of his primary issue in the 1972 election; Perhaps seeing his overarching goal fulfilled would even dissuade him from running. And, it would give Nixon the imprimatur needed to rise to the latest Soviet triumph and surpass it. He and America would tough it out, and respond to the latest Soviet move with more in kind, and paint those who sought cancellation of Apollo as defeatists.

Conversation between Nixon, Ehrlichman, Haldeman, and Colson, Oval Office, 1 August 1969 [From Nixon Presidential Library Archives, declassified 1 November 2007]

P: [unintelligible] cut off Teddy Kennedy's [expletive deleted].

E: You think he's going to take this buy-out?

C: He has to. He's been whining about a national health system for years. He can't turn it down, not with his buddy Moynihan writing the bill.

P: All of this is a pain in the [expletive deleted]. It's going to [expletive deleted] bankrupt us.

H: You can't back down and let the Russians own the Moon. Won't look good in '72.

P: Yeah, I know [expletive deleted]. At least I won't have to worry about Teddy then.

E: What if he doesn't go away?

C: Don't worry. Liddy and a couple of others, we've got that one covered.

General Viktor Malenovsky (ret), head of KIK (Command-Measurement Complex). Interview with Jonathan McAtee, 14 June 1995

Malenovsky: The big problem we had was how to make it *look* real. We could say we'd launched a rocket and a mission, but the Americans had a ground radar tracking network, so did the British. And so did the Chinese, who in '69 would be just as happy as the Americans to expose a fraud. So there were two problems. How to make it look like we'd put a lunar mission in Earth orbit, for rendezvous and docking, and departure, which meant fooling ground radar and radio facilities. The second was how to fool the spy satellites into thinking that we'd done it.

McAtee: Start with the spy satellites.

Malenovsky: It's no secret that the Americans had Corona spy satellites watching the launch complex at Baikonur since the mid-'60s. In early 1969, we had two N-1s on the pad, plus the Proton carrying the Lunokhod. We had to hurry to put another

Proton on the pad, after we launched the first Proton. It was a big Chinese fire drill, I believe you call it.

McAtee: Or bait and switch. It must have been pretty tricky.

Malenovsky: Right. That's why we did night launches so often. It was easier to hide things. And we had some favourable weather, overcast, all of which let us do it undetected. The circumlunar mission was problematic. We'd sent the unmanned Zond 5 around the Moon in September '68. In fact, we took the first pictures of the Earth from the Moon, before Apollo 8, but never released them. The flight itself was filled with problems, the 101K Earth Sensor failed, and the guided re-entry system shut down.

McAtee: Meaning?

Malenovsky: It meant we couldn't land Zond 5 in the Soviet Union, so we sent it into the Indian Ocean. Some heads rolled over that, since we couldn't have the lunar lander with the rock samples sit at the bottom of the ocean.

McAtee: What about the N-1s?

Malenovsky: We actually launched one a few hours later. It exploded seventy seconds into the flight. But it wasn't detected by Corona. We'd timed it right.

McAtee: And the transmissions from the supposedly manned spacecraft?

Malenovksy: Easy enough. We put a relay transmitter on board. We beamed signals from ground control to the Zond, and then those got looped back. It also meant that ground-based transmitters could pick up the signals. We were a little less strict about protocols that restricted interception of the signals. But not too strict, since we didn't want to appear too eager to have everyone listening in.

McAtee: It sounds like just as much ingenuity went into pulling off a fake moon launch as it would have taken to do it for real.

Malenovsky: You're probably right. But what choice did we have? It was a race, after all.

Sergei Kamarov, Soviet film producer, Mosfilm studios. Interview with Jonathan McAtee, 1 February 1996

McAtee: The stages where the lunar television transmissions were faked were at Baikonur?

Kamarov: No. The schedule was too tight. I mean, Afanasyev called me in the middle of January '69, summoned me to his office in Starry Town[7], and let me in on it. All of our equipment was in Moscow, at the Mosfilm studios, so it wasn't a big move. We had the Red Army at our disposal, so it got hauled out there in a day.

McAtee: The security must have been tight.

Kamarov: We were told that if word leaked out, we would be lucky if all we got was twenty years in the camps.

McAtee: Intimidating.

Kamarov: It was a great motivator. We had to have everything right, make it look convincing, or else we would disappear. Anyway, we set up in a building at the cosmonaut training center. They had mock-ups of the lunar lander there, as well as a mock-up of the modified Soyuz for the interior shots.

McAtee: You built a miniature lunar surface in one of the buildings there.

Kamarov: Right. It was amazing how easy it was, once the money started flowing. We had whatever we wanted, so money was no object. I had some of the best special effects people at Mosfilm at my disposal. We created a space one hundred by one hundred, taking up almost the whole building. The walls we painted flat black, with the ceiling. We carted truckloads of gravel and sand, crushed to a fine powder, and dumped it three feet deep on the floor.

McAtee: What about the horizon problem? The Moon's smaller, the horizon is nearer?

Kamarov: And with no atmosphere, there's a clarity to mountains ten miles away. Our prop people were the best, and did a fantastic job. We had to pile the crushed gravel just right, more in the middle. They trucked in the LK lunar lander in the middle

---

[7] The astronaut training complex around the Yuri Gagarin Cosmonaut Training Complex near Moscow

of the night before the launch was supposed to take place.

McAtee: What about the exterior shots, the docking of the L3 Soyuz and the LK? Khrunov had to do an EVA to transfer from the living compartment to the lunar lander, and that was broadcast.

Kamarov: They had a simulator, and we made a few additions to it, to make it more realistic. Add in some distortion effects, and it was entirely convincing. That was the docking. As for the EVA, we used wires. Khrunov flew around the Soyuz just like Peter Pan.

Interview with Vasily Mishin

McAtee: The LK lunar lander didn't exist in full form at the time you began the mission?

Mishin: No. Another wonderful example of the Soviet system. We had the whole N-1 and L3 system designed by late 1965. Korolev and OKB-1 bureau wanted to have an integrated programme, with the circumlunar vehicles and landing vehicles the same design. Chelomey wanted to do it piecemeal. So for a while we had *two* lunar programs, run by two different bureaus—Korolev's manned mission, and Chelomey's circumlunar mission! We had hearings, and finally Afansyev went with Korolev's design, after wasting time and money on Chelomey. No sooner had we done that than we had to redesign the Soyuz, chopping off the forward spherical compartment, leaving a bullet-shaped craft that could only be circumlunar. So the development of the lunar lander was delayed. By late 1968, we didn't really have a functioning model. It was a mess.

McAtee: How did you solve the problem?

Mishin: We had the film people and the OKB-1 staff working around the clock. The basic design was there. We only needed a mock-up that *looked* like it worked. The instruments didn't have to *do* anything.

McAtee: So behind the control panels?

Mishin: Nothing. Just wires leading to a battery. All those pretty flashing lights and gauges and dials—dummies. Every one of them. But pretty convincing.

McAtee: And what about the low gravity?

Mishin: That was harder. We put springy material in the heels of the boots that Khrunov wore—

McAtee: Why wasn't Leonov chosen to go in the lander?

Mishin: He refused. He said he wasn't going to do any more for this fraud than he had to. The only reason he got away with it, wasn't taken off the mission and sent to the camps was that he was already a Hero of the Soviet Union, for his first spacewalk back in '65. He wasn't some unknown trainee we could kill off in a jet crash or training accident. So Khrunov got the honours.

Interview with Sergei Kamarov

McAtee: How did you make the moonwalk look real?

Kamarov: It was a real feat. Khrunov's boots were filled with a springy material we had stolen from one of your shoe companies, and then we put real springs inside. The real trick was that the feeds weren't in real time.

McAtee: They weren't?

Kamarov: No. We taped it all, ran it through some distortion, and then slowed the tape down on replay. It looked real, and if it hadn't been for Bugova's defection[8], it wouldn't have come up.

McAtee: What about the wire?

Kamarov: (snorts) Minor. It didn't even get noticed until the whole thing was in full swing and the CIA and NASA were going over the tapes with every bit of image-enhancing technology available. But that wouldn't have done it. People talking about wires and strings would have been written off as cranks, up there with the flying saucer nuts.

Interview with Valeriy Mishin

McAtee: What about the wire?

Mishin: (sighs) Look, we had to make it appear real. So we figured

---

[8] Lev Bugova, 1948–

that planting a camera outside, and showing the upper stage of the LK-1 taking off would be even more proof. So we hauled in a huge crane, punched a hole in the ceiling, dropped a steel cable through, and on signal when the "rockets" fired, the crane lifted the upper stage. There was a small jerk, but that was about it. We covered it with signal distortion. But one of the fucking geniuses we used on the crew hadn't painted the cable. There were spots that were left bare, or barely covered. They showed up in the lights that we were using to simulate the sun. But the picture was so grainy that no one really noticed until much later.

The New York Times, 12 February 1973
MOON HOAX!
DEFECTOR SPILLS BEANS ON '69 MOON LANDING
MISSION SHOT FROM STUDIOS IN MOSCOW
APOLLO 18 MAY BE REDIRECTED TO SITE

Mexico City (UPI)—A Soviet defector today at a press conference claimed that the Soviet Moon landing in February 1969 was a hoax, televised from sound stages near Moscow.

If Lev Bugova is to be believed, Americans Neil Armstrong and Buzz Aldrin really were the first men to walk on the Moon on July 20, 1969...

Interview with Lev Bugova, CGI designer, Lucasfilm studios, by Jonathan McAtee, 22 June 1994

McAtee: You didn't defect to tell the world about the moon hoax?

Bugova: Of course not. I had intended to take that to my grave. Telling them about faking the first moon landing was a way to save myself. I wanted out because I was a Jew, and being a Jew in the Soviet Union was only slightly better than being a Jew in Hitler's Germany. I was at a film festival in Mexico City, slipped away from my KGB escorts, and took my wife to the American Embassy.

McAtee: You were initially denied an entry visa?

Bugova: Right. You Americans had a habit of handing defectors back. Remember Simas Kudrika?

McAtee: Somewhat. He jumped overboard in Boston—

Bugova: Martha's Vineyard. He was Lithuanian, jumped off the Sovetskaya Litva and landed on a Coast Guard cruiser, back in '70. The State Department messed around, and after ten hours the captain let the KGB board. Kudrika got ten years in a gulag, but he got to emigrate in '74, only because his grandmother was an American citizen. That was *détente* for you.

McAtee: Wasn't there an exception for Jews?

Bugova: Jackson-Vanik[9] wasn't passed until a year later. And it never really amounted to anything. Nixon was forced into signing it, but he and Kissinger were so focused in managing relations through appeasement that it was never really enforced. So I was looking at being sent back, with a bunk at Kolyma waiting for me, unless I could give them something big.

McAtee: What did you have in the way of corroboration?

Bugova: Physically, nothing. The security was tight. We weren't allowed to take photos, and we were searched by the KGB every night before we left. I had the information in my head.

McAtee: Did the CIA believe you?

Bugova: Not at first. But then some of their analysts began looking at the footage, and it began to add up. Apollo 18 launched two weeks after I showed up at the American Embassy. That gave the Americans the opportunity to prove me a liar.

Interview with Dr James C Fletcher, NASA Administrator (1869-1976), by Jonathan McAtee, 5 January 1995

McAtee: Bugova's story must have presented a problem with the Apollo 18 mission.

Fletcher: You have no idea. Apollo 18 was set to land in Copernicus Crater. The computers had been programmed, the crew had been planning landings on simulators with Copernicus, and almost literally at the last minute the CIA, NSA, NRO are

---

[9] The Jackson-Vanik Amendment granted most-favoured nation status to countries who granted their citizens the right of free movement abroad and emigration

telling us to land in Ptolemaeus. I told them it couldn't be done. They began saying that didn't sound like NASA's can-do spirit, and I told them it was simply endangering the astronauts.

McAtee: What changed your mind?

Fletcher: Joe Engle, the mission commander, immediately changed the simulators, they began preparing round the clock, so by the time they launched in April '73, Engle was ready to take it down in Ptolemaeus.

McAtee: The Russians wouldn't give you the exact coordinates of the landing, either.

Fletcher: No. They denied the whole thing at first, said Bugova was a drug addict, mentally ill, the works. But the CIA guys debriefing him said he was perfectly sane, no sign of drug use. Then they began claiming that the site, and the property left there, a flag and a few scientific instruments, were property of the Soviet government, and we would be trespassing. That's when we began getting suspicious.

McAtee: But the moon rocks were a problem.

Fletcher: Right. Our guys at NASA looked at a couple samples, compared them to the stuff that the Apollo missions had returned, and they matched.

McAtee: So Bugova might have been a plant.

Fletcher: There were some in the CIA who were pushing the idea that Bugova was another Penkovsky, a double agent sent to misdirect us. But we never could figure out a motive. But Bugova told us that they'd sent an unmanned rover there, to pick up some rocks and bring them back. An unmanned rover was within their capabilities, they'd sent a couple more of the Lunokhods in '70 and '71. So the NRO and NSA got hold of the telemetry from those missions, compared it to the Zond mission, and there was a match.

McAtee: But that still wasn't enough.

Fletcher: Right. They began running the footage from the surface back, comparing it to the Apollo footage. The Soviets hadn't shot a lot of film on the surface, maybe a few hours, poor quality stuff. Their lander was only on the surface for six hours before it lifted off. The CIA did some analysis, found the horizon wasn't quite right, the footage of Khrunov on the surface didn't match up with the shots of Armstrong, Aldrin, and the rest. But that wasn't going to be enough...

Transmission between Apollo 18 Lunar Module Endeavour and Mission Control, 21 April 1973 1734 hours CST

Engle: Contact light on.

CAPCOM: Roger that, Endeavour.

Evans: Shutdown.

Engle: Roger. Engine stop.

Evans: Mode Control, both Auto. Descent Engine Command Override, Off. Engine Arm, Off. 413 is in.

CAPCOM: We copy you down, Endeavor.

Engle: Smooth as glass. Master arm on, descent vent cleared.

CAPCOM: Roger. We read you two hundred, two-zero-zero south of Zond site.

Engle: Roger that. Looking through the port here. Can't see a thing. No flag.

[END AT T+ 108:35:40]

[BEGIN T+ 123:09:00]

Engle: We're approaching the coordinates on the rover, Houston. Ron's got a real leadfoot here.

CAPCOM: Roger. Ron, you're not driving your 'Vette. Slow down.

Evans: Engle's an old lady, I'm fine. We're there.

CAPCOM: What do you see?

Engle: Nothing. No flag, nothing. You sure they got it right?

CAPCOM: Positive.

Evans: Tell Neil and Buzz I owe them a hundred bucks. And congratulations.

New York Times, 30 April 1973

BREZHNEV OUT AS GENERAL SECRETARY

CPSU CENTRAL COMMITTEE OUSTS AFTER MIDNIGHT SESSION

UPROAR OVER ZOND FRAUD SAID TO BE MAIN CAUSE

ANDROPOV, HEAD OF KGB, NAMED AS REPLACEMENT

Moscow (UPI)—Leonid Brezhnev was removed from his post as General Secretary of the Communist Party after a late-night session of the CPSU's Central Committee. It was widely believed that confirmation by Apollo 18 astronauts that the Soviet Union's moon landing four years ago was a hoax was the prime motivating factor.

Other sources inside Moscow claimed that the move had been building for some time. Brezhnev's regime has been seen as corrupt and doing little to combat economic stagnation at home.

Brezhnev's replacement is Yuri V Andropov, fifty-nine, who has served as the Chairman of the KGB since 1967...

Stephen Ambrose, Nixon: Vindication, 1973-1977 (New York: Doubleday, 1994), p 98

The revelation that Armstrong and Aldrin had, after all, been the first men on the Moon had repercussions far beyond the space program. The most obvious was the toppling of Leonid Brezhnev after the New York Times first broke the story, and his replacement by KGB Chairman Yuri Andropov. Brezhnev had been seen as a reincarnation of Khrushchev, a peasant given to blustering, but manageable with a certain degree of flattery and concessions. Andropov was not to be so easily manipulated.

The shake-up in the Kremlin provided Nixon with a golden opportunity on the domestic front. The Watergate scandal had been gathering steam for a couple of months, since the Washington Post began covering the innocuous burglary of the Democratic Headquarters at the Watergate Hotel in June 1972. A slow drip or revelations had taken a mounting toll. On January 30, 1973, Liddy and McCord pleaded guilty to conspiracy charges, but whether a massive campaign of espionage against opponents had taken place, and if so who had ordered it, remained unanswered.

The accession of Andropov provided Nixon inspiration and a chance. In a meeting on February 25, 1973, aide Charles Colson told Nixon that the Administration would have to come clean. "If Brezhnev can't get away with it," Colson said, "You can't. And

Brezhnev counts himself lucky he didn't get shot." Haldeman and Ehrlichman reluctantly agreed.

After a retreat to Camp David, Nixon faced the cameras on March 3. He divulged that his orders had been misinterpreted by overzealous aides, and that he accepted personal responsibility. He announced the resignations of these aides, and promised cooperation with the US Attorney investigating the break-in, but declined to name a special prosecutor.

He followed up the speech by meeting with members of the House and Senate, focusing on Southern Democrats. Strom Thurmond (a recent defector to the GOP, but who still held influence over his fellow Southerners), John Stennis, Sam Ervin, John East, and Herman Talmage all came out in support of Nixon, and were joined by over forty members of the House. Any further moves by the Congress, such as an investigation, thus faced formidable obstacles.

Thurmond recalled that Nixon hinted that if the investigations turned up evidence of corruption, Nixon's actual complicity would be irrelevant. The Times and the Post, he liked to point out, had hated him since his uncovering of Alger Hiss as a Soviet spy back in 1948. With trust in the Presidency eroded, one of two options would present themselves: impeachment and trial by the Congress, or a resignation to prevent further damage—either of which would leave Spiro T Agnew as the thirty-eighth President to face the Communists' top spy.

That prospect brought the Southern Democrats around, joining forces with GOP stalwarts. Liberal Democrats fumed, and eventually moderate Republicans like Howard Baker of Tennessee fell into line. The public did as well, especially after Nixon's press conference of March 3, 1973.

Responding to Dan Rather of CBS News, Nixon, in a stunning *mea culpa*, admitted mistakes had been made. "They fall at my doorstep. Look at Russia—their leader isn't immune from taking responsibility for the actions of his subordinates. It's no different in a democracy. In fact, the standard is higher. People have a right to know if their President is a crook. Well, I'm not a crook. But if the Congress and the public believe that I am guilty, that I have committed high crimes and misdemeanors, then I will gladly offer up my resignation, effective immediately, rather than put the nation through the trauma of impeachment. I would only ask that this be done as expeditiously as possible, to prevent an erosion of world confidence in the United States in these critical times."

"Finally," the Los Angeles Times opined, "Nixon has confirmed what was long suspected—that Spiro Agnew is not only Nixon's life insurance policy, he's impeachment insurance as well." Similar sentiments echoed even in such former Nixon backers as the Wichita Eagle-Beacon, which began with "President Agnew—Eeeek!" In the end, though, it worked.

Nixon's poll ratings suffered, falling to 49% in March 1973 and bottoming out at 39% in October 1973, after the resignation of Agnew on corruption and bribery charges dating back to his days in Maryland. But the impeachment inquiry fizzled out, and Nixon completed his term.

Richard Nixon, Mandate for Leadership: Memoirs, Vol. 2, 1973-1977, pp 114-116.

Brezhnev's ousting from power by the Politburo in February 1973, coming on the heels of the revelations of the moon landing hoax, came as no surprise. Khrushchev had been undone by his failed bluff in Cuba, which had damaged Soviet prestige. The sudden discovery that Americans had, after all, been the first men on the Moon, proved too much for the Party leadership.

His replacement, Yuri V Andropov, made me wish for a fleeting moment that the hoax had never been discovered. Brezhnev was a typical Russian peasant, like most of the Communist leadership left over from the Revolution. He was a peasant, not a terribly educated man, simple in his tastes, and had a head easily turned by flattery, either real or hollow.

Andropov was the head of the KGB. He had a technical college education, and was a literate man. He had directed partisan guerilla activities during their Great Patriotic War (what we call World War II). He served as ambassador to Hungary in the 1950s, and led the brutal suppression of the revolution there in 1956, personally convincing Khrushchev that military intervention was necessary. When Imre Nagy and the rest of the Hungarian leadership were led to their deaths by Soviet duplicity, it was on Andropov's orders.

Andropov was more dangerous than Khrushchev, more even than Stalin, both peasants given to heated passions that blew furious one moment and were forgotten the next. Andropov was cold, calculating, something that came across at our summit in Washington several months after he was named General Secretary, and again in Moscow in 1974 and Reykjavik in 1975.

What America needed at that time of crisis was firm leadership, unencumbered by the distractions of scandals real or imagined. The stakes were never higher than in March 1973, when I finally confronted the issue of Watergate head-on. I had done much thinking over how to handle it. As President, it fell to me to take responsibility for the actions of my subordinates, and if they had done wrong, the law would deal with them. If the Congress believed that I was responsible, then I challenged them to take the appropriate measures at once, or forego the death by a thousand cuts of endless investigations. At that time, America deserved a firm, steady hand unencumbered by the distractions of petty political games.

Conversation between Nixon, Ehrlichman, Haldeman, and Colson, Oval Office, 1 March 1973 [From Nixon Presidential Library Archives, declassified 29 February 2008]

P: [expletive deleted] Rodino, and these [expletive deleted] subpoenas.

C: It's nothing. We've gone over this. We've got executive privilege.

E: Are they gonna buy that?

C: Ike used it. So did FDR. And I'll bet we can show that Kennedy used it.

P: The press will love that. But they'll never go for it. This is going to get out of control.

C: Raise the stakes.

H: What?

C: This is a poker game. They're putting their chips in, Mr

President. You've got to raise the stakes, get them to fold.

E: What sort of raise?

C: You go on TV and tell Congress that unless they wrap this up in ninety days, you're going to resign—

H: Preposterous.

P: Let him finish.

C: They close this up in ninety days, either shutting down the hearings or impeaching you, or you'll resign.

H: [expletive deleted] are you thinking?

E: You've lost it, Chuck.

C: Who the [expletive deleted] wants Agnew as President? Head to head with the head of the KGB? It's perfect. You've got to have bigger [expletive deleted] than Rodino and the rest of the Democrats.

P: It's a risk. But you're right. No one wants Agnew sitting here. [expletive deleted] We should have ditched him in '72. But the conservatives would have killed us. I should've gone with Connally.

H: You'd have to sell it to the party first.

P: We can get some of the Southerners in here. Strom can bring them around, just like he did in '68.

E: You're actually going to do this?

P: It'll shut down Rodino and Ervin and the Democrats.

E: What about the Post?

C: We'll deal with that. And we'd better do it now, because Agnew's got problems of his own back in Baltimore. If we're going to do this, it's got to be now.

New York Times, 17 November 1973

DEATH RULED ACCIDENTAL

Washington (AP)—The Virginia Highway Patrol today ruled that the death of Washington Post Reporter Bob Woodward in a car crash last week was not the result of foul play. The police report indicates that a combination of fatigue and bad road conditions led to the accident on a Virginia highway. A toxicology report is pending, and police did not eliminate alcohol or drugs as a contributing factor.

David Remnick, The Shadow of Lenin (New York: Viking Press, 2011)

It may be fairly said that the monumental embarrassment of the exposure of the Soviet Moon Landing as a fraud in February 1973 ultimately saved the country. In the short run, it caused no end of headaches for the Party leadership. Most visibly, it almost certainly cost the Soviet Union the chance to host the 1980 Olympics. When the IOC met in October 1974 in Vienna, it chose Los Angeles as the host city; the Russians would have to wait until 1984 to host the Games.

Late-night comedians had a field day with the matter. It even became the inspiration for a now-forgotten 1978 movie, Aries One, about a Soviet Mars mission that succeeds, but is not believed (also remembered for a minor role by OJ Simpson as the first African cosmonaut, before his later notoriety).

In the long run, though, the Moon Hoax gave the Soviet Union the leadership it needed, and the kick required to shake off the encrustations of the slow stagnation of the Brezhnev years. Yuri Andropov was by no stretch of the imagination a liberal democrat; *Glasnost* would have to await the accession of Boris Yeltsin in 1988.

Andropov's call for *perestroika*, or an economic restructuring, fell on fertile ground. Some hard-liners, notably Alexander Yakovlev, resisted the changes, insinuating that it amounted to a "return of the nepmen"[10]. Given Andropov's former title, and his ongoing ties to the KGB, such criticisms were muted.

The Soviets, pushing ahead in the Space Race, first to orbit, then to the Moon (for real in 1985), and then to Mars, carried a double burden. They had to be ahead, they had to do it right, and there could be no question whatsoever about the genuineness of their accomplishment. When Andropov ceded the Kurile Islands,

---

[10] Nepmen were those who, under Lenin's New Economic Plan of 1922, profited from the quasi-capitalist reforms that were necessary in the wake of the Revolution and the Civil War

taken at the end of World War II, back to Japan in 1982, in exchange for a treaty that guaranteed a huge transfer of high technology and machine tools, it was a huge leap forward for the Soviet Union as a whole. The Reagan Administration could bluster all it wanted, but the Soviet Salyut and then Mir stations, the Buran shuttles, and the later Zond lunar craft were all run by Japanese computers, their parts tooled by Japanese machines.

What occurred with Apollo in the United States soon replicated itself in the Soviet Union—the spillover of technological know-how from the military-industrial complex to the civilian sector. Although it took longer, and was not as widespread, by the beginning of the twenty-first century the average Soviet citizen enjoyed a standard of living comparable to that of the average Westerner.

Interview with Vasily Mishin

McAtee: So in the end—

Mishin: In the end it was beneficial. But it was an accident. The thing you have to understand about the whole system is that it was enormously wasteful. Those first launches, Sputnik, Vostok, Voshkhod, and then Zond, all of them nothing more than publicity stunts.

McAtee: But they were successful, weren't they? Didn't you demonstrate the apparent superiority of Soviet science and technology?

Mishin: Not necessarily. Sputnik happened because Khrushchev was new in power and needed a spectacular triumph to cement his hold on power. Same thing with Vostok, take away some of the spotlight from Kennedy telling the world the Americans would go to the Moon. And then after Kennedy made that speech, well, Khrushchev just couldn't sit back and take it, no, he had to push Korolev to build a moon rocket. I'm convinced it was all the pushing that finally killed Sergei Pavlovich [Korolev] back in '66.

McAtee: I thought it was the botched surgery—

Mishin: Which he had because Khrushchev kept making all these demands on him, and then letting Glushkov hamstring the operations. And his years in the camps under Stalin did him no good. But I digress. The whole thing was a big political show, from beginning to right now. The damned politicians, I don't care whose side they're on, they can't let well enough alone.

McAtee: But haven't the governments provided the funding? Without that, none of the missions could have occurred.

Mishin: But the money always comes with strings. With short-sighted idiots who only care about braying their greatness to the public, rather than making true progress. Without all that, the process would have been fairly orderly. First develop orbital transports, establish permanent stations in orbit, use those for jumping-off points to the Moon and Mars, and finally the outer planets. Then the stars themselves.

McAtee: It sounds like what von Braun laid out in his Collier's articles in 1951.

Mishin: (with a sound of disgust) Unfortunately, yes. But even for an unregenerate fascist, he was right about that. So here we are, sitting in a climate-controlled room, looking out at the lunar surface, and all of the signs of progress that Soviet Power has brought to the stars.

Pravda, 4 July 2017

TSIOLKOVSKY LEAVES EARTH ORBIT

Moscow (TASS)—The SS Konstantin Tsiolkovsky departed its orbital dock at 0530 GMT, headed for the planet Mars. The pulsed xenon ion drive will accelerate the ship to several hundred thousand kilometres per hour. Glavkosmos has set arrival time in Martian orbit for 1 November. The Tsiolkovsky's crew will then descend to the surface on 4 November, to mark the centennial of the Revolution.

A crew of international observers was on hand at the Gagarin space platform to watch the mission's departure...

Sam Kepfield was born in 1963, and raised in western Kansas. He graduated from Kansas State University in 1986, and received his law degree from the University of Nebraska in 1989. He later completed post-graduate work in history at the University of Nebraska and the University of Oklahoma. He practices law full-time in Hutchinson, Kansas, in order to support his writing habit. His work has appeared in Science Fiction Trails, Aiofe's Kiss, Electric Spec, Jupiter SF, as well as a number of anthologies. In 2009, his story 'Salvage Sputnik' was a winner in the Robert A Heinlein Centennial Short Story Contest.

THE TAKING OF IOSA 2083

CJ Paget

"AH, HERE HE is. In this corner," says Xilou. Boris floats in the centre of a poorly-made web. The basic instincts assert themselves even out here where there's nothing for Boris to catch. Em stomps up the wall in her gecko shoes and scoops him up in her hands. Boris is one of the few non-human creatures to have made it this far from Big Blue, having gotten himself flash-frozen into a shipment of medicines. A big old spider, slow-moving, possibly blind, probably female, and missing two legs, but Emily loves him. Xilou, who's always despised Earth's creepy creatures herself, takes this as a good sign that Em is developing down her own path.

"You're a bad boy, Boris," says Em, "always running away." She jumps to the makeshift vivarium, confident in the only gravity she knows, and drops Boris back in his home. He falls dream-slowly in the near non-existent g, scrabbling madly at the air as he goes.

"He is naughty, isn't he?" says Xilou, crouching next to the child. "He should scan that sometimes you have to do as you're told by people who know best, hmm?" Hard to believe it, here she is pushing the same bilge that command fed them during the wars. But that's motherhood.

Em looks up and smiles, making Xilou's chest ache. Em's face is that of the child Xilou might have been, but never was, as Xil was born full-grown from a jar. Em came from a jar too, for Xilou lacks the natural equipment to produce her. Xil brushes back the child's hair, remembers being asked what colour she wanted it to be. She said 'purple', one of those embarrassing mistakes you make when you're a neut who never grew real hair of your own. Filling all the gaps in Xil's DNA has cost her a small fortune: cloning's not cheap, especially not for an old neut who's a deserter from the Warring Moons and runs on the wrong side of the law.

"Now," says Xilou. "You stay in here with Boris, honey. Mommy's got some business to attend to."

Em runs to her only other real possession, the old cookie-cooking toy, a present from one of Xil's surviving wing-sistas who gave it to her that day, back on Ganymede, when Em came screaming out of the jar. You feed the toy scraps and it breaks them down to chemistry, and reassembles them to approved, customisable templates from its internal database, mostly cookies. It takes time to cook though, and Xilou can tell Em uses the device as a means to prolong their time together, to delay the inevitable abandonment. She suspects that Boris's frequent escape artistry has a lot to do with Em's need for attention, a need that Xilou struggles to provide.

"I progged a new flava, innit?" says Em, concentrating furiously as she selects options on the device's touch-sensitive skin.

"Where did you learn to speak like that?" asks Xilou, making her voice sharp like she's heard teachers and other mothers do, getting a startled look from Em that tells her she's doing it right. "I've programmed a new flavour," she corrects, "and never say 'innit', I won't have you talking like a dodger." She puts an arm round Em to take the edge off the reprimand, and together they wait for the 'cooking' lights to stop flashing on the device. The cookie launches from the slot in the top, sailing upwards in the low-g, varicoloured with clashing greens and reds: one of Em's experimental concoctions. Fortunately one of the things they didn't give neuts, because you don't need it to fly a warboat, is a sense of taste.

✦

"Thank you all for coming," says Xilou. "Sorry to keep you waiting."

The people anchored around the table keep their faces blank and expectant. She's "Madam Xil" here, and gets the most respect she's had since leaving her wing-sistas and being a coffin-dodger for the Ganymedian Republic, a lifetime and millions of kilometers ago. Like all neuts she bought the hair implants, boobs, learned to speak 'proper', tried to act 'normal', tried to conceal her birdlike, low-mass form. Wasted money. Now she knows: power, that's what brings respect and acceptance.

She sits between Mr Black and Mr White, the only members of her tiny organisation that she'll be taking with her. Deserters like her, but normals trained for boarding actions and those still-born ground assaults on Europa. They've been her most loyal foot-soldiers since she got them off the Warring Moons. Black is White and White is Black, though the skin colour's surely cosmetic in both cases. They spend so much time in each other's pockets that Xilou suspects they're an item, not that she really understands what that means. The others are carefully chosen as useful and sane people who, like her, do what they must, having found their choices limited wherever they've run.

"I have bad news," she announces. "Titania isn't working out. This colony is failing, dying. Most of the people will die with it." She sees reactions flicker across faces like gas giant lightning, microexpressions too complex for a blank-faced neut to parse. "The seedstock we bought with us was telomere-locked to only reproduce for a fixed number of generations. I don't know by who, or how far back in its ancestry. I know that we haven't been able to source alternatives, and that the hydroponics yields are now failing. The administration's keeping it quiet, but soon it'll be obvious and then things'll get ugly. They're already bartering our own fuel supplies for food. I plan on getting out. You're all here because you have useful skills and no real family. You can't bring anyone with you, this is a very limited escape plan. That rule doesn't apply to me, I will be bringing someone. If you have a problem with that, then I suggest you leave now and make other arrangements."

None of them go. She pushes, "Go now, or you're in this to the death."

None of them go.

"If you talk, to anyone, then Mr Black and Mr White will have a talk with you," she warns. "Now, Mr Latimer has an escape plan for us. If you would, Mr Latimer?"

Latimer stands carefully, he's an Earthwor— an *Earther*, with an Earther's physique, and prone to accidentally springing himself into the ceiling. He smiles his "let's make lots of money" smile. He's not, in Xilou's opinion, a good thief, but he's always the man with the plan. He taps the table and it bursts into pixellated life, displaying a lumpen, pockmarked thing with a shining tail.

"IOSA-Twenty-Eighty-Three," he says. "Arriving here in about two hundred hours."

"A comet?" says Sang-Anne. "What do we do with that?"

"Someone's already done it." Latimer operates menus displayed in the table's surface. The comet becomes a cutaway schematic, showing internal chambers. "While we've been bleeding into this worthless moon the smart money's been on comets. The ice shields you from cosmic radiation and provides minerals, hydrocarbons, drinking water, oxygen, hydrogen, and reaction-mass. A couple of radioisotope heaters jammed into the surface will give you an effective steam rocket. You want faster: install a fission reactor. The big comets are hollow worlds, cities in flight, homes to tens, or hundreds, of thousands of people. But they stay out in the deep black, don't risk themselves. This is a pebble, two hundred metres long, part of a fleet operating out of one of the cities. It's coming here to trade."

"Crew?" asks Mr White, who knows what's coming.

"Ten, maybe. But most of them will be in deep hiber, saving resources. They'll hibernate in shifts, only all coming awake when they visit somewhere significant, and we're not significant. Titania has two automated surface-to-orbit lighters, one's being loaded now with anything we can strip and sell. Thirteen people is the most extra payload we think we can get away with. The lighter should compensate for the extra mass automatically. Plan is: we ride up and take the ship."

"We take the ship, and it takes us where we want to go, then we give it back and say we're sorry," says Xilou. "And no one gets hurt. We have no quarrel with these people, and this isn't something I want to do. It's survival. If anyone does get hurt without good reason, the person responsible will answer directly to me." She sweeps her gaze slowly round the table over each of them. Disconcerting stares are easy when you're a neut, it's the natural state of your face.

✦

The lighters look more like buildings than flying machines. In Titania's airless night they've no need of wings or streamlining, or elegance, they're just black boxes with a hypergolic firecracker buttressed to each corner, the brute application of Newton's second law. Xilou's suit HUD displays infrared, ultraviolet and photo-multiplied optical in false colours, overlaying the dim scene with a garish colour-scheme like corrupted video. Without the suit's electronic senses, the darkness would be nearly total. Suit-vision always reminds her of her dodging days, when data was fed straight into her wired brain. She still has the skull-jack, of course, but ironically there's nothing out here advanced enough to interface with it.

They ride, hidden among crates and canisters, on a flatbed made of ice with independently powered smart-wheels bolted to it. A child-sized suit slumps in the circle of Xilou's arm. Xenon is one of their few exports, it's good fuel for ion thrusters, but also works as a general anesthetic. Xilou monitors Em's breathing mix and bio-signs, not trusting that task to anyone else. The lies she's told Em about how she makes a living are brittle things that must be protected, and the xenon is one way of doing that.

"Can't see no one," says Mr White over suit-link. "Don't like this, Latimer will have talked, he never stops talking. They'll be waiting."

Just two days ago, Latimer got caught trying to convert local currency into something more widely tradable and illegal. Typical of him to over-reach and crash out of his own plan.

"No, he'll stay sealed," says Xilou, "he'll know he's got a sleeper contract on his ass." Automated systems will handle the announcement, bidding and payment for the hit, unless Xilou sends a 'cancel' transmission in time. Still, she lays Em gently down and picks up her gun. Homebrewed by Black and White from scavenged materials, it has bullets powered by electrically triggered aluminium/ice nanopropellant and one of those multipurpose automation processors for targetting and data. When the thumb of her suit touches the processor's data-contacts her HUD says she's got twenty shots and overlays a targetting grid.

The flatbed shudders to a halt and they drop from it, pushing themselves downwards, falling like snowflakes and landing with the grace of fairies. Automated sleds are loading the lighter with bundles of uranium fuel rods, their major export. The rods, slightly warmer than the ambient 80 Kelvin, shine a little in Xilou's infra-red vision.

They're not getting in the main hold with that.

Black and White make a big show of 'sweeping the area for hostiles', but find nothing and no one. Xilou feels a little sorry for them, it's a reminder of the war, in which only neuts and starved-thin girls lying in goo-filled g-coffins see any action, and ground-grunts march about or sit in tin-can troopships, and if the action finds them, they never even know it.

The lighter's side is curtained with kevlar webbing, simple pockets to hold low-mass loads when the main hold is full. Jumping up the sides of the craft is easy in Titania's weak gravity, then you just undo the zips in the webbing, climb in, and hold on. Xilou makes sure Em is firmly secured, then sends the message to cancel the sleeper hit. Latimer will live to lie another day.

When it comes, it's not so much. The engines don't roar, they burp. There's a brief flicker of brightness, shocking Xilou's dark-adapted eyes and then the ground falls away. The launch-field shrinks to a dot; the chasm the colony hides in spools out below her; then it's like looking down on a map, she can pick out the famous features, like the giant ridiculously-named crater, Gertrude.

Titania becomes a thrown ball, a discarded thing speeding away into the endless night. The universe crowds in. Out here on the perimeter there are more stars than you ever believed, out here there's an endless wrap-around vista of sparkles, of possible worlds held forever out of reach. The memories come back, the ones she's buried down deep. Memories of what she was made for, of the warboat that was her true body, of tactical lighting up her brain with its pretty patterns, of the power and terrible glory of being a thing that hunts through this endless darkness, savage and unthinking and alive. Oh, she aches for it, oh the night calls to her, telling her to throw herself into its endless embrace.

Xilou turns her back on the universe, presses her visor against Em's, stares at the sleeping face within, and tells herself,

That's all behind me now.

Overhead something swells from a dot, to a fingernail, to a fist. A fist of ice and darkness.

✦

In their suit's photo-multiplied vision the comet is a vast rainbow-filled black diamond, rather than an ugly, flying mountain of ice and crap. Titania's scarred face looms below, showing no sign of human presence. The colony could be airless ruins already for all you can see. They clamber up the lighter's side, holding onto the kevlar webbing or using their grip-gloves to make sure they stay fixed to something, don't bounce themselves away into the endless night. Xilou carries Em securely strapped to her back. The sound of sleeping breath fades in and out over their suit-to-suit link. Em's possessions, the vivarium and cookie-cooker, float in a webbing-bag clipped to her suit. Xilou doubts Boris will survive the coming journey, how long do spiders live anyway? She slaps one hand, then the other onto the great wall of ice, triggering her grip-gloves. Thousands of tiny electroactive polymer tendrils shoot into the cracks and crevices of the ice. In the next instant a current flows and the tendrils expand to many times their original diameter, filling those cracks. Her hands are stuck as though frozen to the ice.

"This thing's huge," says Mr Black, his voice raspy over their suit-link. "Crew of ten? It could hold thousands." Their suits form a line-of-sight optical comms network, they can speak without fearing detection.

"This one's a baby," says Xilou. "Not even that." She mutters the 'left release' command and the tendrils flow back into her left glove. She reaches as far forwards as she can, palms the ice and triggers the glove once more. "Right release," she says.

They crawl swift and easy over the ancient, space-worn surface. Only once does Mr White hiss "Down!", and they freeze, watching something run along the small horizon, something that looks like Boris but mechanical and big as Em herself. Black and White track its motion very precisely with their guns. Xilou copies, unable to resist her neut programming: *if you don't know what to do, mimic someone who does.* But if they shoot at it, the comet's crew will be alerted and that's game over.

The thing scuttles on its way, leaving them to scuttle away on theirs.

Eventually the disposal lock, slightly warmer than the ice it pokes out of, shines in their suit-HUDs. This is Sang-Anne's show. Sang-Anne is very definitely a good thief. She works with mysterious tools and swift precision around the outer edge of the circular lid. There's a flicker of electrical sparking and the lid opens, slowly. Mr Black and Mr White do a strange dance, taking it in turns to point their weapons down the shaft. Move, stop, wait. Move, stop, wait. Xilou is never sure what she's seeing with Black and White, but she knows it's very good, that they're highly trained, you can see it in the choreography.

White pushes himself up, launching himself over the opening, and Black grabs his shoulders and thrusts him down into it, there being no real gravity to do that job. Black sits back from the edge, furtively peering over it at irregular intervals. Eventually they hear White say, "Clear".

"Sang-Anne, you're next," says Black. "Come here."

Sang-Anne does as she's told. As soon as she's close enough Black picks her up and throws her down the shaft. Her shriek is cut short when the suit-link loses line-of-sight connection.

"What did she think was going to happen?" says Black, bemusedly. "Amateurs. Okay, Leif, you're next."

One by one by one they are thrown down the shaft, into a darkness so absolute that the only things visible are the heat-traces of each other. They collect at the bottom of the shaft like beans in a can. Xilou imagines one of those spider-robots charging down this shaft, would they even know before it slammed into them, pulping them against the ice-floor? But no, that's not the way it'll happen. This is a disposal shaft: a chamber under the floor can be explosively filled with ice-steam, launching the floor and everything stacked on it up the shaft and into the black. That's how it will happen, if the crew detect their presence.

Sang-Anne is already hacking the entry-system that's embedded in the ice, just holding her suited hand against it, unmoving, like she's trying to break in by magic or force of will. Most of what she's carrying is software, and that mostly just secret lists of backdoor passwords for various systems. Not big, not clever, but she can name her price while no one else has the password list.

A white light pulses within the ice beneath Sang-Anne's palm. The outer door of the airlock slides open. Xilou checks Em's bio-status. Black, White, and a couple of the other tough guys crowd into the lock. It closes behind them. Everyone else waits for the other door to open, disgorge the advance party, close, the lock to cycle, and White to announce "Clear" to the rest of the team. Sang-Anne does her magic again, and the next group go through.

Surely they must know we're here now, thinks Xilou. But maybe not. Latimer says the parts of these makeshift ships aren't always joined up. Stand-alone systems are distributed throughout the vast bulk of the ice, sometimes smart and swimming in a sea of mutual radio-chatter, but sometimes dark and unmonitored. Perhaps this airlock is unsupervised, unwatched, undefended. It must be, or they'd surely have been thrown into the weightless night by now.

She goes through with the last group, into a maze of dark corridors. Their suits provide directions, following Latimer's schematics. Xilou wonders if all these comets are dug out into a standard topography, or if Latimer obtained details of this one in particular.

Eventually, ahead there's light. Dim light, too weak to see by if not for their suits' enhanced vision. Audio too: voices. Laughter. A girl's voice. Xilou feels that new creepy feeling that she never felt in the war: guilt. White's voice whispers over the suit-link, "We all go in together, a show of force. There's no point doing it any other way, we've nowhere to retreat to and they control the systems, once they know we're here, it's over. I'm downloading a tactical program to everyone's suit, you just follow the arrows and prompts, like a game. If anyone starts firing, you start firing, but if you start firing and you can't justify it after, then you'll be chewing vacuum. Most importantly, walk don't run, trying to run will spring you off the floor."

A countdown appears in Xilou's suit-HUD, just like a launch sequence in her dodging days. "Get ready. Go in three... two... one..."

"WALK!" it commands, an arrow pointing the way. But Mr

Black doesn't walk, he launches himself into the chamber, flying, looking down the barrel of his weapon. Xilou marches after her arrow, following the directions *go here, aim there*. Mr White stays standing in the corridor, monitoring them through the data-links of their suits, switching between them, deploying them like pawns in a chess game.

The chamber's cathedral-big, filled with blue lozenges that look like her warboat's g-coffin. So many of them, hundreds at least. One of the tough guys tries to run, despite the warning, and is off across the room, spinning end-over-end like a discarded booster. The three people, two girls and a boy alike as triplets, lock dark eyes onto him and watch bemusedly as he pinwheels before them. Xilou names them in her head, One-girl, Two-girl, and Boy. They're clones, pretty and genadapted, eyes with large pupils and eyeshine that says they have a reflective tapetum, like cats.

Xilou's suit walks her to them, and the HUD says "TALK!" By the time she arrives Mr White has himself anchored, his gun leveled at their faces, and they have their hands on their heads. Two-girl is clearly the baby of the group, she looks close to blubbing. Boy looks proudly defiant. One-girl looks strangely amused.

Shouldn't they look surprised?

"All we want is a ride," says Xilou. "In-system to Jovian space. After that, we'll leave you. How many people can you carry awake for that long?"

"What?" says One-girl. "Are you crazy? None!"

"Don't lie to me," says Xilou, "or I'll hurt your sister." She swings her gun to point at Two-girl, and hopes One-girl doesn't call her bluff.

"It's true," says Boy, his words coming out so fast that they trip over each other. "That's an eight-month journey. Do you know how many calories a person needs when they're out of hiber?"

"How. Many. People?" says Xil.

"One," says One-girl. "Two at a pinch, but by the end you'd be eating—"

"I'll manage," says Xilou. Neuts are low-maintenance: designed that way. "Now, put your sister into hiber. No funny stuff, I want to watch the procedure."

"But—"

"Do it."

One-girl takes her sister's arm, and leads her to one of the hiber-coffins. Xilou is struck by how calm they are, normals usually get agitated, imagining all manner of improbable things, but the girls act more like neuts: comfortable as long as they have orders to follow. Shock, Xilou assumes. Two-girl lies in the casket, snake-like tubes grow from it, sliding through vents in her clothes, biting into her flesh, finding arteries, pumping in drugs. The lid closes as Two-girl's face slackens and her breathing slows.

"It's mostly automated," says One-girl, seemingly annoyed at Xil watching over her shoulder. "You just put them in."

Xilou watches the casket's status display, watches One-girl's hands. Contrary to popular belief, neuts are perfect mimics, that's why they're so bad at emulating normal behavior, because they can only repeat, perfectly, what they've been shown. But show a neut something once...

"That's it?" says Xilou.

"That's it," says One-girl. "She's under."

"Okay. Everyone, pick a casket, strip to your underwear, get in," says Xilou. "Quickly now, once the lighter finishes unloading we'll be on our way." She gun-waves One-girl back to her brother. "Mr Black, keep an eye on these two, if you would. Any funny stuff, shoot them, we can always wake one of their brothers or sisters; I'm sure there's more than a few of those in these caskets, right?"

One-girl and Boy nod their clone heads, disturbingly calm. Xilou wishes they'd act more, well, 'normal', less neut. One-girl gives her a sideways look that Xilou can't parse, and that at least is normal.

Xilou moves quickly from casket to casket, operating the controls as she saw one-girl do. The casket-lids close. Soon everyone is sleeping, except her and Black and One-girl and Boy. "Now you," Xilou tells Boy. She walks to one of the remaining caskets.

Boy walks to a different one.

Xilou feels the hairs stand up on the back of her neck. She

doesn't have hairs, she's a neut, but phantom follicles prickle across her skin all the same. "Where are you going?" she asks.

Boy looks at her like she's being stupid. "Not that one," he whispers, like he only wants her to hear it.

But Mr Black hears anyway. "What does that mean?" he asks, swinging his gun to point at Boy. "Some caskets are special?"

One-girl emits a piercing, inhuman scream. Black swings his attention, and gun, to her.

There's the bang of a hiber-coffin lid being kicked open, Two-girl rises from the cryptobiotic dead like something from a corny dreamadrama. There's a loud, mechanical rattle. The bullets lift Black from the deck, globs of blood exploding from the ruined face-mask of his suit. Xilou points her own weapon at Two-girl, who freezes, watching her sideways.

"What the fuck did you let them bring guns up for?" asks One-girl.

The silence rings around them. Xilou wonders why they're still talking to her. Who do they think she is? "They wouldn't come otherwise," she says.

Two-girl's looking at her funny, like she's a diagnostic that doesn't scan. "You're Sawyer, right?"

Xilou thinks fast, fast as she would in her warboat when it screamed 'Incoming!' and pumped her full of nutterdrine. 'drine changes you, you never really slow down again, and fear, fear's nature's own 'drine. If she says she's 'Sawyer', she'll have to prove it, some code-word, some piece of shared knowledge that she ought to know. When she doesn't... "No," she says, "Sawyer won't come up here, Sawyer don't trust no one. Sent me instead."

"Tell him to come up with a less fucking elaborate plan next time," says One-girl. She goes over to where Black floats in a nebula of red jelly, grabs him and starts dragging him to a hiber-coffin, unclipping suit-clasps as she goes.

"What are you doing with him?" asks Xilou.

"Most of him's still good," says the One-girl, stuffing Black's body into the coffin.

"Why would you ask that, if you knew Sawyer?" says Two-girl.

"What is this?" asks Xilou, voice calm despite the thudding in her chest. She keeps her gun and attention on Two-girl, and hopes no one else is aiming at her from the darkness.

"What do you think?" asks Two-girl.

Xilou takes an optimistic guess, "You're slavers." It makes some sense, new societies need cheap labour, it's all there in the history blits. It wouldn't be so bad, she figures, so long as she and Em were sold to the same keeper. It'd be life, better than staying here to starve.

"We've got machines," says Two-girl. "No one needs slaves."

Xilou backs up, needing space to think, and collides with a casket. So many caskets. Something bumps against her side and she puts her free hand on it, keeping her eyes on Two-girl. She recognises the shape, Em's cookie-cooker. "You've been sold locked seed-stock too," she guesses.

"Everyone has. Long-term investment strategy by some group called Biocorp. They sowed their seeds to the sky when the first dreamers went up, and those seeds have bred and spread, generation after generation, until now a thousand new nations find their harvests failing. Oh, eventually someone will engineer a solution, something edible that breeds true, but till then Biocorp can name their price, and the single most precious commodity after anti-matter," she glances to hiber-coffins arranged in ranks around them, "is going to be protein."

The thing strapped to Xilou's back stirs, and she hears a sleepy whimper through the suit-link.

"Alas, there's only one source of protein that ships itself, wide-eyed and hopeful out to the far edge. And us," says Two-girl. "Most of the far colonies have started selling their surplus."

"Surplus?"

"People who are no use, who are just a burden on the colony. New arrivals, mostly, incomers looking to make their fortune on this dark frontier."

Xilou thinks of Ganymede. Home, that was. She remembers how, every time the warring stopped, people started talking about the 'neut problem': *what do we do with these things we've made to fight our war for us?* She knows who'll be 'surplus' if things start getting tight back Jovian way.

"It's survival," says Two-girl. She drops her gun, pushing it so it floats down into the casket, and steps out, her gecko-shoes connecting to the floor with a sound like kisses. "Shoot, or don't.

You know you're not getting off this ship."

Somehow, while her attention has been focused on Two-girl, One-girl and Boy have vanished, like fish that can flick their tails and disappear into the night.

"Maybe not," says Xilou, "but I can take you fuckers with me." She pulls out Em's cookie-cooker, depresses the activation stud. Its big red lights strobe in the sepulchral gloom.

"And what's that?" asks Two-girl.

"Souvenir of where I'm from," says Xilou, she holds the flashing thing up to her faceplate so Two-girl can clearly see her neut face. "Cubane bomb. Once I release this stud, we've got thirty seconds to enter the deactivation code."

Two-girl looks hard into Xilou's visor, eyes narrowing. She's looking for those secret signals that normal people have, the ones a neut can't really see; the ones neuts try to spot, so they can practice them and pretend. *That's right, bitch*, thinks Xilou. *Look into my neut face for answers, and good luck with that.* She smiles, one muscle at a time, like she used to, back when she was learning to do it, back when her wing sistas would laugh and say, *Not like that Xil, that's just creepsy, innit? Like this*, and she'd try again and still get it wrong.

"You're bluffing," says Two-girl.

"You scan what I am, innit?" says Xil. Her dodger's diction is coming back to her, that verbal shield that you hid behind when you were a neut among normals, a dodger among c-darts, a statistic waiting to happen. "You scan why I's here? Runnin'. Time's when the warrin' stops and everyone's gotta be besties, they need someone to blame for the things they done. Always they blame a neut, 'cos we got no mas and pas to stand up for us. I was just followin' orders, but they said I done a crime, so I ran. Took this in case they ever come lookin', 'case I was ever cornered. This much cubane will bust this ice-ball like an egg and blow us all to dodger's dock, 'ceptin you ain't one of us, so you'll be goin' someplace else. Someplace cold, I imagine." She takes a step forwards.

Two-girl takes a step back, and Xil knows she has her.

"Well?" asks Xilou. "What's it gonna be, bitch? Stay, or go?"

Two-girl looks up and to one side, Xilou suspects she's somehow conversing with the others, like Xil used to hear her sistas' thoughts when they flew as a wing, like she'd hear her boat telling trajectories and threat evaluations. *Come on*, she wishes. *Believe, believe, believe.*

The decision comes. "Go," says Two-girl, pointing the direction with her chin.

"Not without the rest of my wing," says Xil.

"It's too late for that. These hiber-caskets... they're not fully operational. They're just killing jars."

So Xilou goes, walking backwards through the maze of coffins, Two-girl following, giving curt directions, the darkness behind her crawling with heat-sources now: they're not alone. Em's breathing seems louder and less rhythmic, Xilou prays she's not about to wake up, that would be one too many variables on tactical. The cookie-cooker begins to steam, the vapour building in a bubble around it, not knowing where to go in the zero-gee.

"We could use someone like you," says Two-girl. "In the coming war."

"War?" says Xilou, hoping that talking will keep Two-girl's attention away from what's happening with the 'cubane bomb'. Unless, of course, she's already noticed and is leading Xil to some place where the trap can be sprung.

"You think we're happy about what we're forced to become, about what's going to happen to everyone out here? No. Biocorp have sown, now they're going to reap. There's a thousand, thousand ice-balls bouncing around out here for us to harvest into a fleet. A fleet unlike any that's ever been seen. We just need people to fly them. People like you. We're going to go back to Earth, and bomb it till they give us Biocorp, every man, every woman, even the janitors."

"No," says Xilou. "My dodgin' days are done. I just want—"

The cooker emits a loud, electronic 'ping!' that Xil doesn't remember it ever doing before. Bite-sized cookies in the shape of eight-legged beasties with smiley marzipan faces explode from the top of it.

Two-girl gives a small scream and jumps back hard enough for her gecko-soles to disconnect and leave her drifting. Xilou presses her back to the nearest wall, briefly forgetting that she's got Em strapped there. She points the gun into the darkness, and wonders, if she started firing now, would she get them all?

Does it matter either way?

Two-girl starts laughing so hard that it folds her up where she floats. Other voices, most like echoes of Two-girl's own, join in from the darkness.

"Go," groans Two-girl, barely able to speak for laughter. She waves Xilou to a door in the ice. It hums open. Beyond it is a familiar docking-corridor: The lighter.

Xilou backs swiftly towards it. Figures leap from the darkness, snatching at the floating cookies, startling Xilou and making her jerk the gun back and forth, tracking them.

"Wait!" says Two-girl, just as Xilou has one foot within the docking corridor. She points to the cookie-cooker. "Leave that."

✦

The journey down feels a lot longer than the journey up. In the dark hold there's no way for Xilou to see the ice-ship as it sprouts a shining tail and moves out of orbit. She unstraps Em and holds her tightly as the old lighter rocks and rattles around them. What now? She doesn't know. Something will present itself. She knows she ought to feel some grief, but a neut is built to get over losses quickly. She should find a way to send a message, at least warn neut sistren of what might be coming. Their wing-sistas will stand by them, the only normals who definitely will. Dodgers are one people.

The lighter's hold doors open, admitting a dim shaft of starlight that creeps and crawls over the shapes stacked within. Xil didn't even realise they'd landed. In the twilight she can see that the fuel-bundles they sent up have been swapped for mysterious containers made from ice. Xilou keeps herself hidden behind one, wondering what might be inside.

A figure slips into the hold, dimly visible in her photo-multiplied suit vision.

"Are we there yet?" asks a sleepy voice over her suit-com.

"No, honey, change of plan," says Xilou.

Em unclips Boris's home from Xilou's suit. She peers in through the viewing window. The inhabitant waves black legs at her, struggling to assemble a fresh web after all the recent shaking and banging. "Boris wants to go home," whines Em, as though the creature's motions are semaphore that only she can read.

The new arrival moves around the hold with an over-cautious bulky care that's unmistakeable. It's Latimer.

It's "Sawyer".

He's clearly looking for something and Xilou knows what: the payment for the 'surplus protein' he sent up to the ice-ship. The whole thing's been a set-up from the start, and with her and Black and White out of the way, the remains of her organisation are his to take over, if he can. Latimer finds something, brick-sized packs that he gathers excitedly up into his arms. Xilou puts her thumb to the data contacts on her gun, and it tells her, 'Full load: Twenty shots.'

"You stay here and look after Boris, honey," she tells Em. "Mommy's got some business to attend to."

Colum sold his soul to science fiction in the 70s, and has never stopped being bitterly disappointed with 'progress' since. He lives in Brummiegum, UK, with many aged but adorable computers that he's rescued from abuse and neglect (but mostly from the trash). He's been published in Daily Science Fiction, Hub Magazine, Fusion Fragment, Kasma SF, Bards and Sages, Jupiter SF, and the Anywhere but Earth anthology. He writes because no one else seems to be writing the shit he wants to read.

A RAY OF SUNSHINE

Bill Patterson

> The days were long and many, space was empty,
> only one man was needed at the controls [...]
> before the asteroids were entirely behind, each
> ship regularly had its off-watch member suspended
> in space at the end of a cable. Isaac Asimov, The
> Martian Way (1952)

IT STILL SOUNDS wonderful, sixty years later. Whose heart wouldn't be filled with awe at floating alone in space? Looking at all those stars in the velvety black. Who wouldn't want to do that for the year and a half it takes to travel from Mars to Saturn? There's only one small problem. If you did 'space float', as the protagonists in Asimov's The Martian Way had, you would arrive vomiting, your hair falling out, and in serious medical danger from radiation sickness.

It really is sad—the destruction of a beautiful story by ugly facts. When the Good Doctor wrote that story in 1952, the first satellites were still six years in the future. The Van Allen belts were still years from discovery. Isaac Asimov may have had an inkling that space was filled with radiation, but he had little data upon which to base a story.

The more we learn about the environment in space, the more deadly it appears to humans. Galactic cosmic rays, solar radiation, bubbles of ions blasted off the surface of the Sun and even the occasional bit of antimatter are zipping past. It makes the hazard presented by micrometeoroids seem trivial. If you manage to survive the journey and slide into orbit around a nice big planet and behind its protective magnetosphere, you're still not safe. Every planet in the Solar System with a magnetic field is also surrounded with belts of trapped energetic particles which constitute a danger all their own.

If you are an avid reader of science fiction, then you are aware of most of the dangers of space flight: microgravity and its effect on human physiology, the impact hazard from space debris, even the boredom of the long trip. If the author ever mentioned the radiation environment, it was usually episodic—the sudden solar flare that louses up communiciations or makes everyone cram into a shelter for a certain length of time.

Yet it is this forgotten danger of space radiation which has the greatest effect on whether we can even get out of Low Earth Orbit in the first place.

But, really, how bad can space radiation be? After all, we've had astronauts up in space on and off for fifty years. Several have had year-long stays, or more, up there. The answer is that we've been very lucky so far. In 2005, the National Research Council, in their report Space Radiation Hazards for the Vision of Space Exploration, laid out the scary reality. Three months after Apollo 16 landed on the Moon in 1972, and four months before Apollo 17 launched, one of the most powerful solar flares recorded blasted from the face of the Sun. Less than forty minutes later, travelling one-fifth the speed of light, highly energetic particles, mostly protons, arrived at the Earth/Moon system. If the astronauts had been in cislunar space at the time, many researchers estimate that they would have received two Grays inside the Apollo spacecraft, and twenty Grays if they had been caught on the Lunar surface. A two Gray exposure is usually survivable, but it requires very prompt medical treatment. Twenty Grays is a fatal dose, even with treatment.

Before we take a look at these three major radiation hazards of space, let's look at what radiation generally does to the human body.

What we see now happened 8.33 minutes ago. But radiation travels the speed of light, so it's already hit the Moon. Oh, Jesus, those poor men! REMs, 5,000, maybe 6,000 total dose? [...] He spread the alarm...that a gigantic solar proton event was under way. James A Michener, Space (1982)

Space Radiation and Human Health

'Radiation' is energy dissipated from a source. Radiation, in the purest sense, refers to the ultrasound that imaged your kidney stone, the radio waves from your mobile phone, the light from your incandescent lightbulb, the X-rays that imaged your hand, and the gamma rays that are being absorbed by the containment dome on the neighbourhood nuclear station. It means the harmless and the deadly. Therefore, we'll break the term 'radiation' down to ionising and non-ionising types.

Non-ionising radiation encompasses the electromagnetic spectrum from radio waves all the way up to visible light. This part of the spectrum is not considered hazardous from a space health concern, since it can be blocked easily by the spacesuit or spacecraft. Non-ionising radiation does not penetrate the tissues of the astronaut to inflict damage. Non-ionising radiation can excite chemical bonds, however. So that microwave or infrared or near-ultraviolet radiation might cook you, but your genes are safe.

Ionising radiation, though, is another matter. The definition is "photons with sufficient energy to knock an electron out of orbit" around an atom. Radiation with a wavelength of 150 nm (1500 angstroms) or shorter is considered ionising, although very little of such Solar far-ultraviolet reaches the ground. Beyond the ultraviolet region of the electromagnetic spectrum lies the X-ray region, then the gamma ray region.

There is no end to the electromagnetic spectrum, so gamma rays in theory can have arbitrarily high energies (yet see the Greisen–Zatsepin–Kuzmin limit, which implies an upper bound of 5×10^{19} electron volts). Thanks to Einstein's $e = Mc^2$ equation, high-energy photons can be considered the equivalent of subatomic particles travelling at a high rate of speed. This becomes important when discussing galactic cosmic rays, as these are usually particles travelling at high velocity, rather than photons.

When a packet of ionising radiation, either photonic or an energetic particle, hits a mass, it will continue passing through it until it has dissipated all of its energy or exits the mass. The most likely way it will shed its energy is ionisation. As it passes near an atom it will energise electrons. Sometimes, enough energy is transferred to an electron to cause it to escape entirely from the grasp of the nucleus. When that occurs, two bad things happen: the now-positively-charged atom is actively seeking another electron, and the escaped electron is ready to hook onto another nucleus.

When ionising radiation strikes the wall of the spacecraft, a defect in the crystalline structure of the metal is created, and the ejected electron becomes part of a roving band of charge carriers. If the atoms are part of an electronic chip, spurious electrical signals can be generated. In 2003, the MARIE instrument carried aboard the Mars Odyssey, an experiment specifically designed to monitor the radiation environment around Mars, was disabled permanently by radiation damage to its electronics from a series of solar flares.

In a living organism, the effects of ionising radiation are far worse. If the atoms affected are in the cytoplasm, the regular contents of the cell, the effects are to increase oxidative stress to the cell, disrupting its function until it can heal. But if the disrupted atoms are in the nucleus, then the chromosomes are far more likely to be affected.

The activated atoms will form improper cross-linkages with other atoms, altering how the DNA encodes proteins for the cell. This is called a mutation. The telomeres, the caps on the end of the chromosomes, can be literally blasted off, leading to cell death. If the cells affected are sperm or egg cells (or their precursors), then there is a chance that the mutation will be passed onto the next generation. The most probable result, however, is a rogue cell, dividing out of control. *Cancer.*

The susceptibility of an organism to radiation damage is governed mostly by its repair capability and structural complexity. Humans are more likely than, say, flour beetles, to be vulnerable to damage to blood-forming organs like bone marrow. Like the 'hygiene hypothesis' which states that the human immune system is best trained by low level exposure to dirt rather than an antiseptic environment, the 'radiation hormeisis' hypothesis states that higher levels of background radiation train the cell repair mechanisms to fix ionisation damage to cells. Both hypotheses are highly controversial and not yet accepted by science.

NASA, by law, is required to set a radiation limit on astronauts in space. Currently, for astronauts in Low Earth Orbit, that limit is a three percent increase of lifetime fatal cancer risk. There is no set limit for voyages beyond LEO, since we lack the capability for such trips. However, since it is a lifetime risk, and cancer takes time to appear after the original radiation exposure, the older you are, the more space radiation you can take. Ironically, it seems the Mars mission, all other things being equal, will be crewed by the oldest active astronauts.

> A hundred million square miles of the Sun's surface exploded in such blue-white fury that, by comparison, the rest of the disc paled to a dull glow. Out of that seething inferno, twisting and turning like a living creature in the magnetic fields of its own creation, soared the electrified plasma of the great flare. Ahead of it, moving at the speed of light, went the warning flash of ultraviolet and X rays. That would reach Earth in eight minutes, and was relatively harmless. Not so the charged atoms, that were following behind at their leisurely four million miles per hour-and which, in just over a day, would engulf Diana, Lebedev, and their accompanying fleet in a cloud of lethal radiation. Arthur C Clarke, 'Sunjammer' (1964)

Radiation Sources

Radiation in space ultimately comes from those unshielded fusion reactors littering the heavens we call stars. The greatest source of radiation in the near-Earth environment is the Sun. Beyond the protective magnetic field of Earth, though, galactic cosmic rays from all of the other stars in the universe begin to dominate the radiation environment.

The Sun is continuously emitting fusion debris from its surface. This 'solar wind' is composed mostly of protons and electrons from ionised hydrogen, plus all of the other reaction products of the fusion process. The solar wind buffets the entire Solar System out to about 100 AU. Occasionally, the magnetic field of the Sun becomes tangled, forming the various surface features of the Sun: prominences, filaments, and sunspots. Energy in the solar magnetic field can build until it is released. Sometimes the fields straighten out slowly, via gradual decay. Occasionally, they reconnect explosively. These solar flares are our first dangerous source of space radiation.

Quite often, a solar flare will accelerate a large quantity of ionised gas in the corona of the Sun and fling it into space. This is called a Coronal Mass Ejection, or CME. If the solar wind is like snow blowing in your face on a winter's day, CMEs are like standing at the wrong end of a snow blower—particle counts and energies can go up by several orders of magnitude in minutes and last for hours or days. Scientists call these episodes Solar Particle Events (SPEs). They occur irregularly, cannot be forecast easily, and a single event can provide forty percent of the total dose for a long-duration mission in a relatively brief timeframe.

The flux of charged particles induce 'surface charging' on the external skins of all spacecraft. The electrons or protons can't get through the skin, so they pile up on it, like pollen on a parked car. If the entire outer skin is not electrically connected, then different areas will receive different charges. In extreme cases, electrical arcs have resulted between these charged areas, resulting in significant damage or loss of the satellite. A spacecraft approaching the space station may be at a significantly different voltage level, and, just like when you touch a doorknob on a dry winter's day, there will be a spark. That spark could be thousands of volts at hundreds of amps. And if you're out in a spacesuit running a cable between the two vessels, you could get a fatal jolt.

The second dangerous source of space radiation are galactic cosmic rays (GCR). The term 'cosmic ray' puts one in mind of some sort of 'super x-ray', or a pure energy phenomenon. In fact, GCRs are made up of subatomic particles from electrons and protons all the way up to ionised atomic nuclei, zipping along at tens of thousands of kilometres per second. At these speeds, you can't just put up a piece of aluminium and expect them to stop. GCRs drill through most shielding materials, creating showers of charged particles in their wake.

The total radiation damage from galactic cosmic rays over an average mission to Mars is predicted to be greater than the total expected radiation from solar particle events. This is because energetic electrons or protons do not penetrate very deeply into the body, whereas a speeding iron ion in a GCR could go most of the way through the astronaut before it is stopped. The iron ion will deposit its energy throughout its entire path length, creating a 'shower' of charged ions in its wake, whereas the electron will damage only a few atoms. Thus, even though heavy nuclei such as iron represent a small fraction of the GCR spectrum, they generate significantly more damage to shielding and humans.

The third source of dangerous space radiation is termed 'trapped radiation'. Some planets, such as Earth, Jupiter and Saturn have substantial magnetic fields that divert the solar wind around the planet, more or less like fanciful force fields in science fiction. The magnetosphere of the planet is not impenetrable, however. The solar wind already bends the magnetosphere of a planet from its spherical shape into a elongated teardrop. A solar flare bends it even further.

This bending of the magnetosphere causes the magnetic lines of force to sweep across the surface of the Earth. When they do, any long conductor, like high tension lines, rails or pipelines, have huge currents generated in them. In 1989, this process led to the blackout of a major portion of Quebec when the electrical grid overloaded from these Sun-induced currents.

Back in space, a significant number of the ionized particles become caught between the magnetic lines of force in the magnetosphere. Once inside, they continue to travel along the lines of force at high speed, becoming 'trapped radiation'. The Van Allen belts of Earth and the Io flux tube around Jupiter are examples of such trapped radiation. Most of the radiation absorbed by astronauts in the ISS comes about when the station traverses a section of the Van Allen inner belt around a region called the South Atlantic Anomaly.

Well, it seems that we're stuck in Low Earth Orbit, aren't we? Maybe not. There are various mitigation measures that can be taken which will allow us to perhaps reach Mars without cataracts.

Mitigation Measures

Avoidance. Your mother always said, "an ounce of prevention is worth a pound of cure". But, like everything else in space, the correct way to do things is counter-intuitive. It would seem that the best time to set sail upon the velvet deep would be during solar minimum, that period of time when sunspots, and solar flares, are at their lowest level. But a funny thing happened on the way to the heliopause, that area of space where the solar wind hits the 'wind' from the interstellar medium. The energetic particles that make up GCRs seem to have a tougher time when they have to go against an energetic solar wind. Hence, the radiation danger from GCRs is highest when the danger from SPEs is the lowest.

Scheduling your voyage then becomes a delicate balancing act. You want to blast off when the Sun is active, but not too active. Flying in outer space really is Rocket Science.

Material Shielding. Ah, but you say, we can load up with shielding! The International Space Station has blocks of polyethylene plastic fitted for just that purpose. Those blocks were in fact a retrofit after astronauts have been living and working up there for quite some time. For a long-duration mission to Mars, the shielding has to be in place before it launches.

Shielding comes down to mass. If we were to shield astronauts to limit them to the same radiation levels as earth-bound nuclear power station workers, NASA calculates it would need three to five hundred grams per square centimetre shielding. Since astronauts would typically have a shorter career exposure, less shielding, in the twenty g/cm^2 range, would be required. Since we're actually going somewhere, increased shielding means higher fuel consumption for the same payload.

There is a substantial debate in the scientific community about how to best shield astronauts. On one side are those who advocate standard aluminium walls. Others support the use of a strengthened polyethylene plastic. It all boils down to those pesky heavy-ion GCRs. When it hits aluminium or heavier shielding, such as lead, it generates huge showers of secondary radiation. However, if one hits a plastic-sheathed rocket, it will generate relatively few secondary particles. The lighter shielding, though, gives the crew less performance for the more common energetic proton events. Again, the question boils down to risk management. Which solution yields the lowest risk while still being able to fly?

Is that it? Are we doomed to Low Earth Orbit forever? Can nothing more be done?

> Nothing, but nothing, can get through a General Products hull. No kind of electromagnetic energy except visible light. No kind of matter, from the smallest subatomic particle to the fastest meteor. That's what the company's advertisements claim, and the guarantee backs them up. I've never doubted it, and I've never heard of a General Products hull being damaged by a weapon or by anything else. Larry Niven, Neutron Star (1966)

Since NASA doesn't have access to General Product hulls, they have to be a little more inventive. There are really only two things you can do when confronted with high energy ions: deflect them or absorb them.

Deflective Shielding. One concept that has been explored is the use of high-strength magnetic fields. Since most GCRs are in the form of high-speed charged ions, a spacecraft sheathed in magnetic fields should, in theory, be able to bend incoming charged particles away from it, thus deflecting away a substantial amount of incoming radiation. Problems with such a system include mass (and consequent higher fuel consumption), power for the electromagnets, and the unavoidable navigational problems when the ship's field interacts with the interplanetary magnetic field.

Bill Patterson

The field strength required to perform this shielding is in the neighborhood of ten to twenty Tesla. By comparison, the magnetic field of the Earth is thirty-one microTesla, and an MRI machine runs about three Tesla. Such strong magnetic fields have problems all their own. Starting up or shutting down the field will induce strong currents throughout the ship, meaning more shielding and thus mass. People have experienced crippling headaches in MRI machines; the spacecraft will be running a field five times higher for months on end. Theoretically, the idea has merit, but magnetic shielding is a long way from any implementation.

Electrostatic shielding is another possibility. Charging the spacecraft with a high positive charge is possible, but like magnetic shielding, the medical implications of life in a high electrostatic field require significant study. As with magnetic shielding, it requires mass and a source of plentiful electrical power.

NASA may intend to re-establish a manned presence on the Moon before it tackles Mars. This is good, for the Moon can supply all the mass required for material shielding. And it also has thorium. Thorium is the oft-forgotten fuel for space-based nuclear power plants. Thorium-based pebble reactors have run for years in the United States without mishap. Given enough incentive, thorium could readily be extracted from the Lunar regolith, packaged into pellets, and stored for eventual use in space-based reactors.

And the Lunar regolith can be easily launched from the surface of the Moon. Since you have to mine the rock of the Moon to get the thorium, why not send the remaining slag, high in iron and aluminum content to the waiting spacecraft? Fashioned into plates, the slag can act as a suit of armour for the spacecraft. The remaining regolith, powdered, can be used for reaction mass in an ion engine powered by the thorium reactor. It's a double win—you get a great source of plentiful electrical power for deflective shielding and propulsion, and reaction mass for the increased material shielding.

It is quite conceivable that one day a spacecraft, launched from Earth, fuelled with Lunar thorium, will unfurl its gigantic magnetic fields, hundreds of kilometres in extent. Safe from most of the hazards of space radiation, it will traverse the lonely deep to Mars, there to begin human exploration. And during the journey, aboard the spacecraft will be the lucky astronauts, drifting in the deep on the end of a cable.

Bill Patterson, 51, has been interested in writing science fiction ever since college. The author of one commercially successful CAD software book, Bill was a magazine columnist in the same area. He has been published in JournalStone's 90 Minutes to Live. He and his wife of 28 years, Barbara, live with their two sons in Central New Jersey. Bill has been an avid space weather hobbyist since 2002.

THE BRAVE LITTLE COCKROACH
GOES TO MARS

Simon McCaffery

for James McCaffery

"HOUSTON, WE'VE GOT a problem."

Mission commander Lee Patterson uttered those prophetic words on Day 152 of our glitch-ridden transfer, twenty-six days from encounter and insertion around Mars. Thank God we weren't transmitting a daily update on the downlink—can you imagine what the cable news talking-heads would say about America's last hope to beat the Chinese landing? It sure as hell got my attention after everything Lee and I had been through: the power fluctuations on Days 44 and 45, the buggy software that knocked out our X-Band transmitter for seven hours on Day 89, and the water purifiers that stopped purifying our recycled fluids on Days 111 and 112. My vomiting episode on Day 123 nearly caused the Houston flight surgeon to suffer a breakdown. He became convinced that a pathogen, Salmonella or E coli, had hitched a ride and then exploded in a surge of near gravity-free virulence.

As it turned out, something else had stowed away aboard the *Vision*. In hindsight, something extraordinary.

I was checking our final course adjustment at the time of the incident. TCMs—Trajectory Correction Manoeuvres—are delicate, computer-controlled sequences we had to complete during approach phase so we didn't skip off the upper atmosphere and go down in history as the greatest NASA failure, a final nail in the programme's coffin. We'd been dialling down the main cabin lights to limit eye-strain, and when I glanced over and saw Lee slam his hand on the aluminium edge of the compact treadmill squeezed next to the tiny stand-up galley, I thought my eyes were playing tricks.

"Shit! I missed it."

For a split-second my mind simply failed to grasp what I'd seen perched there before it scuttled away.

Periplaneta Americana. A cockroach.

"You saw it, too—*tell* me you saw it, Dave," Lee said. His eyes were bloodshot and he had several days of stubble. The inside of the command module smelled like ass but we'd lost the capability to notice weeks ago.

I stared at Lee, and giggled.

I clapped a hand over my mouth but I couldn't stop. Any flight psychologist would tell you it was a bad sign, but I couldn't stop laughing.

✦

We named him Archy, after the free-verse poet reincarnated as a newsroom cockroach in the Twentieth Century 'Archy and Mehitabel' New York Evening Sun columns by Don Marquis. We stopped trying to kill him once the shock wore off. Besides, who packs a can of Raid on a sixty-million-mile-plus voyage to a sterile planet? Archy became a pet, a fitting mascot for the mission.

You're asking how an adult cockroach could stow away aboard an American spacecraft constructed in high-tech clean rooms, but before you pass judgment on the fine folks at Lockheed and Boeing, consider the events that led to our historic mission. The Chinese had caught us with our britches down—hell, we were going commando. NASA was operating on the smallest fiscal budget in its history. Private aerospace firms were boosting eighty percent of payloads bound for orbit. The Orion missions to the Moon had been scrapped nearly a decade ago and the latest Mars rover had dug another billion-dollar crater when its Rube Goldberg skycrane yo-yo landing system malfunctioned.

When the president was informed that the People's Republic of China planned to launch two taikonauts to Mars in a highly modified Shenzhou spacecraft, the *Lei-zi* (named for a goddess of thunder), he nearly blew an O-ring. An election year was approaching, to be fair, and he already had plenty of domestic crises to manage. The European Space Agency quickly announced a joint mission with the Russians. So did JAXA, though they never made it to the pad. The president had no choice but to throw in, his administration hanging in the balance, and the timetable was lousy. NASA dragged two Ares-based Jupiter boosters out of mothballs—one to test and one for launch—and set about extensively modifying old Orion spacecraft designs into a stretch command module with a single-pilot lander. Unproven luxuries, like a VASIMR, a Variable Specific Impulse Magnetoplasma Rocket engine that could have halved our transit time, were jettisoned. Not enough time to develop and test. The engineers also nixed slower but more efficient solar-electric prototypes. It was a rush job to the launch pad and everyone knew it, including Lee and I. But we'd been sitting on the sidelines for years waiting for a new launch vehicle, and who was going to refuse to be the first man on Mars?

As a kid growing up on the poor side of Oklahoma City, I'd ask my older brother to identify the glowing red dot on the power pole transformer drum outside our shared bedroom window, and he'd tell me it was the "Angry Red Planet." He was trying to spook me, but all I felt was excitement; some day I was going to fly there.

On launch day some smartass technician piped the Sanford and Son television theme into the suit-up room, but we made it through third-stage burn without a hitch, on cruise control to Mars.

A few weeks later, the glitches started. We coped, and now we had something to take our minds off of the tension and boredom.

"Archy has adapted to zero-G," I told Lee five days after the little guy narrowly missed being terminated from the mission. It was another glitch—a computer fault fired the attitude controls and halted the command module's rotation. We'd lost ninety percent of centrifugal gravity for several hours.

It turns out that cockroaches possess one of the most efficient and incredible locomotion systems in nature. Robotic engineering teams have tried for years to mimic it in hopes of designing a planetary rover that can traverse rough terrain and rapidly react to danger. Who knew?

"He sure has," Lee said. "The first roach in space is doing his race proud."

Lee grew up in a small town across Lake Pontchartrain from New Orleans, and I thought he had done a terrific job of suppressing his innate loathing of the big, fat waterbugs.

"He's not the first, actually," I said.

Archy flicked his reddish brown eight-centimetre body from the fire suppression master switch to a soft landing on the rim of the starboard viewport.

"A Russian cockroach named Hope gave birth to thirty-three babies," I said. "They were conceived during a two-week trip aboard a bio-satellite back in '07."

Lee gave me an odd look.

I grinned. It was undeniably a giant leap forward for a species that had been introduced to North America from Africa in the early Seventeenth Century and was universally despised.

I began quietly relaying data and observations to a geeky Stanford entomologist named Tevis. The guy seemed to know more about cockroaches than humanly possible. Roaches are funny creatures, breathing through spiracles in their sides. A few species are known to be parthenogenetic, reproducing without the need for males. Cockroaches have been known to live up to three months without food and a month without water. Maybe the first generation ship sent to the stars should be manned by a colony of Archy's kin? Any intelligent life on the other end had better use clips and keep their sugar in airtight canisters.

Some of the earliest writings about cockroaches encouraged their use as medicine. Pedanius Dioscorides (First Century), Kamal al-Din al-Damiri and Abu Hanifa ad-Dainuri (Ninth Century) all offered medicines that either suggest grinding them up with oil or boiling them. The list of ailments to be treated included earaches, open wounds and "gynecological disorders". Cut off a cockroach's head and it can survive for days since much of its nervous system activity takes place in nerve ganglia located throughout its body.

I spent my spare time watching Archy manoeuvre about the cabin, delighted.

We kept the module cabin lights low more often since Archy, like the rest of his species, is "negatively phototactic". That's the scientific way of saying that when you flip on the kitchen light any cockroach in the vicinity is going to disappear underneath the refrigerator at nine-tenths the speed of light. After weeks of monotony punctuated by moments of ice-in-the-gut dread, my spirits were lifted. Was this how career criminals felt in prison, training bugs to drag race and mice to roll wooden spools, to keep from going insane, knowing they might never step outside gray cells only slightly smaller than *Vision*'s command module?

"He's got pitch, roll and yaw down," Lee said.

I made a mental note to ask Dr Tevis about Archy's physiology of balance. But we never had that stimulating discussion.

Six days later, Lee Patterson lay strapped to his cot, dying of a mysterious disease we couldn't diagnose.

✦

Day 163. Lee is strapped to his bunk, unable to hold down food, drifting in and out of consciousness. He exhibits flu-like symptoms, but no high fever or coughing. Mars is growing closer, a dusky orange marble, and our pilot might not make it to orbital insert. Worse, I've started to feel like crap, although at first I cannot be sure whether it is the mounting stress or mental suggestion. I am filled with dread.

I spend hours on the downlink relaying Lee's symptoms and debating causes and procedures with Mission Control, made all the more frustrating because of the ten-minute round-trip delay. It isn't faulty air or water filtration. Our room-temperature food concentrates were not contaminated.

We check for spikes in GCR (galactic cosmic radiation) and SEP (solar energetic particles). On April 27, 1972, John Young and the crew of Apollo 16 returned to Earth from an eleven-day lunar mission, three months before the start of one of the largest sun flare SEP events of the century. If they had flown earlier they would have met with disaster. But our GCR and SEP readings are registering low-normal. There have been no detected sun flares producing coronal mass ejections. We aren't being exposed to energetic particles trapped in a planetary magnetic field or secondary neutrons from a malfunctioning Cosmic-ray Shield Toroid (proposed for the *Vision* but also ixnayed by mission engineers as too expensive).

So it isn't radiation, either. We come up empty on a root cause.

Worse, my subconscious is not concocting phantom symptoms—whatever is attacking Lee is beginning to affect me.

I'm enveloped in the worst fear of my professional career. My entire body breaks out in sweat and I hear a high ringing in my inner ears. I develop a rash. I force myself to stay calm, to eat and stay hydrated, to go through the motions of monitoring the onboard systems and prepare for insertion, but I'm weakening.

Archy looks down from the top shelf of the galley, shiny antennae waving.

I think we're really screwed this time, buddy.

✦

Day 166. Or is it 167? I come awake in the gloom, disoriented; something is wrong. The cabin lights are dimmed but I see an odd, flickering light near the Waste Collection System—the suction toilet that freezes and jettisons solid waste and reclaims all fluid for purification.

I get up and fight a wave of dizziness. I've been getting sick a lot, like most astronauts feel for the first two days of a mission as their gastro-intestinal system becomes acclimated to periods of weightlessness. But we've been in deep space for more than five months. I stagger toward the toilet alcove, and stop.

Archy is running in an erratic circular pattern on the decking, stopping and darting forward, clearly uncoordinated. I rub my eyes and kneel beside him. The edge of Archy's thorax and abdomen beneath his wings are glowing a phosphorous eldritch blue. So I wasn't hallucinating.

Something the Stanford entomologist had told me tries to surface in my mind but it cannot penetrate the muzziness. I evacuate my mainly empty stomach, and then transmit a message on the downlink to Mission Control. I hunker down to wait.

It takes some time, but they manage to get Dr Tevis on the uplink.

"Commander Keener, this is extremely interesting. I know of

a species of Amazonian cockroach that produces a glow within the abdomen to attract a mate, similar to a firefly. This is a chemical reaction involving luciferin, luciferase and oxygen..."

He drones on excitedly and I cannot tell him to shut up because of the transmission delay. Eventually we decide that I will transmit a video clip of Archy for analysis.

I check on Lee, who is nearly comatose, and then I fall back on my own bunk. I never do remember what it was that I wanted to ask the entomologist.

I have a strange dream. I am exploring a deep underground mineshaft cut through solid granite. I turn a corner and find Dr Strangelove sitting in that silly wheelchair, grinning up at me, his traitorous gloved hand writhing at his side. He rattles on about magnetic fields, mineshaft depth and absorption tables, and that's when Archy climbs out of my breast pocket-flap, his carapace glowing like one of those plastic stars you glued to the ceiling of your childhood bedroom—

I struggle up and look for Archy, but cannot find him. I open the squeaky galley pantry door, our version of a cockroach dog-whistle, and wait, but he doesn't appear.

When Dr Tevis and I first discussed Archy's adaptation to life in deep space, I asked whether cockroaches could truly survive a nuclear holocaust.

"That's an urban legend, that cockroaches are impervious to extremely high levels of radiation," Tevis said. "They can withstand a lot, say 67,000 rems, but they're actually not as resistant as several other species, including some types of fruit flies."

Cockroaches are well suited to hide in cracks and rubble, could subsist happily on the detritus of our annihilated civilization, but they probably wouldn't inherit the Earth.

But suppose Archy's exoskeleton is reacting to an unknown form of cosmic radiation? New anomalous particles accelerated on the solar winds that now, far from home, are penetrating both the ship's aluminium skin and radiation shield fashioned of a thin layer of hydrogen-rich plastics? We have been sending robots to Mars and the outer planets for over forty years, not living organisms. The quantitative biological effects of cosmic rays aren't fully understood, and are the subject of ongoing NASA research.

I share my theory with Mission Control, and I can tell they think I'm losing it. Cracking up.

Arthur C Clarke once famously wrote that for every technical problem, there is a technical solution. Unfortunately there are no spare parts lying around inside the spartan Command Module to construct a cosmic ray shield and test my theory.

It's difficult to remain alert. My head aches and my muscles are sore and weakening. I'm urinating frequently: another bad sign. I hope the water reclamation system can keep up.

And that's it. There is one procedure I can try. I don't need to construct a shield at all.

First I stop our rotation, then ease Lee out of his bunk restraints and carefully manoeuvre him aft to the small pod enclosure behind *Vision*'s water supply and filtration system. The old International Space Station had a similar cubby, called a storm shelter, used as a "potential mitigation strategy" in case a major sun flare occurred while the astronauts were stuck in orbit. I empty it of its spare gear and supplies. Huddled inside, Lee and I are surrounded by thin curved walls of recycled water.

And water is an excellent shield against radiation.

I rest for a ten minutes, then return to the main cabin to gather supplies, food packets and water, and send a status message streaking toward Earth. I pray it isn't our last contact with home. In that moment I understand what it must have felt like to stand in the shoes of Jim Lovell or Lindbergh when things looked bleakest, straddling a razor-thin line between survival and extinction.

While gathering meal packets I see Archy floating motionless in midair. I cup his body in my hand and carefully slip him inside a jumpsuit flap. I restore gravity, and head back to Lee.

✦

I wasn't the first man to step foot on Mars. Sorry, mother; and tell my brother I'll buy him that bottle of Johnny Walker Black

Label when I get home.

That honour went to Lieutenant Colonel Gérard Talbot, the ESA *Aurora 3* lander module pilot. I was second, followed by Lt Colonel Hui Chen of the *Lei-zi*. The flags of the United States, Russia, China and the eighteen member states of the ESA, including Canada, are planted in the Martian soil. Global stock markets have surged. The president won re-election in a landslide. And for a brief time, people around the world have stopped fighting with one another so they can stare up at the heavens in wonder.

I send a message to my brother and Mum, trying and failing to express Mars's beautiful desolation.

Lee has remained in orbit and seems to be making a full recovery, though we cannot be sure of any long-term effects until we're back on Earth. It will be a bitch of a return flight when the transit window re-opens. Opposition-class missions mean you pay on the back end. To be safe we'll have to spend a lot of time in the water-shielded storm shelter. More data for the flight psychologist.

During my thirty-day stay on the surface I conduct surveys and monitor the life-support aux pod, which captures carbon dioxide and hydrogen to replenish our water supply. The in-situ fuel generator inhales Mars's thin atmosphere and is steadily cooking up a fresh batch of methane/oxygen $CH_4 + O_2$ rocket fuel for the long flight home.

Mars is everything we dreamed it would be: butterscotch boulder fields and endless rust-veined vistas. Earth is a faint star.

In the year 1000 CE, King Olaf I of Norway sent Leif Eriksson sailing from Norway back to Greenland, but the expedition was blown off course. On the eve of despair, legend has it the Viking explorer beseeched the Norse gods for assistance and released a trained falcon to bear his message. The falcon flew from sight and later, under a moonless black sky and glowing heavens, Leif's men resigned themselves to their fate. But the following morning the falcon returned with the dead body of a field mouse, and Eriksson ended up in North America instead of Greenland.

If Archy hadn't invited himself aboard, if Lee had had better aim, if the cuticle of Archy's exoskeleton hadn't fluoresced from the collisions of those unearthly cosmic particles, Lee and I would have died before we hit insertion, and no warnings would have been transmitted to the crews of the *Aurora* and *Lei-zi*. All three missions would mysteriously have been lost—a monumental blow to man's collective long-delayed exploration of deep space.

Archy never got his ticker-tape parade down Fifth Avenue.

I buried him on a sandy ridge overlooking a vast, rock-strewn plain leading to the southeastern edges of the Tharsis Montes region, whose main landmarks are three volcano remnants including the Pavonis Mons. Among the souvenirs given to us by schoolchildren I found a small plastic American flag. I planted it proudly by his grave. It will degrade in a few decades from cold, swirling Martian dust devils and the savage ultraviolet, but my silver astronaut wings will remain for all to see.

Archy had earned them.

Simon McCaffery writes SF, horror and hybrids of both genres. You can blame his father, the artist James McCaffery, who bought him George R. Stewart's Earth Abides when he was ten, and Warren's Eerie and Creepy magazines instead of the four-colour, cheaply printed comic books of the day. Simon's stories have appeared in Black Static, Tomorrow SF, Alfred Hitchcock Mystery Magazine, Space & Time and in a number of anthologies. He is currently completing a novel that mixes elements of horror and emerging medical technology. Drop him a line at simonmccafferyfiction.blogspot.com

SEA OF MATERNITY

Deborah Walker

I HAVE TWO real-time images on my bedroom walls. One shows the blue and white-swirled glass eye of Earth. It was a trompe d'oeil, what I would've seen outside, if Lunar's domes were made of glass instead of being a regolith sandwich with a ten-metre-wide filling of fungi. The west-facing wall showed an image of dusk-yellow Titan, sent from the People's Space Collective probe. The two images in my room showed where I had come from and where I hoped to go.

I stared at the computer and let the data wash over me. My head moved slightly as if I were listening to music. It *was* music to me: the music of biology. Oh yes, biology has music: listen to the hammer of your heart, the back-beat of blood pulsing through your veins. But my work took me into the deep music, into the multifaceted sounds of biochemistry.

About a hundred years ago, at Chernobyl, out of that terrible disaster, we found a new melody, a black mould in the reactor bins that thrived on radiation. Just like a plant it broke the bond of water, but instead of sunlight the fungus fed on radiation and instead of chlorophyll the fungus used melanin, the same melanin we find in our skin.

I pulled up a 3D image of the melanin molecule, looking at the proposed active sites of the latest variety. Melanin is a miracle of adaptability. It's able to absorb all kinds of radiation. Here on the Moon, we sandwich it over our domes. We give it water; it gives us oxygen. We give it carbon dioxide and it gives us carbohydrates.

Such an elegant solution to life in this sea of radiation.

I develop new strains of fungi, looking for enhanced efficiency and different absorption spectrums. What I really wanted to do was to develop a strain which would be active in very cold conditions, say 95K, maybe something that could thrive on a liquid methane sea. Yes, I was dreaming of Titan. That's my pet project. My colleagues thought I was crazy. How could a multi-cellular organism survive under such conditions? But I was getting very interesting results at increasingly low temperatures.

My theory is that when pushed to the extreme, life creates new music. It happened at Chernobyl. I was trying to make it happen in my lab. We were about to move beyond Lunar, and we needed a better repertoire to protect us. Think what it would be like if we could move outside the domes, if we could create a strain that could alter the atmosphere of an ice moon.

I admit it. It's a wild dream. But I was making progress. I only needed to create the perfect conditions to initiate the correct mutation in the melanin.

As I worked, other, more prosaic, thoughts distracted me. While thinking about a new biochemical song, trying to see, deeper and deeper, I was also thinking about my daughter Alicia. I was thinking about my meeting tonight with Philip. I was thinking about Makhul, who was becoming increasingly irritated with my procrastinations. All those worries were tangled up in my speculations; I was good at multi-tasking.

I heard the door clattering open. That could only mean Alicia; and that meant, no doubt, another argument, another ridiculous pointless argument. I wanted to keep my door shut and just *think*. In many ways, I prefer the world of the biochemistry. We might not know exactly how melanin works, we unwrap more questions as we narrow our focus, but at least we can use it to our advantage. Recently, my dealings with my daughter were just as strange as anything I'd encountered in my experiments, yet I couldn't see any practical applications to our endlessly repeated arguments.

"Sheila, I'm home," Alicia shouted. I reluctantly turned off the computer and walked into the living area.

Alicia was wearing her suit. She stamped her feet to shed the moon dust that clung to her over-sized boots.

"You know what I hate, Sheila?" she asked.

Alicia always called me Shelia. I've asked her many times to call me Mum, like a normal daughter. "What do you hate?" I said, while looking in the cupboard for the hoover bot. Moon dust is a devil to get rid of, if you let it settle.

"I hate the fact that I can only ever date boys who are younger than me. Did you ever consider that? I mean, come on." She unfastened her suit and shrugged out of it. She left it on the floor, and flounced down onto the settee, dressed only in a vest and shorts. My daughter; thirteen years old, a slender frame, a smart girl with raging hormones and a talent for whining and winding up her mother. I could almost see her calculating, just thinking of things that would push my buttons. "Unless," she said, "I go for someone considerably older than me."

Alicia was the first child to be born in Lunar. In a population of five hundred colonists, there were only fifty children. It was a lower birth-rate than we'd projected. It seemed as if many of the colonists had waited to see how Alicia turned out before they had their own children. Once she passed her seventh birthday and it became clear that she was as healthy as an ox, the birth-rate began to rise. But that meant that Alicia had very few dating opportunities.

It was an old argument, "I sympathise, Alicia, I really do, but I don't know what you expect me to do about it."

Alicia turned on the TV, filling the room with the blaring music she liked. She was quite willing to continue the argument, though. She was like me: good at multi-tasking, "I just thought that you should know how I feel. That's what you're always asking, isn't it, Sheila? How do you feel? How do you *feel*?"

"Why don't you date some of the boys from your fan club?"

"One: they're all nerds, science geeks; and two: I don't want to date someone half a million miles away. It's just not the same."

"There's always Mitchell." Mitchell McConnell was only six months younger than Alicia.

"Yes, there's always Mitchell." Alicia had elevated sarcasm to an art form. "That would be so convenient for you all, wouldn't it? If I paired off with Mitchell and maybe had a baby. Then everyone could study my baby. A lovely little third-generation Lunar baby. Well, I'm never doing that. I would never be as selfish as you—Sheila."

"I really haven't got time for this." It was an effort to remain calm. I picked up the suit and nearly dropped it. "That's cold," I said, throwing the suit onto the settee. "Where have you been?"

"The Shoemaker ice mines," said Alicia.

That made sense. Temperatures at the base of the crater can reach 100K. The outside of the suit was still freezing, but Alicia never seemed to feel the cold. I glanced at the life-support display, just checking that she hadn't been pushing things. "What where you doing there?" I asked.

"The school field trip, remember? I told you about it last week? You never listen to me."

"Did you enjoy yourself?"

"It was okay, bit boring." That was a lie. My daughter loved going outside the domes. "We saw Malapert."

"Oh yes?" I really needed to get back to the lab.

"Are you even listening to me?"

"I'm sorry, darling. I've got some work I want to get finished. Your dinner's in the machine."

"Did you even think about what it would be like for me?" shouted Alicia. "It's so boring here. There's nothing for me to do."

I sighed as I walked to my room. It wasn't easy being a first-generation space mother.

✦

We have always dreamed, as we looked out into space. We have always wanted to see everything. Dreamed about it for our children, that they might walk, step by slow step, beyond the pathways that confine us. That they might escape, minute by slow minute, beyond, into the space of dreams. Was that wrong? Was that so wrong? How am I different from any other mother, who wants the best for her child, who wants her child to be able to reach out of the dark night and touch the light of the stars?

✦

"How do you feel?" asked Mira, the base's psychoanalyst. She had the typical smooth-silk reassuring voice of her profession. I found it quite irritating.

I'd learnt to be careful with my responses, "Oh, just great. My work has been progressing well, I feel like I'm on the edge of a breakthrough. The alignment of the active sites on this new strain of melanin is unusual, but I've got a feeling that—"

Mira interrupted me, "Do you realise, Sheila, that whenever I ask you about your psychological well being, you start to talk about biochemistry?"

"Do I? I'm sorry, Mira."

I hated these weekly therapy sessions. I should have been used to them. They were mandatory for everyone in Lunar. Fourteen years of psychoanalysis, and I still resented them. I imagined my responses, piped down to Earth and analysed by the finest space-psychologist minds. I didn't like the loss of privacy, or the loss of control.

"Your daughter says there's been some tensions at home," said Mira.

"Did she really?" I wondered what else she had said. "Look, I'm sorry, Mira, but can we skip this week's session?"

"If you wish, Shelia." She was disappointed. "But remember that these are for your benefit."

"Thank you, Mira," I said wondering if my skipping a session would be a black mark on my record, but at that moment I just wanted to be outside. I wanted to suit up and get as far away from my life as possible.

✦

But before I could escape, I needed to put in some hours in the factory. Lunar works on a co-operative model. We all need to put in a required amount of time doing the routine jobs. Pretty much all of the five hundred colonists were scientists of one type or another. We can't just sit around all day doing experiments. Things needed to get done.

In addition to working in the fungi labs, I worked as a mechanic in the regolith processing plant, and I also taught music in the school. When I called up my schedule, I saw that I owed the processing factory the most hours. That was hardly surprising. It was my least favourite job, maintaining the bots that extracted the water and volatiles from the moon dust.

✦

I was wrestling with the circuitry of a particularly recalcitrant bot when Xambe found me, "Rough day?" she asked.

"This little creature just doesn't want to do its job. I know how it feels."

"You look terrible," she said with the brutal honesty that only your best friend can deliver.

"Yes, it's been a rough day," I agreed. "I had another argument with Alicia this morning, then a pointless therapy session. And my day is not going to get any better because I've got a meeting with Philip tonight."

"I had a drink with Makhul last night," said Xambe.

"Well, that's fine. We're not exclusive." I tried hot-wiring the bot. It gave a series of bleeps of incipient life but they quickly fizzled out.

"Hey," said Xambe. "You know I wouldn't go for another woman's fella. He just needed a shoulder to cry on."

"I wouldn't care if you *did* date Makhul." As far as I was concerned the bot was beyond hope.

"That's the problem isn't it, Sheila? I had a long talk with him."

"Oh, spare me."

Xambe pulled the bot out of my hands and set it to one side. She put on her serious face. "When are you going to wise up, Sheila? He's a good man, and he's applied to the Titan project. You're throwing away your future."

Sometimes you need your best friend to tell it how it is. I knew she was right: I liked Makhul, I really did, but I just wasn't ready to commit. I tried to explain it to Xambe, "It just ended so badly with Philip. I'm not sure if I want to go through it again. And there's Alicia to consider. She's bad enough as it is, how would she react to a new daddy?"

"The People's Space Collective like married couples, and Makhul's applied to go to Titan."

"You're not suggesting that I get married to him, just to improve my chances to get to Titan?"

She shrugged. "It's worth considering, Sheila."

Sometimes you need your best friend to tell it how it is, and sometimes they just get on your nerves sticking their noses into your business.

"Xambe, do me a favour?"

"Anything you want, honey."

"Just leave me alone. This is something I need to figure out by myself."

She nodded and left me alone for the rest of the shift.

✦

I don't know how much I achieved, but I put in the necessary hours at the factory. At last, I was free.

"I'm going onto the surface," I told Xambe.

"Do you want some company?" she asked.

"No, I just want to be on my own. You know, sometimes this place... it all gets on top of me."

She nodded, "I know. I know. You don't have to explain to me. But if you need anybody to talk to, I'm there for you, honey." She took my hand. Xambe was a good friend. I was going to miss her if I went away. Xambe hadn't applied to the Titan colony. She was settled here, in fact, and she was looking forward to the changes that the open boundaries would bring.

✦

I took my favourite moon mover from the port. I loved to explore the surface; it was one of the few things that I had in common with my daughter. Moon movers are a little bit like caravans—there were sleeping accommodations, exercise facilities, enough supplies and equipment to keep a person fit and well for a couple of weeks. Before I set off, I linked into Lunar's database and checked the forecast for solar flares. There'd been a level X warning for a couple of days and I didn't want to get stranded by an unpredictable radiation storm. The forecast told me I should be safe for the next couple of hours.

I drove up the slope of Shackleton; and along shielded dark road that cut though the Peaks of Eternal Light where the mirror-polished solar panels fields harvesting energy, relaying the excess back to Earth to repay the massive debt we had incurred building Lunar. I drove past the acres of domed farms, which grew food to feed us all, and more besides, as they stockpiled supplies for the coming wave of immigration. I drove past the Malapert Mountain, where bots had assembled sheets of nano-embossed metal into the skeletons of the new colony domes. Bots crawled over the metal micro-fusing the lunar regolith into glass-like bricks. Work was progressing well; the bots had already seeded some of the domes with the radiosynthetic fungi, possibly one of my own strains.

I drove until I had removed myself from all sight of colonisation. When I judged I was far enough away from civilisation I parked the mover and stepped out, into the bleak, inhospitable and starkly beautiful landscape of the Moon. It was so quiet here, so still. I felt myself relaxing and my breathing growing steady. I indulged myself in the fantasy that I was alone, on a distant world. I looked up the Earth just above the horizon. How many people were looking back at me and dreaming? The Moon was a place of wonder; it was easy to forget that sometimes, as I got swept away in the minutiae of my life. The unspoilt, savage, bleakness of the Moon touched something deep inside of me.

I explored the terrain, walking over the crushed and broken rocks that made the crater's ejecta blanket; and down the terraces which lined the crater wall; until I stood on the basin floor. In the distance I could see the crater's peak. This was an unnamed crater. Areas of the Moon had been designated as sites of natural beauty and would remain untouched as national parks, but this crater and the thousands like it, would no doubt be lost, sooner or later, to the wave of colonisation. It saddened me, the changes that were coming to this wild landscape. Perhaps I would be gone by then, building a new colony on Titan. And there's the contradiction, I spend my days trying to develop an organism that will re-shape the environment, and yet I value the untouched landscape. When we stepped onto distant worlds, we brought our alien biology with us. We needed to shape the world to fit our needs. Colonisation came at a price.

I headed back to Lunar and to the last item of my day: the meeting with my ex.

✦

I changed and showered, then walked across the habitat dome to the bar. Philip was waiting for me. I wasn't late, but Philip had a pathological need to be early.

"Hey," I said, taking a seat. He had chosen to sit by the window which relayed a real-time image of the view outside.

"Hello, Sheila. How are you?" said Philip. He rose slightly in his chair, as I sat down. He was an old-fashioned type of a guy, something that had attracted me to him in the first place. He was English, very upper-class. You could etch glass with his accent. It said a lot for Philip that his personality had over-rode these obvious defects. I admit it, I'm a reverse snob, anything that smacked of money and privilege just turned me off. But in Philip's case, I had made an exception.

"I haven't seen you for a while, Sheila," said Philip.

"No?" I replied, acting surprised. It was astonishing how easy it was to avoid someone, with a little effort, even if there were only five hundred or so people to hide amongst.

"What are you drinking?"

"Oh, I better have lunar hooch," I said. The colony only had a small amount of imported stuff, although I noticed that Philip was drinking his usual Gordon's G&T. Everything that Lunar produced was free. I had plenty of credits, but there wasn't any point on wasting it for a meeting with my ex.

Philip went to the bar to order my drink, while I looked outside. I could see someone in the distance examining the old Russian base.

Philip came back with my drink. I took a sip and winced slightly. Lunar hooch was drinkable, but it was undeniably an acquired taste. The pineapple juice took the edge off it. The marketing team thought that hooch would be a prime export item when we opened up the boundaries with Earth. They said people would go crazy for a drink from the Moon. I had my doubts.

"How's the research going?" asked Philip.

"Oh, really great. I'm right on the brink of something big."

"Fine. Fine." Philip's eyes glazed over, as they always did when I talked about my research.

"Is that Cho?" I asked, pointing outside.

"Yep. Cho thinks the base will be one of the key sites for tourism when the boundaries open. He's assessing the site for damage."

"Wow. He's really into this tourism thing, isn't he?" I said. I supposed that the tourists would want to see the old base; the habitation modules, the solar power ovens; the In-Situ Resource Utilization unit.

"Hmmm," said Philip noncommittally. I knew that Philip, like many of the other colonists, had doubts about opening up our colony. But that was the remit; after fifteen years of isolation, Lunar would be open to immigration. Those years of isolation were important. We were the guinea pigs for Earth's plans to colonise the Solar System.

"They look so small, don't they?" I said, pointing to the habitation module outside, "Could you imagine living in them for six months at a time?"

"They're sites of special historical importance," said Philip. "I don't know if we should Disnefy them."

"It's going to happen if you want it or not."

"A lot of things happen whether I want them or not, Sheila."

I refused to feel guilty; he was the one who had had the affair, not me. "Let's just stick to the point, shall we? I assume you asked me here to talk about Alicia."

"She's really unhappy, Sheila."

"I know that. I *do* live with her."

"She really wants to go to Earth."

"Well, she can't."

"Just like that?" asked Philip.

"Yes. Just like that. If she were on an outer world colony she couldn't just go to Earth. I don't understand what her problem is. She's only got to wait a year, before the boundaries open."

"It's tough for her. She's only thirteen. She says it's boring here. She says she's fed up of talking to the same people over and over and over again."

"And if she were living in Paris or Tokyo or London, she'd be miserable too. She's *thirteen*, Philip."

"I think you should consider it properly, Sheila."

"What would it mean if she went back? It would mean the failure of this entire experiment. You know that, Philip. I hope you haven't been encouraging her. Have you? Have you?"

"Well, I said that I'd discuss it with you."

"Oh, that's just great, now I'm the bad guy. Thanks a lot. Thanks a lot, Philip." I stood up and downed my drink.

As I stormed out of the bar, I noticed Makhul, sitting by himself, watching.

✦

Alicia was waiting for me when I came in, "Well?" she asked.

I cursed under my breath, "No. No, you can't go to Earth. I don't know what you were thinking. Have you thought about everybody on Earth?"

"I don't care about the people on Earth."

"Well, that's obvious, You don't care about anybody except yourself." I was fed up of pussy-footing around. "What about all the people who bought space-bonds to fund this project? What about the hundreds of thousands of people on Earth who are tithing, giving up one percent of their income to support us. You don't care about them. What about the people who can't afford one percent of their income, yet who still want to contribute? The people who work in the People's Space Collective projects? This is bigger than you, Alicia." I was on a roll. "What about the people who came before us, the pioneers of the Russian base, and the JAXA base, the helium-3 miners. You live in luxury compared to them, and you want to go home, because there's nobody you can date?"

"You are so smug. I suppose you'd prefer it if we lived like that, like the real pioneers of the Moon." said Alicia. "It was their choice to come here, can't you understand that? All you care about are your bloody mushrooms. Dad understands."

"Well, then, let him go home with you. I just don't care anymore, but don't expect me to give up my dreams because of you."

"Yes, it's all about you. All the time. It's like you've kidnapped me or something. I want to go home, but you won't let me. Thanks, thanks a lot."

She wrenched the door open and ran out of the room. I sighed; I could have handled that better.

✦

Five minutes later, Makhul phoned me, "I saw you with Philip tonight," he said.

"Yes."

"Did you tell him about us?"

I sighed. I'd agreed with Makhul that we'd keep our relationship private, until we knew how things were going to work out. "We were talking about Alicia, Makhul."

"Oh." It seemed like I was disappointing everyone today. "I thought you were talking to Philip about us."

"I told you that I wasn't ready to do that, Makhul. Don't push me too hard."

His voice became angry. "When are you going to decide, Sheila? Seems to me like you're still hoping to get back together with Philip."

"Don't be ridiculous."

"Well, you're not ready to settle down with me, are you? Are you?"

I said nothing.

"Well then, let's just call it a day."

"You don't mean that, Makhul."

"Yes, I do. I'm tired of you, Sheila. You're just stringing me along."

"Fine."

"Fine."

I put the phone down: the perfect end to the perfect day.

✦

Next day, I was scheduled for a whole eight hours in the lab. What bliss. I left Alicia in bed, and promised myself that today would be about science. I checked the cold-treated fungal strains, and took samples to check the production rates of the metabolic intermediates. Even now, after a century of research, we still didn't understand the trigger mechanism for radiosynthesis. In the classic experiments, exposure of *Cryptococcus neoformans* to increased radiation levels altered the chemical properties of its melanin within twenty to forty minutes. I was hoping to induce a similar effect in *Cryptococcus sheila* with a combination of cold exposure and radiation.

I lost myself in my work. It seemed to me as if this was the only part of my life that was going according to plan.

The base-wide com interrupted me, "This is an X solar flare warning. Please do not leave the base."

I put in a call to Alicia, intending to tell her to return to the flat. Even though we were well-protected in the base, I liked her at home during a solar event. There was no answer from her comm. I asked the computer to locate her.

"Alicia Reginess is not in the Lunar base," came the reply.

"Has she taken a mover out?" Even if she had taken a mover out she'd be safe, even though a small amount of radiation might slip through the vehicle's magnetic shields. I just hoped that she'd make it back to the base in time

"Negative. All registered movers are accounted for."

Where was she? Where was she?

"Computer, is she walking on the surface?" Without the protection of a moon mover she would be vulnerable to the radiation in the solar wind. A touch of fear walked along my spine.

"Alicia Reginess cannot be located within a five-kilometre radius of the base."

Philip called me, "Alicia's missing."

"I know, but where is she? Has she deactivated her com?" That was almost unthinkable.

"I've had a call from Mitchell's parents. He's missing, too."

"She's out on the surface." And with a certainty I could not account for, I said, "She's gone to Malapert."

"But we know where all the movers are," said Philip.

Suddenly it came to me: "What about the old rovers?"

"She wouldn't have taken one of those, would she?" asked Philip. "They won't provide adequate protection during a storm."

"I'm heading over to the port. We've got to find them."

"I'll meet you there," said Philip.

I put in a call to Makhul. I wanted him with me, too.

Mitchell's parents joined us at the port. "You were right, Sheila, they must have broken into the storage sheds and hotwired one of the rovers," said Theodore, Mitchell's father. Eleni, Mitchell's mother, was white-faced. She didn't speak.

"I'm going to find them," I said. "I'm sure they're gone to Malapert."

"Did she tell you that?" asked Theodore.

"She mentioned it yesterday. I'm pretty sure that's where she'll be."

Philip nodded. "I think you're right, Sheila. But we need to widen the search, just in case. Security are giving us three movers. They're taking the other ten." He looked over to Makhul. "I appreciate you being here, Makhul, but I can't allow you to risk your life."

"I'm going," said Makhul.

I put my hand on Philip's arm, "I want him to go, Philip."

We suited up. The security teams were faster, and we watched them leave the port. Mitchell's parents took one mover, Phillip took another, and Makhul climbed in beside me.

"We're going to find them," he said.

The rovers were slower than the modern movers. We estimated that they could only have travelled about twenty-five kilometres in the time that they'd been missing. Still, it was a lot of distance to cover.

Communication between the movers was patchy. I heard only fragment of the conversations.

"...biggest storm since 1989."

"100 million electron volts of energy."

"Please God. Let us find them in time."

"Maybe 100 rem of ionising energy, maybe more."

I shuddered, exposure to 300 rem of ionising energy was fatal. What effect would 100 rem have? The longer they were exposed, the more dangerous it would be. We need to find them quickly.

I pushed the mover to the limit of its capabilities. The thin atmosphere of the Moon was so tenuous it provided little or no protection against the proton storm. We were forced to rely on our eyes to scan for Alicia and Mitchell; the scanning sensors of the movers were functioning sporadically due to the interference.

I drove over my assigned territory in a daze, willing the

mover to go faster. I half-listened to the fragmented words of the comm. I scanned the surface. The lunar landscape which had seemed, only a few hours ago, so wondrous, seemed malignant, dead, malicious. Waves of ionising radiation swept over the Moon. The proton storm raged, sleeting hostile particles onto the surface. If I was wrong and we were heading in the wrong direction... I couldn't be wrong. I couldn't allow myself to even consider that.

Ever moment they were out brought them closer to the death.

"This is my fault," I said in a dead dull voice.

"No. Don't think that," said Makhul.

"Yes. What kind of mother am I, Makhul?" I moaned. My fault. All my fault. "I should have listened to her."

"Wait. We see something," Philip's voice came over the com. "You were right, Sheila. They *are* at Malapert." He gave us the exact co-ordinates.

We were close. Within minutes I saw the gleam of the metal rover, looking so small, so fragile against the shadow of that massive lunar mountain.

I exited the mover and ran out into the storm. Philip was carrying our daughter in his arms. When I saw her I thought... I thought that... My heart slipped through my body, dropping endlessly towards the moon dust.

Makhul ran to rover and grabbed Mitchell.

"We've got to get them back to the base," said Philip pushing past me.

I saw Alicia's arms move slightly. Alive. We took them back to Lunar and to the hospital.

✦

The days passed in a blur. I remember shouting a lot, insisting that they ship Mitchell and Alicia to Earth for treatment. They refused. I remember Makhul holding me. I remember Philip and the doctors trying to reason with me.

It wasn't until Alicia recovered consciousness and asked for me that I finally believed that she wasn't going to die. I was holding her hand when she opened her eyes. A wave of relief rushed over me, so intense I felt as if I were drowning. When she slipped back into unconsciousness, I went home and started packing.

✦

It was puzzling they both showed no signs of radiation sickness, even though they'd endured a significant dosage of radiation.

"There should be signs," said Doctor Akrem. "Vomiting, fatigue, low blood counts; but apart from their extended periods of unconsciousness, neither Mitchell nor Alicia show any symptoms."

"And the periods of unconsciousness, you said that they're not dangerous?" I needed constant reassurance.

"You understand what I'm saying, don't you, Sheila?

"Certainly, they've had a lucky escape."

Dr Akrem shook his head, "I'm saying that they've demonstrated an extraordinary radiation tolerance. Quite extraordinary. I want to do some more tests."

✦

A few days later we had the answer.

"Are you saying my daughter is radiosynthetic, like a fungus?" asked Phillip incredulously.

"No. He's not saying that," I explained. "There's no evidence that she can fix carbon dioxide."

"But the other part: absorbing radiation and water splitting?"

"Yes," I said. "I've confirmed it. The melanin in their skin absorbs radiation. They're tolerant to radiation in a way that we could never be. In fact absorption of radiation is actually beneficial to them, in term of increased ATP and NADPH levels."

"Is that safe," asked Mitchell's mother. Both Mitchell's parents were astrophysicists. It was down to me to explain the biochemistry.

I nodded slowly. Even for me, it was difficult to take in. "It appears to be. Our bodies create those chemicals when we digest food. They're perfectly normal biochemicals."

"But why didn't we know this before?" asked Philip. "They've

Deborah Walker

been tested all their lives."

"I'm theorising that the altered melanin only activated during exposure," I said. "It's been dormant. I think that this mutation was caused during gestation. Living in Lunar means exposure to enhanced radiation. Both Alicia and Mitchell were exposed in the womb."

"Perhaps all our children have this ability," said Dr Akrem.

"It's certainly possible," I agreed.

"But it's safe?" asked Mitchell's mother.

I nodded. "It saved their lives."

"It's an evolutionary step," said Dr Akrem. "I'm going to run more tests."

"Not on Alicia," I said. "We're returning to Earth."

"But Sheila, this is important information that could assist future colonies."

"Then they can do the same experiments on Earth."

"But Sheila..."

My mind was made up. "I'm taking my daughter home, Dr Akrem. There's nothing you can say to convince me otherwise."

✦

We are, it seems, an adaptable species, able to grow tolerance to extreme conditions.

✦

"I'm a freak, huh, Mum? Some type of radiation absorbing super-girl?"

I smiled and held her hand. She looked small and young, lying in the crisp white sheets of the hospital bed "I've got some good news for you, honey."

"What news?" Her voice was still frail from the ordeal she'd gone through.

"We're going home."

"Home? We're going back to Earth? Because of what has happened?"

"Yes. I'm so sorry, Alicia. I should have listened to you. We're going home."

"We can't," she said. Her hand plucked nervously at the bed sheet.

"We can, and we will. I don't care about Lunar. You're much more important than that. I'm only sorry that you had to show me how unhappy you were in this way. I should have listened."

She sat up slightly in the bed, "It was an accident. We didn't realise the rovers wouldn't have proper shielding. It wasn't a cry for help."

"Well, no matter. We're going back to Earth."

"I don't want to," she said.

"What do you mean? Don't worry about me, Alicia."

"I don't want to. I don't want to be the reason that Lunar fails."

"Don't worry about that, Alicia. The People's Space Collective has collected enough data. Colonisation will go forward, even if we do go to Earth."

"There's another reason, Mum."

"What is it?"

She had the grace to look embarrassed. "Me and Mitchell—well, we've become close. We're dating."

I was speechless.

"And what about Titan?" asked Alicia.

"You know about Titan?"

"You've got a picture of it on your bedroom wall. I didn't have to be a genius to figure it out."

"I've applied to go, but nothing has been arranged yet."

"I want to go."

"You do?"

"Mitchell's parents are applying," she said, smiling

"You can't go to Titan, just to follow your boyfriend, Alicia."

"I know. I know. It's complicated, but I really want to go."

"No, absolutely not," I said. "We're going to Earth, the Moon is not safe, and forget about Titan."

"What about Makhul?" asked Alicia.

"You know about him, too? What else do you know?"

"I know he went out into the storm to look for me. That's pretty special."

"Yes. Yes it is."

"And Mum..."

"Yes, honey," I was dazed by her sudden change of heart. She was crazy, crazy.

"Just thank you, Mum."

I smiled as I looked at my daughter. My daughter, the first child born in Lunar: changeable and unpredictable as a solar flare. My daughter, Alicia, second-generation Lunar child.

Deborah Walker grew up in the most English town in the country, but she soon high-tailed it down to London, where she now lives with her partner, Chris, and her two young children. Find Deborah in the British Museum trawling the past for future inspiration or on her blog: deborahwalkersbibliography.blogspot.com. Her science fiction has appeared in Nature's Futures, Cosmos and Daily Science Fiction.

THE NEW TENANT

Dr Philip Edward Kaldon

SHE FLOATED ABOVE Amazon Rain Forest Zone 23, snapping pictures, then comparing them to the ones she'd shot last month. The erosion had increased and this whole section would probably be lost.

"You have a call," her phone said.

"I'm busy." And expected that to be that.

But the phone didn't take no for an answer. "It's from Fourier. A Mr Ethan Hurd."

Sally Weilland smiled at hearing the name of her old college friend. Her phone knew her better sometimes than she did. "Ethan, how the hell are you?"

"Probably not having half the view you do, Sal."

"Ugh. Most of it isn't going to be here next year. You might be getting the better part of the deal. Speaking of deals, what's happening with the NASA proposal?"

"We got it."

"You mean you got the bid in?"

"No. I mean we got it. You want to get away from it all for a while? We need to have a caretaker on board."

Despite the importance of her work here, it took Sally no time to make her decision. After years of extensions and another ten years past anyone's estimated lifetime, NASA had chosen not to retire the International Space Station, but to sell it. And Fourier Rocketry had won the damned thing.

"When do you want me?"

✦

This wouldn't the first time she'd been in space. Sally's father had managed to cash out stock options from three successful software startups, and so had given her a trust fund with a huge annual allowance. One year, she'd spent the entire allowance on two weeks aboard Virgin Galactic's Earth Sphere One hotel. Another, she went around the world single-handedly in a solar-powered boat and never once put into a port. This year she'd bought an airship and floated over the ravaged Amazon. She'd put up much of the seed money Fourier Rocketry burned through in the beginning, trusting in CEO Ethan's dream and vice-president Ross Perkins' thoroughness.

Five of them had dreamed up the concept of Fourier Rocketry years ago at MIT: Ethan, Ross and Sally, along with Judd Washington and Rajit Gupta. They could hardly know the ISS itself was in their future, it had been continually manned since before they were born. Living in space was a reality for them and they wanted a piece of it.

"The whole point of a Fourier series," Ethan had said, "is that you can make any function from an infinite series of a complete set of Fourier functions. Make a square wave out of sine waves, whatever.

"But more to the point, you can get close in many cases with just a few terms."

The proposal was simple: five rockets, each one carrying a payload up to ten times that of the previous. From seventy kilograms mass on the Fourier-5, to 700 tonnes on the yet-to-be designed Fourier-1. Miniaturisation of technology had opened up the market for microsatellites of less than seventy kilos—Rajit had built two in grad school. They'd already launched eight of the Fourier-5s and then brought in some welcome revenue with one of the Fourier-4s. Tonight, here at a rented launch pad at NASA's Cape Canaveral, Fourier Rocketry was about to test their Challenger crewed capsule atop the first Fourier-3.

"It is only fitting," Ethan told his colleagues, "that on the doorstep of our greatest triumph, we debut our path to the stars for ourselves."

"Not exactly the stars," Ross said. "Just Low Earth Orbit."

They all smiled. If Ethan was the visionary, then Ross was the realist.

"And no one is aboard," Ross added.

"True. But when Sally goes up to the International Space

Station..."

"The *Fourier* International Space Station," Ross corrected.

This time Ethan didn't mind the interruption. "Yes, now it's the Fourier Rocketry International Space Station."

"One used obsolete space station, only one valid bid," Judd said. "Brilliant strategy, Ethan, to out-manoeuvre the big names in aerospace."

"Some of us just read the rules," Ross said.

"And NASA's still pissed that we bought it for a song."

"Pretty expensive tune, if you ask me. But the other bids wouldn't have differed much in price—we still had the better business plan."

"Have your fun," Ethan said. "But Sally will go up as our caretaker in a rented Ariane seat. We'll go up on our own rockets and others will rent from us."

"Hear hear!"

The Fourier-3 launch and test flight were a perfect success. They breathed a sigh of relief, and hoped that Wall Street investors, and potential clients, would take note of the new kid on the block.

✦

"Ms. Weilland!" "Ms. Weilland!" "Sally!"

She was besieged by reporters at the airport on her way to South America for her launch. Apparently Fourier Rocketry hadn't considered its new-found newsworthiness. Sally could have used a handler.

"All right, all right. I'll take two questions," Sally finally said. "You—yes?"

"Ms. Weilland, how have you prepared for this flight?"

"I'm assuming you're talking about going into space and not Air France. One of the things I did was get this buzz cut. I didn't want the hassle of dealing with long hair in space again."

The reporter pounced on her last word. "Again?"

"Yes. This is my second time."

"But you were a tourist then."

"Actually, I had two research experiments that were approved by Virgin Galactic so I worked on that mission. Very similar to some of the work and photography I expect to do on the Fourier International Space Station. Next question."

"How do you feel about ripping off the taxpayers by buying a multi-billion dollar space station for just a few million?"

"I don't think Fourier Rocketry ripped off anyone. NASA and its international partners have gotten their money's worth out of the International Space Station and they've moved onto their new station. Closing down the ISS and abandoning it would not only be a waste, but normal procedure would have been to deorbit the whole thing and burn it up in the atmosphere, which entails its own risks. Instead, they boosted it back up to a slightly higher orbit and solicited bids from anybody. We happened to win. And that means everybody won. Thank you very much, I've got a plane to catch and a rocket launch to space." Sally managed to end the discussion before the whole bidding debacle issue was raised.

When she finally settled into seat 3A, her phone had a message from Judd: *Sorry about not having someone with you at the airport. Our fault. Won't happen again. You did great. Regina's being flooded with P.R. requests and Ethan couldn't be happier-J.*

Sally smiled. The stubborn little engineering girl from Boston did good.

✦

With a clang of the hatch, Sally was alone on the FISS. Twenty minutes later there wasn't another human being within hundreds of miles in any direction.

After the announcement that Fourier Rocketry had bought the ISS, the press went on a feeding frenzy, trying to figure out who these upstarts were. Sally had missed some of that, having been busy preparing for her mission. But after her airport ambush, the press bombarded her with questions, filling her public email inbox. During a lengthy pre-launch press conference in Guyana, she pointed out that between the medical tests at NASA, training in the ISS simulator in Huntsville and the stack of technical manuals from decades of ISS construction and operation she had to review, they'd have to wait for some of their answers until she'd reached the calmness of space and settled into her new home. Ethan's wife, Regina, stepped in and handled the rest of Fourier's PR. All the same, Sally cringed at some of the ways she was being portrayed.

Sally Weilland holds engineering degrees from MIT and a Masters in Crisis Engineering from the University of Illinois. She also has a PhD in Sustainable Science from the University of Tokyo, making her one of the most qualified astronauts to ever fly in the International Space Station and the perfect candidate to bravely operate the ISS alone until Ethan Hurd brings the Fourier Rocketry Gold Crew aboard.

The last ISS crew were clearly concerned for her welfare. They'd kept all the supplies stocked up, especially the precious triad of air, water and food. And having pulled tonnage out of Earth's gravity well at great expense, there was no desire to bring home a lot of old gear. Amongst the old and obsolete cameras, lab gear and computers, Sally had a large selection of American and Russian spacesuits, should the need arise for an EVA.

Before the last NASA astronaut left, she asked Sally, "Are you ready for this?"

"Is anyone?" Sally replied. "Yeah, I'm good."

"Godspeed then."

✦

Sally's one large luxury item was her beloved and obsolete 200-600mm f9.5 AI-S Zoom-Nikkor lens. She'd found it in pristine condition years ago, and become intrigued by its strange pedigree and its ability to take stunning photographs. It'd been CPU-chipped and worked with all modern digital cameras. Today, she floated in the Cupola and, after adding a 2X multiplier, looked down on the Gobi Desert and started taking pictures. There was a market for fresh photographs from the Fourier International Space Station, as well as a contest to come up with a better name than FISS.

"Judd is calling from Huntsville," her phone said.

"Hey, Sally. Have you bothered to eat today?"

She smiled. "You've been checking the camera feeds?"

"Just me and seven million online users. You've been taking pictures for a few hours."

"It's fascinating."

"Don't overdose and get tired of it, now. You'll be there for a while."

"I don't think it's possible to get tired of it."

"You still need to eat."

"Would it help if I had a roommate to nag me? I can put an ad on Craigslist."

"Well, while you're waiting for that to pan out, Rajit would like you to go to the Kibo module and check up on Experiment 13. Looks like it needs some TLC."

"Actually, it probably just needs some reagents."

"Same thing."

"All right, I'm on it, boss. Let's keep the paying clients happy."

She fitted the cap on her lens, removed the memory card and velcroed the camera to a support. No one else was up here to mess around with her gear, but something could always float by and ding the glass. Nikon wasn't likely to make a service call and FedEx didn't pick up reliably from here.

✦

For the most part dinner fare aboard the FISS consisted of processed food pouches. Though there was more to assemble and a greater variety than the various pastes and mashes consumed by the earliest astronauts, Sally didn't have to do much in the way of cooking. But today, Arrival Day for the new Fourier Rocketry crew, Sally had something special in mind.

There'd been two boxes in the last Fourier-5 cargo pod which she'd stashed away. Now, rigging up a camera at the mid-deck dining table, Sally began recording her latest commercial tie-in.

"This is Sally Weilland on the Fourier Rocketry International Space Station. I've got company coming up from Earth today. I've cleaned up the place and prepared their sleeping spaces. Now we're going to have some surprise fun.

"This is the New Kenner Super-Sized E-Z Bake Oven. Toys 'R' Us will have it in for Christmas, but they sent one up early. And now we're going to put it together and show you that it's so easy to use, you don't even need gravity to bake a cake."

She hadn't had much in the way of girls' toys growing up. But some of the guys in the Crisis Engineering Lab at Illinois had brought in an E-Z Bake Oven and spent a couple of days rigging their own units out of spare parts and old-style hot filament light bulbs. Tiny pans of brownies had entertained the lab for weeks, which had given her the idea.

"You got that download, Judd?" Sally asked when the eighteen-centimetre-diameter cake was baked and the frosting had been applied.

"Sure thing. Looks good."

"And Ethan and the rest of Gold Crew don't know anything about it?"

"They've been too busy getting ready for launch to worry about anything outside their checklists. Surprise will be total. And by the way, Barry loved it."

"Barry?"

"Barry Simpson? The VP at Toys 'R' Us? Says you're a natural. They want to send some more toys up before Christmas."

"Nothing that's messy," Sally warned. "This one worked because the batter is so thick and, frankly, chocolate cake smells damned good after a couple of weeks up here."

"Understood."

✦

"Florida's coming up," Sally said. She reset the magnification on telescope T4 and adjusted the focus.

"Beautiful picture," Judd said.

Thirty seconds to launch... main fuel and oxidizer tanks are pressurizing... refill boom is fully retracted. Twenty seconds...

The computer locked the telescope on the launch pad's coordinates. The Fourier-3 rocket was barely visible against the surrounding tower and structure. There was a bright flash.

"What was that?" Sally asked, as the launch pad disappeared in a white fog.

Standby... standby...

"Uh... uh..." Judd was unable to talk.

There's been an event. Clock stopped at T-minus 13.381 seconds. We have no telemetry from the site.

271

"Shit! It blew up, Sally. The goddamned thing blew up! Fuck! Fuck-fuck-FUCK!"

Sally floated in cold silence. The FISS passed over Florida, while T4 continued to track backwards. As the angle shallowed, she could just begin to see how high the towering dark cloud had grown where the rocket should've been. The computer screen updated. NO MISSION TRACKING DATA, it reported. It might as well have said, ALL YOUR FRIENDS ARE DEAD.

The smell of chocolate cake lingered unwelcome in the air.

✦

"What do you want to do?" Ross asked. "We'll understand if you want to come home, but there are some issues."

"Like what?" Sally asked, not particularly wanting to abandon the FISS *or* stay aloft in limbo.

"The Soyuz lifeboats are old and the Russians don't even use them anymore. I guess there are concerns that either of them might not work properly."

"And they have a long checklist I'd have to do myself."

"There's that. But everybody else is scheduled. In a pinch, if you were in a real emergency situation, someone might do a rescue, but we're not there. I do have one other proposal."

"Okay. Sounds like I won't like it."

"You could stuff yourself inside a Fourier-5 pod. If we leave the ceramic nose cone on, it's capable of reentry."

"I know that. But I don't think I want to be on the first test. Besides," Sally said firmly, "we can't abandon the station now. If I go, there's always been the issue of whether anyone can get back in. Or whether it'll drift out of control without supervision."

"There are the robots."

"And they're old and temperamental, too. I spent two hours getting Fred to boot yesterday. No, Ross, I committed to being up here for as much as a year. You've got to figure out how to bring up the next crew."

"If we're allowed to."

"Every programme has setbacks."

"Yes, but we also lost our CEO and one of our major engineers. I should never have let Ethan and Rajit be on Gold

Crew."

"We're a small company, Ross. Everybody has to pitch in. What I'm doing isn't exactly safe either. And Ethan was adamant that he wanted to be the first president and CEO of a space firm *in* space."

"It looked good on paper," Ross admitted. "But now the money's drying up."

"You'll find a way. Ethan was a dreamer and a good talker. But what the investors need right now is the voice of calm and reason. And that's you. Just be yourself. No sugar-coating, but no doom and gloom. Got it?"

"Thanks, Sally, for the vote of confidence."

"Ross, that boat sailed a *long* time ago—or I wouldn't be up here right now."

"Point taken."

✦

Sally roused herself to regroup. Whatever else was going to happen, including whether Fourier Rocketry was going to survive, she was still on the FISS and still had jobs to do.

She'd just led one class of Earth students through a demonstration of the two Austrian exterior robots, Hans and Franz. Now she was showing them her two interior assistants.

"Ginger does everything Fred does, but backwards and in high heels."

Ginger wears high heels?

"No," Sally said. "It's a joke. Actually, Fred and Ginger don't have legs."

Oh.

✦

When the next Fourier-5 pod arrived, Sally contemplated the tiny interior space and wondered what it would be like to be crammed inside and ride it back down to Earth. Not that it mattered, this pod didn't have the heat shield or reentry fuel. She'd also run a check on one of the Soyuz lifeboats. Someone had sent her a report pointing out how long it had been docked and speculating on the likelihood that the docking rings wouldn't separate. The author proposed that Sally use one of the Canadian robot arms to pull the Soyuz off and then redock it, but she agreed with another analyst who considered that option far too risky.

One of the new small commercial ventures paying for Sally's time aboard the FISS consisted of a tiny Epson video projector and a rolled-up screen. They wanted her to do movie reviews from space. She fumed for a minute about this. When would she have time to sit through a bunch of movies? Besides her other jobs, it was taking four to five hours a day to keep the station running by herself.

Then she saw the Post-It note from Judd stuck on projector. *Remember to stop and have some fun from time to time.* Maybe he was right. Here she was, marooned in Low Earth Orbit on an aging space station, working for a company which had just lost nearly half its founding members *and* had no working heavy-lift capacity at the moment.

Perhaps stopping and ripping apart a good movie or two might be fun. She hadn't even given herself time to read a book in weeks.

And when she finished unpacking the supplies from the pod, she discovered that Judd had sent up a large bag of popped popcorn.

✦

LOST IN SPACE. Psychologists say that stress and loneliness could be affecting civilian astronaut Sally Weilland, abandoned on the International Space Station three weeks ago.

"Honestly," Sally told Judd, "I don't know why I read these articles about me. It's not like they bothered to find any facts or talk to anyone who knows anything."

"You haven't felt like giving many interviews," Judd pointed out.

"I've been too busy trying to round up new clients and do the jobs we've already contracted for."

"I know, I know."

"And frankly, Regina's not been ready to face the press,

either. For which," Sally hastily added, "I can't blame her."

"Ross is trying to get some new help. But money's tight just now. So if you could..."

"I'm sorry, the connection has been lost," the phone reported.

Sally brooded for a while. The FISS was in a communications dead-zone for the next twenty minutes. Fourier had acquired access to the old Space Network and the last of the TDRS satellites when they bought the FISS—NASA's new station used a totally new network. But the old system was breaking down and cost too much to maintain.

✦

"You have an urgent message."

"Sally here."

It was one of the younger ground controllers. "Get on your cameras, Sal. There's a 6.2 earthquake in the Pacific and we have a report of a tsunami wave heading towards New Zealand. You'll be overhead in seven minutes."

"Got it."

This was the sort of opportunity which not only gave them visibility, but if Sally could get the photos on the market fast enough, news organizations would pay handsomely. She tasked a telescope to start a live feed and then set up her cameras.

"How are the transmissions going?" she asked her phone.

"I'm sorry, the network connection is down."

Dammit, she thought. *We're losing time and money. Again.*

"Estimated connection time in twenty-three minutes."

Sally could punch someone in the throat, she was so mad. But it was hard to have a tantrum floating in micro-gravity. She had the pictures, she had the video of the tsunami from space. Breaking news and she had to wait. Even worse, the Google Space equipment attached to FISS used its own frequencies and Fourier was probably being scooped even as she waited. Twenty-two minutes now.

To her surprise, the main comm monitor bleeped, indicating a new connection. Curious to see what had changed, she floated over.

FINC-203 ONLINE
NEW INTERNET CONNECTION
FISS-0 TO FINC-203 TO FINC-201 TO DOWNLINK
AUTOLINK PROTOCOL AP:1.199.199.201.5 ENGAGED
NEXT INTERNET INTERUPTION IN
4 HOURS 17 MINUTES 08 SECONDS
NEW CELLULAR CONNECTION
VIA AUTOLINK PROTOCOL AP:1.199.199.201.5 ENGAGED
NEXT CELLULAR INTERUPTION IN
4 HOURS 17 MINUTES 05 SECONDS

Within seconds Sally was on the phone. "Judd, you bastard! You did it."

"Uh, did what? Sally, it's 3:13 in the goddamn morning and..."

"And I'm supposed to be in a comm blackout. But you launched, didn't you? FINC-203 is aloft and online!"

She could hear a yawn and a few assorted other noises in the background.

"I guess it did."

"You didn't know?" Sally couldn't believe that.

"Well it was scheduled. But it got late and I'd been debugging the RAID backup array and... I guess I forgot about the launch."

"You forgot about a Fourier-5 rocket launch?"

"We've done a bunch of those."

"Seventeen, so far."

"And they're reliable. Besides, Tina and The Kids are running those launches. I don't have to babysit. But it sounds like the autolinking protocol ran correctly."

"Damn right it did. I've got Internet! And cellphone. Do you know what this means?"

"Um, you can wake me up in the middle of the night?"

"That's just a bonus," Sally quipped. "No, it means that we're just about independent. We can get by without TDRS."

"Huh. Yeah, I suppose that's true."

"With three FINCs we still have some dropouts, but once -204 and -205 get up, we'll no longer have either comm drops or be dependent on the remaining TDRS sats."

"NASA will be pleased."

"Screw NASA. This means the world for us, Judd. Literally."

"Well, since you're up, go write a press release or something.

Blog about it. Get the word out."

"Will do. Right after I download these tsunami pictures."

"There's a tsunami?"

"About to run into the coast of New Zealand. Bye. Get some sleep."

"As if. I suppose I have to call Tina and tell her congrats."

"Wake up Ross and have him do it."

She heard a laugh from half a world away. "I think I will. G'night, Sally."

✦

She shouldn't really bother with this stuff, but Sally was one of the founders. So she read the financial reports from Ross and winced at the eroding of their capital.

What else could she do? They still needed investors. They still needed money. Hell, they still needed a heavy-launch capability and a new crew.

"What I need is a roommate."

She'd said it aloud, but rather than worrying about it, Sally suddenly embraced the concept. Maybe it was as simple as that. She had Internet, after all.

ROOMMATES REQUIRED

SPECTACULAR VIEW

INTERNET ACCESS

NO SMOKERS NO DRUGS

MUST PROVIDE OWN TRANSPORTATION

Only half amused with herself, and half hoping something would come of it, Sally posted the rest of her ad to Craigslist. Then she went back to work.

✦

"You have a call from Sanj Gupta. He is Rajit Gupta's cousin in Mumbai."

"Hello?"

"Greetings, Miss Weilland. I am Dr Sanj Gupta, Rajit's cousin. Rajit spoke very highly of you and of Fourier's futures. I wish to offer my condolences on your losses."

Sally wasn't sure where this was going. "Uh, and I offer mine to you and your family."

"Thank you. I wanted to apprise you of some discussions going on about tasking a mission to supply you, or rescue you, from the International Space Station. If that is what you wish."

"Gee, thanks. But I'm not in any trouble at the moment. And Fourier Rocketry is still around, though I have to admit we don't know for how long. All I can say is that we haven't closed our doors yet."

"That is good to hear. ISRO has its own efforts in space, as do China, Russia and the Europeans. But those of us in the Indian aerospace community feel much as Rajit did that the International Space Station is too large and too valuable to neglect. We are looking to invest in Fourier Rocketry, if that is possible."

"Possible? It would be wonderful," Sally said. "Let me get your contact information. You'll get a call from Ross Perkins, vice-president... um, our new president and CEO, within the hour."

"Oh, thank you very much, Miss Weilland."

"No, Mister Gupta, thank *you*."

No sooner had she disconnected when she had another call. "Marion Hope from Greenpeace is calling about the Craigslist ad."

✦

Arrival Day: Take Two.

NASA inspectors signed off on the third Fourier-3 booster. The fault had been located and addressed at the subcontractor level. For a time Sally thought that Green Crew would be arriving on rented transport from either the Europeans or the Chinese. But everyone had agreed the loss of the Gold Crew mission wasn't a systemic flaw in Fourier Rocketry's designs—and had pushed for the integration and assembly of the next rocket.

The new crew was a mixed bag. Greenpeace was sending its own environmental monitor aloft. Two Chilean astronomers. An Italian crystallographer to take over the research in the Kibo module. And a biologist from Barbados. Three more small countries and six international businesses had already signed on to either run experiments or send new modules up. In six months Blue Crew would be launched to relieve Green Crew—and Sally would be able to return to Earth.

"Welcome to your new home," Sally said when the hatches were finally opened.

"Glad to be here. Say, do I smell chocolate cake?"

Sally blushed. "It's a housewarming gift for you."

"We brought wine! Cake or wine first?"

"How about a safety tour?" Sally suggested, and they all had a good laugh.

Suddenly the space station felt crowded. Busy. Alive.

"You have a call from your father, Sally."

"Excuse me," Sally said and spun away. "Hey, Dad. I've got company."

I know. Just wanted to know if there was anything else you needed.

"You didn't happen to supply a couple hundred million to Fourier Rocketry the other week, did you? I heard on Wall Street Week that there was an unknown investor—and Ross isn't talking."

Guilty as charged.

"Thanks."

It's good business.

"I think it is."

Fourier Rocketry and the FISS—newly rechristened the Second Chance—were finally in business.

When are you coming home?

"I am home, Dad," Sally said. "I've got another six months on this lease. Then we'll see."

She disconnected and rejoined her new roommates. There was a lot to do. But first there was cake.

Dr Philip Edward Kaldon

Dr Philip Edward Kaldon teaches Physics at Western Michigan University in Kalamazoo by day and writes of the great wars of the 29th century and elsewhen at night. His stories have been published on three continents on this planet, appearing in Analog, Writers of the Future XXIV, Andromeda Spaceways Inflight Magazine, Abyss & Apex and 100 Stories for Haiti, among others. His website can be found at www.dr-phil-physics.com

WAVERIDER ENTRY SPACECRAFT:
A HISTORY

Duncan Lunan

IN MAY 2010, the US Air Force successfully tested the X-51 prototype of an air-launched, scramjet Mach 6 cruise missile. To minimise risks to serving personnel, the production version is intended to be launched from a B-52, to take out targets identified by unmanned drones sixty miles away. The vehicle's novel feature is a nosecone shaped to generate an attached shockwave at hypersonic speed—a 'Waverider'. In November 2010, Time Magazine hailed Waverider as number four in the fifty best inventions of 2010[1]. Nobody would have guessed from the item that Waverider was actually invented fifty-three and a half years before, at Queen's College, Belfast, for peaceful purposes.

Waverider was devised in March 1957 by Prof Terence Nonweiler of Queen's College, Belfast[2], during work commissioned by Dr WF (Bill) Hilton of Armstrong-Whitworth on the 'Pyramid Wing' re-entry vehicle, intended for a manned spacecraft in the British space programme based on the Blue Streak missile[3]. The Blue Streak programme was cancelled by the Macmillan government, but work on Waverider continued at the Royal Aircraft Establishment, Farnborough—mainly examining

---

[1] Richard Corliss et al, 'The 50 Best Inventions of 2010', Time, 176, 21, 48, 22 November 2010.

[2] Terence RF Nonweiler, 'Some Reflections on Waverider Design', Asgard, 3, 2, 19-22, Association in Scotland to Research into Astronautics, June 1997.

[3] Kenneth Gatland, 'Commonwealth Astronautics', The Aeroplane, 28 August 1959, pp 51-53.

Waverider's potential as a Mach 6 airliner[4,5]. In the same period there were tests of X- and Y-winged projectiles—in effect, four or three Waveriders mounted back-to-back—at NASA's Ames Research Center. Terence Nonweiler believed that in 1962-63 at least one Waverider was tested at the Woomera Rocket Range, mounted on the nose of an air-launched missile, possibly the Blue Steel stand-off bomb. Actually, Blue Steel was steered by forward-mounted canard fins and would not have been stable in such a configuration, but attempts were made in 1965 and 1967 with X-wings attached to an Australian research rocket, the Jabiru. Both failed due to misfiring of the rockets' upper stages.

In the late 1980s, regrettably, Dr Hilton claimed that he had invented Waverider himself and that Nonweiler had wrongly taken the credit for it. Gentleman that he was, at NASA's 1990 Waverider Symposium at the University of Maryland, Nonweiler said that he no longer remembered how it came about. At a conference in Glasgow two years earlier, however, he had demonstrated with the original piece of paper ("a well-worn teaching aid") how he had invented Waverider by origami, while trying to simplify the shockwave calculations which Armstrong-Whitworth had commissioned. In Dr Hilton's own book Manned Satellites (Hutchinson, 1965) on page 89, he unequivocally credits the idea to TRF Nonweiler[6].

In 1962, Prof Nonweiler became Professor of Aerodynamics and Fluid Mechanics at Glasgow University, and in March he spoke on 'The Future in Space' to the Scottish Branch of the British Interplanetary Society. He became a member of the

[4] (Anon), 'Around the Stands… Waverider', Flight International, 17 September 1964, p 528; 'RAE Bedford Open Days', Flight International, 4 June 1964, p 943; E Colston Shepard, 'Shapes for Still Faster Aircraft', New Scientist, 22, 394, 599-600, 4 June 1964; J Pike, 'Efficient Waveriders from Known Axisymmetric Flow Fields', in "Proceedings of the 1st International Hypersonic Waverider Symposium", NASA/University of Maryland, 1990.

[5] AJ Eggars et al, 'Hypersonic Waverider Configurations from the 1950's to the 1990's', in "Proceedings of the 1st International Hypersonic Waverider Symposium", op cit.

[6] WF Hilton, Manned Satellites, Hutchinson, 1965.

branch, and remained one the following year when it became ASTRA, the Association in Scotland to Research into Astronautics. In 1977, it adopted Waverider as its flagship, which has appeared in many versions of the ASTRA logo since then.

Nonweiler's classic paper 'Delta Wings of Shapes Amenable to Exact Shock-Wave Theory' was received by the Journal of the Royal Aeronautical Society in September 1962[7], and earned him that society's Gold Medal, but it was two to three years later before the concept briefly came into the public eye. Newspaper articles featured the Mach 6 airliner work and the prospect of reaching Australia in ninety minutes, leading to an extremely contrived appearance on an Scottish Television programme, in which news figures of the day were supposedly discovered in a restaurant: Prof and Mrs Nonweiler just happened to have brought a Waverider model with them to dinner. Afterwards, I asked Nonweiler about the obvious geometrical problems of launching it and landing it as an airliner, but was disappointed to learn that Waverider was still a theoretical concept, which didn't yet even include control surfaces.

In 1967, Prof Nonweiler took part in an ASTRA discussion project which led to my book Man and the Stars[8]. His brief was to discuss interstellar travel and navigation, but we went on to discuss the problems of landing on an Earth-like world, and he included a description of Waverider. Nonweiler strongly advocated winged space vehicles for delivery to planetary surfaces, and for landing in unknown terrain, he insisted on 'time to enquire' over the landing site—best attained with a low-wing-loading glider such as the Waverider. He dismissed arguments that more sophisticated systems than wings would become available: where you have a planet with an atmosphere, he maintained, a wing, making use of that atmosphere's properties, is more elegant than anything which wastes energy staying aloft by other means.

In April 1970, Nonweiler lectured to ASTRA on 'The Apollo 13 Disaster', with a detailed criticism of US and Soviet manned

---

[7] T Nonweiler, 'Delta Wings of Shapes Amenable to Exact Shock-wave Theory', Journal of the Royal Aeronautical Society, 67, 39-40, January 1963.

[8] Duncan Lunan, Man and the Stars, Souvenir Press, 1974.

spaceflight design philosophy, for which his kindest word was
'pragmatic'. In his view the Space Race had forced the adoption
of aluminium-and-ceramic materials technology and
aerodynamic shapes from the Intercontinental Ballistic Missile
programmes. Sophisticated aerodynamic shapes and the
advanced materials technology to go with them, in the X-15 and
its unmanned counterparts, had been brushed aside; the X-20
Dyna-Soar was cancelled before glide tests of the prototype.
Serious design errors like putting all the oxygen tanks in the
same bay of the Apollo Service Module were only to be expected
in the circumstances. Although much slower, a development
programme of winged vehicles would have been preferable.

We followed Man and the Stars with a project on the
exploration and development of the Solar System, eventually
published as my New Worlds for Old, and Man and the Planets[9].
The first contributor was Prof Nonweiler, on 'The Role and
Future of the Space Shuttle', in November 1973. By then the
Space Shuttle design had been finalised and Nonweiler said the
march was continuing down an extremely chancy road—the
major constraint now was cost, not time. He went on to predict
the factors which would delay the entry of the Shuttle into
service in 1979, and which led to the losses of the Challenger and
Columbia. Sad to say, he was right on all points.

But Nonweiler had an alternative to suggest. He went on to
outline the Waverider principle to the meeting, in more detail
than we'd heard it before, and it captured everyone's
imaginations. Even on the night, novel ideas for Waverider
applications flew around; by our seminar at the project midpoint
in June 1974, a good deal of headway had already been made and
preliminary artwork by Ed Buckley and Gavin Roberts was on
display.

At airspeeds above Mach 2.4, a Waverider wing would
generate a plane shockwave below it, attached to the leading
edges; the energy normally dissipated in a sonic boom is
harnessed to generate lift. The shape of the cavity and the
planform of the vehicle are directly related: a delta planform

[9] Duncan Lunan, New Worlds for Old, David & Charles, 1979; Man and the
Planets, Ashgrove Press, 1983.

dictates a shape called the 'caret wing', because from the rear it looks like an inverted 'V' or a printer's caret. A Concorde-type planform requires a cavity shaped like a Gothic arch, which the Royal Aircraft Establishment evolved for their Mach 6 airliner design. For best performance the wing-loading should be low, making the Waverider a very efficient glider.

We proposed planetary missions dubbed 'gliding entry', to distinguish them from the direct entry missions conducted or planned at that time[10]. Waverider could be used for prolonged exploration of the upper layers of Earth's atmosphere, so far sampled only by vertical sounding rockets; but it could map the ionosphere of Jupiter, which is multi-layered and deep, whereas the Galileo entry probe went through it in seconds. Because the most intense plasma would be concentrated below Waverider during atmosphere entry, it should be possible to maintain contact from overhead, or from Earth in a planetary mission, through the entry phase. By 1988, the TDRS satellites could receive data from the Space Shuttle from above during re-entry; later missions achieved speech contact, although the Shuttle was immersed in plasma to a much greater extent than the Waverider would be.

For extended missions in the atmospheres of Venus, Jupiter and Titan, balloons are at the mercy of the winds, limiting the study to one airstream, unless reaching another by rising or falling; their usefulness for surface studies is limited. When deployed over Venus in 1986, their lifetimes were short. Waveriders could cut across airstreams for more comprehensive sampling, and at low speed, would remain aloft almost indefinitely in denser atmosphere layers. (Nonweiler remarked that at two to three atmospheres' pressure a Waverider's stalling speed would be so low that "you could get out and walk beside it.")

On Mars, Venus and Titan, Waveriders could deliver payloads accurately to preselected targets. Since they travel at a high

---

[10] Duncan Lunan, 'The Role of Nonweiler Waverider Spacecraft in Exploring and Developing the Solar System', L5 Society (Western Europe) Conference, 1977; reprinted Spacereport, ASTRA, 1981; (abridged) Journal of the British Interplanetary Society, January 1982.

angle of attack during entry, we believed that landers could be carried as 'deck cargo', without having to fit into thermally protective aeroshells—although Gordon Ross of ASTRA, and JPL and the University of Maryland, later discovered independently that even at high Mach numbers there has to be smooth flow over the upper surface to realise Waverider's theoretical performance. As Nonweiler said, "one would stop short of having an open cockpit."

Waveriders could perform extended gliding missions over Mars, flying down Valles Marineris and other chasms, for example, or spiralling down Olympus Mons for close-ups of the mysterious cliffs at its base. Stalling speed in the Martian atmosphere would be about 400 kph, comparable to the touchdown speed of the Space Shuttle on Earth—not good for landing conventional payloads, but a caret Waverider makes a very effective penetrator.

There's concern in the developing world that the poorer countries won't benefit from exploiting the Solar System's resources, and the gap between rich and poor nations will widen. The United Nations Moon Treaty hasn't been signed by Britain or the USA, but the 1967 Treaty on the Peaceful Uses of Outer Space specifies that extraterrestrial resources are "the common heritage of mankind". When the resources of the Moon and the planets are developed, it will have to be on an international basis, with safeguards for developing nations' rights. Waverider's low wing-loading gives a landing 'footprint', descending from space, which literally envelops the Earth, and touchdown speed less than 160 kph; a delivery vehicle which can land anywhere on Earth, on ordinary runways, will have great political importance. Other ideas from the Man and the Planets discussions suggested that Waveriders' future role could be comparable to Containers in the late Twentieth Century.

In January 1982, Gordon Dick (now Gordon Ross) and John Bonsor proposed an ASTRA Waverider Aerodynamic Study Programme for low-speed work, as Nonweiler had said for years that some British group should do. The first stages recapitulated the RAE research, moving towards an M-wing configuration. This proved highly unstable in pitch, on its one test flight, and ended its days as a rocket-powered boat. Counting the basic caret wing as 'Mark I' and the M-wing as Mark II, the Mark V was a caret wing with a vertical stabiliser like the RAE airliner's, but optimised for Mach 3.

In 1983, Rocket Propulsion Systems offered to launch a model at over Mach 4, at 30 km. altitude, on a flight of their planned 'Tiger' rocket. The offer came to nothing, but ASTRA conducted smaller-scale tests in 1985 and 1988. The first, witnessed by Dr James Randolph of the Jet Propulsion Laboratory, Pasadena, released a small Waverider into spiral descent from approximately one thousand feet, and although the glider wasn't recovered, we claim the first rocket launch of a Waverider into stable free flight. We also claim the first free flight, hand-launched earlier that year, but the USAF disputes this: they claim to have achieved an attached shockwave with the prototype XB-70B hypersonic bomber[11], but even if they did, it wasn't a true Waverider because it had a conventional aerofoil wing. No such claims have been made for Blue Steel, though it flew even earlier at over Mach 3 and had turned-down wingtips.

In June 1984, I mentioned Waverider's possibilities at a symposium in California, and was invited to speak at JPL. Dr Randolph was interested in Waverider as a carrier for the Starprobe project, to send an instrumented vehicle to within four solar radii (three million kilometres) of the surface of the Sun. It could be accomplished by Jupiter slingshot, but radiation hazards and very long flight time made that unpromising. Aerogravity manoeuvres in the atmospheres of the inner planets could give the probe a trajectory with solar encounters every two to three months, but required a carrier with a very high lift-to-drag ratio at high Mach numbers—for which Waverider was the best candidate.

In July 1986, I was invited to Energy Sciences Laboratories in San Diego, to discuss tether-launch of a Waverider from the Space Shuttle. Dr Joseph Carroll of ESL put this notion to Dr Fletcher, the Director of NASA, while John Bonsor, Ross and I put it to Roy Gibson, Director-General of the British National Space

[11] AJ Eggars et al, 'Hypersonic Waverider Configurations from the 1950's to the 1990's', in "Proceedings of the 1st International Hypersonic Waverider Symposium", op cit.

Centre, who would have to sign any Memorandum of Understanding on our behalf, and he approved. NASA required the Tiger/Waverider flight test first, to demonstrate Waverider's capabilites (and our own!). In April 1988, we met BNSC and Ministry of Defence representatives to discuss it, but RPS no longer had backing for the Tiger airframe, only the motor, so it couldn't be done, and we had to continue on a shoestring as before.

In 1985, we had tested models on a rig mounted on top of a Ford Cortina; press coverage led to wind-tunnel tests of a basic caret wing, at Mach 2.4 in a wind-tunnel of the Royal Military College of Science, Shrivenham, by courtesy of British Aerospace. We later learned from Clive Smith, the backup Juno astronaut, that BAe was considering Waverider as a shape for the HOTOL single-stage-to-orbit vehicle: because of its large wing area, advanced materials composites would be needed to keep the weight down and Waverider might be a candidate for a later generation of HOTOL.

In 1989, we flew a radio-controlled model, another first for ASTRA. In April 1990, Jim Randolph lectured in Glasgow; the audience was entertained beforehand by singer-songwriter Meg Davis, since when Jim's forced-orbit hypersonic interplanetary aerogravity manoeuvres at above Mach 125 have been known to us as 'megasonics'.

In October 1990, the University of Maryland held the First International Hypersonic Waverider Symposium, co-sponsored by NASA. Ross gave a presentation on our work and ideas, unveiling his new Mark 10 shape, with equivalent capacity to the Space Shuttle but with much superior glide performance[12]. (Thereby, physically much larger: it would accelerate to forced orbital velocity in atmosphere by external fuel burning.) Ross also announced his 'subtractive control' system for controlling the Waverider by segmented tip-fins.

In one respect we were unique: no one else reported on flying real Waveriders. When Ross showed his first six Waverider

---

[12] Gordon J Dick & Duncan Lunan, 'Amateurs' View of Waverider Applications', in "Proceedings of the 1st International Hypersonic Waverider Symposium", op cit.

models lying on the grass, a voice from the audience said, "My God, hardware!" Almost everything else in the intensive three days of the conference was computer graphics. A lot of theoretical work had been done, but many of the studies generated wing shapes which would fit within the shock cones from a point source travelling at hypersonic speed. Instead of a caret profile these produce a scalloped contour for the underside—Jim Randolph christened the family 'lips'. They would be very unsuitable for low-speed flight and landing, a key factor in ASTRA's efforts to design a Waverider shuttle, though not affecting it as a carrier for interplanetary transfers.

We also learned that a new class of re-entry vehicle gave Waverider a possible military role. 'Evaders', very loosely defined, were meant to perform high-stress, high-temperature manoeuvres during atmosphere entry, possibly as target drones for ground-based SDI. There had been tests with biconic designs, like NASA's for aerogravity manoeuvres in the atmosphere of Mars. But Waveriders might be used, and there were people (in civilian clothes) casually saying things to us like, "of course, we've cracked the control surface problem you're working on, but we can't tell you about it."

Evader was a joint effort by McDonnell Douglas and the USAF Ballistic Missile Organization. In late spring 1993, they tested a full-size research model in a US Navy Hypervelocity Wind Tunnel, at Mach 10, 14 and 16.5[13]. The model's upper surface closely resembled Ross's, though the underside was nearer the Maryland configuration. To everybody's surprise except Ross's, the performance turned out to be excellent even at well away from design speed. The model was instrumented for flight, and McDonnell Douglas tried to persuade NASA to launch it on a sounding rocket as a research vehicle. Knowing it to be part of a military programme, NASA was not so inclined, partly because they now had their own. In 1995, a large Waverider was tested at

---

[13] Mark E Kammermeyer, Michael L Gillum, 'Design Validation Tests on a Realistic Hypersonic Waverider at Mach 10, 14 and 16.5 in the Naval Surface Warfare Center Hypersonic Wind Tunnel No. 9', Naval Surface Warfare Center, Dahlgren Division, White Oak Detachment, 5 May 1994.

NASA Langley Research Centre[14]. Design Mach Number was 6, like the 1960s RAE Waverider airliner, and the model resembled it closely—but instead of a vertical stabiliser it had tip-fins like Ross's shuttle design! Following that, on in August 1996, NASA and the US Air Force unveiled a research vehicle, claimed to be the first of its kind, but shaped like the test models we had been flying in the UK for over ten years.

The new vehicle, LoFLYTE, was to perfect control systems for a Waverider which would operate at Mach 5[15]. (The Space Shuttle re-entered at Mach 25; megasonic interplanetary transfers would be at Mach 125 or more.) LoFLYTE was eight feet four inches long and uncrewed, but its 'intelligent' control system would become increasingly independent as it 'learned' from a pilot on the ground. It was built by Accurate Automation Corp. of Chattanooga, Tennessee, with Japanese participation in the control system, according to our US sources.

Since 1991, there's been speculation that the US military already has an operational Waverider, possibly the 'Aurora' spy-plane alleged to be operating from airfields in Europe, including Macrihanish on the Kintyre peninsula. In August 1991, the Sunday Times suggested it was responsible for sightings of 'wedge-shaped' or triangular UFO's, including one which had buzzed a British Airways Boeing 737 near Manchester in 1990. But the speed ranges quoted, from Mach 0.5 to Mach 2.0, were in just the area where Waverider work had still to be done—there would be no need for LoFLYTE or its successor if they were already mastered. And the 'evidence' for Aurora at Macrihanish consists of mysterious sonic booms, which a Waverider wouldn't generate. Almost certainly the traiangular UFOs were early Stealth aircraft.

In 1992, Ross and I drafted an article, 'Flight in Non-

---

[14] (Anon), 'Langley Probes Hypersonic Waverider Flight Concept', Space News, 6, 32, 28 August-3 September 1995.

[15] Dan Nolan-Proxmire et al, 'NASA to Hold Briefings at Oshkosh Air Show', NASA HQ Public Affairs Office N96-50, July 30 1996; 'Intelligent Test Aircraft Unveiled in Wisconsin Today', N96-154, 2 August 1996; Ian Sheppard, 'Towards Hypersonic Flight', Flight International, 26 November-2 December 1997, pp 44-46.

Terrestrial Atmospheres', including a Waverider carrier for a Venus surface explorer, a flexible aircraft for Mars exploration, and a Waverider factory for the atmosphere of Jupiter[16]. Analog editor Stanley Schmidt asked us also to consider worlds which would be like Earth, yet sufficiently different to need different designs. Following an earlier suggestion by LH Townend[17], Ross came up with two flexible Waverider shapes, the Lucifer Plane and the Altair, allying his previous experience in sails and hang-glider design to Nonweiler's theory.

At the 1995 Edinburgh International Science Festival, Ross unveiled two new 'Shapeshifter' flex-wing designs, for a space shuttle cargo vehicle and an interplanetary probe carrier[18]. The latter was tested in the Architecture Department wind-tunnel at Glasgow School of Art, where he worked in the industrial design unit. He went on to a whole new family of flexible airfoils, some tested in subsonic and supersonic tunnels at Imperial College, London, and investigated manufacturing a sample of the woven carbon-fibre fabric he designed for the Shapeshifter, for thermal testing at the Art School, which has the plasma torch equipment needed.

At the Astronomical Society of Edinburgh in January 1996, Ross and I proposed a flex-wing Waverider as a one-person escape craft for the International Space Station[19]. It would bring an individual back, for personal or medical reasons, without evacuating half the ISS crew by Soyuz, or all of them by Shuttle or a lifeboat like the cancelled X-38. A wrap-around life-support garment would maintain cardiac stimulus, intravenous drip or other medical needs during return to Earth; highly manoeuvrable, with a large cross-range footprint, landing vertically by steerable parachute, the craft would deliver a casualty straight to the best hospital to deal with the problem. A

---

[16] Gordon J Dick & Duncan Lunan, 'Flight in Non-Terrestrial Atmospheres', Asgard 2, 4, ASTRA, April 1992; shorter version Analog Science Fiction/Science Fact, January 1993.

[17] LH Townend, "The Waverider", APECS Limited, 1983.

[18] Gordon Ross, 'Hypersonic Flexwings as Ultralight Waverider Vehicles, a Conceptual Study', Asgard, 3, 2, 23-33, June 1997.

[19] Duncan Lunan and Gordon Ross, 'Mayday in Orbit', ibid, 35-40.

simplified version would have let the crew of the stricken *Columbia* return individually to Earth; the life-support system would have major spinoff applications. But to date it hasn't attracted funding, despite presentations to NASA and to Astrium UK.

Meanwhile, the University of Maryland and the US Air Force continued to develop their alternative concept, eventually incorporating it into the nose cone of the X-51 tested in 2010. Terence Nonweiler would have hated what's happened to his invention, sacrificing its positive features except for the hypersonic manoeuvrability, and as a pacifist he would have hated what the X-51 concept stands for. In his 1970 lecture to ASTRA he had attributed the lack of interest in Waverider to its lack of military applications, and considered it a small price to pay.

In December of 2010, I said as much to Prof Richard Brown, who held Nonweiler's Meechan Chair at Glasgow University, before moving to the University of Strathclyde as Director of the Centre for Future Air-Space Transportation Technology. Having examined Ross's flex-wing designs, he's interested in taking them forward. We look forward to further meetings on this and to reclaiming the territory for Nonweiler's version of the Waverider and its peaceful applications.

Duncan Lunan is an author, researcher, tutor, critic, editor, lecturer and broadcaster on astronomy and spaceflight, plus a wide range of other subjects. He has published four books, over 700 articles and thirty short stories, was SF critic of the Glasgow Herald 1971-92 and as Manager of the Glasgow Parks Department Astronomy Project, he designed and built the first astronomically aligned stone circle in Britain for over 3000 years. He is a Director of the educational company Astronomers of the Future, and his next book, Children from the Sky, is scheduled for publication by Mutus Liber in late May 2012.

DREAMING AT BAIKONUR

Sean Martin

Moscow, 27 June 1938

THE TREES ALONG Konyushkovskaya Street were heavy with scent. After a light rain earlier, the paving stones glistened with the last of the evening's light. Trams made their last journeys of the night, their bells ringing to signal the end of another day.

Up on the sixth floor at No 28, Sergei Pavlovich Korolev waited for his young wife Ksenia to come home from the printers where she worked. He had put Natasha, now three, to bed, and was waiting to show Ksenia what he had been working on that afternoon: rocket trajectories, his notepad a thicket of calculations, crossings-out and pencil marks. It was nearly nine. Tram bells from the street were replaced by a new sound: Mussorgsky's Pictures at an Exhibition. Sergei watched the gramophone intently. Almost as soon as the piece began, he heard footsteps on the stairs, followed by a key scratching at the lock. The door opened and Ksenia hurried in.

His smile vanished as soon as he saw her expression.

"Sergei Pavlovich, there are men downstairs," Ksenia said, half out of breath. "Two men. I saw them get out of a big car."

"They came for Glushko," Sergei said, his colleague's fate only too clear in his mind. Men had called at Glushko's apartment one day in March, and no one at the Design Bureau had seen him since.

"And now they come for me."

Sergei stepped forward and held Ksenia close. They closed their eyes and let the Mussorgsky fill the room about them. The eighth piece, 'The Catacombs'. All too apt, Sergei thought.

A harsh rap at the door brought them both back to the present. Sergei and Ksenia looked into each other's eyes and then Sergei moved towards the door as the music faded, letting go of his wife's hand. He opened the door.

"Sergei Pavlovich Korolev?" asked a man in a trench coat.

"Yes," Sergei replied.

"We have a warrant."

The man held up a piece of official-looking paper. Sergei nodded, and let them enter.

There were three of them. NKVD. They had done this many times before. And they set to work, going through drawers, shelves, alcoves, while Sergei and Ksenia sat on the sofa, holding hands, listening to the needle on the gramophone stuck in the run-out groove of the record. Books removed from shelves, waste paper baskets emptied, clothes examined. Sergei looked ahead, trying to distract himself with the pattern of a tree on the rug in front of him, imagining rocket flight paths in the curlicues of the leaves. At one point Sergei looked into the bedroom to see one of them examining Ksenia's underwear, then take his cufflinks from the dresser and pocket them.

The ordeal lasted all night. At six o'clock in the morning, the men sealed the study and told Sergei to collect his things.

Ksenia, more scared than she had ever been before, put Sergei's toothbrush and some clothes into a bag for him.

They would not let him see Natasha.

"How long will you be away?" Ksenia asked.

Sergei shook his head slightly. "You do know, don't you, that I'm not guilty?"

Before she could answer, the head NKVD man stepped forward and locked his arm under Sergei's.

"Let's go," was all he said.

Ksenia heard their footsteps die away on the stairs, and then ran to the window. She saw them push Sergei into the back of a car, and drive away into the Moscow dawn.

✦

Baikonur Cosmodrome, Kazakhstan, 8 April 1961

"Sergei Pavlovich," a voice said. "Time to get up!"

Sergei opened his eyes. His whole body ached with tiredness. How long had he been asleep for? He could barely remember getting on the plane in Moscow.

"Sergei Pavlovich, we have landed at Baikonur," the voice said, and now Sergei could see that a junior officer was talking to him. He shook dreams out of his head. His limbs felt like iron. Heaven at that moment would have been his bed in the villa at Podlipki, his little corner of the institute. How far he had come, in these twenty-odd years. It was not real, part of him felt, as he stumbled out of the plane into the warm evening air of Kazakhstan. But it was real, he knew. Whatever was real was now, his life was now; whatever his country had become since the end of the Great Patriotic War didn't matter. What mattered was talking to Grechko and the other fuel engineers, and to see that things were running to schedule. And then he must talk to Yuri Alexeyevich Gagarin.

The control bunker was a squat, massively-concreted building. Angular spikes jutted abstractly from the roof, designed to break up a rocket should one crash during a launch; a rocket in pieces would cause less of an explosion. The arrangement was known as "the hedgehog". Sergei nodded to the structure as he entered the bunker, as if to honour such a simple but effective device. He liked simplicity. Simple was strong.

The control room was well lit. White-coated technicians moved quietly between rows of desks like orderlies on a hospital ward. The computer was off in rooms of its own, computing trajectories, yakking out tickertape on the hour.

Sergei's key men lined up to greet him: Yuri Mazzhorin, his guidance trajectory guru; Mstislav Keldysh, who had plotted the route Gagarin would take in Vostok 1; Oleg Ivanovsky, who had designed Vostok; fuel engineer Georgi Grechko, a mathematical prodigy and the man Sergei most trusted with a slide rule; and then, finally, Valentin Glushko. The man who Sergei believed had denounced him in '38, now running his own part of the rocket programme. Glushko was also an engine designer of genius. Sergei could not do without him. But the past was never discussed. The two men liked to believe it was an administrative error; a minor miscalculation made by a nameless functionary within the NKVD.

"Moscow has given us the all-clear," Sergei said. "They were impressed with Ivan Ivanovich, and his safe return."

The group laughed. Ivan Ivanovich, a human dummy in a

spacesuit, had flown into orbit two weeks earlier, accompanied by a dog, a cockpit full of mice and guinea pigs, and a tape blaring out a choir singing Berezovsky's Vespers and a fishwife from a small village in the Urals reciting her mother's recipe for cabbage soup. As a ploy designed to fool the Americans, who might be listening in on Soviet ground-to-air communications, it was genius. Ivan and his fellow 'cosmonauts' had been recovered safely after landing in a field near a village two hundred kilometres from Baikonur.

"Now we are on the verge of history, comrades. You know your duties. Please tell me at once if there is an anomaly, however small. Now I have to go to the Summerhouse, for the pantomime."

✦

Moscow, June–July 1938
They took him to an underground room—it was still in Moscow, he was sure of it, probably a dungeon in the Lyubyanka—and denounced him for two days on end. He was given no food and drink. He was parched and weak. They accused him of sabotaging the Soviet rocket programme, like his turncoat friend Glushko; who had named names, among them Korolev's. Their bosses, Kleimenov and Langemak, were already dead. Sergei explained that he had done nothing wrong.

"You swine are all guilty!" shouted his interrogator.

Sergei asked if he might have a glass of water. A guard approached him with a water jug, and smashed it in his face.

Sergei signed a confession the next day, more fearful that harm would come to Ksenia and Natasha than he was of dying. He was sentenced to ten years of hard labour. And then he was put on a train to Siberia.

✦

Baikonur, 9 April 1961
The Summerhouse, built the previous year by Marshal Nedelin to celebrate the success of Russia's space programme, stood on the banks of the Syr Darya. The river flowed sluggishly below the

willows at the edge of the lawn. Korolev paused before the marshal's picture, already yellowing on a wall in the conservatory. Poor old Nedelin: trying too hard to please Khrushchev, he had rushed preparations for a launch. Things went wrong with the fuel supply; the rocket exploded on the launch pad. Nedelin—watching from a specially-constructed dias—had to be identified by his medals, there was so little left of him. The crew on the gantry were completely vapourised.

Sergei Pavlovich Korolev would not suffer the same fate, he was sure of that. He had already suffered enough and now there were only three days to go before all that would be history. All that promise, all that work, all that future, would be represented by one man: by Yuri Alexeyevich Gagarin. But where was he? Korolev looked down corridors, past blue alabaster pillars, through arches that would not have looked out of place in the palace of the last Tsar. Sergei found it ironic that the Russia of the Tsarists and the Whites had been swept away only for some of it to be recreated by the Communists. What was once good for Mother Russia was always good for Mother Russia, it seemed.

Sergei Pavlovich came into the main hall. The place was thronged with Party bigwigs, reporters from TASS, and men in long coats despite the spring weather, the KGB descendants of the NKVD thugs who had come for him that warm summer night twenty-three years earlier.

"You are to stand at the top table," a puffy Party boss told him, sweating in a suit a size too small. Sergei nodded. This was unusual. He made his way through the crowd to the dais. Normally he had to remain in the wings, the unseen, anonymous Chief Designer. His daughter Natasha, once they had been reconciled, joked that had he been in the USA he would have enjoyed the status of a Super Hero. Sergei had laughed, knowing how true that was. *Captain Korolev!* But in America, Wernher von Braun enjoyed celebrity status. Sergei knew they had to act quickly, send a man up before the Americans did.

Glasses chinked, throats cleared, a hush descended. Marshal Moskalenko, a humourless man, commander of the Strategic Missile Forces, spoke first. He praised the man who would be the first Soviet in space, a "high and important task given to you by the Motherland". Korolev nodded in agreement—Yuri's task was indeed important, and the Motherland would rejoice. Sleep was tugging at Sergei's sleeve: he yawned and felt his body deflating. He thought he would collapse from tiredness completely when one of Moskalenko's apparatchiks pushed him on the shoulder.

"You must make a speech, Mr Chief Designer," the man said. Korolev stepped forward onto the dais to louder applause than he had heard in years. He could barely hear himself as he spoke about his hopes for the future, how there would soon be a space station fully manned by cosmonauts, how they would soon be on the Moon and Mars, how going to such places had been in his blood since he was a boy watching aviators grace the skies over Odessa.

Sergei felt it was a pedestrian speech; he could have given it in his sleep. He was virtually asleep anyway. He had even reversed his no-vodka policy tonight, hoping that a few shots would wake him up. Then Yuri Alexeyevich was invited to the microphone.

Sergei smiled with a father's affection at the farm boy from Smolensk. Yuri saw him across the melee and winked. Sergei watched as Yuri received his commission from Moskalenko, bowing with all due servitude and vowing to honour the people with his flight. Moskalenko and his cronies looked. Even the halting of Yuri's speech by Vladimir Suvorov, the official cameraman, who asked the cosmonaut to wait while he loaded a fresh spool of film, failed to dent the sense of occasion.

Sergei backed away, wishing he could get on with work, rather than these stage-managed antics. He looked out across the lawn. Beyond it was the river, and, on the other side of that, the distant towers of the launch pad.

✦

Eastern Siberia, Summer 1939
On his first day in the transit camp, he had asked for a piece of paper and a pencil. The guards joked that it was too late to write his will, and punched him to the ground. He stood up again and repeated what he had said.

That night, he wrote to Ksenia. It was a short note, just to say he was alive. And then he doodled a few thoughts on trajectories:

if you were going to launch a man into space, where would you best do it from? The poles? The equator? But then he returned to writing to Ksenia, wondering if he would ever see her again, and trying to put his misery into words.

The transit camp was not his final destination. That lay further east, towards the Kamchatka peninsula. Maldyak. One of the Kolyma camps. They moved him out there as the weather worsened. Autumn in eastern Siberia. He couldn't believe the cold. Sergei lived in a tent with other prisoners: people from the rocket programme, and writers, musicians, engineers, even Party members, all starting their working day at four am. They worked in the mines, gangs of criminals overseeing them, effectively running the camp. They worked sixteen hours a day and then were fed soup, battling to get a place near the stove in the tent. Punishment was arbitrary; everyone lived in fear. One morning in the third week, a gang dragged Korolev out of the mine and beat him. He was left on the hard earth, jaw broken, teeth missing, his mouth full of blood.

They refused his requests for paper and a pencil. Who was he to think he could take time off to write or draw? But he wanted to jot down a few ideas for an engine or a fuel tank; it would take his mind off the pain and the tiredness and the cold and the hunger.

They would not give him a pencil, and beat him again.

✦

He could barely walk. His legs were swollen, one eye was sealed shut. He had problems turning his head; his neck felt like a vice. The world had forgotten him. Time passed. How much he couldn't say. But one thing was very clear: he was on his grandmother's knee in the house in Kiev. She was reading him a story from The Arabian Nights. Aladdin soared high above the kingdom on a magic carpet. As his Grandmother read, Sergei could see golden deserts, oceans of deepest blue, red sunsets and white mountains. Aladdin flew so far he reached the Black Sea, where Sergei could now picture himself as a boy swimming across the bay to watch the great aviator Sergei Utochkin fly his biplane at the fair in Odessa. As he stood on the shore, water dripping from him, he spoke to mechanics who had stopped working on their own planes to watch Utochkin loop and dive.

"That is our home," one of the mechanics said, pointing. Sergei thought he was pointing at Utochkin's plane; but the mechanic, somehow reading his mind, explained: "We come from the sky. All the way out there is our home, past the clouds, among the stars."

✦

Baikonur, 10 April 1961

Grechko, clutching a mass of loose sheets of paper, approached Sergei's table in the canteen. Sergei had finished his stew and was drinking a cup of tea. Beside his plate was a sketch for a space station. Once Yuri had gone up, Korolev had plans: another cosmonaut, probably Gherman Titov, would go up, then a woman, then a whole team, in a ship bigger than the tiny Vostok.

"Sergei Pavlovich," Grechko said. Korolev turned from the waist to look at Grechko. Since the beatings in the gulag, Sergei could no longer turn his head. Korolev indicated for Grechko to sit down.

"Are you happy with the fuel supplies now?" Korolev asked.

"Yes," Grechko said, and showed Korolev the calculations. Endless rows of six-figure numbers in smudged pencil. This was all Grechko had, the computer being out of bounds.

Korolev nodded. A good man with a pencil and a piece of paper was all he needed to put Gagarin in orbit. He, Sergei Pavlovich, supplied the other ingredient: the dream.

"Sergei Pavlovich, there is something else," Grechko continued. "There is a problem with my room."

Sergei nodded. Grechko lived, like most of the engineers, in the sleeping cars of a disused train that was rusting happily on overgrown sidings at the far edge of the cosmodrome. The engineers hated it, and would only fly down to Baikonur for launches at the last minute, returning to Moscow as soon as their work was done.

"What's wrong now?" Sergei asked, concerned that his staff should be experiencing possibly debilitating discomfort. Nothing should stand between them and their ability to work.

"I have bedbugs the size of rats," Grechko said.

✦

Maldyak, Eastern Siberia, Summer 1939

"Here is a king, a weakling," a rasping voice mocked. Sergei Pavlovich lifted his head, expecting the leader of the gang to come over and hit him again. One more beating would finish him, he was sure. He wanted them to get it over with. Then he could close his eyes, see those mountains again, meet Utochkin in the clouds.

"Sergei Pavlovich," said a quite different voice. "Korolev."

Sergei couldn't focus on the second figure. All he could see was a man who was tall, well-built. And who knew his name.

He woke in a bunk at the camp doctor's. He felt far too warm. He retched, but nothing came.

The man who had saved him was Mikhail Alexandrovich Usachev, ex-head of the aviation plant in Moscow. Like Sergei, they had come for him in the middle of the night, no time to pack. People at the plant noticed his absence the next morning, too scared to say anything about it.

Sergei spent a week in the doctor's hut before he saw Mikhail Alexandrovich again. Usachev gave Korolev something he said would aid Sergei's recovery: a sheet of paper. And a pencil.

✦

One morning in late autumn, Sergei was taking dirt from the mine workings to the spoil heaps. Pushing a barrow was tedious and backbreaking, but at least he spent most of his day standing upright, which wasn't too painful. Across the compound, Sergei could see an old man too frail to push his barrow. Everyone looked old at Maldyak. But this man moved as though the reaper were already at his shoulder, guiding him. The guard, one of the criminals, ordered him to push with greater vigour, indicating all the spoil still to be shifted. The man teetered on a brink only he could see. The guard punched him. Not hard, but it was enough to send the man down.

Korolev put his own barrow down, and walked across to the

guard. He gave Sergei a smile, too proud of his knocking the man down to order Sergei back to work. In that moment, Korolev hit him. With a look of surprise on his face, the guard collapsed next to the old man. Korolev bent down and helped the old man to his feet.

Sergei was summoned to the commandant's office. He said goodbye to the men in his tent. One of them gave him his coat. It was frayed but warm. Korolev thanked the man, expecting they would take the coat off him once his bullet-riddled body had been discovered somewhere out in the woods, just the other side of the mine.

The commandant was talking to Usachev. The office was not as warm as the doctor's hut. Sergei did not feel sick. He knew he would start to feel sick once they had told him that he was going to be shot. He was surprised he had lived this long, in fact. He could have been shot for asking for a pencil. If they gave him a last request, it would be to do one last diagram, one last calculation.

"Sergei Pavlovich," the commandant said. "Mikhail Alexandrovich has been telling me you are a great rocket designer."

"Yes." Korolev had his pride and so tried to be as factual as possible. Now was not the time to show weakness. He had just punched a guard, and now must face the consequences.

"I was just telling Mikhail Alexandrovich that the head of the NKVD has fallen. Nikolai Yezhov has been arrested."

So: the man behind Korolev's arrest and ten-year sentence was now himself a victim.

"The new head has ordered your case to be re-examined. You are to go back to Moscow."

"The new man?" Korolev asked, as if he was having trouble understanding.

"Your saviour, Sergei Pavlovich," the commandant said. "His name is Lavrenti Beria."

✦

They could not drive him to Magadan where he could catch a boat across the Sea of Okhotsk, so Sergei had to hitch a lift with a lorry taking cabbages and engine parts into town. The driver was bearded and toothless, his skin greasy with engine oil. Sergei wondered if he had been in a camp. Everyone around here looked like they had.

"Where are you going?" the driver said as the lorry bumped down the road.

"Moscow," Sergei replied. "They are going to re-try me." At the next turning, he noticed a bird perched on a tree. He pointed it out to the driver. "That is freedom. Only the birds have freedom."

The driver asked for payment in Magadan. Sergei had no money.

"I'll take the coat," the man said. Sergei gave it to him and watched the lorry drive off. He looked around him, his eyes drifting from the dilapidated houses up to the tree-tops. Three birds sat in the bare branches—Ksenia, Natasha and Sergei. But he wasn't sure if he recognised himself any longer.

At the dock, they told him the last boat had left for the winter. He slept in a barn the first night, burrowing himself into the hay. The old coat might have been tattered, but it would have helped keep him alive. It snowed overnight. A light dusting of white coloured the farmyard when he stepped out. In the camp he would have had cabbage soup and a piece of stale bread by now. He wasn't sure this was any better. At least here he would die of cold, rather than at the hands of the gangs.

He spent the day wandering, getting colder and hungrier. He tried to picture summer in Odessa, talking to the mechanics and admiring the beauty of their seaplanes. Sometimes, in his dreams, he would be swimming, drifting on his back, looking up at the big blue freedom above him, and a plane would pass over. He would close his eyes and imagine that he was flying in the plane's wake. The longer he kept his eyes shut, the stronger the feeling became. Other times he would notice the shadow a plane made on the water; it was especially good—lucky—to be able to swim through a plane's shadow. Somehow, he knew, he would one day work out how to climb the shadow and reach the plane, uniting the freedom of water and the freedom of sky.

Odessa faded. He was on a narrow track that lead out of town. A thin copse of trees lay ahead. He could feel himself swaying, losing balance. There was movement in the trees ahead. Was it a gang of brigands, waiting to jump him and take his life—all he had left? He didn't care. They could have it.

Then he noticed it. Over by the well. A loaf of bread. He walked over, using what felt like the last of his energy. If this is not real, he told himself, I will die. Cold, hunger, brigands, birds—they can all have my bones. Sergei reached down and touched the bread. It was real, warm, freshly baked. Who had left it here? Had someone dropped it? He looked around, expecting an irate baker to run up. But no one did. He was on his own. Even the figures in the trees seemed to have melted into the gloaming. He ate.

That night he slept in a storage hut on the perimeter of the local army camp. He woke early, frozen to the floor.

✦

He spent the winter odd-jobbing in Magadan, sleeping where he could. Blizzards gave way to fogs, but the cold never left. One day in March, news came that the boat to the mainland had arrived. Sergei hobbled to the harbour and watched it dock in the fog. It was almost as beautiful as a seaplane.

After reaching the other side of the Sea of Okhotsk, he made straight for the railway station. He explained to the guard that he had to get to Moscow. The man nodded, chewing his pencil. Then Sergei had an idea.

"I must write to Comrade Stalin. And to my mother."

The man nodded, and gave Sergei the pencil.

The compartment was cramped, the seats painful. But the sounds of the carriages clunking over rusty rails was music, a song of westwards, of home. He wrote a letter to Stalin, explaining his innocence once more. Sergei explained his love of rockets, of flight, of summers in Odessa. The letter was tatty. His hands were too cold to write properly. He wrote to his mother, thanking her for the campaigning she had done on his behalf.

The world once more seemed to float. He was on the Black Sea, on a magic carpet over the Urals looking down with love on the Motherland. He was in a cold train, crunched in a corner, half-crippled, crying. He stopped writing and slept.

When he woke, he realised he was still clutching the pencil. But he felt worse than he had ever felt. His gums were bleeding. A guard was summoned. At Khabarovsk, Sergei was taken off the train.

"This man is dying," the guard said. "He has scurvy. He cannot die on my train."

They put Sergei down on a bench on the platform. A doctor might have been called for, but no one was sure. The guard waved to the driver and the train slowly pulled out.

Sergei ran his tongue around his upper gum. One tooth was still left. The rest was sore, small holes where his teeth had been. They were in the ground at Maldyak, along with other people's bones. It reminded him of Bruegel's The Triumph of Death, with skeletons mowing the living down, or the old story of the three kings who meet three skeletons while out hunting.

"As you are now, so once were we," the chief skeleton said. Sergei imagined himself one of the kings. But all he had to show from hunting was his suitcase, which was nearly as battered as he was. The lock no longer worked.

The skeleton drew closer. "And as we are now, so you shall be." The three laughed.

Sergei nodded, knowing the skeletons were right. He had survived the Lyubyanka, the transit camps, the hell of Maldyak, only to leave this world on a railway station platform. At least I'm dying like Tolstoy, he thought, as the skeletons' laughter became the sound of a child crying and its mother trying to shush it. He opened his eyes.

There was a small crowd of people looking at him. The woman wiped her child's nose. No one spoke. And then an old man stepped up to Sergei. He smiled.

"I can make you better, sonny," the man said. He led Sergei out of the station. A boy came with them, carrying Sergei's case. But the pencil Sergei refused to let anyone touch.

The man sat Sergei down under a tree.

"It is warm here," the man said. They were facing the sun. It was not yet midday.

The man and the boy went away. Sergei slept, too tired for dreams. When he woke, the man was back with some herbs. He told Sergei to open his mouth, and then rubbed the herbs on

Sergei's gums.

"This is *kolba*," the old man explained. "Kolba is good. Makes you better."

Sergei nodded, realising he had dropped the pencil. He looked down, searching for it with a tired hand. He stopped when he saw a butterfly flitting over the grass. A small tentative freedom. Sergei was dumbfounded by the creature. It was doing what he had always wanted to do, to fly, to get away. He looked back to the old man.

"I'm alive," Sergei said, weakly.

✦

14 April 1947, Moscow

Sergei was summoned to the Big House. An audience with Comrade Stalin. In less than three years, he had gone from being a prisoner to walking the softly-carpeted labyrinth of the Kremlin. He had written to Stalin after the re-trial. His sentence had been cut by two years, and he had been assigned to work in a *sharaga* prison, or Central Design Bureau 29, as it was euphemistically called. Nothing in the Soviet Union was named for what it was; everything meant something else. Sergei designed liquid-fuelled rocket boosters for the Pe2 dive bomber. He felt kindness and gratitude toward Comrade Stalin who, while not answering Sergei's letter, had evidently seen to it that Sergei was never sent back to the frozen circle of Maldyak's hell.

The conference room was full of Party men, politburo functionaries. Sergei was part of a team who were now working on studying captured German V-2s, one of the wonders of the war. Stalin did not offer Sergei his hand, and acknowledged him only with a slight nod. Sergei wanted to thank him for commuting his sentence, to urge him to clamp down on the NKVD thugs who had been ruining the country, but he held himself in check. Now was the time to sell his dream to the most powerful man Russia had ever known.

Stalin paced the room. The V-2 was obsolete, Sergei argued. Russia must look to the future if it was to compete with America. And the way forward was liquid-fuelled rockets; the work he had done in the *sharaga* proved that.

Stalin was not so sure. Maybe Comrade Korolev and his team should perfect a Soviet copy of the V-2 first? The meeting ended. Sergei was to develop a missile for bombing the Americans and their capitalist allies. Space travel would have to wait.

✦

Baikonur, 11 April 1961

Sergei walked slowly, listening to the launcher's engines rumble as it inched along the rail tracks linking the main assembly shed with the launch pad. He did not look up, his eyes instead focusing on the ground ahead of him, his body dwarfed by the shadow of the huge R-7 rocket lying on its side on a hydraulic platform. Moving at less than walking speed, Sergei had to check himself to stop himself overtaking the launcher. He listened. Anything that sounded abnormal could cause a delay, but the launcher's huge engines rumbled happily.

It was four kilometres from the assembly shed to the launch pad. There was so much Sergei still had to tell Gagarin; but that would have to wait. For now, he gently willed the railcar to deliver its huge payload safely to the pad. As soon as it was there, the gantry team would go to work, checking, endlessly checking: life support systems, propulsion systems, navigational gyros.

It was a warm day and the steppe was in flower. The best time of year to be at Baikonur. The rocket's shadow comforted him the same way the shadows of the biplanes at Odessa had thrilled him when he was a boy.

That afternoon, Sergei Pavlovich, Yuri Alexeyevich, and his ever-present back-up, Gherman Titov, ascended the gantry. There was barely enough room for them to look into Vostok's capsule at the same time, that tiny space filled with status indicators, switches, chronometers, gyroscopes, accelerometers, temperature and pressure gauges, gauges to measure oxygen, temperature, carbon dioxide and radiation, a little globe that represented the Earth, the food locker and the TV camera which, Sergei explained, would be trained on the cosmonaut for the entire flight. Yuri—or, in the case of unforeseen developments, Gherman—had to spend that time scanning the dials at intervals, taking notes and reporting the readings back to the control bunker via the radio up above the pilot's seat.

"Don't forget your pencil," Sergei joked. The two cosmonauts laughed.

"Where would we be without pencils?" Yuri replied.

Sergei froze, the joke no longer funny. He clutched his chest, breathed out and looked down at his shoes.

"Sergei Pavlovich, shall we call a doctor?" Gherman asked. Yuri's hand was already on the gantry's intercom.

✦

Moscow, Autumn 1948

A summons came. A recall to the Big House, to see Lavrenti Pavlovich in Room 13. Beria. The man who had saved him from the *gulag*, and had taken the NKVD to new depths of brutal depravity. Now he was overseeing the Soviet Bomb. Sergei dreaded to think what Beria would do with an atom bomb. Why bomb the Americans, when your own people were so much closer to home, so much more trouble?

Sergei banished such heretical thoughts as he entered Beria's department. All the secretaries in the ante-room looked like they were about to be shot. It took Sergei a moment to realise that they were not going to be killed; they were simply working for Beria. This was normal.

Sergei was ushered into Beria's office. A big, balding man sat behind a heavy oak desk, checking paperwork and scribbling notes with the harsh stub of a pencil. He looked up at Sergei. His eyes were completely obscured by the thick lenses of his pince-nez.

"Your rockets keep crashing, Comrade Korolev," Beria announced coldly. "When was the last explosion?"

Sergei explained that they had indeed been having trouble with the R-1, the Soviet remake of the V-2. It was not possible to get it right first time. Even men captured in 1945, who had worked at von Braun's Peenemünde complex, had admitted as much.

Beria was not interested in von Braun's early difficulties. "There is another rocket team."

Sergei thought for a moment Beria was referring to the

German, but then realised his error.

"The other team's results are much more satisfactory. They have not had a crash at all. Their rockets fly all the way to Kamchatka."

Sergei nodded. He was not aware of another team. He was sure Beria was lying; there was no other team. But he could not accuse Beria of lying.

"You might find people knocking on your door in the middle of the night," Beria announced, like a music-hall star delivering his punch line to an audience who'd heard it all before, but still feared the humour.

Sergei nodded again. Beria dismissed him.

✦

Baikonur, 12 April 1961

The telephone rang. It was shortly after five am. Startled from a fitful sleep, Sergei sat bolt upright—the times Beria would phone late at night to shout abuse, threatening him with re-arrest, a vivid presence in the dawn's half-light.

"Sergei." It was Nina, his second wife. "Have I woken you?"

"Yes," Sergei said, looking at his desk, scattered with papers and last night's notes, relieved Beria was long-dead.

An empty tea-cup sat by the vase of lilacs his housekeeper had placed on the table, but the flowers had not had their usual calming effect on him. Sergei had come back from the gantry to see the doctor, and after taking some pills and having his blood pressure taken, he lied about how well he felt. The doctor left, reassured that Korolev was well enough to oversee the launch. Sergei could not sleep, and spent the night worrying through problems that might occur in the morning. The first forty seconds after ignition were crucial. If they could get through those without Gagarin having to eject, it would bode well for the remaining one hundred and seven scheduled minutes of the flight. Korolev finally dozed off in his chair around four am.

"I slept very well," Sergei told Nina. "I feel fine."

Thirty minutes later, Sergei called at Yuri's cottage. "What's this? A lie in?" he joked.

"Everything will be alright, Sergei Pavlovich," Yuri said as he was being assisted into his spacesuit.

Korolev nodded.

An old woman presented Yuri with some flowers as they walked out to the bus. "I used to live in that cottage," she said. "Before the rockets came. My son was a fighter pilot. He died in the War." Yuri thanked her and got on the bus carrying a bouquet of roses.

Crowds mobbed Yuri as he alighted from the bus at the gantry. Someone asked him for his autograph.

"Is this really necessary?" Yuri asked, but signed anyway. Then someone else asked. As he was signing, Titov was told to go back to the cottage. He would not be needed.

Yuri spoke to the crowd in the bright, early morning air. "Dear friends, compatriots, and people of all countries and continents! In a few minutes a mighty ship will carry me aloft to distant space. What can I say to you in these last moments before the launch? At this instant the whole of my life seems to be condensed into one wonderful moment... to be the first to enter the cosmos, to engage, with nature—could one dream of anything more?"

He turned to Sergei Pavlovich, who forced a smile. All these crowds. More people getting in the way.

"Well, Yuri Alexeyevich, it's time to get aboard," Sergei said.

"Don't worry, Sergei Pavlovich," Yuri said. "Everything will be fine."

Yuri had to spend over two hours in the capsule before the launch, timed for seven minutes past nine. Korolev radioed him from the bunker.

"This is Dawn, how do you read?" Sergei said.

"This is Cedar," Yuri replied. "All is well."

Sergei knew they had to make light of things, fearing the doctor might be called again if the strain he was feeling got any worse. He broke off from routine checks to remind Yuri he was not to go hungry on the flight.

"You have sixty-three tubes of food in the storage locker. You will get fat!"

"The main thing is that there is some sausage!" Yuri replied. "Sausage and vodka!"

"We'll have the vodka tonight when you get back!"

Yuri looked over Vostok's controls again. He put his hand on the keypad to the left of his chair. Korolev had told him the secret code that morning in the cottage. If Vostok began to deviate from its flight path or, worse, start to spin, Yuri could gain manual control of the ship by typing in 3-2-5.

In the bunker, Sergei was getting updates by the minute; dozens of pairs of eyes scrutinized readings, print-outs, cross-checking telemetry systems. Sergei could feel his breath getting heavier, more laboured. His heart thudded inside his chest like a fist. He took more pills. There was as much chance of him dying during the course of the morning as Gagarin.

They could all hear Yuri whistling a song inside the capsule. Then he began to sing:

Today you bought me not a bouquet of roses
But a bottle of Stolichnaya
We'll hide it in the bulrushes and
Get drunk out of our skulls
So why do we need these goddam lilies of the valley?

Sergei had heard Yuri sing this many times before in training. It brought a smile to his lips, though he noticed Glushko looking disapproving.

"Cedar, this is Dawn. Ignition is about to start," Sergei said.

Yuri stopped singing. "This is Cedar. I read you."

He sounded calm. His pulse rate showed normal. Sergei was reassured.

Now, at six minutes past nine, time seemed to have stopped. It was the longest minute in Sergei Pavlovich's life. By noon that day, he knew Yuri would have seen something no other human being had ever witnessed: the Earth from space. He imagined Yuri speechless at the beauty of the Earth, the mountains and valleys, the rivers and seas, as if he were on a magic carpet from one of Sergei's childhood stories. Yuri would be dazzled by the strength of the sun, and quietened by the shadow of night across half the globe. He would experience true weightlessness. He would need to keep hold of his pencil, in case it floated across the capsule and out of reach. And then, when one orbit was complete, he would come back to Earth, parachuting down onto the steppe in the Saratov region, nearly three hundred kilometres west of Baikonur. He would explain to suspicious villagers there was no cause for alarm: he was a Soviet, had come from outer space and needed to telephone Moscow.

It was now seven minutes past nine. There would be no countdown. That was something only the Americans did, for show. Sergei gave the signal.

"Ignition," he said.

The bunker was loud with the R-7's engines blasting. Korolev and Glushko exchanged glances. Grechko clutched his slide rule. It felt like an earthquake.

And then they heard Yuri's voice over the intercom. "Let's go!" he shouted.

And as the rocket went up into the clear April air, Korolev turned to watch it on one of the monitors. Suvorov had positioned his cameras, with more than enough film loaded this time, at a safe distance from the inferno of the blast pits. One screen showed the R-7 forging into the heavens on its column of fire, while another was trained on the rocket's shadow, and Korolev saw it moving across the gantry, away from the bunker, over the steppe, escaping upward.

Sean Martin is a writer, poet and filmmaker. He is the author of The Knights Templar: The History & Myths of the Legendary Military Order, The Cathars: The Most Successful Heresy of the Middle Ages and Andrei Tarkovsky, amongst others. His films include Lanterna Magicka: Bill Douglas & the Secret History of Cinema. He is also the winner of the 2011 Wigtown Poetry Prize. He lives in Edinburgh.

RECOMMENDED FURTHER READING

FICTION

_Barton, William: Dark Sky Legion (1992)
_Barton, William & Michael Capobianco: Iris (1990), Fellow Traveler (1991), Alpha Centauri (1997)
_Baxter, Stephen: Voyage (1996), Titan (1997), Moonseed (1998)
_Hartmann, William K: Mars Underground (1997)
_Jones, Gwyneth: Life (2004)
_Kerr, Philip: The Second Angel (1998)
_Landis, Geoffrey A: Mars Crossing (2000)
_Locke, MJ: Up Against It (2011)
_McAuley, Paul: The Quiet War (2008), Gardens of the Sun (2009), In The Mouth of the Whale (2012)
_Mercurio, Jed: Ascent (2007)
_Mixon, Laura J: Burning the Ice (2002)
_Moriarty, Chris: Spin State (2003), Spin Control (2006)
_Nagata, Linda: Tech-Heaven (1995), The Bohr Maker (1995), Deception Well (1997), Vast (1998)
_Robinson, Kim Stanley: Icehenge (1986), Red Mars (1992), Green Mars (1993), Blue Mars (1996), The Martians (1999)
_Sargent, Pamela: Venus of Dreams (1986), Venus of Shadows (1988), Child of Venus (2001)
_Slonczewski, Joan: The Highest Frontier (2011)
_Sterling, Bruce: Schismatrix (1985), Holy Fire (1996), Distraction (1999), The Caryatids (2009)
_Williams, Sean, with Shane Dix: Echocs of Earth (2002), Orphans of Earth (2003), Heirs of Earth (2004)
_Zubrin, Robert: First Landing (2001)

NON-FICTION

_Armstrong, Neil, Edwin 'Buzz' Aldrin & Michael Collins: First on the Moon (1970)

_Butricia, Andrew J: Single Stage To Orbit (2003)

_Chaikin, Andrew: A Man on the Moon (1988), A Passion for Mars (2008)

_Chown, Marcus: Solar System (2011)

_Collins, Michael: Carrying the Fire (1974)

_Cox, Brian & Jeff Forshaw: The Quantum Universe: Everything that Can Happen Does Happen (2011)

_French, Francis & Colin Burgess: Into That Silent Sea (2007), In the Shadow of the Moon (2007)

_Gilster, Paul: Centauri Dreams (2004)

_Gott, J Richard & Robert J Vanderbei: Sizing Up the Universe (2010)

_Kluger, Jeffrey: Journey Beyond Selene (1999)

_Kondo, Yoji, ed.: Interstellar Travel and Multi-Generational Space Ships (2000)

_Krone, Bob, ed.: Beyond Earth—The Future of Humans in Space (2006)

_O'Neill, Gerard K: The High Frontier, 3rd edition (2000)

_Orzel, Chad: How to Teach Quantum Physics to Your Dog (2010)

_Roach, Mary: Packing for Mars (2010)

_Schmitt, Harrison: Return to the Moon (2005)

_Schrunk, David, Burton Sharpe, Bonnie Cooper & Madhu Thangavelu: The Moon—Resources, Future Development, and Settlement, 2nd edition (2008)

_Stafford, Thomas: We Have Capture (2002)

_Stenger, Victor J: The Fallacy of Fine-Tuning (2011)

_Wolfe, Tom: The Right Stuff (1979)

_Zubrin, Robert: The Case for Mars (1997), How to Live on Mars (2008)